Cultown

Cultown

Duncan Smith

V
Ψ
Γ

Alfadex Books

Published by Alfadex Books, Sydney, 2017.
Copyright © Duncan Smith 2017.

A CIP catalogue record for this book is available from the National Library of Australia.

ISBN 978-0-9872228-3-1

1. Fiction 2. Drama 3. Psychology

Lighthouse XIII band: www.vortexwinder.com
Alfadex Books orders and information:
matthew.alfadex@gmail.com

Cover design by Ivan Hruszecky.

Duncan Smith is guitarist and songwriter with the band Lighthouse XIII, whose albums include *Waves Upon Waves*, *Vortex Winder*, *The Maelstrom Ascendant*, and *Cultown*.

He is the author of the books *The Vortex Winder*, *The Maelstrom Ascendant*, and *Hammer and Heat*.

Website:
www.vortexwinder.com

Cultown

Part One

Part Two

Part Three

"When, at this point now, of mankind's development, his emerging unconscious knowledge is denied by his institutions, then it will rise up despite those institutions and annihilate them. Cult after cult will emerge, each unrestrained by the use of reason, because reason will have denied the existence of rampant unconscious knowledge, disorganised and feeling only its own ancient force.

If this happens, all kinds of old and new religious denominations will war, and all kinds of ideologies surface."

Jane Roberts, 1974, The Unknown Reality Vol.1.
Amber-Allen edition, 1996, p 85-86, San Rafael, CA.

Part One

1
Debunked

Follow me to the end of the Earth. Then further.
Revelations of Milinish

When they first called us a cult, it was an insult. Now I take it as a compliment. See? Even my enemies' barbs turn to roses. A cult, you say? Damn right we are, the best there ever was. We're the ultimate, the cultimate. And it's all thanks to me, the accidental messiah.

Yes, it is I, Thomas Swan. Accept no substitute. I've decided to finally tell the story of how I formed the Milinish, and the glorious debacle that followed. And why, you ask? I'm just sick of the lies. Not from me, for I value truth above all things. It's the lies of others. The press, the government, and the pathetic ex-members who were too gutless to face the apocalypse with us.

That's what hurts the most. You expect the tabloids to lie, that's what they do. It's the betrayal of old comrades that gets me. See, I heard there's another book about the Milinish set to come out. It's by a young fool named David McHugh who was only with us a few months. McHugh? More like McWho? I'm racking my brains just to see his face.

It's not hard to guess the sort of book it is. It'll be one of those bullshit exposés. You know, 'how I was brainwashed and victimised by an evil cult,' that type of caper. The really outrageous thing is the title. *Milinish: The Inside Story.* The inside story? This clown has the audacity to write the history of the Milinish when I, Thomas Swan, can't even remember him. You might as well get some faceless Nazi private off the Russian front to write the inside story of the Third Reich. What a joke! So look, people, if you want the real inside story of the Milinish, listen to the guy who created it in the first place - me.

A word of warning, though, it isn't a very nice story. But why should it be? This ain't Sophie's world! No, you're in Tom's world now and a twisted place that is, to be sure. Still, the tale of the cult to end all cults is one that even the squeamish should hear. If there's a moral of the story for you surviving humans, it's to ponder the kind of spiritual climate in which something as mad as Milinish could arise in the first place.

Some will find this tale disturbing, others will find it amusing. Most of all, it's enlightening. Yet enlightenment comes at a cost. I had to steal your children to make you listen to me, and they aren't coming back. No, the children are mine, and with the likely fallout to follow publication of this account, it's kinder to take them with me. With me? Where are we going then? Into the great void of non-being, the vast caverns of extinction that are the destination of all. One day you'll join us there.

Before we proceed, let us clear up the important matter of pronunciation. Come on, it's really not that hard. Once and for all, it's M'linish with the emphasis on the *in*. The first syllable is not stressed, it's just a short stab as in m'lord. Have you got that? It's not melon-ish, but mer-*lin*-ish. The name has no great meaning, it's just a corruption of the phrase 'my lineage' that struck me in an idle moment. When events took the surprising turn they did, I was stuck with it.

I am thirty-nine years old as I write this, and I was thirty-three when the Milinish began. Of my life before that time - school, family, work - I will not speak, but the press has already described me as a drifter who went from job to job after dropping out of uni.

Technically, they are correct, and so what? I may have rejected formal schooling, but I got my learning elsewhere. There's no denying I dabbled in many pursuits along the way, some noble, some nefarious, but wisdom was never gained by sticking to the straightest paths. I've been many things - artist, traveller, entrepreneur. Just before the Milinish, I was playing guitar in a rock band, but I won't go on about my earlier life here. Most of you humans are too self-centred to pay attention for more than two minutes so let's cut to the chase, which was about the time I wrote my first book.

Please don't think I have always been a cynic. When *Old Religion, New Science* came out, I was still a young man, full of the idealistic belief I had something important to give the world. The book was directly sparked, so to speak, by a mystical near-death-experience in my own home.

I was living alone in a one bedroom flat in Bronte, a beach suburb in Sydney, Australia. One fine morning I was about to have a blast on my electric guitar when I got a blast of a very different kind. When it comes to replacing frayed electrical cords, you really shouldn't procrastinate. *I'll do it next week*, I thought as I shoved the cord into the back of the amp and got the shock of my young life. It was very nearly over for Tom Swan right then and there. I copped a piercing dose of voltage and dropped my guitar.

With an agonised shriek, my consciousness fled from my body. Next thing I knew, I was rushing through space towards a vast fiery triangle out among the stars. As I neared the triangle, a thousand voices and images reached me, all in an instant. Then there was an explosion of light and I was back in my body.

As I lay humbled on the floor of my little flat, a revelation came to me with complete certainty. I was an immortal soul who had lived before, I was divine, and after death I would return to my true home in the hereafter. I was not alone in this. In fact, every person alive was a spiritual being visiting the planet in physical form.

A profound cosmic awareness enveloped me. I felt the presence of all Earthly beings: the beauty, the hunger, and the love. If only everyone could share this awareness there would be an end to suffering. It was up to me to show the way. I'd use my spiritual vision to start a new science of mental health and unite the planet.

Now that I had the truth, it had to be communicated to the world at once. I stood up, walked to my desk, and immediately began to write my great book, *Old Religion, New Science*. It was the story of my life, my death, and my vision for humanity. What a

5

glorious future awaited the world when it learned the truths gained from my near-death-experience.

How naive those hopes seem now, yet at the time there was no doubt about the importance of my revelations. Here, finally, was proof of life after death. I wrote the book in an extraordinary burst of creativity over seven days, working up to eighteen hours a day. In that unstoppable frame of mind, and using contacts gained during my time as an entrepreneur, I signed a deal with Millennium Books, a 'New Age' and self-help publisher. Sure, I had to chip in for the costs, but so what? I gladly paid them extra just to hurry things along. Like a man inspired, I rushed through the publishing process until the book was out. Then, bristling with expectation, I returned to the solitude of my Bronte flat and waited for the book to sell and to change the world.

It did neither. To my dismay, my little work of genius sold barely a dozen copies. So to the twelve people who bought the book, thanks. To the rest of you, thanks also - without your stupendous apathy I would never have gone on to form the Milinish!

Wisdom comes with hindsight, however, and at the time I was aghast at the fate of my work. What use is it discovering profound truths if no one knows about them? The book sank without a ripple, although Millennium Books didn't seem to care. They assured me this wasn't unusual for a first time author and my second book would do better.

The reassurance meant nothing. It was clear the book was limping into oblivion, and with it the incisive wisdom of my vision. I can barely convey the sense of outrage that gripped me as the book continued to be ignored. It was this emotion, however, that led me on a circuitous route to ruin and then salvation.

The turning point came one evening after I made a visit to Spiral Architect, a New Age bookshop in the city. This was several years ago, of course, when there were still a few bookshops around the place. Not that it did me much good, because clearly my work continued to be shamefully ignored. Not a single copy had been sold during the week since my last visit. What's more, the moronic look of the shop's customers made me want to grab a copy of *Old Religion, New Science* off the shelf and slap their stupid faces with it.

But I didn't do that. Instead, I went straight to the nearest pub and got blind drunk.

God only knows what tirades of retribution the poor patrons had to put up with that night. I must have stepped over the line at some point, because through the blur of that evening I do recall getting thrown out. I stumbled into a taxi and ended up at Bondi Beach. The last thing I remember is hurling an empty beer bottle into breaking waves, and from there it's a blank.

I woke in darkness on the sand. The tide lapping at my ankles prompted me to seek higher ground. I limped up to the parkland above the beach and made a bed under a park bench, complete with newspaper for blankets. My last thought before falling back to oblivion was the realisation I'd become a living cliché.

If any joggers had spotted me the next morning they may have thought, 'the apprentice winos are certainly getting younger.' Then they would have jogged by and got on with their smug, non-book-buying lives. Unfortunately for me, that was the high point of the day. It was all downhill from there.

The fact is a calamity was about to happen - but it was also a miracle from the Lord above. He truly moves in mysterious ways, for he spoke to me that day through a newspaper. That in itself was a minor miracle. Last century, the winos had it easy - there were papers everywhere. With everything online now, newspapers truly were thin on the ground these days. And yet the good Lord chose to speak to me through this antiquated medium.

It happened like this. As the violent rays of a new dawn began to wake me, I opened my eyes and wondered where the hell I was. My bedroom had certainly changed since the day before. Then it all came flooding back - the book, the pub, the waves, the whole debacle of the night before.

It seemed advisable to ease my way back to consciousness, one sense at a time. Let's see, there were five of them weren't there? Taste (ugh, dry mouth), touch (ugh, wet grass, hard ground), hearing (ugh - traffic). Three duds, better try sight. I decided to focus on the fine print of the newspaper which had warmed me in the night. That way I'd be able to gently coax my awareness through the post-alcohol minefield of that morning.

My eye drifted over the front page. It was the usual rubbish - money, war, fear-mongering and the like. It was nothing but conflict - no wonder I never followed the news these days. But as I flicked through the rest of the newspaper, my eye was drawn to a small article at the bottom of page 13, I was stung into wakefulness by something amazing - mention of my book, the very book which had triggered the calamitous events of the night before.

Surprise turned to dismay when it became clear the mention was anything but flattering. The news item was headed 'Scientist Slams Dummies.' Some guy named Rudolph C. Orantor had chosen my book as an example of the growing number of non-scientific works masquerading as science. I learned that the full article appeared in the latest edition of *Real Science* magazine. Sickened and stunned, I went straight to a newsagent, and paid money to find my spiritual vision vilified in print. Here is the article in full.

Science: Dinkum, Dumb, and Dodgy
by Rudolph C. Orantor.

I am not the first person in recent years to lament the low level of scientific literacy in society, or the depiction of scientists in pop culture as either lunatics or socially inept nerds. But when a recent survey shows that nearly fifty percent of adults believe in some form of religious creationism, questions must be asked about the type of future we are creating for our children. Are they to inherit a world where astrologers are more valued than astronomers, and faith healers are preferred to medical practitioners? Whatever happened to modern science?

Somebody recently sent me a book which exemplifies the whole problem. Thomas Swan's *Old Religion, New Science* is the sort of pseudoscientific nonsense I would normally ignore, but the credence now given to such questionable publications forces me to examine it with a somewhat sterner eye.

Mr Swan claims to have 'written this work in a burst of revelatory vision over a seven day period,' causing one to wonder if he actually wrote it in six and took the seventh off as a day of rest. Whatever Mr Swan's working methods, he advances some highly dubious claims. Not only does he purport to have survived death and found proof of reincarnation, he also implies possession of the

8

full range of psychic abilities - precognition, clairvoyance and the rest of the usual suspects.

Unfortunately, Swan's work demonstrates, by default, the strength of the scientific method. Where is the thought-out hypothesis tested under controlled conditions; the careful and cautious piecing together of the data; the cross referencing with previous findings in any area of study; the rigorous skepticism applied to one's findings? More simply, where is the evidence? Not only does Swan apply no critical perspective to his 'revelations,' he fails to satisfy that small and inconvenient need for evidence in support of his extraordinary claims. All the reader gets are assertions, and it is with dismay that one realises most readers will accept these assertions as uncritically as they are given.

Is our species to revert to a Middle Ages mentality where charlatans rule the credulous? Are we, some time down the road, to face the prospect of Mr Swan's 'science' being taught in schools? Are we 'evolving backwards'? We, the science community, are at risk of becoming obsolete in a world that ever reaches for the quick fix, the easy answer. It is high time that not only do we collectively raise the public perception of scientists, but also the level of real science education in the wider community. Otherwise, we are headed for a new dark age. So strongly do I feel we are under threat, it is necessary to adopt a more forceful tone than is customary for this journal. The mentality that produced *Old Religion, New Science* is deluded. It is dangerous, it is irrational, and it must be combated before civilisation falls into decay.

Thud! My morale hit the pavement and bounced into the gutter. So much for my efforts to help humanity. But the immediate question was, why me? Why my book out of the hundreds of New Age or religion books out there? Maybe because I had the audacity to use the word 'science' in the title. Yes, that must have been what stirred up old Orantor, who after all was a 'real scientist.' I slunk off home to my little flat and collapsed onto the bed.

You may wonder why I did not shrug my shoulders and dismiss Orantor's words as simply the opinion of one man against another. Did I have so little faith in my own vision? The sad truth is that in those pre-messiah days I still had enough self-doubt to see another person's point of view. Perhaps if the hangover wasn't so bad, I wouldn't have taken it as hard, but the rest of that day I could barely rise from my bed of gloom. What if Orantor was right and

9

my great insights were no more than deluded fantasies? I re-read his article obsessively, seized by humiliation and even remorse.

I lay bedridden all day and half the night. At 3am, I rose from my sickbed and wandered city streets as a penance. I searched my spirit for guidance, but nothing came. No visions, no lights, no wise words. There was only emptiness and the growing suspicion Orantor was right.

The next day I conceived a response. I resolved to confront my nemesis head on, at least intellectually. It turned out Rudolph C. Orantor was an author himself. Indeed, he almost seemed to have his own shelf at the local bookshop. There was no doubt about it, old Rudolph C had the pop science market by the throat! If he wasn't holding forth on evolution, he was pontificating on physics. One minute he was glorying in the history of science, the next he was waxing lyrical on the origin of humanity and the universe itself. No topic was too large or small to escape the supreme scrutiny of Lord Orantor.

Perhaps it was excessive self-flagellation, but I bought them all and sat down to read. If my hope was to find signs of weakness, I was sorry to find that the man was no fool. In fact, in the light of his lucid conjecture, my own *Old Religion, New Science* began to seem profoundly unsound. The sense of dismay grew in me like a cancer.

Was Orantor right in judging my book to be hollow, sensationalist, and quite without foundation? It seemed he very well might be. It was clear now that my near-death-experience had been a delusion. My 'revelations' were nothing more than wishful fantasies based on a fear of death. It was Orantor, not I, who understood reality. The scientific worldview he described in his books was the correct one. The implications for me were immense.

My life was not, after all, a spiritual journey into matter. No, it came from the pairing of gametes in my mother's womb after the evolution-driven fornication of my father and mother. That, it seemed, was my real genesis. Granted there was a larger context within the expanding universe and the evolution of life, but the specifics of me came down to the random coupling of one among millions of sperm with an egg. All my characteristics of body and 'soul' could be explained by the genetic material - the DNA - that formed them. That was why I was. And I should be grateful for having been that sperm, that one in a million chance. I should feel wonder at the miraculous complexity of it all, and seek to make a saner and better world for all humanity. In facing up to the truth, I should feel renewed vigour and a sense of hope. Of course, Orantor was right.

There was just the small matter of my imminent demise.

Not - with any luck - next week or next year, but inevitably sometime in the next fifty years my services would be dispensed with and I would return to the earth from where I came. This regrettable mortality could perhaps be overcome by having children. There was - apparently - some consolation in knowing that while I would die, my DNA would live on in the form of descendants. Somehow, a hollow feeling remained at the thought that this complex genetic machinery would discard me into the pit of history. Yet it was clear that Orantor was right - there was no evidence for anything else and it was wishful thinking to conclude otherwise. I had simply been wrong.

If only Thomas Swan had been a good loser.

I have in my time flung chessboards, abused racquets, and violently torn up losing betting slips. Once I hurled a golf club fifty metres skyward where it lodged in the upper branch of a tree to surprise passing golfers for the rest of the day. Now, having been humiliated by Orantor, I began to pace deliriously around my tiny flat.

I had been debunked by science to add insult to the injury of being ignored by the New Age community. Deep in the seething resentful chemicals of my brain, a terrible revenge bubbled up into some half-formed impulse.

If religion was no more than an institution for achieving social control, perhaps it could be inverted to achieve chaos. And if it was true, as science said, that I was just a piece of physical debris flung out in the wake of an ancient and accidental explosion, then I might as well wreak as much mayhem as possible before returning to nothingness. If Orantor wanted to paint me as a religious crank,

11

I'd give that learned gentleman all that and more - a caricature of all the beliefs of the world in their chaotic and meaningless glory. And in that moment, the Milinish was born.

2
Revelations

One search, one quest, one sceptre to wrest.
Descend to ascend, helix eternal.

Cultown Album Lyrics

I never thought anyone would take my second book seriously. *Revelations of Milinish* was a hoax tossed off in a few days - yet it went on to become a bestseller and the Milinish bible. Here's a shortened version of its creation myth. Those familiar with Orantor's work will spot his influence.

Orantor's readers will know that DNA is the self-copying material that carries genetic info from one generation to the next. I have given it a new explanation.

Extract from Revelations of Milinish:

The world was not created in seven days by God. Nor was life made in millions of years by evolution. Those stories are only echoes of a greater truth.

In the beginning was oneness, love and light. God made the Earth with a committee of seven angels to assist him. Two of those angels were Adamcas and Evelyn, and a third was named Satan.

The Earth was newborn. Life had not yet appeared in its mighty oceans or on the land. God created a new race of super-beings to inhabit the world. It was God's wish that Adamcas and Evelyn act as spiritual

13

guardians to this race, without ever taking material form themselves.

Then one day brother Satan came to Adamcas and Evelyn and tempted them with the taste of physical life, saying 'the pleasures of Earth are unknown to you in your spirit form. Only by becoming flesh can you know the delights of matter. Look - I have stolen God's magic.'

This was no apple, it was a vial of DNA Satan stole from God's laboratory. DNA was the divine substance with the power of creating physical form. All three angels drank some of the magic potion. Thus did they taste the fruit of physicality - but the real fruit was damnation. God came and cursed them, saying 'if physical life you desire, then so shall you be, body and soul.' He cast them down to Earth and transformed them into primeval slime, where they lived in a hot, bubbling little pool of water.

The race of super-beings that was to have ruled Earth was sent to another world instead. Life of a very different type arose on an Earth now cursed by the betrayal. Adamcas, Evelyn, and Satan were angels and could not be killed, but they were joined together as a gestalt entity who would suffer over and over again. Although their spirits were immortal, their punishment was to live and die as mortal, physical creatures. They were cast into an endless cycle, doomed to perish and be reborn again and again until their souls became purified from the original sin. This cycle of reincarnation would take aeons.

Satan was the most powerful of the three, and the most guilty for his theft of the DNA. Yet he did not meekly accept his fate. Having been turned into slime by God, Satan swore revenge and vowed to evolve into a physical being powerful enough to challenge him. He would survive, progress, and ultimately defeat God. Out of this hate-fuelled desire, Satan kicked off the whole process of the genetic evolution of life on Earth.

The three fallen angels and DNA were now one, and together they pursued Satan's evil ambition. First, single-celled organisms arose, reproduced, and died in the primeval mud. After a while, they evolved into more complex life forms. Having been cast into physical life as DNA, Satan feared death. Yet with every re-birth, he strived to create ever more powerful bodies. These bodies were battle machines, organic robots that allowed DNA to survive. All manner of vile forms emerged from Satan's fear of mortality, and so did DNA create all species in its desire to live. All these forms of DNA competed in the struggle for survival to see who was the strongest.

Eventually the sinful race of man emerged, and this was Satan's greatest triumph. As never before, murder and war were unleashed upon the Earth by Satan's children. Conflict was everywhere, and not just in the struggle for survival. Adamcas and Evelyn also had their part to play. It was Adamcas who had committed the original sin, and so terrible was the burden of guilt that he wanted to banish the memory of it. Evelyn acted as his conscience and did not let him, yet he repressed her forcibly. Adamcas became the conscious mind and Evelyn the unconscious mind - the place where all repressed memories were buried. So began the oppression of the mind and of the female principle and women in general.

Separate social and economic classes also formed and were constantly at war. Another part of Adamcas became the proletariat - the working class - and Evelyn became the bourgeoisie - the middle class. There was constant class conflict and every other kind of strife. In each nation of the Earth, the proletariat fought the bourgeoisie, the conscious mind fought the unconscious, and men enslaved women. All in order to survive, reproduce, and ensure genetic survival. Sexes, nations, and religions fought one another. Life was nothing but war.

God looked down upon the planet of suffering that Earth had become and took pity on its creatures. Once every two thousand years, he sent a son to Earth to remind the descendants of Adamcas, Evelyn, and Satan of their origins. The task of the messiah was to remind everyone they were at core spiritual rather than physical beings, and that salvation could only be reached by transcending physical form. In that knowledge lay the only hope for all humanity.

Reading that now, it's not a bad creation myth. Well, no worse than plenty of others! Yet despite the prophecy implicit in the last paragraph, I had no real inkling the messiah would turn out to be me.

No, there was no reason to think this book would be any more widely read than the last one. Having written it, I fell back into despondency. I'd made a flippant mash up of Christianity and Orantor's beloved evolution, but so what? It did nothing to alter the fact that my real book, *Old Religion, New Science*, was a complete bomb. Nothing had changed. I was again gripped by futility and there seemed nothing left to do but fall on my sword and exit the world for good. But I did, after all, have a two book deal with Millennium, so I gave them *Revelations of Milinish*.

I doubted they would even publish it. Perhaps they'd think the book too outlandish, too different to my first one, or realise it was a joke. But no, *Revelations of Milinish* was accepted for publication, which just shows that in this sort of genre, anything goes. In any case, they weren't complaining when the book started to sell.

To this day, I'm not quite sure how it happened. My first book was a heartfelt statement of truth and was ignored. My second was a parody and went on to launch a new religion. How can I, the accidental messiah, explain this? Destiny? God's will? Well perhaps, but in practical terms, it came down to some promo and a little luck.

I dropped off the manuscript to the office of Millennium Books and was surprised to find hardly anyone about. The only occupant was a dozing middle-aged man named Philip, who until then I'd only spoken to on the phone. His desk was even messier than my own at home, and my arrival didn't inspire him to tidy it. I cleared a space on the desk and dumped a pile of papers and a USB stick.

'There you go, Phil, that's the new book. Hard copy and digital files.'

Philip inspected the topmost sheet of paper, titled *Revelations of Milinish* by Thomas Swan.

'Aha. Your latest bestseller.'

All too aware of the dismal performance of my first book, I reacted to his remark.

'We might sell a few more if you bastards did some promo. That's your job, isn't it?'

'Not really. Once we print the book we've done our bit. The rest is up to you.'

'Is that right? You didn't mention it before. I should have read that contract more closely.'

'Tom, I'll give it to you straight. In this day and age, publicity is up to the author. We've got enough to do as it is.'

'What about me?' I replied. 'Don't I have enough on my plate writing the thing without having to promote it as well?'

Phil shrugged, making his thoughts on the matter quite clear.

'Well,' I said, 'what do you suggest?'

Phil raised his eyebrows and said the first thing that popped into his head.

'I don't know. You're a muso, aren't you? Why don't you write a song?'

And with that, he seemed to lose interest in the conversation, if he had any in the first place. I cut my losses and went home. Yet strangely enough it was Phil's half-baked suggestion that did the trick. The Lord must have been using the idiot to send me a message. A song? OK then.

I tossed off a little ditty called 'In Nihilum.' The music took ten minutes and the lyrics a touch longer. I recorded it at home and

17

posted it on YouTube with a cool video showing an extract from my book. From there, it was a link back to my website for free download of the song and two sample chapters. I sent a link to a few old contacts who promised to upload it to social media.

That was enough to start a trickle of interest. When I noticed this a few days later, I actually went back and re-did the song in better quality and paid a cluey pal for some SEO shenanigans to get it higher in Google searches. Next thing you know, people are ordering the book from my site and requesting it at shops. And a few weeks later, blow me down if I don't walk into the same accursed bookstore from before to find *Revelations of Milinish* stacked up at the front desk as feature book of the month!

Those were the circumstantial reasons for the book's success - luck, a good song, a little basic promo, and the quick contagion of the internet. Yet the deeper cause only became clear when I read through some of the feedback which showed up on my blog and in the mail. This was reaction from actual people, something for which I wasn't at all prepared.

I read through it fearfully at first. If this was in response to something I'd written as a hoax, would it be fan mail or hate mail? Yet as I read through it alone in my little flat, the true implications of what had happened began to sink in. Surprise and a spark of megalomania danced a jig through my once jaded mind. Here's a sample of the response.

• Thank God for the day your blessed book came into my life. For an old Catholic, it was a sad day when the Pope said 'evolution is more than a hypothesis.' The atheists smirked, but now with your revelation of Milinish our faith is redeemed. Scientists said there was no God but you explained how he created Eden and the devil corrupted it. You have confirmed what true believers knew all along, that God created the world but Satan made evolution. Or rather, the revelation that struck like a bolt from heaven, that Satan IS evolution. So all who believe in evolution believe in Satan. I am now an ex-Catholic converted to the church of Milinish. Where do you hold your meetings?

• As a scientist who believes in God, your book is of tremendous interest. I've long been frustrated by my colleagues' attitudes. They either dismiss entirely the spiritual dimension of the world they study, or adopt a feeble agnosticism where science and spirit can never meet. You, on the other hand, have seized the nettle and unified the two. Well done, sir! I'll be keeping an eye out for you on the lecture circuit.

• Dear Sir, As I read Revelations of Milinish, I felt a surge of truth like never before. I am speechless. It is wonderful, that is all I have to say, that is my last word on the subject.

That was the first paragraph of an eight page letter - and still on the low end of the lunacy scale. It was nothing compared to this next one. The guy who wrote it should start his own religion.

• Sir, I charge you this - and the truth can NOT be forged or denied, nor can, or SHOULD any cover ups ever be concealed from the truth, but basically the 'prophecies of Milinish' is the work of vision and that is a FACT! But the fact remains, you are gutless for not giving a powerless reader the chance to defend himself against any hint of fidelity or breach of promise. The question of circles and squares on page 45. Is this an obvious red herring or a veiled reference to 'starships' of light? Or are you an imposter after all? Come sir, the reckoning day is closer than I think and that is in all humility, but please I beg you to take these matters to heart, and keep WRITING the TRUTH without fear or favour. The governments of the world are trembling because they know the TRUTH and the truth cannot be denied. I salute you.

Of course – my thoughts exactly! Apart from those cryptic writings, there were a couple of smartarses who wrote in. One of them wanted to know if I had any knowledge of Gnosticism (not really but I got the joke), and the other one simply said:

- I thought your book was very funny.

Speculating on the success of my second book, I had two explanations. The shallow one was that it was due to luck and a bit of basic promo. The deeper one was that I had touched some kind of nerve in the mass psyche. My little hoax had, by an accident of cosmic proportions, crossed that fine line between stupid and clever, thrown a rope bridge over the chasm between credibility and incredulity, and fallen into that never-never valley where science and religion meet.

Was *Revelations of Milinish* the missing link between God and evolution? Perhaps, in the minds of many, it was. It seemed that science and religion, those institutional stalwarts, had gotten drunk at a party and tumbled recklessly into fornication. And the bastard offspring was Milinish! Judging by the response so far, it looked as if the embarrassing brat wasn't going to vanish discreetly up some country orphanage, but was going to emerge kicking and screaming into the sunlight. More amazing still, the bastard was going to be publically hailed as the return of the prodigal, to the mortification of both parents.

Yet the family tree of Milinish extended further than science and religion. If evolution and Christianity were the parents, the cousins were Marxism, psychoanalysis, and Eastern religion. No wonder my book was successful, it had gobbled up all the great theories of life in one go and become the mother of them all!

It looked like I'd had the last laugh on old Rudolph C. Orantor. One of his books had a chapter on 'chaos theory' - something to do with large scale events being caused by the far reaching effects of tiny initial variables. The famous example he gave was the flapping of a butterfly's wings over Asia spreading out to eventually cause a hurricane in Europe.

Perhaps the Milinish would never have come into being if not for such tiny variables. Just think - if Orantor had not written his article, if the newspaper hadn't featured it the day after my night

20

out at the pub, if I'd not staggered up to that particular park bench and used the paper for a blanket - well, I'd probably never have written *Revelations of Milinish* in the first place. A little chaos goes a long way.

Either that or it was all part of God's plan.

It wasn't long before Millennium Books had a conversion of their own and decided to promote my book - now that it was already successful, that is. The usual deal, in other words. Mind you, it would still be me doing all the work. They suggested their latest guru had a duty to educate the public, so they proposed a lecture tour of the major Australian cities.

My first impulse was to refuse. It's one thing to sit alone in a darkened room writing flights of fantasy, something else to front a crowd of people who've taken it for divine reality. And what if people came who were hostile? Scientific and religious fundamentalists who wanted to stone me? You never knew with these fanatic types.

More practically, how would I stand up to the trials of acting and oration in presenting my case? To some degree I would have to convince *myself* of the credibility of my doctrines before I could convince others, and this posed problems on creative if not moral grounds. Just what reserves of invention would I need to pull it off?

I studied myself in the bathroom mirror. I still had my long rock star hair, and as I'd not bothered to shave for a couple of weeks, a very passable beard. I'd never gone so long unshaven before. The facial hair really transformed me, almost as if I were someone else. Then all of a sudden it hit me - I looked rather like Him.

There was no doubt about it. By some accident of DNA, I bore a striking resemblance to you-know-who. The fair skin, soulful blue eyes, and dark flowing mane. It was the beard that really brought it out. That and my height, six feet tall in my sandals. Of course, they say the real McCoy was a five foot, dark-skinned Arab, but what kind of appearance is that for a saviour? No, my resemblance was to the Renaissance, Europeanised version. It gave me a strange feeling.

21

Millennium Books also wanted to re-release *Old Religion, New Science*, but I forbade it. In fact, I told them that if they put it out behind my back, I'd not only sue them but go to another publisher. I did promise to write them a brand new book instead. Trouble is, I'd written two books, one I believed in, the other I'd tossed off as a sort of joke. As it was the latter which had caught on with the public, that's the one I'd flog to them. It was all they deserved.

I suppose that in moral terms the whole enterprise was a bit dodgy, but three factors swayed me down the rocky path of messiah-dom. First was that I couldn't believe what was happening - it was all too silly for words. Perhaps it was one of God's little jokes. Well, I'd go along with it for now. Second, the nihilistic outlook I'd adopted since Orantor's slagging made me rather indifferent to moral questions. After all, in the bigger picture nothing really mattered, so what the hell? And finally, this event was bigger than me, and to be swept along by destiny, chaos, or God's will was easier than to resist it.

Hail Milinish!

3
On Tour

It's better to be an anti-hero than a non-entity.

Cultown

'So you're saying Satan is in everything?'

The size of the room turned eighty people into a crowd. Like painted figures, their eyes followed me around the room.

'Yes,' I replied. 'It's become fashionable to say God is in everything - and that's true - but it was Satan who physically made all living things. Any creature that walks, swims or flies was created by Satan through fornication and DNA engineering. The saving grace for humanity is that God the spirit is also present. Any more questions?'

A bearded man in the third row raised his hand.

'Who controls this world, God or Satan?'

'The whole history of planet Earth is the battle between spirit and flesh. God made one and Satan the other, and they've been fighting for control ever since. The battlefields are the hearts and minds of you, me, and every other person on Earth. God wants us to become spiritual beings again but Satan cares for only one thing - survival, fornication, and the reproduction of genes.'

'It all seems very complicated.'

'Not at all. Many people want to make life *seem* complicated. They like to spin intellectual webs, theories and hypotheses to dazzle and confuse one another. There are whole libraries of them! Let me assure you that life is simple. You follow the spirit or you

23

follow the flesh. There is no grey area. Grey areas are only for people who lack the courage to see things for what they are.'

A chap in John Lennon glasses and a leather jacket piped up, in an American accent.

'Mr Swan, I love your spiritual take on evolution, but you can't expect scientists to know anything about Satan's role in it. That's not what they do. Same for Marxism and psychoanalysis. These guys are specialists. How could they know where all these other theories fit in?'

'That's a great comment and really, you've put your finger right on the problem. You see, in the last two centuries, all sorts of theories have been flying around. They're useful in a way as small pieces of the puzzle. Trouble is, none of these specialists can put all the pieces together and see the big picture. The polymath doesn't get a look in these days. Well, what good are specialists? They're no better than fleas on an elephant. Each flea can only see its own piece of the elephant and no one's got a clear view of the whole animal.'

'Oh right, the old elephant analogy. Don't you mean blind men instead of fleas?'

'I'm sorry?'

'It's usually explained as a team of blind men, each of them touching a different part of the elephant and no one can see the whole animal.'

'Well, it all comes to the same thing. Perhaps they were blind fleas. The point is that these specialists are about as useful as one hand clapping. If you'll permit a few liberties taken with dates, the trouble with Marx is he never said anything about Freud, and the trouble with Freud is he never said anything about Marx. And neither of them said nearly enough about Darwin or Buddha! Of course, scientists do have a superficial grasp of evolution, but they fail hopelessly to address the role played by Satan. Yes, genes do strive to selfishly reproduce themselves, but this is so Satan can survive on the Earth and eventually rule it.'

And so on. A mish-mash of theories given rapid fire in ringing tones of conviction. Everyone loved it! My fears about audience hostility proved unfounded. Each day, I'd bound onstage in my thousand-dollar-suit like a coked-up game show host. I'd soak in the applause for a while, raise my hands to quell it, then throw down my new catchphrase - 'I'm Thomas Swan. Welcome to reality.'

Sure, the venues were small, but all the better to sell them out. The entry fee was just enough to deter any critics from bothering to show up. It's true there were a few queries from Christian souls uneasy about the liberties I'd taken with the Bible - but I dealt with these in the question period after my talk.

'Why didn't Jesus say anything about DNA in the Bible?'

I winked.

'Come now, brother, electron microscopes were pretty thin on the ground in Jesus's day! He had to speak in the language of his time for people to understand. Now I have to speak in the language of my time. If Jesus were alive today, he'd tell you all about Satan's connection to DNA.'

'Are you saying you are Jesus reborn?'

I raised both hands in a cartoon gesture of surrender. 'Whoa, brother, don't go there! Let's just say we're related!'

Applause and whooping followed this remark. A woman in the front row swooned. When the commotion died down, someone called out from the back.

'Why are Adamcas and Evelyn called Adam and Eve in the Bible?'

'Wait til my next book, sister. Don't worry - all your questions will be answered when the time is right. The sad fact is much of the Bible has been changed and corrupted over the years. That's one of the main reasons I've come among you at this crucial time in history, to separate fact from fiction. Be patient and the truth will come.'

It seemed enough to placate them for now, at least until the word of Milinish evolved further. Thankfully, the word was rarely challenged on scientific grounds, as I feared this may have been harder to shrug off. Yet every now and then, some know-it-all scientist showed up. It helped me learn important lessons for dealing with insubordination.

It happened first at one of the Melbourne dates. I called for questions and a fanatical-looking young man stood up and demanded to know what qualifications I had that entitled me to lecture on the DNA molecule. The room hushed, curious to see how the messiah would deal with a heckler. The guy was sweating and shaking, whether from nerves or anger I couldn't tell. I paused for a long ten seconds to give him the spotlight, then favoured my assailant with a patronising smile.

'Well, well. How nice to see a scientist in attendance. Did Orantor send you?'

'I'm a post-grad in microbiology at Monash University.'

'So how long have you been a Satanist? I mean a scientist.'

The audience laughed and I did a little shimmy at the podium. The young man flushed.

'As you're clearly an expert on DNA, *Professor* Swan, I'd like to know if you agree with Jenkins' theory on trace-mitochondria and its implications for evolutionary drift.'

'Old Jenko, eh. You want to know what I think of him?'

'Or how about Fraser's theory of secondary genetic masking? Surely you have an opinion on that.'

'Enough of the name dropping. Think that'll impress anybody? Stop trying to intimidate us with knowledge! Why don't you save it for your next coven meeting, my boy? There are many people today who want to make life very complex. They like to spin intellectual webs, theories, and hypotheses to dazzle and confuse each other. There are whole libraries of them! Let me tell you that life is very simple ...'

Alas the angry young man lacked the courtesy to let me finish, bursting in with more of his fanatical obsessions.

'Do you have any idea of the beauty, wonder, and complexity of the DNA molecule?'

'I do indeed. And the unfortunate thing, my child, is you've got too *much* an idea of the beauty, wonder, and complexity of the DNA molecule. While God is beautiful, Satan is clever and you, my boy, are too intellectual by half. The sad thing is your intellect is impeding your spiritual growth. If you turned half your brain off, you'd be a lot closer to God. Open your heart. Stop thinking and start feeling. The entire history of Western culture is riddled with over-intellectualisation. It all started with the Greeks and we know what a depraved lot they were.'

'I suppose you'll be telling us next the world is flat and the sun travels round the Earth!'

'Did I say that? Is that all you can do - take cheap shots at spiritual people with your caricatures? Look at you having your little tantrum, trying to get attention in front of an audience. You look like you're about to burst into tears. Call yourself a scholar? You need to raise your intellectual game - and until you can stop being so emotional and come up with a more thoughtful approach, I think we'll stop wasting everybody's time. Let's move on. Next question please.'

At that, my assailant walked out, having learned the folly of trying to argue with me. By the way, I don't recall the *exact* details of what the young guy asked me. It wasn't 'secondary genetic masking.' I just made that up. It was some scientific gobbledegook or other. You get the general idea.

You know what - I was hooked on this new game. It wasn't a bad racket at all. You'd walk onstage to thunderous applause, give your lecture, then answer a few easy questions before spending the night in a hotel room. Not a bad life at all. It was so much better than going on the road in rock n roll. At least I didn't have to sit in a tour bus with a bunch of roadies, and I got to stay in five star hotels instead of two star vans.

There aren't many photos of me from those early days of the Milinish. Frankly, I was still trying to get the beard right. Let it get too long and I started to look like a Viking; too short and I lost the coveted resemblance to Our Saviour. I'd sit in my hotel room googling images of my predecessor, trying to find the perfect model. In the end, I kept going back to the old masters. The classic Renaissance paintings can't really be topped for this sort of thing.

By the back end of the tour, I finally got it right. The inky-black hair and beard against pale skin really brought out the ocean-blue of my eyes. Hell, some nights I'd look in the mirror and think maybe I *was* the messiah after all. With my expensive suit, there was a nice mix of the contemporary and the classical. No wonder they loved me.

After coming off tour, I felt a bit flat. I missed the crowds, the applause and excitement. So what now? For want of a better idea, I started work on the next book. To some degree, it had already taken shape on the tour. It turned out a surprising number of audience questions were about New Age beliefs, rather than Christian or scientific matters. It had been, 'Do you believe in reincarnation?' or 'What do you think of UFOs?' Or astrology, or crystals, or karma? And while I was answering those questions with evasive eloquence, I was asking myself: 'what *do* I think about them?' And gradually, the answers began to form.

4
Amnesiac
Awake

*The mob, as a rule, has all the intellectual
and emotional maturity of a toddler. Treat it
as such, and it may grow up to thank you.*

Reality Explained

I came off tour and sensed the fragile potency of the moment.
Sure, the book was hot, but fad is only one letter away from fade.
I had to seize this chance - and not just by writing another book.
No, I sensed a pull towards something greater. Musing on the
conundrum, my hands picked up a guitar and the Lord sent me a
song. The chords came to my fingers and the words to my lips.

> Amnesia, tell me who I am.
> All I have known,
> I no longer understand.
> I feel a change is coming,
> I feel it building up inside
> Changing you, changing me,
> Mind blowing reality.

Then it hit me - I *was* the messiah after all! My revelations of
Milinish weren't a joke, they were cold hard fact. *Now* I understood.
My first conversion was only a prelude to my second. *Touché*, Lord.
Oh, his mysterious ways! He'd sent me Orantor's article so I could
unconsciously stumble on the *real* truth. My next move was clear.

I'd form a new religious order called the Milinish and take that truth to the world through my books.

And my music - yes, of course! My ailing career as a rock n roller wasn't going anywhere. Then let it rouse from its slumber in service of this new calling. Thomas Swan, the rock n roll messiah. Why ever not? I had a ready-made audience and a message to give it.

It all made sense. I always knew my life had a greater calling. There'd been signs since infancy. Yet to be the messiah to lead humanity forward? That was a destiny even I had not imagined.

I sang the new song 'Amnesia' again, imagining thunderous drums and bass driving it forward. Then I rang Jamie.

He'd showed up in the crowd at one of my Sydney talks, dressed like a young CEO. He had a stack of questions but cornered me privately after the talk, rather than airing them in the public forum. Even then, I noticed the sad eyes behind the enthusiasm, the haunted sideways glances. Sensing a resource to be tapped, I made sure he signed up for the mailing list. Now, just hours after my phone call, here he was at my front door answering the call to arms. He was still suited up. Well, I *had* implied this was a job interview.

After his eager entrance, Jamie looked round in surprise at my modest abode.

'Underwhelming, isn't it?' I said. 'Still, there's no shame in humble beginnings. Jesus was born in a stable.'

'Of course, Mr. Swan.'

'Buddha was the other way round. Born a prince then took his vow of poverty. That's the spiritual path for you - many roads, one destination.'

My guest didn't reply. I saw nothing to contradict my first impressions. Physically, he was a regular matinee idol, yet there was something deflated about him.

'As for you, Jamie,' I continued, 'you're more Buddha than Christ. You're from the palace, that's clear. But Buddha left of his own free will, there's the difference. Not you. I sense a classic fall from grace narrative. Some tragedy spurred your departure.'

'How did you know?'

'I can read you like a street sign. Where you've been and where you are now - which is some kind of Purgatory, if not Hell itself, right? But here's the good news - your suffering's a gift. Embrace it. Pain has sent many a pilgrim onto the spiritual path.'

The droopy eyes lifted slightly, as a chained dog looks up at the sound of its master's car in the driveway. 'Why does it have to be like that?' he said.

I gave him a sympathetic smile.

'Church of hard knocks, ain't it. Fact is, you're one of the lucky ones. See, there are two main paths to spirituality; one long and straight, the other a sudden fork in the road. Sure, there's lives seem perfect on the surface. There's a career, material comfort, the happy home - you name it! Yet a seed of discontent gnaws away all the while. For decades, in some cases. That's the slow burn route to conversion most folks endure. I pity them their long road to the Lord. Then there's others flung violently onto the spiritual path by some trauma. And this, Jamie, was your route and your blessing. It's saved you thirty years of wasted time.'

Jamie took off his jacket and tie, and discarded them onto the sofa. He opened his wallet and took out a photo of a beautiful young woman. I peered at the tiny image.

'So it's one of Evelyn's daughters at the heart of the matter. Who is this fair maiden?'

'My ex-wife, but it's not her fault, I can only blame myself.'

'We're all guilty, my son.'

Although Jamie was less than ten years younger than me, I had already assumed a paternal role. At any rate, he continued his sad tale.

'My whole working life, I cared for only three things - my family, my party, and my country.'

'Party, is it? Am I invited?'

'The Labour Party. I won pre-selection at the first attempt.'

'Aren't you a bit young to be in politics?'

'That's exactly it. I would have been the youngest ever Member of Parliament. I could've been anything. MP at twenty-five, PM by forty. That's what they told me.'

31

Looking at him now, I had my doubts. Sure, he was textbook dark and handsome, and had the boyish good looks to get a start. In time, those looks might ripen into those of a statesman. He'd need a tinge of grey to attain any broad appeal. Maybe he could get some grey hair dye. Even so, I sensed he was just too nice to make it all the way up the ladder. He lacked the ruthless self-confidence to carry him to the very top. Yet Jamie seemed convinced his destiny had been snatched away from him. He sat there, slowly shaking his head.

'I don't get it. You work twelve hours a day, six days a week, and all for the betterment of self, party and country. But you text one silly selfie ...'

'Oh no.'

'... one indiscretion in a moment of weakness and it all comes to nothing.'

'Sexting, was it? Aren't you a bit old for that?'

'One dumb photo at the end of the week when I was half-drunk and too tired to think straight. A set up, of course. That's obvious now. One mistake and they forget all the hard work you did.'

'That's the downside of your youth, Jamie, and your technology. Wouldn't have happened in the old days. Phones were for speaking.'

'So, next thing you know I'm making a public apology.'

He pulled his wife's photo out of his wallet and tossed it in the air. It performed a flaccid loop and landed face down on the floor.

'She stood by me at first. So did the party - for about five minutes. I got punted soon as the polls came in. Then a few weeks sitting around the house and my wife says this wasn't what she signed up for, and moved out.'

'Oh fickle Evelyn.'

'Years of service, years of my life. All gone.'

'Don't blame yourself, Jamie, it was Satan acting through you. As a scientist, I take a rational approach to morality. *God* doesn't want you to sext anyone, it's Satan's DNA driving the urge to copulation. It goes all the way back to the ancient swamp and you're just one more fallen prey to those primal urges. We're every one of us a mini-battlefield in the great struggle between spirit and flesh. Still, battles are not wars. There's a way back for you yet.'

'Too late - I'm damaged goods. The party won't touch me. My wife won't answer my calls.'

'Then they've lost the right to your talents. There are others who can use them. Look at you. Handsome, fit, hard-working. Why squander all that over a trifling DNA battle? Satan beat you once - so what? I'm going to take him down once and for all, and you're the man to help me.'

'The damage is done.'

'To your political career, sure. Still, I reckon there's a higher calling in the wings. What's politics up against the greatest religious movement ever formed?'

'What do you mean?'

'This is *my* party. The Milinish. I've just formed it. We're far more important than a political party. Never mind governing a country, we're going to rule the world. We'll be the fastest growing religion since Christianity. It's my calling to lead, of course. But you, Jamie, you'll be my trusted lieutenant. I don't care about your past, there's a place for you right here by my side.'

My grandiose claims had pricked his interest, yet Jamie looked doubtfully around once more at my cluttered apartment. I placed a firm hand on his shoulder.

'Never mind the present, think of the future. The only certainty in life is change. You've seen how fast a man can fall. Stick with me and you'll rise up higher than you ever were before.'

'You really think so? But why me?'

'For a start, you understand the doctrines. That was obvious from the kind of questions you asked that first night. Don't think I didn't notice - you went straight into my black book. And now I'm getting a handle on your back story, well, it's case closed. Satan made you send that text but God sent you to me.'

Jamie's face was already regaining the confidence it must once have possessed. I sensed the future prime minister he might have been.

'You're serious?' he said. 'I didn't even know you had your own group. I thought you were just a rogue academic with a way out theory. So, the Milinish, you say? You're really going to build up the numbers?'

'Like I said, it's humble beginnings but wait and see where we are in twelve months.'

'But how to get there?'

'God will guide us, of course, but the real work has to come from us. *Both* of us. Messiah I may be, yet no one can work alone. Jesus had his disciples, Buddha had his followers. I'm the same. Give me staff, an organization, and recruits. It's the same as a political party, only ten times more meaningful - and that's where you come in.'

'It's a big job starting from scratch, Mr. Swan.'

'Then let's get on with it! And call me Tom - we're a team now. Look, all you have to do is kick things off and it'll take care of itself. Once you get a few recruits, you can subcontract the job out.'

'Sure.'

'We'll all have our role to play. I'm the leader, you're the organiser. This is where your political experience will be put to good use. Who cares about your little photo scandal? Not me, Jamie. I'm not fool enough to squander your energy and organizational skills over such a petty matter.'

'I really appreciate that, Tom.'

'What else do we need? Funding! We can do it top down or bottom up, doesn't matter. Bottom up, we do it through recruits. Top down, get sponsors, a patron. Ideally, both at once.'

By now, my spark of enthusiasm had fully infected Jamie. He sat visibly taller in his chair and looked ready to begin work at once.

'So there's your brief,' I said. 'Get me staff! Recruits! Funding!' I banged on the table with each command. He nodded eagerly.

'First thing you do is get some recruits. Then find me a patron. We need a new HQ. This flat won't cut it.'

'I'm on it, Tom.'

'It's a noble cause, Jamie. Not only are we doing the Lord's work, you'll find personal redemption too. Who'll you be in five years? The man who helped save the world. Forget your wife. Given time, you can take your pick for a new one.'

'But what about the photo?'

'I couldn't care less. For purposes of discretion, you can work behind the scenes at first. You're the organiser, I'm the face. In due course, you'll step up as a leader. And if anyone does bring up your past, you'll wear it like a badge of honour. All Satan did was prepare the ground for your rebirth. So who's laughing now?'

I stood up and extended my right hand. Jamie leapt to his feet and we shook on the deal. Then I sent him on his way to begin the Lord's work and mine.

5

Vagrant to Vaucluse

God works in mysterious ways, and I am one of them
Old Religion, New Science

A patron, converts, a new HQ - did we pull it off? Did we what!
How did we do it? Well, I'm not going to bang on about the details.
As Confucius say, 'logistics, logistics, as boring as statistics.' Actually,
that wasn't Confucius; it was me, which is even better. The point
being, never mind the practical details. I leave all that to Jesus.

Long story short, the Lord sent me Rose. Jamie went scouting
in the posh suburbs and met her through a book club. A rich
divorcee with a spiritual bent and a big house in Vaucluse, she was
a prime prospect to pluck.

Jamie set up a special Thomas Swan lecture just for her. We
had enough converts by now to make up a crowd, yet the deluxe
performance I gave was only for Rose. I thundered, charmed, and
cajoled, and by the time it was exit stage left she was up on her feet
with the rest of them. Couple of days later and I'm ringing her
doorbell, come to inspect what could soon be the new Milinish
HQ. She didn't know that yet. All she knew was that backstage
after the show, she'd found herself asking me to dinner.

When Rose opened the door, I was disturbed to find her much
more attractive than I'd noticed the other night. Her dark brown

hair was done up in a sort of bun, and with the hair pulled back, the natural comeliness of her features came to the fore. Her skin was a touch darker than mine, yet her eyes just as blue. And while Rose must have been at least ten years older than me, it was refreshing to see that a few lines of life experience had not yet been botoxed out of existence. It was a face, not a mask, one that showed generations of good breeding in both the cultural and Darwinian sense.

She was wearing a light blue gown that, to my untrained eye, looked fit for the red carpet. Whether this was normal evening wear for wealthy Vaucluse women, or put on for my benefit, I didn't know. It was slightly unsettling, to be frank. I hoped this wasn't going to put me off my game.

I clasped Rose's warm hands between mine, kissed her cheek, then followed her inside to the drawing room. She was a good ten inches shorter than me, and it was only when we sat down that I noticed rather more cleavage on display than at our first meeting. This set off a most un-messiah-like blush. To cover up, I bent down and made a show of rummaging about in my bag. When the heat at last went out of my cheeks, I pulled out a book and straightened up.

'Here it is, my dear. The signed copy of *Revelations of Milinish* I promised you.'

Rose beamed.

'Oh, how wonderful!'

Rose took the book and held it up with reverence. She opened the cover and squinted a little at the inscription I'd scrawled. She reached into her handbag and took out a pair of spectacles, then paused rather self-consciously.

'I do love a women in glasses,' I said. 'I probably shouldn't say this, but I always wanted to date a librarian. Before I took on my mission, of course.'

It was Rose's turn to blush. She laughed a little too loudly and put on her specs. Then she read the inscription aloud.

'To my dear Rose. Long may we walk the spiritual path together.'

It was only a trifle but she looked up in pure delight.

'Oh Tom, I will treasure this.'

37

A short time later, we were walking a different path together, making a tour of the house. And as the philosophers say, it's amazing how two people see the same thing so differently. While Rose saw the downstairs drawing room, I saw a temple where we could hold services. What she thought was a home theatre, I knew to be an 'education centre' for training people in my doctrines. The dining room? That was just fine the way it was. After dinner, I gazed at my host through candlelight as she topped up my wine glass.

'Thank you, my dear. I do enjoy the material world, illusion though it is.'

My host giggled as if she were twenty years younger. 'I thought you'd be teetotal.'

'Not at all. We're no ascetics by any stretch - and why should we be? Don't forget Jesus at the wedding feast. Water into wine and all that.'

Rose spilled a few drops over the side of my glass onto the table. She put down the bottle, then I took her right hand in mine to steady it. Slightly flustered, she picked up a cloth with her left hand and patted down the spill. Her cleavage jiggled as she patted.

'You must come again, Tom,' she said, sitting down.

'My dear Rose, if only I lived closer, or the Lord had blessed me with a car, you'd never get rid of me.'

Rose bloomed.

'But you're only in Bronte, Tom, I could easily send a car to pick you up.'

'How delightful! But I'm afraid my Bronte days are coming to an end. The owner's renovating and I've had notice to leave.'

'What a nuisance.'

'It's no bother. I'm going to bunk out in Fairfield for a spell until we find the movement a new office.'

'Fairfield? That's western suburbs, isn't it? How frightful. Isn't it dreadfully rough?'

'It's the Wild West, no doubt. Still, Hunter's Hill or Rouse Hill, makes no difference to me. Here or there's neither here nor there, far as I'm concerned. Jesus lived among the poor. So did Buddha.

If it's good enough for them, I'm hardly going to put on airs, am I?'

'But is it safe? One hears the most awful things on the news.'

'Do you really think the Lord would let anything happen to me? After all, it's his work I'm doing.'

'But what a shame you're leaving just when I'm getting to know you.'

I took Rose's warm hands and gave them a gentle squeeze.

'My dear, I'd like nothing more than to dine with you every night, but my mission must always come first. Fairfield will do for now. Mind you, you're welcome to come and visit.'

Rose looked alarmed. I removed my hand.

'Strange, isn't it?' I said. 'I can be happy in a slum but you're here in this enormous house all alone, suffering. Money doesn't mean a thing to me. Real wealth is in the heart.'

Seeing that I'd hurt her, I softened my tone.

'I'm sorry, Rose. Sometimes my preoccupation with the spiritual life makes me forget what it's like to be human. It must be awfully lonesome after a divorce.'

Rose hesitated before answering.

'To be honest, I didn't see much of Alan the last couple of years. It's the children I miss.'

'He has custody?'

'Oh no, they're quite grown up.'

'Shouldn't they be here for you at a time like this?'

'They would be,' Rose said, without much conviction, 'but they're both overseas.'

I affected a look of disapproval.

'I see. The post-divorce world tour, is it?'

'It's not just for fun, they're both trying to work. Steffi's in New York trying to get into fashion. Michael's in LA, starting off in acting.'

'Surely they don't make a living out of that. How do they support themselves?'

'Their father and I are helping them out for now.'

'Ah, children, the gift that keeps on taking.'

'I'm just glad they're doing something with their lives. Steffi says she's really getting somewhere.'

'And good luck to her. Starting a business is she? Aren't we all! Long as they don't forget who's funding the junket. Still, if they're going to plunder the family treasury it wouldn't kill them to keep in touch at your time of need.'

'We're all a little self-centred at that age. I certainly was. It's not their fault.'

I smiled benevolently.

'Perhaps you're right. Youth is their crime. We must lower the bar considerably in our expectations, for they know not what they do. Still, the nails sting our palms, just as they did our saviour. And your husband - are you still in contact?'

'Hardly. He's ... moved on, shall we say. Traded me in for a younger model.'

'Ah, the old cliché. Still, no reason you shouldn't do the same. I'm sure you'd have no trouble. Good Lord, Rose, if I wasn't a man of the cloth, I'd make a move on you myself!'

I laughed as if merely making an outrageous joke. She pealed along with me, even as my fingers brushed hers on the way to the wine bottle. I splashed a generous amount into her glass.

'Are you *sure* you have to move away, Tom? I mean, the western suburbs!'

'I need somewhere to stay while the Milinish goes to the next level. If I have to sleep in the streets, so be it. The material world is nothing to me. But if I may speak frankly, you seem awfully attached to it.'

I surveyed our opulent surroundings with a look of deep sorrow.

'I'm not judging you, my dear. Still, let me ask you a question - could you leave all this behind? What would you do if I asked you to come and live with me in Fairfield as my disciple?'

Titillation and horror grappled for control of Rose's face. Words seemed to be forming but did not emerge. I raised my eyebrows and an accusing finger.

'Your silence speaks for itself. You think you've made a spiritual commitment, but your only real commitment is to all this. Your

40

wealth is your burden. I'm afraid you have a good many lives of suffering ahead before you understand that.'

'Oh Tom, you're probably right - but what can I do?'

'Do, Rose? You can do anything you set your mind to - but you don't. You sit alone in your big house and the world passes you by. You know what though? This house may be an illusion but I don't *want* you to walk away from it. The *Lord* doesn't want you to walk away - he wants you to *do* something with it. Something for the greater good of the world, not just for your two kids off indulging themselves at your expense.'

'What do you suggest?'

'I don't know, Rose. That's a question only you can answer.'

I looked at my watch, then stood up and kissed her - on the lips this time.

'A truly enchanting evening, my love, but duty calls. My bus is due.'

Rose scrambled to her feet.

'Don't be silly, Tom, let me call you a cab. Oh, what am I saying? There's plenty of space here. You can stay in Steffi's room.'

'I couldn't possibly impose upon your hospitality any further. You've been more than generous. I really should go and start packing for Fairfield.'

I turned to leave and began a slow walk down the hallway to the front door. I'd only gone a few steps when there was a flurry of movement behind me. Rose made an awkward half-run down the hallway and tripped over her high heels. I turned, made a desperate lunge, seized her violently and pulled her into a warm embrace. Then, as if embarrassed, I released my grip. She stood in front of me and put a hand on each of my shoulders.

'Wait, Tom, I've just had a marvellous idea! Why don't you move in here for a while?'

'Here? What do you mean?'

'I mean here with me. Why ever not? I've oodles of rooms. I mean of room,' Rose said tipsily.

'Here, Rose? Why, what an idea.'

'Why not? I've got all this space and it's going to waste. Just stay a while until you find somewhere permanent.'

41

'I've already given my word to my chum in Fairfield - and my word is my bond. I couldn't possibly let him down. But thank you, it's most kind of you to suggest it.'

'I wouldn't dream of letting you move out there, Tom. You'd be taking your life in your hands. Oh please, just think about it.'

I paused, brow furrowed, as if considering the idea for the first time. I walked into the drawing room and sat down in a plush armchair. Rose stared at me with the imploring look of a girl asking for a pony. I frowned.

'You've got me thinking now, Rose. Maybe it's not such a bad idea after all. Not for my sake, that's neither here nor there. For the good of the movement, that's a different story. Perhaps I do have a higher obligation than my own selfish desires. You know what we discussed at dinner about the huge changes the world is facing? It's up to the Milinish to guide people through. Fact is, we do need a temporary base to run services. What do you say I set up camp here for a while until we find somewhere else?'

'Oh how wonderful!'

'But if it's going to work, I'll need more than just a bedroom.'

'No problem. Just tell me what you want.'

'Well really, all I need is a large room to run services, an office for admin, and a study where I can write the new book. Give me those and we're in business - and I suppose moving in would make everything easier.'

'Tom, you're welcome. I'd be honoured.'

'Then I accept. It's win-win. The Milinish has a stable base to build to the next level, and you get to use your wealth for a higher purpose - thus sparing yourself a couple of lifetimes of karmic suffering. By Heaven we'll do it, Rose! And the sooner the better.'

'I agree. You're not going to change your mind now, are you? Because I certainly won't.'

'Not at all. I can see it's going to be brilliant. Do you have a spare key handy?'

'Of course.'

'Then hand it over and call me a cab! I may as well go and collect a few things right away. When it comes to doing the Lord's work, there's not a moment to waste.'

6

The

Lab-Oratory

"As a scientist myself...."
Milinish in the New Age

The very next day, I was in residence. The first thing I did was ask Rose for a part of the house where I could work undisturbed. This would also allow me to keep my patron at arm's length. She was enamoured with me for now but overexposure could harm that. It's not wise to muddy one's aura with the daily banalities of breakfast. I tried to put it tactfully.

'This is ideal, Rose! A stable base for a while. It's exactly what we need to grow the movement.'

'Glad I can help, Tom.'

'And I really couldn't imagine a more charming host. But for the sake of full disclosure, let me take the confessional. Every man has a vice. Me? I'm a workaholic.'

'Ho hum. I'm used to that.'

'I'll bet. Still, given that my work is all about serving the Lord, I trust he'll forgive me. I only hope you can too. You must understand, Rose, my work will always come first. While it's a great support to have you nearby, it's imperative I'm free to get on with it undisturbed.'

'What are you working on now?'

'The new book's due in a couple of months. Until then it's head down, I'm afraid.'

'I quite understand.'

'What I really need is somewhere to write.'

'Why don't you take Alan's study?'

Rose led me upstairs to an executive office. On its own, it was nearly as big as the flat I'd just vacated. I smiled.

'Perfect! Now, if you can just get rid of Al, I'll get to work. That's him, right?'

An oil painting of the room's previous owner stared down at us. Rose laughed sourly.

'His Archibald portrait. I'd forgotten that was still there. Shows how long since I've been in here.'

'You should burn it, my dear. A symbolic letting go of the past. Unless you're still in love with him?'

My tactless remark had its effect. A strange look came over Rose. She picked up a paperweight from the desk and slung it at the painting. It smashed into her ex-husband's left eye, causing a tear in the canvas.

'Oh bravo, good shot!' I called out a little too loudly, trying to cover my surprise. And now she'd begun, it was clear she might as well finish the job. Rose advanced on her husband and jolted the frame from its resting place. There was a crack as it met the floor. Then she picked up the painting and carried it to the window, looking to me for approval. I gave her the emperor's thumbs up, then flipped it down to signal the *coup de grace*. With an unladylike grunt, Rose heaved the portrait out the window. We heard it crash onto the ground a full storey below.

The sudden violence so contradicted my idea of Rose's nature that I was for a moment struck dumb. Again, I tried to cover up with a joke.

'Well, that's one way to do an eviction. Now you can paint one of me to replace it!'

To my further surprise - and increasing unease - she took me at my word.

'I'll phone Lionel at once!'

'As Rod Stewart might say, I was only joking, my dear.'

45

'He may as well paint someone who deserves it.'

'Rod Stewart?'

'Lionel, for heaven's sake.'

'You're serious? Oh. Well, why not? Thank you, my dear Rose, that's most kind. Look, one more thing, while we're at it. Can you spare an office for Jamie?'

'Is he moving in too?'

'Good Lord, no. He'll just drop in during the day to do all the boring admin stuff I don't have time for. Two or three days a week should be enough. You won't even know he's here.'

'Let me have a think.'

Sure enough, Rose found a downstairs office for Jamie. The following week he was in Monday to Friday, treating it like a day job. By now he was mentoring a couple of whiz kids he'd roped in. They'd head in for brainstorming sessions then go out on recruitment missions of their own. The Milinish was well and truly in business. Membership was already into the hundreds and with our flash new HQ there was no telling where it could go from here.

I was still kipping out in Steffi's bedroom, the best one in the house. Looks like old Steffi had grabbed it for herself. Well, she was OS, so I might as well use it. As for the rest of the house, the downstairs drawing room was a no-brainer for the temple. With its high ceilings and chandeliers it was quite the showpiece. Did I mention it was large? Let's just say if Rose had been around in Jane Austen days, she could have thrown a ball, so to speak. For the Milinish it was ideal for church services, workshops, and so on. Under my supervision, Jamie and his offsiders set it up just right. All we had to do was bung in a few chairs and a PA system, an altar and a pulpit up the front, and the temple of Milinish was in business.

The final touch was the portrait. Rose followed through on her idea. Indeed, she paid the artist double to begin at once. It was a bore sitting for it but my word, Lionel certainly pulled it off. There I am, the visionary prophet staring into the future, dark mane flowing, blue eyes intense, the light of inspiration illuminating my outline.

For the modern touch, certain props were painted into the background - a microscope in the top left corner, a copy of *Revelations of Milinish* in the top right. I'm wielding a sword-like crucifix, my steely gaze fixed upon a double helix shape - which is DNA, of course. Later editions of *Revelations* have a small reproduction on the cover, but it's nothing to the glory of the original at full size.

As a bonus, the artist painted the other great visual icon of Milinish, the simple, minimalist image of just six straight lines. An M topped by a cross - stark, but strikingly effective. You might say anyone could paint that, but as with many things in life, it's all about how it's done. At any rate, both these visual treasures took their place at the front of the new temple.

It was officially named the 'House of Adamcas' but I thought of it as 'The Lab-oratory.'

Oratory is a word with two meanings. An oratory is a small chapel, a place of worship. Oratory is also the art of eloquent public speaking. These two meanings have no connection, but I found one, for it was here that I honed my growing powers as an orator to persuade others to accept my doctrines.

Through speech, I learned how to coerce minds. It was easy enough dealing with people one on one, as with Jamie and Rose. Large groups were something else. To a degree, my church services were experiments in mind control. In that sense, the place was not just an oratory but a laboratory. A scientist needs a lab and this was mine.

Blame Orantor. He'd inspired me to take a more scientific approach to spirituality, so that's what I did. I formed a theory and tested it. My hypothesis was that when traditional religions fall apart all sorts of new ones spring up - and if I could gauge the spiritual climate correctly, I could launch the biggest new religion in the world.

My theory just needed a little testing and some guinea pigs. Luckily, people love structure. Once the Milinish became an official organisation, we attracted a steady stream of recruits. They became my experimental subjects. Some signed on as members, others were merely flirting with us - at first, anyway. Jamie put them all on a database and sent out invitations to our services, now held every Thursday and Sunday.

The Sunday group was closer to a normal church service, while the Thursday nights had a New Age or Eastern bent. Thursdays were for testing new material. As mentioned, the lecture tour had shown that interest in New Age matters was as high as in trad religion. For the new book, the question was whether to play up to this or stick to the subject matter of *Revelations*. It's the old showbiz conundrum. You want to reach a new audience without alienating your existing fan base. That's what the experiments were about. The idea was to test concepts on the Thursday group then ease them into Sundays to gauge crossover appeal. Results would influence the next book.

Meanwhile, Rose's patronage proved to be a mixed blessing. Like everyone else, she was caught up in the buzz of those heady early days, yet her excitement became rather too personalised in its focus. However much I tried to keep my distance, her visits to my part of the house became more and more frequent. It was pretty clear my comments about being a man of the cloth had done nothing to deter her amorous impulses.

I had no aesthetic objection. Rose was still very much in bloom and her ten years seniority didn't faze me at all. Yet the complications bound to arise - the awkwardness, the slippery slope of involvement - would be no help at all. Quite the contrary. Having just scored the perfect premises for the Milinish, it would be madness to risk them for the sake of some erotic shenanigans, no matter how diverting.

I was sitting at my computer one night, refining Milinish doctrine for the new book, when Rose came up from behind and began massaging the back of my neck. It was clear that matters were coming to a head. Quickly checking there was nothing controversial onscreen, I let her continue for a minute or so.

'Rose, I'm working,' I said at last.

'Don't mind me, Tom, keep going. Your neck's awfully stiff. Just pretend I'm not here.'

'That's easy for you to say.'

I felt a delicate, lacy material brush against my right ear. As for the scent, clearly in her position Rose wasn't going to bother with the cheap stuff. I changed to a black background onscreen and saw a reflection of Rose in some kind of exotic white nightie. She'd untied her hair so that it flowed down freely, its dark colour standing out against the pale outfit.

I felt a sudden urge to give in to this act of folly. Yet that was not the only danger of the moment; an abrupt refusal would hardly be a wise course either. A woman scorned does not a good patron make - and I saw what happened to her ex-husband's portrait. It was quite the Scylla and Charybdis. Best not do anything rash. Returning my focus to the new book, I read over the latest chapter and allowed Rose to gently knead and caress my neck and shoulders. Then I tried again.

'As wonderful as that feels, my dear Rose, I really should ask you to leave.'

'Why, Tom?'

'You know I can't do this.'

In answer, Rose undid my top button and slipped a hand inside my shirt. Her hair lightly brushed my cheek. This was getting harder by the moment.

'Please, Rose, think about what you're doing. Would you do this to Jesus?'

She kissed my ear and again I felt the urge to capitulate, tempered by the fading voice of restraint. They grappled briefly until prudence regained its hold over hedonism. Yet I sensed one more bout might produce a different result. In frustration I stood up, threw my host's hands from my body, and turned to rebuke her.

The angry hurt on Rose's face made it clear I'd gone too far. Again I recalled the smashed painting. My own portrait could easily go the same way. Then where would I be? Out on the street, the new HQ quickly won and as quickly lost.

That vivid flash of my beautiful portrait in pieces on the pavement sent me into sudden damage control. I seized the benightied Rose in both arms and kissed her on the lips, a deep and passionate kiss. She responded in kind and for long seconds we surrendered to our lustful desires. I began to undress her. Then all of a sudden I jerked back as if invisible hands had seized me by the scruff of my neck, wrenching me away. I staggered backwards against the desk, then threw myself prostrate upon the floor as if cast down by the Lord himself, weeping bitter tears. This dramatic turn of events shocked my seducer from her ardour. After some coaxing, she helped me into an armchair and put a consoling arm around my shoulders. I managed to speak through my tears.

'Forgive me, Rose, I may be the son of God but I'm still half-human. Please don't tempt me. The human side is all too real.'

I groaned aloud, as if in the throes of passion.

'Believe me, Rose, there's nothing I'd like more than to ravish you right now on Steffi's bed - but what sort of example would that set for my followers? No, my love, we must control ourselves and sublimate this sexual energy to a higher cause. Some tantric energy wouldn't go astray to power our mission.'

I allowed Rose to soothe and caress me, to wipe away my anguished tears. It seemed to satisfy her for the moment.

'But why?' she asked, her scented cleavage only inches from my face. I took the opportunity to bury my face between her breasts. Even now, I was perilously tempted to take a nipple into my mouth.

'Really, Tom. There are plenty of gurus who aren't celibate. Why should *you* be the ethical one?'

'I'm better than them, Rose. At least I want to be, God willing. Sleazy gurus are a dime a dozen. I want to be a better man - for you, for the people, and for Jesus.'

'But what's wrong with sex? What harm does it do?'

'How's it going to look if I warn my followers of Satan's temptations, all the while giving into them myself? I can't allow Satan to beat me, Rose. I just can't.'

I rubbed my face against Rose's cleavage, and softly howled.

'Oh Tom,' she said sadly, 'you're perfect.'

I lifted my head and gave her a rueful look.

'Far from it, my dear. That's exactly why I can't go there. And you know exactly where *there* is.'

Rose stood up, ardour replaced by melancholy, yet full of admiration for my enormous strength of character. I decided to end on a positive note. I drew myself up to my full height and embraced Rose, placing both hands firmly on her lower back. I kissed her again on the lips, more chastely this time.

'I wouldn't rule it out, Rose, not entirely. I will turn to Him for guidance. Perhaps He will permit it at a later date. But not now. I really feel we must lay a foundation for the movement. For the good of humanity and the world. Isn't that what really matters? Now go off to bed, I implore you.'

My host departed, sad yet strangely satisfied. As soon as she'd gone, I surrendered to Satan's evil temptations. Damage control phase two.

The next day, we tried to carry on as if nothing had happened. Awkward - but not as awkward as it *might* have been.

Now back to the services. There was no such thing as a typical Thursday night meeting. After all, Thursdays were experimental in nature. We usually played some mood music over the PA and burned enough incense to trigger an Eastern frame of mind. A good airing would clear the atmosphere by Sunday for the more traditional service.

The idea was to bombard people with pleasing stimuli of all five senses. There was the music and the incense - and not forgetting the hugs and the chocolate. Everyone got one of each when they arrived. As for the visuals, the temple had been done up beautifully, with the focal point our two great visual icons above the altar.

Sometimes, Jamie led a guided meditation for fifteen minutes, after which patrons opened their eyes to see that I'd manifested in the pulpit. Other times, it was Thomas Swan, the singing messiah bounding into the room with a guitar to lead a stirring rendition of our anthem, 'In Nihilum.'

Here's my swansong
but I'm not going anywhere soon
I'm just a cygnet, this is my Signet,
the signature of my decree
From my point of view,

51

it's a doctrinal stew for the ages
Skim the cream off the top,
we're the cream of the crop,
flee your cages

Lead us on into the dark
Cresting the sky in a bright, shining arc
Into nihilum we go
Into forever
and ever we go

And so on to the end. Everyone sang along, at least on the chorus.
Got to love those evangelical churches! Next we had a brief 'love
meditation.' That was me speaking over a New Age soundtrack:
you know, babbling brooks and birdsong over bland acoustic guitar
music. I'd intone a few words about spirituality and love over the
top of it.

With everyone now in a calm state of mind, it was time to
teach. I'd free associate on some topic based on my whim of the
day. The discussion period which followed helped me gauge how
well each one was received. If the response was enthusiastic, I'd
note the topic down for further development. If it was lukewarm
or drew awkward questions, it was placed on the backburner or
dropped altogether.

In the same way, I controlled the length of our closing social
sessions, when we wound down with some tea and snacks. If it had
been a good service with lots of energy, social intercourse could go
on indefinitely. If it had been a below par night, I found an excuse
to wind up proceedings and send everyone home.

Material for the next book began to accumulate.

Meanwhile, the Sunday services were slowly changing. To the
original mix of old style Christianity and Evolution with a hint of
Marxism and Buddhism, I was slowly adding New Age material
which might feature in the new book. One may wonder how on
Earth I managed to blend all these diverse doctrines. Basically my
slant was not 'showing the underlying unity in all religions' but
'showing all religions as cultural distortions of the Milinish.' For it

was the Milinish, of course, that was to end as the ultimate faith after swallowing all its competitors.

Eventually my own doctrines would rule supreme, but it took time to wean people away from their current beliefs. The congregation had to be softened up first, eased away from the traditions they were used to. This wasn't as hard as one might think. If people hadn't already sensed problems in their faith, they wouldn't be looking for alternatives in the first place.

More drastic changes were on the way in the new book. I warned people to be 'open-minded' about their beliefs because great social reforms were ahead. Finally, on the eve of the book's publication, I let loose a wrathful rant upon a packed temple. It doesn't quite come across on paper; you really had to be there to get the full effect. As with the painting, it's all in how it's done.

Remember how the German people were taken in by Hitler at the Nuremberg rallies? Don't misunderstand me - his crimes against humanity are unsurpassed - but when it comes to his skill as an orator, you can't deny it; what a showman. I've seen footage of him onstage, this 'greatest' of all cult leaders, and truth be told I ripped him off blind when it comes to technique.

The bewitchment of the audience happens in stages. You start by saying nothing. Simply command the audience with the silent strength of your aura. Look out at the crowd, make them beg you with the potency of their hunger. Feel the power of every eye focused upon your singular strength, every mind concentrated on the point of your command. Begin with measured tones and ominous pauses. Slowly build intensity of pitch and volume, finish with maniacal yelling. The words don't matter, it's all in the delivery.

While style will always trump content, this speech was clearly setting up for the doctrinal changes of the new book. The sermon of that apocalyptic Sunday was given to a full house at the temple, just before *Milinish in the New Age* came out. I looked out into the crowd, which filled every nook of Rose's large drawing room and spilled out the doors into the hallway.

'Sisters and brothers,
(Slowly and quietly).

We are few but we are many, and there are many more to come. We live at a time when great changes are transforming the world. And we're changing too. There are those among you who've been coming here each week, but after tonight there are some who won't be coming any more.

(Getting louder).

When Jesus spoke in the Bible, he spoke about the concerns of his day, in the language of his times. When I speak in this temple, I speak in the language of *my* day about the concerns of *my* times. Yet there are many in the old churches who refuse to accept that the world has changed. They still think we're living in the Jerusalem of two thousand years ago.

(Suddenly yelling).

They are fools! Hey you in the old church, let me give you the news. The Roman Empire has fallen! Let me give you some more news. Your churches are emptying!

(Softer again).

The old church cannot speak to the people of today. They've got no idea about what God wants. They haven't a clue what the people want, and that's why their congregations are shrinking. Truth is, there *will* be a new age of spirituality as God's kingdom comes closer. Most of you have heard about this so called 'New Age' that's all the rage. All this astrology and crystals and spirit guides and Christ knows what else. I could go on all night. But I've got to warn you there's a lot of rubbish out there. A lot of evil and lying and trickery. Who can you trust in today's crazy world? Well, you can trust in God to somehow tell you the truth.

(Loud).

I am sick and tired of religions fighting among themselves because they cannot admit the world has changed! God is sick of factionalism and fanaticism. God is sick of his children fighting together in the sandpit over who's right and wrong. It's all a load of crap! And that's why it's time for all religions and faiths to come together and join as one with the only true religion there is - the Milinish!

Any one of you not ready to open your heart and change your faith, you may as well leave. Any one of you not ready to believe in God's truth for today, get up and walk out! Take a look around you. Just look around, brothers and sisters. There's folks hanging from the rafters, beating down doors, begging and pleading just for the chance to get into this joint and what we're building here. So if you don't want to be part of it, get out now. Go on, get the hell out! You can *go* to Hell as far as I'm concerned! Anyone here who still wants to pretend Jerusalem is alive, get up and go back to your stick-in-the-mud old churches. And believe me, there's plenty of room for you! All of those who want to join in God's New Age, stay and be saved!

(Quieter again)

From now on there will be only one service of Milinish. All will join as one. My new book is out at midnight tonight. Anyone who has not read and understood it by this time next week should find themselves a new church to go to. There's a very long list of people trying to get into these services, so your places are easily filled. Now, you may go, but you should all depart with light hearts in the knowledge that at midnight tonight, the New Age of the Milinish begins.'

7

Aliens and Hash

There's more than one way to bend a spoon.
Battle of the Planets

'What do you mean you don't hate your parents? Everyone else does. Why not you?'

The hapless young man looked up and stammered some excuse. Literally. What a mess. He needed a massive shake up so he could turn his life around, and by Christ he was going to get it. But wait, I'm getting ahead of myself. Before I talk about our groundbreaking therapy workshops, I'd better say something about the new book. Here's an extract from *Milinish in the New Age*.

People keep asking for my views on 'New Age' concepts - reincarnation, spirit guides, and a bunch of other weird stuff. What does Thomas Swan have to say on these matters? Everything!

Some have asked why Adamcas and Evelyn were named Adam and Eve in the Bible. It was too early to explain this in *Revelations of Milinish*, but now it's time to reveal the whole story.

When God made Earth, he also made another planet called Primo. This was Earth's sister planet in another galaxy, far beyond Pluto. At the time of the first sin, Adamcas and Evelyn weren't just sent here. God divided their souls into two. One half was sent to Earth, the other went to Primo. God renamed them too. The part that came to Earth was called Adam and Eve, while the part that went to Primo was Cas and Lyn.

Life evolved on Primo, as it did on Earth, with a humanoid race at the top. And just like on Earth, the Primons were always fighting each other. Primo had four continents and their names were Ruanglia, Quavisia, Ismismo, and Fundamentia. The continents were at war with each other for so long that one day a bizarre geological event happened.

You may have heard of continental drift. What happened on Primo was continental split! The home planet broke into four pieces so there were four planets instead of one. I will speak about Fundamentia and Ismismo later. For now, I'll tell you about the planets Ruanglia and Quavisia.

The Quavisians are a scientific people with advanced technology. They're also a godless race who believe in physical life only. They don't believe in life after death, so they fear death immensely. Much of their research is aimed at conquering disease, and the Quavisian holy grail is finding an antidote to aging. On reaching the age of forty, the richest Quavisians are frozen in cryogenic chambers where they wait until the antidote is found. Everyone else just gets older.

Life expectancy on Quavisia has risen due to medical advances, so the planet has become hugely overcrowded. As a result, and because they are an aggressive, imperial race, spaceships have been sent out in search of new worlds to colonise. Some time ago these ships detected Earth from afar and chose it for colonisation. There have been several alien abductions recently. These are the work of Quavisian scout ships selecting humans for study in their laboratories.

Quavisia is at war with Ruanglia. That is no surprise because the civilisation on Ruanglia could not be any more different. The Ruanglians are a spiritual race with great psychic powers. They too are travelling

57

to Earth, not to conquer but to save it. Unfortunately, because Quavisian technology is so much more advanced, the Quavisian scout ships arrived in our galaxy first. So far the Ruanglians have only been able to project their spiritual bodies here, but in doing so they planted the seeds for many of the New Age practices. They telepathically sent us these ideas which are now so popular. They also sent out spiritual energy which solidified into crystals. Anyone with these crystals is protected from abduction by the Quavisian scientists.

The Ruanglian spaceships may be slower, but they are coming. Yet so is the Quavisian mother ship. In just a few years they will all reach Earth - and when they do, there will be a final conflict. Fire, famine, flood, and pestilence will rage, laying waste to the land. Three quarters of the world's people will be wiped out, but Ruanglia will win the war and together with the Ruanglians, we the Milinish will found a new kingdom on Earth. This is God's plan for humanity. I, Thomas Swan, am in the process of making psychic contact with the Ruanglian High Command and will brief everyone when this is achieved.

While this is God's plan, the result is far from certain. The final result depends on how well we combat evil. I warn you not to be complacent. Satan has drawn Quavisia here, and together they plot the enslavement of Earth. You must beware the Satan in your own hearts and bodies, and fear the skies.

Naturally, the book made quite an impact on our members. I'd prepared the ground with my 'Nuremburg address.' Once people were over the initial shock, most of them got on board. Sure we lost a few but for every soul that strayed, another five or six signed up. We were pulling in more members than we could handle. It was no longer enough for me and Jamie to run the show, we had to put on more admin staff just to keep up. For one thing, we were about to start the weekend encounter workshops. Rose was hesitant at first.

'Thirty houseguests! All weekend?'

'I know it's a lot of bother but just think of the progress we're making. We're recruiting thirty people a week for the Milinish army.'

'It's too much, Tom.'

'Look, they're paying four hundred bucks a head and a quarter of that's yours. Three grand a week in your pocket. I know you don't really *need* it, but a bit of pocket money doesn't go astray, right?'

Rose paused, then answered in a quieter voice.

'But where will we put them all? I don't have that many spare rooms.'

'Never mind that, they'll be camping out in the grounds. A bit of rough living will break them down quicker. We'll wack a few Portaloos out the back, so they'll hardly even have to come inside except for the actual sessions.'

'Oh, that's not so bad then - and if it's for the good of the movement. It does seem to be going awfully well.'

'My dear Rose, we're flying, and it's all thanks to you. I couldn't ask for a better patron.'

'You couldn't have done this in Fairfield.'

'Not on this scale, and nowhere near as quick - we'd be months behind schedule. Look at us now - we're really on the brink of something. Can you feel it?'

'Yes, I can. I really can.'

'And not just here. Guess what? *Revelations* is out in America. We're going international, my dear!'

'Wonderful!'

I placed a warm hand on the back of Rose's neck and gave it a gentle squeeze. Then I gasped in surprise and squeezed harder.

'Wait! I'm getting something.'

I shut my eyes for a few seconds.

'Rose, I just had the most amazing flash. I'm seeing you as our first queen in the new world! You look radiant.'

'Oh Tom! Really?'

'Radiant! I can see you all resplendent in robes of purple and gold, the colours of royalty.'

I removed my hand.

'But we're nowhere near that yet. It's going to take some hard graft first. That's where these workshops come in. Put everyone together for two days and we can fast track to instant psychic healing. The healthier people are mentally, the safer they are from Quavisian abduction and the more troops we'll have for the last battle.'

'Of course. I understand.'

What was the real purpose of the weekend workshops? Apart from being a recruitment drive, they allowed me to continue my experiments in mind control. Sessions were held in the lab-oratory, of course, and this scientific project had the bonus of being self-funding. Even after catering costs were taken out, plenty of cash was flowing into the Milinish coffers. The course had no shortage of applicants. On the contrary, with hundreds of people keen to attend and only thirty spots free, the rest had to go on a waiting list.

The workshops were billed as 'An Intense Psychological Encounter With God.' I'm not sure if God was in the building but the sessions were certainly intense. It was all about stripping people down and rebuilding them. There was some pain in that but it was worth it. People had been mollycoddled far too long. It was my job to give them a big spiritual kick up the arse.

Yet creating lifelong allegiance to the Milinish didn't just happen, it took some work. When I came off the *Revelations* lecture tour, I went straight into research mode about new religious movements - and found some fascinating material about cults. Yes, even at that early stage, I had an idea where this was going. Anyway, far as I can tell, the great Renaissance of cults was in the 1960s and 70s.

One of the most interesting books was on 'mind control.' It was written as a warning against the manipulative techniques used by cults, but for me it was pure textbook. I adopted it as a how-to manual. The very techniques the book warned against, I put to deliberate use in my workshops.

Let me explain, albeit briefly. When it comes to mind control, it's not just about the mind. One must address the whole self - body, mind, and emotions. The spirit will follow. That's what I did in the workshops.

First you disrupt the body's natural rhythms - and it all starts with sleep. Making people camp out the back was part of that. I kept them up late and woke them early. When folks are tired they're less resistant and easier to break down. As for food, the caterers were told to prepare high carbohydrates meals, boosted by caffeine and other legal stimulants. This made people high strung so they could be more easily played.

With the body prepared, the next step is to overwhelm the mind. To this end I gave long lectures which switched rapidly from one topic to another - reincarnation, UFOs, genes, the unconscious mind, and the Bible - all in the course of a single session. It was a game of hot potato and people tried to gobble it up, even if they couldn't digest it. Then there were the propaganda films. Jamie put together a geek squad to find and assemble footage, to which I added my own music and narration. It was all part of the workshop experience.

Yet the clincher was the emotional shakedown. I worked on the theory that most people are emotionally repressed. Now they were encouraged to release their emotions in explosive fashion. Catharsis is a wonderful enzyme - it liberates then it binds.

I can see it like it happened yesterday. I'm waiting at the door of the lab-oratory. There's Jamie, immaculate as ever in his CEO suit. I'm just as smart, but more flamboyant with my scarves and jewellery. Jamie's up the front of the room, about to cue the applause with a showbiz intro. 'Ladies and gentlemen, he's a scientific genius, he's a guru, he's the son of God. I give you the next president of Planet Earth, the man himself Thomas Swain!'

I'd bound into the room to a blast of rock n roll, strutting like a boxer, then raise my hands to absorb the applause.

'Thanks, Jamie, for those kind words. But you know what? I may be the son of God, but that don't make me special - because you're the son of God too. We're *all* the sons of God. Anyhow, never mind that. I'm not here to preach but to heal.

61

What do you guys think I do all day? Do I sit around praying? Well sure, I guess that's the day job, right? And I don't mind tossing off the odd Nobel Prize-worthy science theory in my spare time. That's my hobby. But there's more to life than work and play. The bottom line is I'm a healer and all I want is everyone to be happy. Not just you guys, not just the Milinish folks, but everyone in the world. Don't matter if you're Christian, Muslim, Jehovah's Witness or Jew. Y'all want to be happy, right? And not many of us *are*, are we? We're all struggling with that one. Well, here's a news flash. I've read and I've studied and I've meditated, and you know what? I've cracked the big one - how to be happy. You want to know my secret? You ready? Then here goes. If you want to be happy all you need is a good dose of hash.'

The workshop participants exchanged confused looks and nervous titters, then looked back at me and Jamie at the front of the room.

'Hash?' said Jamie, in mock surprise. 'What are you talking about, Tom? We don't do drugs here.'

'Course not,' I replied. 'I haven't done drugs since my life in third century Persia. Been straight as an arrow ever since, praise the Lord. See, when I say hash, I mean H-A-S-H. It's nothing to do with getting stoned, it's my new science of mental health.'

'Awesome,' said Jamie. 'What's it all about?'

'Well, guys, I've stripped it down to the fundamentals. The actual nuts and bolts - the DNA if you like - of human emotions. It all comes down to HASH, the four primary emotions. Happy, Angry, Sad, and Hope. HASH. See, everyone wants to be Happy, but there's always something in the way, right? And that makes us Angry. Behind the Anger, what we're really feeling is Sad, a great well of sorrow. If we can somehow move past that, we complete the emotional cycle and return to Hope. Then you're almost back to Happy again, hopefully this time for good! And there you go - that's the principle of HASH - my revolutionary new science of mental health.'

'OK Tom, I get it,' said Jamie, with a slight frown. 'Happy, Angry, Sad, and Hope. But hang on, can I ask you a question?'

'Lay it on me, brother.'

62

'Isn't that a bit simple? You know, to reduce everything to HASH like that?'

'On the contrary, Jamie, if anything it's not simple *enough*. I think of it as the Zen of Human Emotion. Look, I've been around the traps a bit and let me give you the scoop on psychology and the way they teach it at university these days. The long and the short of it, it's pretty much a racket. You want to do a psych degree at uni? Strap yourself in for four years of complicated crap with a lot of bullshit stats. Four years? I could teach their whole course in four days and still have time for a Star Wars marathon on day four. I'd put those monkeys out of business, pretty fast, don't worry about that.'

'So you're really saying all human emotions come down to Happy, Angry, Sad, and Hope?'

'Ultimately, that's what they boil down to. It's like the primary colours. You've got red, blue, and yellow. Every other colour is just combinations of those first three. In the same way, all the fancy emotions are combinations of HASH. They're the primary colours of the emotional spectrum.'

'Oh, right.'

'Or like DNA too, if you want a scientific analogy. The four building blocks of DNA are adenine, guanine, cytosine and thymine. All genetic combinations come from those four. Well, emotions are like that; it's all different mixes of HASH.'

'I get it, Tom. So how do we put HASH into practice?'

'It's really not as hard as you might think.'

I walked over to a whiteboard on the wall behind us, and wrote 'HASH' in big black letters.

'What are we aiming for?' I said. 'It's the double H, right? We all want Happy and Hope, It's the other two that get in the way, especially Anger. It's always Anger causing the energy block. What we need is a way to release it - but how? We've got to find a way to go right to the heart of the problem.'

'So how do we actually do that?'

I smiled and drew a circle around the letter A on the whiteboard.

'Here's where I'm gonna get a bit clever. Thing is, all you folks are angry for different reasons - but we've only got one weekend. Am I gonna do a bunch of one-on-ones with you guys? Have I got time for thirty private interviews? Hell no. Not with that Quavisian mother ship on the way. And at the end of the day, the details don't really matter. It's the *emotion* we have to release and all we need is a tool to release it. So I'm gonna go to the one thing we all have in common when it comes to Anger. You know what I'm talking about, Jamie?'

'No idea.'

'Let me give you a hint. There's two of them, they're the first things you see when you come out of the womb, and they got you into this whole Goddamn mess in the first place!'

'You don't mean ...?'

'Yep, good old Mum and Dad. If any one of you folks want to stand up and tell me you've never been pissed at the oldies, I'll call you a liar to your face.'

'But Tom, surely we all love our parents.'

'Course we love 'em. Didn't say you didn't? Doesn't mean you don't hate 'em too, and with good reason. Maybe they said no to lollies in the supermarket when you were toddlers. Or maybe they railroaded you into some soul-destroying career path as a teen. There's no lack of reasons to hate your parents, it's a no-brainer. Well, it's about time they gave something back after all the trouble they caused - they can help us get rid of the Anger. Goddammit guys, I want y'all to have the tantrum from Hell right here, right now. If you want to get rid of your Anger and be Happy, fire up. If you don't want to be Happy, the door's over there, and when it hits you on the arse on the way out, just think of your mama's heavy hand.'

Off they went - and by Christ it worked! It was tantrum central in the lab-oratory - and didn't they all feel better when they finally got to release all that Anger! When they were done, I'd go straight up and rub the 'A' off the old whiteboard. Once people had their tantrum, however, they realised they loved their parents after all and felt terribly Sad, so they had a good old cry. Let's just say we were singlehandedly keeping the Kleenex company in business.

After that, people were urged to 'strip away the bullshit' and face up to their own weaknesses. Everyone had to stand in front of the group and denounce themselves. They had to admit the only reason they weren't getting what they wanted out of life was they were too gutless to take it. Giving themselves a good tongue-lashing was the first step towards success. If anyone found it hard to get started, I gave them a helping hand. Might seem harsh but the tough love was for their own good. Sometimes the old hash can be a bit harsh on the throat when you're sucking it down, but you still get stoned. At least that's what I remember from my life in third century Persia.

For example, there was a young guy by the name of Luke Simons who just wasn't getting into the spirit of the workshop. He was too repressed to have a tantrum against his parents. He'd mumbled some weak excuse about not hating them and now here he was in front of the group stuttering like a fool, too proud to denounce himself like everyone else.

Yet denunciation was just what he needed. His life was a mess. He'd even been rejected by the army, discharged for trying to keep a pet dog on base, which was against regulations. His mother, a regular at our meetings, was worried about her boy and paid for him to take the course. But he was wasting her money. He needed a good psychological head-kicking - it could well be the turning point of his life. All he had to do was face up to his own failings. Trouble was, he couldn't even get to square one. Like I said, he needed a helping hand.

'Luke,' I said. 'This weekend, twenty-nine people had the courage to change their lives. Twenty-nine people had the balls to get up in front of the whole damn group and confess their weaknesses. But not you. Why? Are you perfect? Are you a role model? I tend to doubt it.'

Simons' military training kicked in and he stood to attention. He was a big lad but timid as a mouse. A milky-haired milksop, six foot nothing. I raised my voice to a sergeant major's shout.

'Who do you think you are? You don't hate your parents, eh! You think you're better than everyone? Everyone else in this room hates their parents. But not you. No, not goody-two-shoes Luke Simons.

Look at you - Simple Simons! Mummy's boy. The sick thing is you actually believe you love your folks. Well - let the conscious mind play its little games. Let Adamcas weave his deceptions. Maybe you do love them with the conscious mind - but unconsciously you want to kill your father and God only knows what you want to do to your mother. Why do you think you joined the army in the first place? So you'd have someone to tell you what to do, for starters. Then to go out into battle and kill your father over and over again, hopefully getting killed yourself at some point so you could stop being such a failure. You think your parents love you? Wake up son! It's Satan protecting his DNA, that's all.'

Simons cowered, as well he should. His lower lip started to wobble.

'And why were you kicked out? For keeping pets. More self-delusion. You really think your puppy loves you? Don't you know animals are 99% DNA controlled and only 1% soul? The only reason an animal loves you is because the gene for love was selected by evolution as an aid to genetic survival.

What if you're drowning and your dog gives its life to save you, is that love? Course not. The gene for self-sacrifice is all about genetic self-interest. You got the dog as a puppy, right? The poor animal thinks you're related, so it's programmed to save you at the cost of its own life. Why? Just so you can live to pass on the genes the deluded dog thinks you both share. It's called kin selection and it's one of Satan's biggest con jobs. Wake up, Luke. Your dog doesn't love you, your parents don't love you. We in the Milinish don't believe in bullshit when it comes to understanding emotions. Why not be honest for once and have the guts to face reality!'

Thankfully, that did the trick. For perhaps the first time in years, Luke felt an honest emotion. He burst into tears and admitted that he hated his parents and himself, and he wanted to change his whole life. Everyone cheered and applauded. It looked like life was going to take a turn for the better for that young man.

It's so important to be able to bond with the group. To strip down to raw, honest emotions. One way to achieve group bonding was for everyone to confess a secret they'd never told anyone else before. Something they were ashamed of, preferably the worst thing they ever did. It was such a relief for people to release their guilt like that in a trusting environment.

Yes, what people needed was a good dose of HASH. They wanted to be Happy, they'd released their Anger and Sadness, now it was time to send them out into the world feeling Hope. At the end of the weekend, everyone was exhausted and ready to hear my message of the Golden Future.

I told them the world was heading for big, big changes and they had a simple choice - they could be part of the problem or part of the solution. Only those who chose to be part of the solution would survive the incredible changes that were coming in the next few years. Which choice would they make?

It was a no-brainer. By the end of the weekend workshop, everyone was united in the desire to serve the Milinish and be saved from the Quavisian apocalypse. Then it was a big group hug and off they went. Wow, this mind control stuff really works.

8

Mutiny

To create is hard, to criticise easy.
Revelations of Milinish

It's rumoured that God moves in mysterious ways. I can confirm it as fact. After a few months of blitzing the field, I was suddenly under siege from all sides. It all started one day when Jamie tapped on my office door.

'Tom, we've got a problem.'

'Not now, Jamie, I'm writing.'

'You'd better take a look at this. Someone's filed a law suit against you.'

'A law suit? Who?'

'Guy named Luke Simons. Do you know him? Says he did one of the workshops.'

I swivelled round in my chair and stared into space.

'Simons ... Luke Simons. No, can't place him. What's his problem anyway?'

'Looks like your techniques didn't work out for him. He's suing for mental cruelty.'

'Hang on ... Simons? Not that army guy, is it? Well I'll be damned. Little bastard's suing me, is he? What for?'

'Reckons he had some kind of breakdown after the session. He's been in therapy ever since.'

'So what? People are *supposed* to be broken down when they come here. Broken down from the pathetic creatures they are and rebuilt as spiritual warriors.'

'It won't work for everyone I guess.'

I grabbed the letter from Jamie. At the sight of a pompous letterhead and some legal jargon, I tossed it aside almost immediately.

'Jesus Christ, I may be a miracle worker but I'm not infallible. For every thousand cured, there's always one Luke Simons. That's not my fault.'

'What do we do, Tom?'

'Stop helping the ingrates, that's what. Why should I bother trying to save humanity anyway? I've half a mind to pack it in and go home. Let the poor fools save themselves.'

'Can't you try talking to him? Offer him a free workshop or something?'

'I'll make him an offer alright. Well, well, sign of the times, ain't it? Everyone wants someone to blame. It's the government, or their parents, or God. Now it's my turn. A lawsuit! You try to help someone and they turn on you. Is it my fault he can't take a bit of tough love? How did his genes ever last this long? That's what I can't figure out.'

'Maybe we should get some legal advice. I can go through the member list, we've probably got a lawyer or two on the books by now.'

'Don't bother, Jamie. I'll handle this myself. But sure, you go through that database. Get me Simons' address. I'll give him some therapy alright!'

When Jamie left, I racked my brains for a solution, then smiled. Of course! Thank God I had the foresight to include those trust and confession exercises in the workshop, and the even greater foresight to record them. And good Lord, I've been around a bit, but even I blushed at some of the titbits served up for confession. The lengths people go to just so Satan can perpetuate his DNA.

I went through the tapes and found just what I was after. For all his innocence, Luke had been party to an indiscretion or two himself. In that wonderful mood of workshop catharsis, it had seemed a good idea to unburden himself - and there I was to lend a sympathetic ear. Succour for the sucker.

Jamie gave me Simons' address. It was now a simple matter of driving over with a couple of burly brethren to intercept him as he stepped out one day. We took a limo for effect and the boys shoved young Luke into the seat opposite me. The poor fool began shaking like a jellyfish in a breaker. I looked at him silently for a minute, arranging my features into an expression of paternal concern.

'Well, Luke. I see the long arm of God's spiritual law has brought us together again.'

Simons shrank and began stuttering like a fool. I'd better edit down his side of the conversation or you'll be up all night trying to finish the book. When he finally cobbled together a sentence, he did manage a small show of defiance. Maybe the workshop did him some good after all.

'Don't touch me, you bully. If you do anything to me, my lawyer will get you sent to jail.'

Oh. On second thoughts it was rather pathetic. I smiled a sad, compassionate smile.

'Luke, Luke, I told you about this during the workshop. When are you going to get over your castration complex and this infantile need for a father figure? You're an adult now. You don't need lawyers to fight your battles. Don't you realise lawyers are one of the most highly evolved of Satan's DNA organisms? Their ancestors were too gutless to fight it out in the jungle with the big predators, so they hid and replicated themselves by stealth. In the modern world, stealth and treachery are the most useful traits around because of all the money and women they bring, so lawyers are evolving in ever greater numbers. Do you realise you're consorting with the Devil's high emissaries?'

'I don't believe in your silly theories anymore. My uncle says they're nothing but pseudoscientific nonsense.'

'Your uncle says! Who are you going to ask next, the cat? For God's sake, it's high time you started thinking for yourself. And don't start blubbing, you're not at your therapist's now.'

I shook my head. Sometimes my love for humanity was sorely tested.

'What's wrong with us all? We've become a nation of sooks. Spill a cup of coffee on yourself these days and the first thing people do is burst into tears and hire a lawyer. By Christ, the founding fathers are turning in their graves at this lily-livered lot we've become. Crossed the sea in no more than a fleet of sailboats, they did, to settle this land. Fought nature, disease, hacked their way through virgin land and built this country up from scratch. Did it without electricity, medicine or Google. Built it up with nothing but grit and guts, on a wing and a prayer, death hovering over 'em like a vulture every step of the way. And look at us now, a shameful pack of sooks without a clue how good we've got it. Sanitised perfection's our natural born entitlement, so we're led to think. It's a sick, sick world.'

I flung open the door of the Limo and bellowed skyward.

'Father, I beseech thee - strike humanity down! Unleash your wrathful retribution upon this race of woodlice! Send a new flood! A fire! Anything to rid the land of this vermin!'

I shut the car door and returned to my normal speaking voice.

'You know what, Luke, I'm sorry you don't listen to the word of the Lord anymore, but here's something else you can listen to.'

I flicked on a recording of Simons' confession from the trust sessions and his face whitened. When the implications had sunk in, I closed the deal.

'I think we've wasted enough time, let's get down to business. Owing to the dreadful trauma you've suffered from my attempts to save your soul, I'm giving you an out of court settlement. But understand this - if I receive one more letter from you about any legal matter, I'll send that recording to your lawyer. See if he wants to represent you then, shall we?'

I handed him a fifty dollar note and opened the car door.

'I'm refunding ten percent of your workshop fee. And my word, when I was a boy, that was a lot of money. Not so much these days, it might get you ten minutes with your therapist.'

My next problem was closer to home. In fact, at home. My righteous deep sleep was shattered one morning by an electric light and a posh young girly voice polished by the best schooling money can buy.

'Oh my God! Who the fuck are you?'

71

Jolted awake, I recognised my assailant from the various photos around the house. Let's just say it wasn't a happy recognition.

'Steffi, please!'

Rose trailed her daughter into the bedroom, face aghast. I looked from one to the other. Steffi had blonded her hair. Other than that, they were cut from the same mold alright - only one was twice as young and half as nice.

'Really, Mummy, did you have to put him in my room?'

'You didn't you say you were coming home. How was I to know? I'm dreadfully sorry, Tom.'

'Who's Tom? Your boyfriend?'

'Steffi! Tom's a spiritual leader doing extremely important work for the world. He's staying here until he finds a permanent home.'

Assuming this would immediately clear things up, I shot Steffi a beatific smile. Yet from the look on her face, anyone would think I'd just run over her dog. I decided to take control of the situation.

'Look, why don't we start over? Someone's got out of bed the wrong side this morning and given that I'm not up yet, it can't be me. Let's get acquainted over breakfast, then I'm more than happy to change rooms.'

To this, Steffi consented. Yet such was her state of sulk, it was an awkward meal, to say the least. I felt like the despised stepfather trying to win over the bratty teenage daughter, with all the futility that entails. She cold-shouldered my efforts to quiz her on the New York fashion scene she was trying to break into. Even my dredged up memory of *Project Runway* on TV didn't hit the mark. I hinted at a close acquaintance with Tim Gunn, but my insinuation I could get her a spot on the show was met with snorts of derision. Before long she'd made a sullen exit. Rose turned to me with a pained expression.

'I'm so sorry,' she said. 'There's no call for this sort of behaviour. I'll have a word with her.'

I placed a firm hand over hers.

'How long's she staying? We don't have time for this. Not now. Nothing can be allowed to interrupt the work.'

'I've no idea. I didn't even know she was coming.'

'Why all this anger? Where does it come from?'

'That's what I don't understand. All her life, Steffi's never wanted for a thing. Her father and I indulged her every wish.'

'And this is how she repays you! I think we'd better get her into one of the workshops quick smart and find out what's going on. No doubt there's some really poisonous material we need to get out in the open.'

Rose picked up a cloth and began twisting it into a spiral. Much like a DNA helix.

'A workshop? Surely that's not necessary.'

'Why not? She's clearly harbouring a great deal of anger towards you. To think that a girl with such loving and supportive parents could end up hating them so much. What a paradox. It'll make a fascinating case study. Just think of the implications and what we can learn. It may make up a significant portion of my next book. I'm going to study this in immense detail.'

'You can't be serious!'

'I most certainly am. This is quite brilliant! I must admit, at first I wondered why the Lord would send your daughter home just when we're doing so well. Now I get it. What an opportunity for research.'

'I'd really rather you didn't.'

'Don't think of yourself, my dear, think of the movement and what we can learn. In fact, when we're done with Steffi why don't you get your son back and we'll start on him too?'

'Michael? Oh no. Please, Tom, there's no need for any of this.'

'If that's the way you feel, fine, but if you're not going to heal her through the workshops, she's got to go.'

'I don't even know why she's here.'

'Neither do I, Rose, nor do I care. Just get rid of her. Can't you give her some money to go back to New York?'

'She never listens to me anyway.'

'Then I put it to you as a direct spiritual challenge: assert yourself!' I slapped my hand on the table. 'Do it for me, do it for Jesus - and above all, do it for yourself.'

'I'll try, Tom. Really I will.'

The next couple of days a cold war settled over the house. Steffi and I adopted the policy that if you can't say anything nice, say nothing at all. We were as ghosts to one another and may have continued indefinitely in this mode. That was until I heard what she was saying behind my back. I wandered downstairs one morning and heard loud voices from behind the kitchen door.

'How can you stand it?'

The reply was too soft for me to catch, so I edged right up to the door and put my ear to the crack. Steffi was holding court like the brat she was.

'It's bad enough having the others here during the day, but he's here all the time.'

'It's no trouble at all, dear. I love having Tom here.'

'Are you sleeping with him? Is that it?'

'Really, Steffi, anyone would think I'm the daughter and you're the mother.'

'Just answer the question.'

'I'm not, as it happens, but it's really none of your business.'

'It is if I come home and he's sleeping in my bed. Why'd you let him move in?'

'If Jesus comes to the inn asking for lodgings, who am I to turn him away?'

'Jesus? He's not Jesus, he's dodgy as. And you know what? I'm going to do some research on this Thomas Swan and find out who he really is.'

'Why do you have to be so cynical? Is this what New York's done to you?'

'Look, Mummy, I know you've gone in for some wacky fads in the last few years, but this is too much. You haven't given him any money, have you?'

Through the door, I heard a defiant laugh.

'If you must ask, it's the other way around. I'm getting a healthy percentage of Tom's workshop fees every week.'

'Oh really? Spreading the wack to others, are you? Brainwashing them - is that it?'

'How would you know, Steffi? Have you read Tom's books, or is this the voice of know-it-all youth passing judgment? At least

Tom's bringing some income into this family rather than draining it like you and your brother.'

'Since you mention Michael, Mummy, I've emailed him about what's going on here. He's thinking of flying home to sort it out.'

'Oh really? You two have quite a nerve, you know that? You're off playing around with your silly careers in the States and you seem to expect me to sit around doing nothing. Then as soon as I develop an interest of my own, you want to interfere when it's none of your damn business. Well you can jolly well fuck off, the pair of you!'

Listening from behind the door, I almost broke into applause - and Rose wasn't finished yet.

'What's so special about you, Steffi? You know, I hope you and Michael do get somewhere in your lives. I really do. But there are plenty of fashion designers and actors already. The world's not going to fall apart if you fail. Tom, though - well, he's gone right to the heart of everything. He's dealing with the deepest issues in life and trying to save the world. If you and Michael think you're going to interfere, you can forget it.'

'Oh my God, this guy has really gotten to you. Are you brainwashed? What's he done to you?'

'Brainwashed? Not at all. Actually, I'm seeing things as they are for the first time in my life. For twenty-five years I let your father tell me what I could and couldn't do - and then the bastard walked out. And if you and your brother think you're going to take up where he left off, then why don't we put a freeze on the trust fund and you can jolly well piss off and start earning a living for yourselves.'

There was a pause, then Steffi replied in a strangely calmer tone.

'Come on, Mummy, don't be silly. We're worried about you, that's all. We just don't want you taken advantage of by some conman.'

'Taken advantage?'

Rose laughed again. There was a note off aggressive liberation in the laugh, like a burst water pipe.

If you really must know, Steffi, I'd gladly give myself to Tom, body and soul. He could have me right here on the kitchen table every day of the week and twice on Sunday - but Tom's the perfect gentleman. He *refuses* to take advantage.'

'That's a relief at least - but I don't get it. If he's not taking sexual or financial advantage, then what does he want?'

'And there you go again with your nasty New York cynicism.'

'All I'm saying is I'm going to check this guy out. Find out who he is.'

'You can please yourself, Steffi, I really don't care. Tom's the best thing to happen to me for years, and nothing you say will make a jot of difference. Feel free to purchase a one way plane ticket back to the States at the earliest opportunity. It's my treat. It won't make a dent in my workshop income.'

Game, set, and match, Rose. I took a few steps backward, then strolled noisily up and opened the kitchen door. I gave a start as if surprised to see Steffi, then beamed radiantly at her.

'Hello, Angel,' I said, 'Isn't it a splendid day to be alive on God's green Earth.'

Steffi shot me a look of pure hatred and exited the room with a violent slam of the door. I raised my eyebrows at Rose and gave her a quick kiss on the cheek, and then the lips.

So there it was, another foe vanquished, another victory for the Lord and his divine plan. At that point, it was all done and dusted, time to get out the brandy and cigars. And it would have been too, if not for Current bloody Edge.

9

Pontius Pilates

He laughed at Darwin in 1859.
Some things improve with time - fine wine!
Continents can never move, if you get my drift.
He will pooh-pooh your views - short shrift!

Cultown Album Lyrics

At about that time I was discovering the dark side of fame. It brings a ton of love and two tons of trouble. We began to get all sorts of bad publicity in the press. We were described as a 'controversial group,' for example. There was talk of my 'eccentric teachings' and 'confrontational workshops.'

Then a tabloid TV show called *Current Edge* did an unauthorised piece on us. That's the first time we got called a cult. I went out in the car one day and came home to see a couple of suited goons blocking the driveway. One had a camera, the other a microphone. The one with the mic stuck it in my car window.

'Thomas Swan, *Current Edge*. Couple of quick questions.'

'I'm sorry, workshops are full this week. Call reception for bookings.'

'Are you a really a church, or just a cult? Any comment?'

'It's my day off. All interview requests go through the office.'

'Is it true you brainwash people?'

'No more than you do.'

I wound up my window, then triggered the automatic gate. Not for the first time, I cursed its slovenly pace in rising, and tried to ignore the young go-getter rapping on the glass at my ear. Finally I gave him the thumbs up and drove in.

They were back the next day. I'd gone out for a morning stroll through the leafy streets of Vaucluse. When I returned they were sitting on someone's fence half a block from home. As I walked towards my assailants, they stood up and prepared to give chase. Clearly, they were used to their targets running away. But instead of retreating, I walked so confidently towards them that they started to back off themselves. I increased my pace and took hold of the mic before looking directly into camera.

'People of Australia, listen to me. My name is Thomas Swan. I am the greatest scientist since Darwin. I also lead the biggest new spiritual movement in the world. But don't just take my word for it. Talk to our thousands of new members. Talk to those I've cured in my therapy workshops. Their lives have changed for the better - so can yours. Come join us. You'll never be the same again.'

I shook hands with the reporter, gave back the mic, then walked calmly through the front gate. You'd think that was the end of it, but the very next day I was upstairs in my study when Rose put through a phone call.

'Thomas Swan?'

'Speaking.'

'Louise Green, *Current Edge*. We're doing a story on you and your group.'

'I don't blame you. We're the fastest growing religion in the world. Naturally your viewers want to know about us.'

'How about an interview?'

'I'd love to, Louise, but I'm absolutely flat out. In a couple of months there may be a gap in my schedule.'

'We're running the story Sunday week so it's now or never.'

'Next week? I may be a miracle worker but there *are* limits.'

'Don't you want a right of reply?'

'What do you mean?'

'There are some pretty serious allegations against you and your group. About your workshops, your services. Surely you'd like the chance to respond.'

'How about I save time and respond over the phone? The Milinish is the salvation of the world and our workshops are setting the standards in human psychology for decades to come. If you

78

can convey that message to your viewers, that'll be of some use. Now I really must get on with my work.'

'Then we'll say you declined to be interviewed.'

'As I said, there may be a spot in my schedule in a month or so. What's your hurry?'

'It's a matter of public interest. You're the biggest new cult of the decade.'

'Eh - what did you call me? A cult?'

'That's right.'

'Really, Louise, if you're going to use such provocative language, I've got to seriously question your agenda. You're doing a story on the Milinish, you say. And what sort of story is *that* going to be? A joyful good news story to showcase our message to the world? A fair and balanced appraisal of our organisation? Or a hatchet job to make me into a bogeyman for the titillation of middle-Australia? And given the nature of your program, that's not a very hard question to answer.'

'We're giving you the chance to put your case.'

'My case, is it? What's this, Thomas Swan in the dock! And that's the thanks I get for trying to save the world.'

'We're giving you a chance to explain.'

'Mighty big-hearted of you. So let's say I invite you round for a full briefing. I can go all night, believe me. Three, four hours, and I'll still be dispensing the wisdom your viewers sorely need. But what's my four hours up against the might of your editor's scissors and those pesky TV time limits? You'll be whittling my four hours down to fit your fifteen minute segment and who knows what we'll end up with?'

'We're giving you the whole hour.'

'What, all forty-five minutes? Rightly so, I suppose. Still, I know what you TV types are like. Surgeons? More like butchers. The hatchet job or the stitch up, it all comes to the same thing. So here's my counterproposal. What say I give you your interview and you give me the producer's chair? You get your story, I make sure it's fair. It's win-win.'

'We can't do that.'

'Course you can. Trouble is, that ain't the story you want to make. Your mind's made up. You already called us a cult. We both know what you want - the dirt. You want me to say I've got a harem of wives and thirty-eight kids. Our church services are pagan rites with orgies in honour of Satan. That's what you want to hear, isn't it?'

'We want the truth. We've been gathering evidence for a while now.'

'There you go again - 'evidence' - like I'm some kind of criminal. I suppose it goes with the territory. They crucified Jesus. You're just another Pontius Pilate. You want to crucify me for the entertainment of middle-Australia. Ha - you're Pontius Pilates, more like. A fitting moniker if I say so myself. Why don't you bring a crucifix to the interview and nail me up?'

'Why don't you tell me more about the wives and orgies?'

'I was being facetious. If you don't understand that, there's little point in us speaking at all.'

'Are you denying the orgies? Do you deny you have a harem of twelve wives?'

'Twelve? I've got a harem of twelve wives? Where'd you get that from? Oh right, the disciples. I've got twelve wives like Jesus' disciples. How's that work then? One wife a month? Or a different one each day for a fortnight with Sundays off to recover. Is that it?'

'So you do?'

'I'm celibate as it happens. Look, I've wasted enough time on this rubbish. You're not getting an interview. What's more, I'm forbidding you to run the story. Your program will be monitored and any report on the Milinish will lead to consequences.'

'I can assure you, Mr Swan, we're going to air Sunday week. The story's ninety percent done.'

'So much for my interview then. Why bother? You've obviously made your mind up. Now I give you fair warning. You're messing with forces greater than you can imagine.'

'What do you mean?'

'Do you realise I could kill you remotely through the power of my mind? Simply through the power of visualisation, I could send radioactive particles down this phone line to stop your heart.'

'Is that so?'

'It's fortunate for you I follow the commandments. Through my Buddha-nature I tread the path of compassion. *By the power of the Swan, all were at peace. And not a bug nor a slug did he slay that day.* That's a quote from my last book. Still, all actions have consequences, make no mistake about that. When your equipment malfunctions next week, don't go looking for technical causes. Just think of me sitting quietly in my office. With the one percent of my mind left over from doing the Lord's work, I'll be sending out quantum waves to sabotage your technology.'

'You must be remarkably powerful.'

'You've no idea who you're dealing with. So understand this - my people will be watching your broadcasts and if you so much as mention the Milinish, I'll cause an immediate national blackout to disrupt all electronic broadcasting. It might cause a wee dip in your ratings. How are your advertisers going to like that?'

'This is all gold. Are you sure you won't give us an interview?'

'Forget it.'

'Never mind, I think we have enough material now.'

'Then I'll bid you good day.'

I hung up and pondered the disquieting implications of the woman's last remark. Could it be I'd gotten a bit carried away? Well, it was spilt milk now. I shrugged and got on with my work.

That lasted until I saw the first promo for the show. There was a shot of me winding up the car window, a look of thunder on my face. The slow-mo made it look worse, and it didn't help that they'd overdubbed my voice saying 'do you realise I could kill you simply through the power of my mind?'

I went straight to our website and placed an official ban on *Current Edge* in the following proclamation.

Dear Friends,

Evil comes in many forms. I've spent my whole life fighting it and thanks to you all, we're winning. Yet Satan has friends in many places, not least the media. The tabloid press has been running humanity down for a long time. Its stock-in-trade is scandal, misery and attacking those in high places. Now it's my turn. I'm sure you've heard of that grubby little show, *Current Edge*. They're running a story on me, and I mean 'story' in the fictional sense. Even the trailer is a complete fabrication, using editing tricks and fakery to run me down.

My friends, I urge you in the strongest possible terms to ignore this shameful attempt to tarnish my good name. I'm placing an official ban on this program. If you feel the urge to watch it, that's just Satan trying to control your mind. Nothing more, nothing less. I put it to each of you as a personal challenge to resist. It should be a matter of conscience. Make sure you stand firm for your own sake, and the good of our noble cause.

A few days later, I sat down and watched the debacle. It was worse than I'd feared. They'd taken about ten seconds of footage, slowed it down to half-speed, and freeze-framed me at the worst possible moment. Then the trademark *Current Edge* bullshit narration began, in all its ponderous retardation.

'He's got twelve wives and thirty-eight kids. He runs weekend rituals at his secret Sydney base. He says he's a messiah here to change the world. And it's all going on in the affluent suburb of Vaucluse.'

On came Louise Green, looking smug.

'We hope you're able to watch this program. Thomas Swan forbade us to run it. He warned us he could use his mind to cause a national blackout to stop it going to air - but here we are. So just who is Thomas Swan? He claims to have found the secret of life. We've turned up a few secrets about him.'

My voice came back on, digitally slowed down a little to make me sound more sinister.

'I've got a harem of twelve wives. Our church services are pagan rites with orgies in honour of Satan.'

In our phone conversation, I'd pronounced the word 'wives' with an upwards inflection to indicate a question. It had been

82

electronically altered to go down in pitch, as if it were a statement. As for my second sentence, that was a joke from earlier in the conversation which they'd placed out of context. Then it was back to Louise Green.

'There are plenty of rumours about what really goes on at Milinish HQ. Those rumours haven't stopped hundreds of people going to Thomas Swan's weekend workshops. Swan says he uses advanced psychology to heal people, but not everyone is convinced.'

On came Luke Simons. His face was blurred out but it was clearly him. I recognised his pissy little voice even through the voice mangler. Then it was time for a rent-an-expert. Dr Rupert Parker, a psychologist.

'These organisations are completely unregulated. Without the proper training, they can do serious harm to people. There have even been cases of suicide. I urge anyone seeking therapy to only use accredited professionals, not these backstreet cowboys.'

Then it was back to my face and voice.

'Do you realise I could kill you remotely through the power of my mind? Simply through the power of visualisation, I could send radioactive particles down the phone line to stop your heart.'

OK, I did say that, but what happened next was a total lie. There was a quick shot of me outside Rose's house, walking towards the two goons who tried to ambush me. I recalled they'd been backing away. Only one problem - the footage was played in reverse so it looked like I was walking backwards, retreating from them! At that point, I swore and turned off the TV.

Well, well, here was the dark side of fame. This certainly wasn't going to help the cause. I was starting to get fed up with Australia. It was one attack after another. First Luke Simons' lawsuit, then Steffi, now *Current Edge*. Whatever next? There was one other attack worth mentioning, given its relevance to later events in this story. It was from a group called the Naysayers society. These people call themselves 'skeptics.'

What is a skeptic? Try thinking Orantor squared and you're getting close. Skeptics groups like to think they perform a social function. Their chosen task is to 'keep society rational.' They want to stop people believing in things like ESP, religion, or the tooth fairy. Skeptics are the watchdogs of science, yet as an organisation they've sprung up quite recently, mainly to combat the spread of New Age beliefs. This calls for a bit of background.

Modern Western societies have mainly accepted the 'scientific worldview,' that is, the one Orantor favours. It's a secular world in which all events have physical causes and rational explanations. The trouble is, since about the 1960s, there has been more and more belief in weird things like reincarnation, near-death-experiences, and other 'crazy' ideas. Skeptics groups have risen to combat such beliefs.

Skeptics are supposedly defined by doubt, but with their belief in science they can be as committed as anyone. Their official journal, *The Naysayer*, has two main aims: first, the debunking of weird things, and second, the veneration of anything that comes under the heading of 'real science.'

Of course, the Naysayers had a field day with me. Skeptics despise religion and the New Age, and their strongest disapproval is for the leaders of religious cults who try to lead others astray.

It came in the post one day - obviously sent by them - a copy of *The Naysayer* journal which showed I had turned into their public enemy number one. At the annual Naysayer prize night, I'd been awarded the 'Bent Fork' award for pseudoscience.

Bent Fork Award
by Gordon Young

The Naysayer Bent Fork Award for 'the most outrageous piece of pseudoscientific rubbish of the year' has been unanimously awarded to Thomas Swan, self-styled guru and leader of the cult of Milinish.

Mr Swan qualifies for the award on so many grounds it would be impossible to list them all, but highlights among his 'achievements' include a laughable misappropriation of evolutionary theory, apocalyptic UFO mongering, and the 'self-help' workshops that help you straight to the lunatic asylum.

It would be hilarious if it wasn't all so dangerous. Swan's books have sold by the truckload, a fact which simply underlines the need for the public to be protected from the type of pernicious misinformation peddled by him and his kind. I propose the first step in this process should be the award to Thomas Swan of not just Bent Fork of the Year, but Bent Fork of the Decade.

I wasn't too upset by this piece. Orantor's original attack on *Old Religion, New Science* upset me when I was a raw rookie. It was all new to me then, but my hide had thickened with each attack. The skeptics were just one foe among many. They could give me a whole drawer full of bent kitchen utensils for all it upset me on a personal level. Even so, there was no denying the publicity was bad for business.

I was starting to get sick of Australia - it was nothing but a nation of knockers. People put you on a pedestal one day and tried like hell to knock you off it the next. Well, they could all go and get stuffed. Bugger lawsuits, bugger meddling bloody daughters, and most of all bugger the blood-sucking media.

While those were difficult times, it's worth remembering that God works in mysterious ways. Life was about to change. Remember chaos theory? A little bit of chaos goes a long way. All the way to America in fact. And like a boomerang, it comes right back. Enter Victor.

10
Sins of the Father

Everyone's got their own cross to bear. Then they meet me.
Milinish in the New Age

We've all heard of a wolf in sheep's clothing, but Victor had it backwards. He'd bought the outfit but no one else did. Not for long anyway, for his true self showed in every limp gesture and intonation. He needed a psychiatrist, not a tailor. Well, he'd come to the right place.

With his gentle manner and dark brown hair cut to military length, he reminded me of Luke Simons. But while Simons was a gentle giant, Victor barely cleared five foot. His untanned skin suggested too much time indoors, while his habit of adjusting his specs was either a tic or an affectation. If you glimpsed him in a crowd, suitably dressed, you might mistake him for a rather attractive, androgynous young woman. In hindsight, it's easy to see why his family life proved so difficult.

Victor had travelled all the way from America to meet me and both our lives were about to change. As he told me about himself, I began to sketch him in my mind. It was a cartoon caricature, yet enough for me to understand and to act. This is the picture I drew.

Victor

It is not easy to be twenty-one and rich. People envy him but they know nothing. Nothing. He sprawls on his bed and looks around the room at all the dumb expensive toys he's got. He considers breaking one but it's the maid's day off.

Father

Victor's dad is the boss of Saborman Industries. Victor is really Victor III. His father is Victor II and his grandfather was the first. Victor III is supposed to one day become the boss of Saborman Industries. At this stage, it's not looking good.

Politics

Victor has a secret place where books are hidden. He studies Marxism on the sly while Father is busy at the office (always). Once Victor bought a socialist newspaper from a young woman on the street and she smiled at him. Back in his room, he reads about all the injustice in the world and resolves to do something about it. He decides to go a meeting of the group that made the newspaper. Perhaps the young woman will be there.

Victor's wardrobe sucks - all his clothes are too new. He goes out and buys a scruffy old pair of pants and jacket from a second hand store. Now he can go to the Socialist meeting. The people at the meeting are full of rage but when he signs up for the group under the name Kevin Jones, they clap him on the back and say 'Welcome Kev.' Now they want him to sell newspapers on the street too. Victor is up all night sweating, tossing and turning. Father has eyes and ears everywhere. Victor decides not to return to the group.

Religion

The secret place in Victor's room now contains books on Eastern religion. He reads about karma and reincarnation, and attends the talks of a yellow-robed guru in the city. Once a week he learns that the material world is illusion, then he returns to his hallucination. Victor donates generously to the guru and is invited to a weekend workshop of fasting and meditation. The early morning starts

87

don't agree with him. He catches a cold and has to return home. He regretfully declines the guru's offer of a pilgrimage to India.

Enlightenment
Victor realises it is his bad karma to be rich, Victor III, and head of Saborman Industries.

Victor's Past
You can choose your friends but you can't choose your family. Victor III was the eldest son of an American tycoon. From the day of conception, he was destined to take over the Saborman business empire. Destiny is a prankster. By a genetic quirk, all the Saborman charisma bypassed Victor and went to his younger brother Edgar, where it was twice wasted.

Victor sweated through school and scraped by. Edgar didn't bother and coasted in with distinction. Although ashamed to be such a dullard beside Edgar, even Victor was charmed by his younger brother. Yet when Edgar was expelled from his last year of school for some grave misadventure, Victor couldn't help feeling justice had been done.

Edgar's expulsion was the catalyst for change in the house of Saborman. It caused Saborman senior to give serious thought to the empire's future. One of his sons would have to take over, but which one? It was a choice between Victor's dogged mediocrity and Edgar's wayward spark. He chose Edgar, taking him directly into the business as his successor.

This decision turned Victor into a philosopher. For the first time he began to ponder fate's dirty tricks. Why is one person born rich and another poor? What causes someone to be handsome or plain, brilliant or a buffoon? Can one blame genetics, upbringing, or karma? It was a complex puzzle indeed.

On the other hand, perhaps destiny could be stolen due to the corruption of those in power. He began dabbling in politics and religion and saw his father in a different light. It seemed Saborman senior wasn't the hero Victor had once thought, but a callous man who oppressed the underprivileged. Victor even fantasised about his father's downfall and the rise of a more just society. How this would happen, he did not know. Then one day Edgar died in a car crash. He took his father's Mercedes for a drunken spin at 2am and drove it into a tree.

For his father, this was almost a deathblow. Powerlessness was a strange new state of mind. Within a year, he too was gone. Perhaps the cancer had been there all along only to rise and strike him at his lowest ebb.

The strange result was that Victor inherited the throne after all, yet what a hollow ascension. As he sat by his father's deathbed he wept in the realisation that death has no prejudices. What was the point of his father's life? He'd amassed a large business empire, but it was no use to him now. What had he really achieved? He'd done little to further the knowledge of humanity or alleviate its suffering. If anything, he'd left the world a worse place than he'd found it. It was a poor epitaph.

The business empire was now in the possession of Victor Saborman III. As he gazed at his father's death-mask, he saw a clear choice between two paths. He could continue to plunder the world as his father had done, or he could try to change it. To his credit, he chose the latter.

Yet he was no leader. A vague desire to save the world is useless without a plan to achieve it. Victor left the running of the company in the hands of administrators and retreated to his father's country mansion in the town of Cull, for he needed to think. Cull was a small upstate town. With a population of just twenty thousand, his father had gone there whenever he wanted a break from city life. He'd taken a shine to the place and invested in several of the local businesses. He had also built a big mansion in the town. It was here that Victor went in his time of need.

Poor Victor. Like an almost-beached whale, he floundered in the shallow sea of his own benevolence. How does one go about saving the world? He decided to take his time, reading his political and philosophical books until a plan occurred to him. Then one day he read a new book called *Revelations of Milinish*.

He was struck by the book's panoramic vision. He had, of course, dabbled in socialism and Eastern religion. He was somewhat aware of other doctrines like evolution, Christianity, and

89

so on - but until now, all these concepts had seemed separate and incompatible. Never before had he read anything which unified them as one system. He was seized by the urge to track down the book's author and speak to him directly. Surely no one could be more qualified than this man, Thomas Swan, to guide him in how to use the power he'd inherited.

Victor took the next flight to Australia and came straight to Vaucluse. When he'd told his story, I rang Jamie and told him to cancel the weekend workshop. I returned to my study where my guest was still reclining on the couch.

'Victor, I knew you were coming today and believed that I could - nay must - help you. But if I am to help you fully, I need to be completely frank with you, and you with me. Is that quite clear?'

'Yes, Mr Swan, of course.'

'Call me Tom. I consider yours a most remarkable case. I mean, look at you - a rich kid with soul who's not a hedonistic, spoilt brat? You don't see that every day. Yet never in all my clinical experience have I observed such a striking dissonance between potential and achievement. Never have I witnessed such a schism between destiny and reality. Allow me to state the obvious - you're a most unhappy young man. You are deeply troubled. Correct?'

'I guess so, Mr Swan ... ah Tom.'

'For the best part of twenty years, your huge soul has been ground beneath a mighty heel. Your wax wings have been melted by the heat of a tyrannical sun. Is this true? Is this real?'

'Yes, yes.'

'By the stars, Victor, you've not even guessed at your capabilities! At this moment, destiny changes, but if I am to take on your case you must to do exactly what I say for the duration of your stay. Agreed?'

'Sure.'

'You will remain here until cured. Treatment begins at once. Lie back on the couch and relax. Together we will probe the very depths of your mind.'

I paused for effect and began pacing back and forth across the floor of the sitting room, as if deep in thought.

'Why have you said nothing about your mother, Victor? Was she not important to you?'

'I hardly knew her. She died when Edgar was a baby.'

'She died in childbirth? In the twentieth century? That is most remarkable. Almost unheard of.'

'It wasn't in actual childbirth. It was about a year later.'

'Close enough. Close enough to count. Did your father ever blame Edgar for this?'

'I don't think so. He always loved Edgar.'

'Perhaps. Things are not always as they seem - we should try to look beyond the surface. Your family, for instance. Three out of four deceased? It just doesn't make sense. Not for a wealthy family in this day and age. In the Middle Ages, sure. Today? It's almost unbelievable. I've a sense there's some extraordinary karmic pattern at work. Some past life curse, most likely. In fact, I'm almost certain of it.'

I gave Victor a stern look.

'Reality is an iceberg, my boy. A small part exists in our conscious vision while the rest remains hidden. Yet the voice of the unconscious communicates with us in its own way. I want you to repeat your account of the dream you mentioned earlier, the one that you've had several times. Tell me exactly what happened.'

Victor lay back on the couch and stretched. He hadn't had this much attention for years.

'It always starts the same way. I'm in a dark forest but there's a voice calling me - a woman's voice. There's a golden key on the ground. When I pick it up, the forest vanishes and I'm standing on a beach looking out to sea. The voice is coming from an island on the horizon. Next thing I know I'm in a boat heading out there. But the sea is stormy, the waves are crashing, and there's a huge lion in the back of the boat watching me.'

'What?' I interrupted. 'Like in that *Life of Pi* movie?'

'Yeah, I guess so. Anyhow, when I finally get ashore, I throw the key at the lion and run into the jungle, where the voice is coming from. But when I find her, it's too late - the woman's dead and there's someone standing over her, grinning. That's when I wake up.'

Victor's body had been taut as he gave this account. Now he slumped onto the couch. I continued pacing from one side of the room to the other, increasing the speed and intensity of my movements until suddenly I wheeled around triumphantly to face my patient.

'Victor! I knew you were a remarkable man. We should be thankful for the clarity of the messages sent to us by your unconscious mind, for your dream is indeed elementary. Listen. The island represents your potential which beckons you on, but you're trapped in the forest of your unconscious fears. The key is knowledge, the knowledge you've sought and found. The lion is your father. Only by using the key can you overcome your father's influence. The ocean is your sexuality. You don't have much experience in that area, right?'

'Not much,' he mumbled.

'I knew it. The stormy ocean reveals the violence of your passion, but you've been afraid of sexuality most of all. So when you do reach the shore, the waters are becalmed. You are impotent. Now tell me, the boat ... what kind of boat is it? Did you say it was a rowboat?'

'I don't remember,' said Victor.

'Think Victor, this is important! Was it a rowboat or a motorboat?'

'I'm not sure. I think it had a motor at first, then I started rowing. The closer I got, the slower it went.'

'Of course! The motor a symbol of potency, yet an oar in each hand alludes to the ambiguous sexuality your father's dominance brought out in you. By the time you reach the island it's too late. The murdered woman is your mother and it's Edgar standing over her laughing. He's destroyed both of you.'

Victor lay back on the couch, too stunned to speak. Finally he said, 'it's amazing. Everything you said is true.'

'The unconscious is always sending us messages, we simply have to know how to interpret them.'

Victor shook his head in wonder. 'What happens now? Am I cured?'

I laughed a wistful laugh.

'Oh Victor, if only it were that simple. When it comes to understanding a personality as complex as yours, it takes more than a simple dream analysis to set things right. I've a feeling we've barely scratched the surface, but let's not rush. You need time to digest all this. I'm going to leave you alone for a while. I suggest that you meditate upon what you've learned - and read my latest book.'

I handed Victor a copy of *Milinish in the New Age*. He looked at it like it was a first edition of the Bible. I smiled.

'You haven't seen that one before. It's not out in America yet. Be warned - it's a pretty heavy book. Not everyone can handle the power of the revelations in there, but I think with the progress you're making, you're tough enough to do it. You won't see me until morning, but whatever you do, don't engage with the external world. That could ruin the treatment. No TV, no internet, and don't leave the house. I'll have some food sent over and a bed made up. On second thoughts, cancel the bed, I'll send coffee. I want you up all night finishing the book.'

I patted his shoulder to let him know it was OK to laugh. Still, he probably took me at my word. The next day, Victor was a changed man. Reading one of my books tended to have that effect on people.

'It's so hard to take everything in,' he said.

'A word of advice,' I replied, 'don't even *try* to take everything in. Not all at once. Our work has barely begun.'

Vic seemed almost in a trance.

'It certainly explains a lot,' he said dazedly. 'Not just about all these alien abduction reports you hear of, but a lot about the world. Quavisia, eh - I always knew there was someone up there.'

'Victor, look at me.'

My tone was gentle, hypnotic, firmly commanding.

'Listen to me Victor. Our work is barely begun. I have some truly remarkable news for you today. Are you listening?'

'I'm listening, Tom.'

'Yesterday, we took a decisive step towards solving your personal problems, yet something bothered me. I felt we were still scratching around on the surface. Today we must go much deeper

93

into your psyche in order for this treatment to have any lasting effect. Are you prepared to face whatever we may find?'

'If you want me to.'

'Then let us proceed. Are you familiar with the concept of reincarnation, the idea that we are born into life after life upon the Earth?'

'Of course.'

'Then you won't be surprised to learn that your current problems stem from a previous incarnation. I've obtained some knowledge you'll find most enlightening.'

Victor leaned forward, eyes wide open.

'Are you acquainted with the history of the English monarchy?' I asked.

'Not much.'

'Oh. I thought you Americans were supposed to be fascinated by it.' I smiled. 'You're going to hear a little story now, Victor, and I think it's going to ring a couple of bells for you.'

Now that the foreplay was over, it was time to get down to business. I paused, and stared off into the distance.

'Do you think life happens by chance? Hardly, for there are no accidents. Indeed, life after life, we play out the same dramas until our karma is worked out. Not just individuals, families too. Fathers and sons, mothers and daughters; we're all born in recurring patterns. It's like a haunting, so to speak, as the old dramas play out in one context and another. This is not the first time you were born with blue blood. You've been tied up in royalty before. Not just with any old king, mind you, but one of the most famous of them all.'

I paused for an imaginary drum roll.

'Henry VIII became king of England in the year 1509. He was nineteen. He ruled England for thirty-eight years until his death in 1547. Henry was a blustering man with a huge ego who always got his own way. He married six wives and murdered two of them. Apart from that, his most famous achievement was an act of religious reform. He rebelled against the Roman Catholic Church and formed the Church of England. This was an almost accidental development thrown up by circumstance, yet its effects last to this day. Are you following me?'

Victor, nodded, wide-eyed as a child hearing a bedtime story.

'He married his first wife, Catherine of Aragon, soon after becoming king. When she failed to produce a male heir to the throne, he decided to divorce her and marry Anne Boleyn, a young woman of the court. He applied to the pope for a divorce. Permission was refused but Henry wasn't about to let that stop him. He formed the Church of England and divorced his first wife. For this he was excommunicated by the Catholic Church.

In 1533, Henry married Anne Boleyn. She was twenty-six years old, he forty-two. Anne fared no better in providing a male heir to the throne, and Henry did not take kindly to failure. She was arrested for alleged adultery and beheaded. It did not take him long to marry again. His third wife, Jane Seymour, finally bore him a son, but died soon after.'

Victor couldn't have been more stunned if the ghost of Henry himself had appeared before him. I continued the story.

'Henry was to marry three more wives during his reign. He beheaded his fifth wife, again for adultery. In later years he lost his health and became increasingly paranoid about his political enemies, until his death in 1547.

We are not once born, Victor. We are placed upon the Earth again and again to learn the lessons we must learn. Listen closely to my words. They will free you from the pain you feel so deeply. Your father was Henry VIII of England. Your mother was Catherine of Aragon, the king's first wife. You were Anne Boleyn, his second, and your brother Edgar was Jane Seymour, his third. When I point out the parallels between your lives then and now, they will seem so obvious you will wonder you had not thought of them yourself.

Like Henry, your father was a powerful leader who wanted a son to take over after his death. Your mother gave him not one but two sons. Strange as it seems, she felt she owed them to him. Remember that as Catherine she'd given him nothing. Yet she soon died, almost in childbirth - give or take a few months - a highly unusual occurrence these days. The death was to punish your father for his past betrayal. She abandoned him just as he abandoned Catherine.

Your father's attention now turned to you, his eldest son. He loved you, yet he was puzzled by your timidity and dullness. It was, of course, all his fault. You loved and feared him, just as Anne Boleyn loved and feared Henry. You tried to please your father but the unconscious memory of Anne's beheading meant fear was always the stronger emotion. This explains your lifelong timidity. You had been charged with adultery before. Now, as Victor, you studied Marxism, all the while afraid of again being charged with disloyalty. This time you weren't found out, but you lived in constant fear.

The timidity extended to your relations with women. Your father had many mistresses just as Henry had six wives. You longed to emulate him, but having been beheaded for adultery as Anne, you felt sexual expression was dangerous.

You were a great disappointment to your father. As Anne, you'd failed to provide him with an heir. Now, thrust into the position of heir to the Saborman empire, you were again found wanting. Like Henry, your father was not one to be bound by convention. Henry defied the Catholic Church, now your father defied expectation and cheated you of your inheritance, choosing Edgar as his successor. He deserted you for your brother, just as Henry murdered Anne to marry Jane Seymour.

Edgar seemed to give him what he wanted - a charismatic heir, just as in that former life, he'd given him a son. But again your father was punished for his selfishness. Like Jane, your brother was to die young.

In this life, you started out trying to impress your father. Then you wanted to surpass him. As Henry, your father was a great religious reformer - he formed his own church. Now you, Victor, are also seized with the desire to enact religious reform, hence your interest in matters spiritual and the problems of the world - and your presence here today.

Your fate is clear. You are destined to be patron of the church of Milinish, the religion that will dominate the next thousand years. In so doing, you'll right the wrongs not only of this lifetime, but those you suffered as Anne Boleyn. Once and for all you can step out of the shadow of your father. As Henry, he created a church, yet you will be a far greater religious reformer than he ever was. You'll be the greatest Saborman of them all!'

Victor stood up and stretched, as if awakening from a long sleep. Then, for the first time since we had met, he smiled.

'You know what, Tom? In a way, I'm not even surprised. I always knew there was something funny going on.'

'You did?'

'I always had a strange feeling I was playing some sort of role. Now I'm finally getting some insight into my relationship with my father, it's all starting to make sense. Everything is becoming clear. If only I'd known this earlier, before I wasted all that time.'

'Nothing is ever wasted,' I began. 'If your father ...'

'What a bastard! He never gave a damn for his family. We were only there to serve him.'

'Now wait a minute.'

'That arrogant pig. He was cruel too. Now I know why he made me go and chop the firewood that time - and the sadistic look on his face! I wish he was here now - I'd spit in that face. What a mess he's made of my life.'

'Wait, Victor. Hate is never justified. It's true your father ruined your past but what you choose to do with your future is up to you. You can be ten times the man he ever was.'

Victor's frenzy receded a touch. He sat back on the couch and asked, 'How?'

Once again I gazed into the future.

'Your father plundered the world, Victor. You can save it. Quavisia is coming. Day by day the Quavisian mother ship moves closer to the Earth. In five years, it will be here. Five years at most. That is how long we have to prepare.'

'But what can we do, Tom? Should we build weapons?'

'With respect, Victor, that is an asinine suggestion. That is precisely the type of infantile arms race mentality that plays into Quavisia's very hands. What is needed is education - we must teach people the truth about their lives. We must teach them about DNA, Satan, Ruanglia and Quavisia. We must psychoanalyse them,

97

regress them to their past lives, and teach them the ways of the Milinish. The more human awareness is raised in the next five years, the better we'll be able to join with Ruanglia to create psychic defences when the Quavisian mother ship arrives. Are you with me, Victor?'

'Yes, Tom.'

'Are you, Victor Saborman III, ready to spearhead the greatest religious reformation in history?'

'One hundred percent.'

'Victor Saborman and Thomas Swan - what a team!'

'What a team!'

'Tell me about Cull.'

He told me that Cull was a small American town, that it had twenty thousand inhabitants, that his father had owned land and businesses there and built a mansion in the town. Then he said I was very popular there.

'What do you mean I'm very popular there?' I asked.

'Well, Tom, it's like this. I own the newspaper in Cull and when I read *Revelations of Milinish* I was so impressed I gave you loads of publicity, and on radio too. I also own the biggest bookstore in town and I let folks buy discount copies. Soon you'd built up a mini fan club. Not everyone liked it, not the old school churches - but who cares about them? They're just a minority now. The people in Cull can't wait to meet you.'

And I couldn't wait to meet them. It was time to say goodbye to Australia. Goodbye Sydney, Goodbye Steffi, goodbye Current bloody Edge. Australia was never quite big enough for me. There were too many knockers and cynics. I felt sure the people in America would be far more open-minded. I called Jamie and told him to organise some plane tickets. The Milinish was going to America.

Part Two

11

Exodus One

It is not the case that the world is in the grip of a delusion. Rather, it is in the grip of an extraordinary range and variety of different delusions.

Old Religion, New Science.

So this was Saborman House, the new HQ? Oh Lord, your blessings come ever sweeter. Victor's father sure knew how to furnish a house. Rose's joint was fine but this was a step up. I went from a place to a palace - added an A and joined the A-list. Five star bedrooms, regal sitting rooms, majestic gardens. Even the bathroom taps seemed to be made of gold. Gold? Gold taps? That's going a bit far - it's only a bloody tap. Who'd this guy think he was - Ramses II as well as Henry VIII?

In any case, he was now just as dead as his reincarnational selves. Dead and out of the way. I wandered curiously through the castle I'd captured. Vic's father seemed to have been some kind of collector, judging by the array of art on display. My favourite was the replica Bayeux tapestry in the library, that woven tribute to the Norman conquest of England. Another past life? I wouldn't doubt it. I *assume* it was a replica, although it did look terribly worn.

There was at least one original Picasso, if Victor is to be believed. As for the library, if it was only for show it was truly a clever deception, although rather light on for fiction in my view. I even found a couple of Orantor's books. Wherever I went, there was no escaping that man, my mentor, my tormentor.

There was a small private zoo in the grounds. Victor Saborman II might have been the head of a blood sucking corporation but to give him his due, if a few species were going extinct through human enterprise, at least he'd save some for posterity. Between the mini art gallery, the library, and zoo, Saborman House almost had the feel of an ark. It was almost as if Victor's father was anticipating some kind of global collapse. All the better, then, as a place to wait out the Quavisian attack and build a new world from the ashes of the old.

I spent a week in Cull but my mind was made up on day one. The rest of the week was just a holiday - and why not? I woke each day to views of a garden with waterfalls and flower beds in the foreground, mighty oaks and pines further back. I spent the morning in an office bigger than the one at Rose's place, the afternoon in the library or the gardens, and the evening with Victor in our own gold class cinema - and all without having to exit the estate. There was no going back to Australia now, that much was clear. Just a quick jaunt to tidy up affairs, but that was it.

Even Cull itself was not as dire as I'd feared. Victor gave me a small lecture tour in the back seat of his car while his chauffeur did the driving. It was a picturesque little town with a certain rustic charm. With its wide streets, clean air, and ample parkland, it reminded me of some of the country towns I knew back in Australia. When we returned to Saborman House, Victor's butler made us a couple of martinis and I sat out in the garden with my new brother in arms.

'I see no reason it can't work,' I said.

'So you're really coming?' Victor asked. There was a note of disbelief in his voice, as if his dream date had agreed to go to the prom with him. I favoured him with a smile.

'I can hardly rule the world from Australia, can I? It's too remote. Cull's perfect. We can really build something here.'

'I thought you'd go to San Francisco or New York like everyone else.'

'What for? Who *isn't* in San Francisco or New York? A thousand faiths, a thousand hustlers. The last thing we want is to shack up alongside that rabble. Let 'em fight it out among themselves, they'll all be out of business soon enough. In the meantime, we'll be building God's own kingdom right here in Cull. It's all about purity, Victor, purity. This time next year, Cull will be one hundred percent Milinish.'

'You don't mind being a big fish in a small pond?'

'Just call me Moby Dick and feed me plankton. I can get total membership here. That'll never happen in the city. Not yet. Once we get this joint sorted, *then* we'll make a move on New York. I'm not such a fool as to do it prematurely. Where'd you think Hitler screwed up? Diluting his forces in Russia, overreaching himself. Should've done with the rest of Europe before he even looked sideways at Stalin, don't you think?'

'I guess so.'

'There's no guesswork involved, my boy, just common sense.'

Victor frowned and fidgeted with his glasses.

'I wouldn't have thought Hitler was much of a role model,' he said.

I gave a dismissive flick of my hand, then finished the rest of my martini.

'I don't buy into his politics but I can certainly learn from his tactical errors. So let's get down to business. From what you said, your old man practically ran this town. Right?'

'Not exactly. I mean, he owned the paper, sure, and a few businesses.'

'Then all we have to do is finish what he started. Local businesses, you say? Great - buy some more. Real estate for one. I want to bring as many of my people over as possible. They're going to need jobs and houses. Do you have someone who can make it happen, someone you can trust?'

'There's this guy, Bob Talbot. Dad let him run a lot of his business stuff when he was out of town.'

'Set up a meeting. I'm heading back to Australia for a week to tie up loose ends, but first I'm going to tell you fellas exactly what needs doing while I'm away. Now, one more thing - we've got to build a recording studio here in the house. The best studio money can buy. You may not realise that before I wrote *Revelations of Milinish*, I was a great rock musician.'

Victor looked surprised, as if I'd told him I used to be a woman or something.

102

'Oh. What sort of music did you play?'

'Heavy duty guitar music. Riffy stuff. You've heard 'Amnesia' and 'In Nihilum,' haven't you? Well most of my songs are a bit heavier than that.'

'I'm sorry, Tom, I haven't heard any of your songs. I had no idea you were a musician.'

'For God's sake! You've got some catching up to do then. And what about you, what do you listen to?'

'Er, nothing really. Pop culture doesn't interest me much. I've spent all my time lately reading spiritual and political books.'

I pursed my lips and sniffed.

'Oh really? If there's one thing you've got to do, Vic, it's put away those bloody books for a while. If you want to be a great spiritual leader of the future, you've got to become more dynamic and charismatic. Once the studio's built, I'll teach you how to play bass. You should buy a bass guitar immediately. '

'Ok, if you think it's best.'

'We can take the message of Milinish further through music. Not everyone reads books, you know. Just think how many illiterates we can reach once we record a few songs of our own.'

'Oh yes, good idea.'

'Don't let me down now, Vic. I'll be back in ten days and I want to see some serious progress. On *all* fronts.'

We shook hands on the deal. Then, from one dream to another, next thing you know I'm back in Rose's house in Vaucluse one last time. Making a goodbye speech. Standing up front in the laboratory, leading a packed congregation, hitting them with the news flash all of a sudden. Maybe I should have given Rose and Jamie a briefing first, but I reckoned I'd lay it on them all in one hit to save time.

There was something in the air that night. You could smell it in the incense - Lilac, Jasmine, and a hint of Jonestown. You could see it on the sea of faces - a fervent froth of fear, faith, and fanaticism. You could hear it in the angry rumble and evangelical roar of the responses. They knew something was up alright. The resolute set of my jaw did nothing to dissuade them.

'Sisters and brothers, buckle up. I've got to warn you - this is gonna be one hell of a meeting.

You know, there's two kinds of people in this world, the doers and the doubters. There's some folks who build and create and light the way forward. Then there's other folks sit on their arses to watch the first lot and criticise what they've done.

I reckon you all know what I'm talking about, right? What we've done these last couple of years is no less than a miracle. And tell you what, we'd never have pulled it off without these two in the front row here tonight. That's Jamie over here on my left, and Rosie on my right. Big hand for these two disciples, alright!'

(Whooping, applause from the crowd).

'Oh yeah, it's a miracle alright. The scientific breakthroughs we've made, the HASH healings, the sheer joy and the love flying around this temple tonight. See, that's why I don't care about the doubters and their trashy TV shows. Let 'em mock and spread their lies and their filthy aspersions. What do they say about me, these gutter crawlers? They reckon I take advantage of people. *Me? I* take advantage of people? Give me a break! Tell you what, guys, the day I let some tabloid TV show lecture me on ethics, that's the day I'll get on the sonuvabitch crucifix and nail *myself* up! And excuse my Hebrew, chaps, but as Jesus himself would say, fuck 'em!'

(Wild whooping and applause).

'They left that bit outta the Bible, folks!'

I raised my hands to quell the laughter.

'You guys are the greatest. You know that? I love you all. Now look, I want you to forgive me for pointing out the bleeding obvious, but I know some of you pilgrims saw that propaganda crap on *Current Edge* the other week.'

(Loud boos and hisses).

'Shameful stuff, weren't it? How can those dogs look themselves in the eye of a morning? Reckon I brainwash people, do they? Gimme a break. I'll tell you something for nothing, guys. Anyone who watches that show for more than five minutes, they *need* their brains washed - and I'll chuck in a shampoo and a blow dry for free. It's a dirty job but someone's gotta do it!'

(Wild applause. Standing ovation).

'Look, guys, I'm once again stating the obvious but you don't have to be Albert bloody Einstein to know where this rubbish is coming from. I never had one word of complaint before *Milinish in the New Age* came out, did I? But ever since I blew the lid on Quavisia, it's been one thing after the other. So what do you reckon? Do one and one and make three? You don't have to be Sherlock mother-fornicating Holmes to figure out who's behind it all. We've got 'em rattled and no mistake. Quavisia's pulling out all the stops to try and shut us down. They're sending plants into the workshops, trying to find excuses to sue me. They're paying off the media to slander us. They're bringing in the CIA and the FBI and the Far Q2. Well I couldn't care less. It's water off a duck's back. Off a swan's back, if you like.'

(Fawning laughter and applause).

'I really don't care. It don't bother me, not in the slightest. We'll just keep on keeping on. Workshops, services. I'm gonna keep on healing you folks, filling you with HASH til you can't smoke no more! But there's something I gotta tell you all. Bit of a newsflash, bit of a scoop. So if there's any Quavisian plants here tonight, I'm gonna throw you a Brontosaurus bone right here, right now. Take it back to your government lackeys and your tabloid hacks, lap up some more pats on the back from that bunch of brats. Hold steady, guys, cos this one's a humdinger.'

(Silence punctuated by a few gasps).

'Put it this way, there's the good news and the bad news. Or to be more scientifically precise, the absolutely wonderful news and the direly cataclysmic news. What do you want to hear first?'

(Confused rumblings, some people calling out).

I raised my hands.

'OK let's get the bad news out of the way. Here goes: Sydney could be gone within a year. That's right - wiped out. The Ruanglian Intelligence intercepted some Quavisian war documents and learned they're going to take out one city per continent. So why Sydney? Why not Melbourne or Canberra or Adelaide? Spite, that's all. The Milinish started in Sydney, so Quavisia's going to bomb it. For any of you property obsessed punters out there, here's my professional advice: don't bother renovating, sell now!'

(Sounds of fear and consternation).

'OK, OK, I shouldn't joke about such a serious matter as your home renovations and property values. I'm just trying to lighten you folks up. But now that's out of the way, let's move onto the good news. We're going global. The Milinish is moving to the USA!'

(Stunned silence, then a few murmurs).

'What do you guys think I've been doing the last couple of weeks? I've been over in the States and found me the sweetest little site to hole up for the apocalypse. We're building a citadel, a holy fortress. I won't name it yet but believe me, it's perfect. It's far from the cities and the danger, a regular Heaven on Earth. Home to twenty thousand souls, half of them already converted to our cause, the other half on the way in. Or else on the way out, know what I mean? The ones who won't get on board, well, it's sayonara and don't let the ark door hit you on the arse on the way out. And guess what? That's gonna leave plenty of room for you true believers to come over and start a new life.'

(A few hesitant cheers, then growing in confidence).

A guy in the front row called out, 'But Tom, I can't go to the States, I've got a job here and the kids are in school.'

'Calm down, brother. Do what you've got to do. Sure, stay here if you have to. I'm not saying Sydney *will* be wiped out, it's just one possible future. You want to risk it, that's your lookout. But any of you other folks who don't want to take the chance, I'll lead you to a wonderful land.'

'What about immigration and visas?' someone else called out. Some other voices joined in. I raised both hands to quell them.

'Now listen you bunch of worrywarts, don't go stressing over logistics. I might be Moses leading you home through the desert, but don't forget who else we've got on board. Only a supreme, all-powerful being by the name of God, and his offsider, Jesus! And on the human side, I've a man of influence over there at Milinish Central. Even as we speak, he's setting up jobs and houses for you guys. As for visas and whatnot, like I said this fella's got powerful connections. So never mind your pedantic paperwork and your bureaucratic bollocks. Meanwhile, we've got our own good people on this side to ease the pain of transition. Brother Jamie?'

106

'Yes, brother Tom?'

'I'm heading over to set up the new paradise this week, but you need to stick around for a month or two and help all these good folks with the nuts and bolts. You up for it?'

'Amen, brother.'

'And you Rosie - I want you to help him. You hold fast and help the pilgrims set up to come over.'

'OK Tom, if you think it's best.'

'The rest of you need to start setting up to emigrate. Those who can't make it to the States, you'd better go bush. Don't matter where, just get out of Sydney within six months. Right, I've said enough. I'm going to conference with Jamie now, and we'll see you all back here tomorrow night for an update.'

My second-in-command wasn't so chipper after the meeting.

'Whoa, Tom, where'd this come from? A heads up would have been nice.'

'My dear Jamie, need I remind you we're at war? As Commander in Chief, if I make an executive decision for the good of the movement, then roll with it.'

'Who's your contact over there?'

'Victor. You met him, remember.'

'That American kid? I thought he was just a rich sap from overseas.'

'You better believe it. He's a goldmine. But you know, I wouldn't underestimate him.'

'We really have to move to the States?'

'You can stay here and be blown up by the Quavisians if you prefer. It's entirely up to you.'

'It's just that ... well, something's come up.'

A sheepish look came over Jamie's handsome face. It reminded me of the day we'd first joined forces. I crossed my arms.

'Yes?'

'It's my ex-wife. We've reconnected.'

'Really? All the progress we've made and you're backsliding to square one? Your timing's impeccable.'

'I still love her, Tom.'

'Do you indeed? How wonderful. I'll add that to my next book to pull in the Mills & Boon crowd. And what does she think of your new vocation? Didn't all the negative press put her off?'

'She's very interested actually. She's asked all sorts of questions.'

'I see. Then let me ask you this, Jamie. Who initiated this 'reconnection,' you or her?'

'She phoned me one night out of the blue. It went from there.'

'Oh for Christ's sake, man, either she's working for Quavisia or the media, or it's the first step in a family intervention.'

'Why so cynical, Tom? What if she wants to join us?'

I snorted, then decided to let it drop for the moment.

'I'm sorry, Jamie, you'll have to work this out yourself. I simply urge you to be extremely cautious about who you trust. All I ask is stay on for a month and help all those pilgrims who want to go to the States. Do whatever it takes to ease the transition. Until then, I'd prefer you delay any reconciliation with your ex-wife. She betrayed you once, Jamie, and as far as I'm concerned, one betrayal per lifetime is all you get.'

There was a knock at the door. We turned to see Rose enter, looking like a faithful dog watching its family packing for the airport. I sighed.

'You'd better go, Jamie. Call me first thing in the morning.'

When the door closed behind him, I looked at Rose. She was dressed up in her Sunday best for the meeting. Black dress, jewellery, the works. As with Jamie, I flashed back to our first encounter.

'Rose, why the mournful look? Aren't you thrilled? We're going global!'

'That's all very well for you, Tom, but what about me? I've never been so happy and now it's all coming to an end.'

'End? What are you talking about? We're just getting started.'

'You're leaving.'

'Our arrangement here was always temporary, you knew that. As the Lord Buddha said, impermanence is the nature of life. Everything passes, everything comes to an end.'

Rose sank into an armchair.

'Fine. Hooray for impermanence. That doesn't make it any easier.'

'Loss is the tragedy of life, my dear. There's no escape, so I've learned to embrace it. Yet death is always followed by rebirth. Don't you recall what I said when we were watching those old *Doctor Who* episodes?'

The ball of misery in the chair shrugged and didn't reply.

'*The War Games*, wasn't it? Patrick Troughton's last story as the Doctor. And there you were coming over all misty eyed as the Time Lords hounded him down and made him regenerate. What did I say to you then, Rosie?'

'I've no idea, Tom.'

'I said if Troughton's Doctor hadn't come to an end, we never would have had Jon Pertwee or Tom Baker, would we? See, the caterpillar must die for the butterfly to be born. Death and rebirth - that's life.'

'I don't want you to go.'

'Neither do I, but the order's come from upstairs, I'm afraid.'

'I love you.'

'And I most assuredly love you, my dear, as a fellow soldier, a fellow human being. As for romantic love, you know it can never be. You knew that from the start. I'm the son of God. I can't betray humanity by confining my love to one person.'

'Oh sod humanity.'

'Those are my very words when I wake up each morning. Then I grit my teeth, make a strong cup of coffee, and get on with it.'

There was no reply, for Rose had crumpled further in the chair, no longer bothering to hold on to her composure. It fair pierced my heart, the very sight and sound, so piteous was it. I picked Rose up from the chair and cradled her in my arms, her salty tears on my neck. I rocked her back and forth for a while, all too aware of the warmth of her body and her full, heaving bosom. Then almost without meaning to, I came to a resolution and heard myself speak.

'All this fuss over a little move. Anyone would think I'd said you couldn't come with us.'

There was a break in the sobbing, then it stopped altogether. Rose looked up, all red-eyed.

'To the States? You mean it?'

'Why ever not? You've proven yourself a fine soldier.'

'Will I still live with you?'

'My dear, Victor would never allow it. But we'll find you a lovely house in town, don't worry about that. Of course you can come.'

'Oh Tom!'

Rose's sorrowful look vanished and was replaced by radiant joy. Even her breasts seemed to perk up. And at that moment, Satan could no longer be denied. The drama and desire, the joy and the lust came over us in a great bestial rush. Then we were kissing and embracing and giving vent to those demonic temptations held at bay all this time.

And Satan felt good. The devil entered us like a bushfire and the Holy Spirit evaporated like so much spilt beer at a barbecue. I violated Rose three times in the name of the Trinity - once as Beelzebub, once as Lucifer, the third time as Satan himself.

My saintly self was cast out of my body, almost literally, for I had the oddest sense of a dual consciousness. My spiritual form hovered bodiless above as I ravished Rose below. I could feel it looking down all righteous like some Witch Finder General who'd caught us holding a coven. Yet the po-faced inquisitor was powerless to impose its puritan reign upon us. It merely hovered in mid-air while Rose and I mocked it with lascivious acts of abandon. I looked up from my work and, with tremendous relish, poked my lecherous tongue out as far as it would go, then added a wink and a thumbs up before resuming my defilement.

It was almost as if Rose was in on the act. She was shameless as a wanton five minutes after confession. The tango took two, for we were equal partners in this Cromwell-mocking display.

Afterwards, I lay there in shock, my saintly self back in my body. I was somewhat astounded at my fall from grace, yet already prepared to shrug my shoulders and move on. I lay face down on the bed, a spent force. Rose kneeled above me, massaging my head, neck, and the rest of my body.

'We must never speak of this, Rose.'

'Are you ashamed?'

'Of course. To think our Lord held out for forty days in the desert against Satan's wiles. And look at me. He tempted me and I failed.'

'You certainly did - three times in a row.'

'Well damn it, if I'm going to Hell, I might as well get my money's worth.'

I laughed a small, embarrassed laugh but Rose did not join in. I tried to regain control of the situation, which was rather hard given my current position.

'Diverting as it was, this mustn't happen again. Do you understand?'

'I'm not ashamed, Tom. It was wonderful. I will always treasure this memory.'

'Of course, my dear. I simply ask, for the good of the movement - keep it under your hat. We must think of my image and my greater responsibilities. I can't be seen as a DNA slave, it would undermine the credibility I've built up all this time.'

Rose put a possessive hand on a part of my body I'd previously denied her.

'I understand, Tom. I promise to keep this to myself.'

'We mustn't think of ourselves, understand? We must always see the bigger picture and my mission.'

With an effort, I roused myself and began to dress, hoping this lapse would not have unseen ramifications. It was spilt milk now, so to speak. As for Rose, having promised she could come to the States, I was not such a bastard as to retract that now. Besides, she might go to the press. With my clothes and dignity at least partly restored, I gave Rose a goodnight kiss, sent her off to pack, then lay down to shut my eyes and dream of Cull.

111

12
Virus

It's my job to heal the sick, whether they like it or not.
Milinish in the New Age

Back at Saborman House, I soaked in a hot, soapy bath. I dried
myself and padded over the thick carpet of my new bedroom,
then through into my new office. I sat down at my desk and gazed
at the majestic gardens outside the window. And all the while, my
mind was turning over how best to manage my kingdom Cull.

The prize was not yet won, not until the town was under
control. Even that was merely the first step towards total conquest.
I mused upon the challenge before me. A military mind might see
it as a battle, a rather obvious analogy. As a scientist, I preferred to
think in terms of a virus - and as I'll explain, the virus was me.

A virus is a tiny organism that invades the defences of a cell
and attacks it from within. From there, it replicates itself and
spreads to other cells and the rest of the body. Think of Cull as
the cell and Milinish the virus. See Cull as a cell within a finger (the
state), and that finger connected to the hand and arm (the nation).
If we could master the arm, that arm could brandish a whip to
control the world.

The vital first step was to conquer the cell, to establish that
base. The host was prepared. Thanks to Victor's canny use of the
press to promote *Revelations*, my profile in Cull was already high. Yet
the newspaper was only one part of it. Saborman Industries had
a hold of Cull long before I arrived on the scene. The company's
tendrils reached into every area significant to the running of a small

town - government and the police, as well as local business and the economy. Now that Saborman and the Milinish were aligned, Cull was there to be had.

Yet I was uneasy. How much power in the company did Victor really have? He was just a boy. Surely a multinational like Saborman has existing power structures, executives waiting in the wings, a hundred complex factors and personalities to deal with. It can't just fall in your lap because you're the boss's son.

Yet strangely, at least for appearances sake - and to the extent that suited our needs - it did. Victor's family believed in the patriarchal succession of power. It must have stemmed from the old boy's time as Henry VIII. So, with monarchy-style recklessness, power was handed on no matter how wicked or incompetent the recipient might be. Hence Victor's control over a business empire he did not understand.

It helped that the company did not take him seriously. I speculate that they let him pose as a figurehead leader and largely ignored him. This was made easier when Victor chose to remain in Cull, rather than going back to the city. My strategic speech had clearly made an impression on him. With Cull more or less isolated, the rest of Saborman Industries were prepared to let Victor and I run it like our own little kingdom, while they conducted business as usual elsewhere. Naturally, a company as big as Saborman has many administrators. We let them get on with it. Their work served to generate profits that would ultimately filter back to the Milinish and *our* work.

Which, of course, was the only work that mattered. The game of economic conquest for its own sake held no interest for me. Nor did business practices. While relaxing in a nice hot bath, sipping a cold beer and plotting world domination, did I want to be bothered with the administration of a business empire? Of course not. In any case, my immediate task was to control Cull. To that end, I drew Bob Talbot into the fold.

Talbot was an administrator who knew the town from the inside. A local man, he'd done his stint in the city. Twenty years ago he'd probably been a young go-getter tearing up New York or LA, looking to make his mark. Now in his mid-forties, starting to sag and thicken round the waist, he was back home looking for a cushy post and some public kudos. Tanned and handsome in a slightly bloated way, he still looked the part to play small town politician. Well, if he'd do the town's book-keeping for me, I'd let him be mayor. A figurehead mayor with no real power, but enough to keep him happy. Victor had already made him the offer on my behalf, as long as he agreed to green light the reforms I had in mind.

On our first big meeting since I got back from Australia, Talbot walked into my new 'War Room' at Saborman House. Even my office was too small for this job, so I'd taken over the games room next to the library. It was a long rectangular room with a bar and a snooker table. On the elongated back wall, I'd placed pictures of inspirational figures - Buddha, Jesus, Darwin, Marx, Iommi, and the like. The front wall I'd reserved for something else. I'd also installed a desk and shelves so as to use the place as a second office. I was sitting at that desk when Talbot walked in wearing his elect-me suit. He already had the job, far as I was concerned. I looked at the front wall and gave Bob the thumbs up.

'I see you and Vic have been busy while I was away.'

Blown up to giant size, spread out on the wall, was a street map of the town of Cull. It was large enough for each individual house to appear as a tiny square.

'No problem, Tom. What's this all about? You got some town planning issues in mind?'

'You'd better believe it. I've got two words for you - independence and purification. Free associate for me - what do those words mean to you?'

'You don't have to teach me about independence. I'm an American.'

'Fair enough, Bob. Then I'll tell you what it means to me. We're going to establish Cull as the 51st state of America. An old fashioned city-state like in Ancient Greece. Better still, a sovereign nation state in its own right. Why should we depend on anyone? We don't need the government, we can set up our own government. We don't need the banks, we can set up our own banks. We can make our own values, our own laws.'

Talbot raised his eyebrows.

'That's your five year plan, huh? You're thinking big, I'll give you that, but how you gonna pull it off? Rome wasn't built in a day.'

'I said Greece, not Rome, and of course it'll take more than a day. Never mind your five years though, give me twelve months and we'll be halfway home. But before we reach independence, the first step is purification.'

Talbot looked uneasy.

'I don't know where you're going with that, Tom. We don't want none of that Klan stuff around here.'

'Klan stuff?'

I laughed and slapped the desk good humouredly.

'Oh right, you mean white power or some rubbish. No, this isn't about racial purity. Anyone can come to Cull - black, white, yellow, red. Hell, if there's any little green men from Mars they can get on board as well, as long as they *are* on board with what we're doing here. No, the only colours that count are sitting right here on my desk. See these four buckets of pins? There's a bucket of blues, a bucket of purples, one of yellows, and one of reds. It's all about the membership system we're going to introduce to the good people of Cull. I guess you're aware plenty of folks are Milinish converts already. What percentage do you reckon we've got?'

'You tell me.'

'I'd say thirty percent, tops.'

'That's pretty good, Tom. Not bad at all.'

'Thirty percent? I can't achieve a damned thing with that. There's nothing pure about thirty percent. And until we make it official, I'm guessing anyway.'

'So this is about membership. That's what you're after?'

'Of course. The only way we can get anything done is through total commitment. That's what I mean by purity. Thirty percent might as well be zero. For real purity, we need eighty, ninety percent, or better yet a neat hundred. But how am I going to know without some hard stats on the matter? I'm a scientist, Bob, guessing won't cut it. We've got to formalise people's commitment. I want everyone in town to sign up as official members of the Milinish.'

'Jeez, Tom, how you gonna pull that off?'

115

'We've just got to get everyone on the same page. Vic owns the press, that's a start. The local rag, anyhow. You know, I don't see why we need the national paper anymore, that won't help us reach independence. Let's stop it coming into town. The local paper's enough, at least we can control that.'

Talbot gave me a scornful look, but quickly turned it into a smile.

'That would have been a great idea twenty years ago,' he said, 'but these days won't people just read it online?'

'Of course, but at least it's a step forward. Give me time - in due course I'll stop the internet coming into Cull entirely. That'll solve *that* problem.'

'You can't do that. It's impossible.'

I stared at him levelly.

'When we reach ninety percent, you'll find the impossible gets redefined. Still, one step at a time. The next thing's incentives. You're the mayor, you're going to introduce the pricks and perks scheme. Make it known that those who sign up as members get benefits - tax breaks, bonuses etc - and those who don't will carry the load. Sure, be subtle about it. At first anyhow. They'll soon get the idea.'

'Benefits? Like what?'

'That's for you to figure out. Go home and brainstorm it and come back tomorrow with some ideas. I don't care how you do it, just make sure signing up as a member is a damn sight more beneficial than not signing.'

Talbot nodded slowly, a spark of cognition in his eyes.

'I see where you're going with this.'

'Good - and that brings us back to the wall map and four buckets of coloured pins.'

I stood up from my desk, selected some pins, and walked to the town map on the wall.

'It's pretty simple, Bob. Every residence in Cull is up on this map. We'll stick a blue pin in every member house and a purple one for those on the verge. A yellow pin can be for neutrals.'

'And the reds?'

'Red pins are for known hostiles.'

116

I tacked a red pin onto the main street, then three of each other colour in straight lines so they formed a triangle around the red one.

'So you've got a map full of coloured pins,' said Talbot. 'Then what?'

'Chemical conversion. Hit 'em with the right enzyme, watch the colour change. We've got to convert yellow pins to purple and purples to blues. And the reds? If they won't change, they'll simply be removed from the map altogether.'

'Hey, wait a minute.'

'Calm down, Bob, we're not mafia. I just mean they can get out of town. They'll be persuaded to leave.'

'How?'

'Start by making them a minority. Victor's already bought up a couple of real estate firms and all the vacant houses in town. I've got a whole bunch of my people moving over from Australia - so there's a nice group of blue pins right off the bat.'

'OK.'

'Not to mention some people from other parts of your own great nation. Plenty of them will want to join us once they know what's going on here.'

'So all we have to do is get the redpinners to sell up and leave town.'

'Redpinners. Ha, I like it! And you're bang on, mayor Bob. Six months and I don't want a single red pin left on my wall.'

'So I guess first thing is to find out everyone's true colours and start filling that map up with pins. What say we announce an official census and send a bunch of doorknockers out to see who'll sign up?'

'Now you're talking - that's why I hired you. Administration is your superpower, that much is clear. Let's get to work!'

We kicked off the scheme right away. Victor had indeed bought every vacant house in town. These were put on a list and circulated to the Milinish faithful in other towns or cities. Even then, demand outweighed supply, as Cull was not the only place in America loving my work. Plenty of folks rushed to join the world's fastest growing religion. Due to the demand, Victor could sell the houses

117

at an inflated price, thus convincing himself what an inspired businessman and a true Saborman he was, and a philanthropist to boot. After all, what was good for the Milinish was good for the world.

But we didn't just let any old riff raff into town. Lots of people desperately wanted in but couldn't afford one of the new houses. We didn't want that type in Cull. Those who fail to learn from history are doomed to repeat it. That's what Jimmy Jones used to say - and damned if I was going to make the same mistakes as him. He took a bunch of poor folks into his Peoples Temple, settled them in a shanty town in the jungle, then had to take care of them. It turned into twelve to a cottage, bad food, failed crops, low morale, and we all know how the story ended.

Yet for every person who couldn't afford a house in Cull, there were plenty who could. There were so many people trying to get in, there weren't enough houses to go round. This could only be good for the economy. There was a massive boom in the building industry as outsiders lined up to buy land and move in. Other local businesses thrived as well. The unemployment rate fell, partly from the demand for labour and also as a joyful response to the new wave of optimism sweeping through town. Oh yes, those were heady days in Cull. And there was no sense keeping the joy all to ourselves. There was plenty to go around. Some people were actually hired as missionaries, and sent to preach the word of the Milinish in other towns and states.

Some weeks into the Purification program, we finally made the big announcement. After weeks of rumour and speculation in the press, planted by us, it was announced that to reward the town's show of faith, Thomas Swan had decide to make Cull the worldwide spiritual centre of the Milinish. It was a tremendous coup for an obscure little town. As was reported in the local press, the news was greeted with joy and excitement. To celebrate, *The Cull Chronicle*, as it was formerly known, was rebranded *The Milinish Times*.

Soon after that landmark event, I was back in my War Room at Saborman House when Victor and Talbot came in. I greeted them, all hale and hearty.

'Will you look at that, boys, ain't that a beautiful sight!'

Bob and Vic turned to admire the street map of Cull, by now resplendent with blue pins, a minority of purples and yellows, and mere flecks of red here and there to mar the perfection.

'I gotta hand it to you, Tom!' said Talbot. 'I didn't know you'd pull it off that quick.'

'It's the power of faith,' I replied. 'It moves mountains. Levels 'em too, if you do it right. But I want to hear from you, Victor. You're the Minister for Believer Housing. When are you going to pull out the rest of these red pins?'

Victor's smile vanished.

'I'm trying.'

I picked up the phone and rang Rose. She answered after two rings.

'Rosie, what's the size of the list?'

I already had a fair idea of the answer. I'd given Rose the job of easing the flow of members from Sydney to Cull. She'd bought a beautiful house in the best street of town and I'd drop in at least once a week to see how she was going. For now, I let Victor stew for a bit while Rose and I chatted. Finally I hung up and frowned at him.

'Look, Vic, we've got five hundred pilgrims from Sydney on a waiting list. Every time I look up and see those red pins on my map, I feel the crucifixion nails all over again.'

'What can I do?' said Victor, with a shrug. 'Some of those families have been there for generations. They won't budge.'

'You're breaking my heart. Come on, let's brainstorm this one. Give me your immediate thoughts.'

Victor sat there fidgeting for a minute, then stood up and made a vigorous walking inspection of the town map, before resuming his seat. He rummaged around in his briefcase, then changed his spectacles for what seemed like an identical pair. Talbot opened his mouth to comment but I held up a finger and returned my gaze to Victor.

'Nothing? Oh well, looks like it's up to me again, as if I don't have enough to do. Anyhow, here's what I reckon. Removing these redpinners is a matter of law enforcement, so let's go good

119

cop, bad cop til they crack. Always play nice first, Vic, give people benefit of the doubt. Then kick some arse. It's the old yin and yang in the Tao of Public Administration. Righto, first gambit - invite them to a free town dinner and all they can drink. Give out toys for their kids. Then ask them to sign up as members. That's good cop. If that doesn't work, go to second gambit - dress up a few guys as FBI and stage a midnight terrorist raid. Give 'em a wakeup call in the name of national security. That's bad cop.'

'Is that legal?' said Bob.

'We make the laws in this town. Couple days later you send a rep and offer them overs to sell their house.'

'How high should I go?' said Victor.

'Value plus a third. Why not? With demand like it is, we'll get it back and then some.'

'What if they still hold out?'

'Go to third gambit. I'll give you a hint - what season is it?'

'Winter.'

'So what do you do?'

'Uh ... free gloves?'

'Cut the power to their homes, for Christ's sake. See if they still want to live there then. Bob's already passed the Environmental Protection Act so if we catch them chopping down any trees for firewood, we can arrest them.'

Talbot chimed in.

'What happened to good cop? Didn't you say you're going to alternate?'

'Oh yeah, I forgot. I'll think of something later. Maybe the free gloves - good one, Vic. Anyhow, once we've cut their electricity in the middle of winter, give them a few more days, then make a final offer. Value and a half of their house and free relocation to another town.'

'You'll do that?' said Talbot, surprised.

'If we have to. I told you, Bob. Purification and Independence. One leads to the other. Whatever it takes, we'll do it.'

As if to illustrate the point, I pulled out a large corkboard with a map of the world on it, stuck with hundreds of blue pins.

'Look at this, Victor! These are our brothers and sisters wanting to come to the promised land. There's brothers in Australia. There's sisters in Europe. We hold their fate in our very hands. I don't care how you do it! You've got four weeks tops, I want every one of those red pins out of my town map. Got it?'

'Got it.'

'Good. So get to work. Give me a high five.'

We slapped hands. It was about time we came up with an official Milinish salute, but for now the old high five would do. Maybe it would evolve into something else.

Victor looked a bit downcast as he turned to go, so I called him back.

'Oh, by the way, Vic - great job on the recording studio. It's really shaping up.'

There was a relieved smile from Victor.

'You like it, Tom? You happy with the gear? I wasn't sure what to get.'

'To be honest, I wouldn't have much of a clue myself. Unlike my father, I'm not omniscient! But if you get top of the range in everything, I'm sure our engineer can cobble together something decent.'

Victor and Talbot walked out and I made one more survey of the town map. The red pins burned my eyes, but I absorbed the energy and sent it right back at them. I visualised them melting and disappearing, quite literally, right off the face of the map. Then I reached out a hand to seize those red pins and cast them physically to the floor. Yet a divine voice stayed my hand. If it wasn't God, it was probably the voice of my higher self. Either that or a telepathic order from the Ruanglian High Command.

'No cheating, Tom. Remove them with your mind, not your hands.'

I swore, then stopped and looked around me in wonder. I laughed and walked calmly from the room.

13
The Inner
Circle

Any fool can hold a gun, or bash someone for fun
Thuggery, skulduggery, intellectual content none
But I attack the mind, those contracts really bind
Conceptual enslavements, they are the lasting kind
Cultown Album Lyrics

Every nefarious group needs an inner circle. The brains trust, the hard core, the black cowled conspirators plotting behind closed doors. It was time the Milinish fulfilled its generic obligations, so I sat down to choose my allies. There would be seven members, each playing a vital role in the organisation. Why seven, you ask? It's a proven empirical fact the number seven has mystical powers. Think of all the things that are seven: seven days of the week, seven deadly sins, seven dwarves, the seventh son of a seventh son. Everything comes back to seven. Hell, this is even *chapter* seven. Oh no, it's thirteen. Whatever.

Seven members to engineer the conquest of the world: who was fit for such a task? All would play a part in the struggle to come. They must be hand-picked with surgical precision. At least the first three were settled. Myself as leader, Victor cos he had the loot, and Talbot to take care of admin. He even seemed to enjoy it.

Alas, empires are not run on bureaucracy alone. There was also the problem of law enforcement. That's where Jim Flynn came in.

I met him one evening after some trouble between cops and redpinners. A redpinner had been badly beaten up and taken to hospital. I called in Flynn, one of the Saborman executives who happened to live in town. He'd not been the first to become a member of the Milinish, but he'd not been the last either. Now we sat across from each other in the War Room at Saborman House. He looked like an actor who's been chosen to play a lawyer in a TV show. Late thirties, tall and tanned, unrealistically handsome. In some ways, he reminded me of Jamie who, I'm sorry to say, had rather fallen out of favour. They almost had the same name. Perhaps Flynn was the new improved version. I stood up and poured him a whisky, then resumed my seat.

'A pleasure to make your acquaintance, Jim, even if the circumstances are lousy. I need to say a few words on a subject very distant from my heart. That subject is violence.'

I adopted a stern look.

'I've never understood the appeal,' I said. 'Aesthetically, it's an abomination, and as a political tool it's as crude as it gets. Doesn't matter if it's schoolyard bully, wife-beater, gangster or cop, violence is the hallmark of every thuggish regime in history and we must go beyond it. I would not besmirch the good name of the Milinish by tainting it with the blood of the dissenter. Milinish is about freedom, not slavery.'

Flynn said nothing so I continued my spiel.

'We must realise that the pen is mightier than the sword. It is words and not swords that make reality. Power is wrought with ideas and language. How do you think I got here? How did I create these lush surrounds, the chair you sit in, the whisky warming your glass. Not by kidnapping Victor Saborman and beating him up! No, I created it all with a drop of ink, just as I am redrawing this entire town. Almost literally.'

I glanced at the map on the wall stuck with blue, purple, yellow, and red pins.

'Why is Cull the fastest growing town in America? Why are people flocking to settle here? Did I send an army of thugs round

123

to intimidate them into joining? No, I seduced them with words and ideas. It's conceptual enslavements that bind, they last longer than chains and prisons. People flock here because they love my words - that is real power. It has nothing to do with guns or bombs. Why do people die in wars? The more relevant question is why they kill. Why do they murder complete strangers on command? Because words have told them this is what they must do. They have been created by words.'

'That's an impressive round of rhetorical questions you've fired off there, Tom,' said Flynn. 'I'm not surprised. Your books are an arsenal of analogies and murderous metaphors. There's no doubt that when it comes to wordplay, your armoury's top drawer.'

'Ah, alliteration - simple but effective,' I said. 'I see you're a man after my own heart, and I daresay when it comes to quick wit, you're the fastest gun in town.'

'I wouldn't know,' Flynn replied. 'But if we're talking real violence, I don't think words can compete. You want to give peace a chance? Fine, but what we've got in Cull is a bunch of old school cops. The only use they've got for white doves is target practice. You can't expect to change the culture overnight and erase lifetime habits.'

'If your cops can't change, then expel them from town and replace them with those who can. I've no use for thugs. And I think you'll find cultural conditioning *can* be changed. Control the mind and the body will follow. That's my way. Reprogram the software and the machine runs differently.'

'How do you do that?'

'Perhaps that's a challenge for a person of your own talents, Jim. Could there be a more rewarding vocation? Not only will you earn promotion to the Milinish High Command, but a place in history. What an achievement - the first totally peace loving police force! You'll go down as one of the great reformers, and all by showing that peace is a better means of social control than violence. Violence is crude, messy and inefficient - and mental cruelty is far more effective.'

'Mental Cruelty?'

'Social isolation for a start. Who wants to be the odd man out, the only one left out of Cull's biggest club. Membership is well over ninety percent now. If all criminals are expelled from the club, the crime rate will take a dive. I won't tolerate violence in Cull, from citizen or cop. That message must be clearly understood.'

'All right, we change the software, but is that enough? There's some who say violence is hard wired into us from genetic programming. After all, chimps are violent too and our ancestors evolved right along with them. It helped us survive just like our simian cousins. If that's true, it won't be easy to change the head kicking inclinations of our local cops.'

Despite myself, I couldn't help a glance through the door to the library where Orantor's books were shelved. Did Flynn think he could lecture me now? I delivered a slight rebuke.

'What is this - pop science? Why don't you leave the Darwinian fairytales to me? I learned from masters, even if they don't have my sense of theatre. Still, I like your style. We can go a long way together if you'll toss your trendy opinions away. There's only room for one trend in this town. You're head of security, but no violence. You won't need it - especially when you say the magic word.'

'And that is?'

'Quavisia.'

The Inner Circle's next member was chosen quite differently. On a whim, I decided someone would be drawn at random from the townsfolk of Cull itself. This was partly meant as a cheap gesture towards democracy and partly just for a laugh. It was announced that a lottery would be held with tickets selling for $10 each, the winner to be elected onto the High Council of Milinish. It seemed like a good idea at the time.

The winner was a guy named Selwyn Clark, a sixties throwback at first glance, though he was so young he could only have read about them. His blondish hair was dreadlocked and complemented by a short, scruffy beard. He wore one of those Indian hippy shirts and a string of beads. He showed up at my office with a guitar strapped over his shoulder - inappropriate, but suitably random. I didn't mind as long as he wasn't planning to break out any Bob

Dylan protest songs at council meetings. I supposed he could always learn some of mine.

'Congratulations on your win, Selwyn. I'm sure your talents will be vital to the future of Cull.'

'Thanks, Tom, but I knew I was going to win.'

'What do you mean?'

'I just had a hunch. That's why I only bought one ticket in the lottery.'

'Do you know how many tickets we sold in the last four weeks?'

'No idea,' said Selwyn, shaking his big dopey grin.

'In a town of 20,000 inhabitants, roughly 400,000 tickets were sold. That's an average of 20 per citizen. One woman alone bought over 200 tickets, yet you tell me you had just one. It's pretty clear you were at long odds to win. 400,000 to 1, in fact. But you 'knew' you were going to win. How so?'

Selwyn shrugged.

'I just had a feeling. That's why I only bought one ticket. And the sheer unlikeliness of it just confirms I was destined to win.'

'Selwyn, you do surprise me. A 400,000 to 1 long shot comes off and you conclude that no other result was possible, that the improbability of the outcome proves its inevitability.'

'Makes sense, right? Doesn't it seem a bit unlikely it could have been an accident? If only one little thing had been changed, I wouldn't even be here. There is plan and purpose behind everything. There are no accidents! I always knew I was special. Looks like I was right.'

'But you've only won a lottery. Anyone can do that.'

'I don't think so. Only a lottery winner can win a lottery.'

'Suppose someone else had won it. What's to stop them getting up here and saying exactly what you said - that it was destiny, it was planned, and there was no other possible outcome. Someone had to get lucky and it happened to be you. If you hadn't won the lottery, you wouldn't be here saying it was inevitable you'd won the lottery!'

'I don't believe that Mr Swan, and neither do you. You're just testing me.'

'Ok Selwyn, I give up. But from now on you shall be known as 'Destiny.'

'Cool.'

'By the way, if a big rock hadn't fallen out of the sky and made the dinosaurs extinct, you'd never have been born in the first place. Or was that destiny too?'

'Definitely.'

'You win. Welcome aboard.'

Two more members needed. One night I was kicking back with a beer, listening to Megadeth, when suddenly Alice popped into my mind. Well, not an actual vision of Alice - we hadn't met yet - but a memory of her letter. Remember all those messages I received in chapter two, the letters and blog comments? Alice's was the one that said *Revelations of Milinish* was 'very funny.' It had been signed Alice White, Brunswick, which is a suburb in Melbourne. Back in Australia I'd already gotten Jamie to check her out. Turned out she was a rogue science graduate who'd ruined a promising career by researching ESP. She'd tried to set up some kind of paranormal research project at university, but been denied funding. She'd then quit and dropped into obscurity.

From time to time, I had idly wondered whether to make contact with her. Well, why not now? I rang international directory assistance to see if they had an Alice White in Brunswick. It was 2am in Cull, so probably daytime in Australia. A female voice answered the phone.

'Hello.'

'Alice White?'

'Yes.'

'I'm calling from America. You don't know me, but I've heard about your research into parapsychology.'

'Oh yeah?' she said, without interest. 'What research would that be?'

'You know - into dreams and parapsychology.'

'That was years ago. Who are you anyway?'

'It doesn't matter who I am. Just answer one question - how would you like to start your research again with a very large grant?'

127

She took a bit of convincing but finally agreed to meet me, although my identity was still a secret. She only agreed to come to the US because I promised to deposit a cash advance in her account and fly her over. I suppose she thought the free flight and accommodation meant a cheap overseas holiday, if nothing else.

I rang Jamie and told him to arrange the cash and a plane ticket. He sounded grumpy for some reason. I was rather concerned about that boy. He'd been a bit sulky ever since missing out on the Inner Circle, but just because he was my number two in Australia didn't guarantee him a place if people like Victor and Selwyn were more qualified.

The real reason I'd not chosen him was lingering doubt over his mental health. As I suspected, his ex-wife's attempt to reconnect was a pathetic attempt at an intervention. The rest of his family were in on it too. They'd all but kidnapped him, and tried to fill his head with lies about me and the movement. Fortunately, they were too late to stop Jamie doing the job I asked of him, which was to enable the flow of members from Sydney to Cull. That was all up and running by the time he got waylaid by his so called family. To his credit, when Jamie found out his ex-wife's true motives, he was so angry he severed ties for good and caught the next flight to the US.

The trouble was that even after we settled him in a nice house in town, he seemed prone to mood swings and odd behaviour. I decided to put him on light duties for a while, simple administrative tasks that wouldn't tax him unduly. As it happened, one of those tasks was ensuring I had a steady supply of dope, coke, and trips.

Now hang on. Before anyone jumps to conclusions, these drugs weren't for my own use. They were for scientific research into mental health. Experiments were already underway in the Saborman House laboratories. Cocaine, was being tested on the timid and marijuana on the uptight. LSD was for those trying to access their unconscious minds. So far the results were promising.

If I did occasionally experiment on myself as well, that was simply a matter of professional ethics. Unlike the cowards who test substances on animals, I made a vow that no drug would be tried on others I wasn't prepared to take myself. So I did. And who says science isn't fun?

Now that I think about it, Jamie was probably indulging in a little experimentation himself. That would explain the mood swings. Unfortunately, someone with mental health issues needs to exercise caution in such matters. Oh well, it's too late now.

In any case, I was working so hard on one thing or another that I quite forgot about having invited Alice to Cull. It was therefore a real surprise when she was shown into my study one morning. She was about thirty, androgynously pretty with her dark hair cut short. She wore black trousers, a white shirt with blue tie, and glasses to complete the scholarly look. I hid my surprise and shook her hand.

'So you're a scientist,' I began.

'That depends,' said Alice.

'On what?'

'Who you talk to. Most competent researchers would call me a pseudo-scientist.'

'Right,' I said. 'Parapsychology isn't much of a career move for a science graduate. But I've been listening to the experts - you know, the proper authorities - and they say there's not a shred of evidence for the existence of ESP, out-of-body travels, or the paranormal.'

'That depends.'

'On who you talk to?'

'You could say that. It also depends on what counts as evidence, and whether anyone wants to find any in the first place. My application for a research grant was dismissed. They said there wasn't enough evidence to justify funding such a study. Funny that. You might say the lack of evidence has something to do with the lack of research.'

'Now now, Alice, be reasonable. ESP incidents are a nuisance. We can't have any of that nasty anomalous data mucking up our nice little scientific paradigm.'

'Of course not. What would the neighbours think?'

'Where would it all lead? One minute it would be ESP research, the next moral ruin. And tell me, does the gender thing come into it at all?'

'What do you mean?'

'How is it for women in science these days?'

'Pretty good really. As long as you have the grades and the right views, it doesn't matter what sex you are now. Any prejudice against me is about my field of study, not my gender. There are plenty of women in science these days. In fact, most of them would be keen to distance themselves from the likes of me. Having finally gotten into the club, they're certainly not going to hang out with a pseudo-scientist.'

'I see.'

'Have we met before?' said Alice. 'You seem familiar.'

'In a fashion. You sent me a letter once about a book called *Revelations of Milinish*.'

'You wrote that? Jesus Christ!'

'Bless you, my child.'

Alice looked around her at my well furnished study.

'So you're Thomas Swan. The press ran a few stories about you - they say you're this big time cult leader.'

'It's all true, I'm afraid. You are now in Cull, a small American town that is rapidly turning into a larger American town because my so called cult is the fastest growing religion in the world. We'd like to make you an offer. Tell me, what's the largest research grant you've ever received?'

'Well, in Australia we have this thing called the dole and it's about three hundred a week.'

'Take a look at this cheque. It's a bit more than the dole.'

'But this is made out for a million dollars.'

'It's the research budget for your new parapsychology department. You'll study ESP, dreams, out-of-body experiences, trance states, and whatever else you can think of. Maybe it's all bunk, but I'll give you a go. If you do happen to find anything, it'll be one in the eye for old Orantor. What do you say?'

Alice took off her glasses and grinned.

'I don't know what kind of racket you're running here, but frankly I don't care. Finally the chance to do some research? I'll take it. A million bucks!'

'Yeah. We had this lottery. It's funny, I suppose, a lottery prize going to ESP research. Oh by the way Alice, one more thing - you are now a member of the Milinish High Command. Congratulations.'

'Thanks, Tom ... I think.'

So there we were, six members down, one to go. She was due any minute. There was a knock at the door. A young woman entered and sat down. I smiled and shook her hand.

'Arianna, welcome to the Milinish Inner Circle. You may be wondering why I've given you the job.'

'Token woman?'

'What rubbish, we've already got one. You're the token black, gay woman.'

'Who said I'm gay?'

'Google.'

'Great. So I'm a PR stunt?'

'That's a cynical way to spin it, I prefer to say you're a symbol of solidarity. Fact is, my story doesn't have enough women or minorities. Including you shows we're inclusive.'

'Well hip, hip hooray.'

'Don't blame me. It would have been handy if Orantor was a woman, but like most scientists of his generation, he's an ageing Caucasian male.'

'Who?'

'Orantor. Oh, never mind. Fact is, the Milinish doesn't discriminate. I treat everyone equally badly. No prejudice here.'

Arianna looked unconvinced. A local woman, I'd headhunted her for the job even though she'd been a yellow-pinner until recently. I think she'd only turned up due to the salary on offer. Even so, she was hardly leaping out of her seat at the prospect. Indeed, for most of our interview she was *slouching* in that seat.

'So what do you want from me?' Arianna said. 'A female perspective on your doctrines?'

'Not really. I think the whole thing's a fake.'

'Your doctrines are fake?'

131

'No, the idea of a female perspective. In fact, the whole male-female thing. I'm so bored with it. Men this, women that, blah, blah, blah. Why can't we just be human beings? This obsessive need to extrapolate psychological traits from people's genitals - I'm over it.'

'What about in your book? You said men and women are at war.'

'It's an artificial war. A cultural creation. The idea that there's some innate difference between men and women - I don't buy it. Never have, never will. Any differences are 90% cultural, I reckon. Behaviour is learned through social indoctrination, then someone makes up a biological theory to justify it. And no matter how many pop science theories try to tie personality to genitalia, my gut instinct says it's all a lie.'

Arianna sat up a little straighter, and ran her fingers through her short black hair.

'Great,' she said, 'but that doesn't change the fact women have always been oppressed by men one way or another.'

'Sure.'

'So why don't you do something about it?'

'I'm liberating humanity. All of humanity. What more do you want? Other than that, as I said, I treat people the same.'

'Surely you realise you benefit from male privilege?'

'So what? I feel no personal guilt. I happen to have been born a man. That doesn't make me guilty of the sins of other men who've lived before me, or the systems they created. On the contrary, I've been the victim myself in plenty of my other lives.'

'Oh really?'

'I've been a woman, I've been black, I've been persecuted more times than I could count. Women have had plenty of oppression through history. That doesn't mean there should be mass retribution against those who happened to be born male now. Why should today's men suffer for the crimes of others? Hell, most of them were probably women in past lives, same as me.'

'So that gives them the right to oppress women now? It's their turn?'

'On the contrary, it should make them more compassionate. They should be the ones leading the charge for gender equality. There's no excuse for mistreating others. Oppression is oppression, it's the same old crap no matter who's doing it or for what reason. Because really, every reason is the same reason - abuse of power. That is all.'

Arianna shook her head slightly, as if not sure what to make of me.

'So how exactly are you going to liberate humanity?'

'In every conceivable way. Getting rid of the tedious obsession with gender is one - and I'll start right at the top. Do you realise many religions still think of God as a man?'

'Not mine. I'm Wiccan.'

'And what have you got - some kind of Female Principle as the primary urge? How's that an improvement?'

'It can't be any worse than the male gods.'

'Sure, but why go there at all? If we have to put up with this male female rubbish in daily life, I don't see why we should impose it on the gods as well.'

'Then what do you believe?'

'I favour a pantheist conception. Spirit in all beings, and certainly beyond our notions of male and female.'

Arianna seemed about to reply, then stopped. I could almost see her mentally shrugging her shoulders.

'Getting back to the job, Tom, if I join your so called Inner Circle, what's our brief? What does the job involve?'

I smiled.

'I generally try to make it up as I go along, then eventually in hindsight work out what I was trying to do. So, are you in?'

This time, Arianna's shrug was quite visible.

'In like Flynn, I suppose.'

'Yes, Flynn's in too. He's head of security. Anyhow, never mind that now. You can meet everyone at the first meeting. Welcome aboard.'

We stood up, shook hands, and with that the circle was complete.

14

Quantifiable Karma

Who the hell is keeping score of all this karma?
The Tom Letters - a Collection

So what was it like living in Cull in those heady days? Ask someone else. I was locked up in Saborman House writing my new book. I was also writing songs in the recording studio Vic had put in. In fact, there was no real need to leave home at all. Everything I wanted was right at my fingertips.

That wasn't the only reason to be a shrinking violet. Who wants to take a stroll down main street with a lot of messiah-struck clowns gawping at you? To keep your mystique, you've got to ration your public appearances. You can't just wander down to the shops for a pack of toilet paper or something.

According to Bob Talbot, Cull was thriving in every way. As mentioned, the influx of citizens had produced a boom for the building industry and the town's economy in general. There was a sense of being a chosen people and that great events were at hand. Despite the imminent threat of the Quavisians, everyone was united in purpose, borne along on a wave of spiritual optimism.

Ah yes, the Quavisians.

There were two security forces working for the social stability of Cull. One was the police force controlled by Jim Flynn. The other was Quavisiaphobia. My prophecies said the Quavisian mother ship was on the way and three quarters of the world's population would be wiped out when it arrived. People realised that by living in Cull, home of the prophet, the chances of survival were much enhanced. In their own way then, the Quavisians contributed a great deal to keeping order in Cull. Anyone who did not comply with my wishes was simply asked to leave town, and to be banished from the protective gaze of the shepherd was no small punishment.

It was Jim Flynn who suggested we play up this fear even more. For Flynn, charged with the task of keeping public order without using violence, Quavisiaphobia was a godsend, and it was his idea that screening certain films would be in the public interest.

'How about *Independence Day* or *War of the Worlds*, Tom? It will help if people are reminded what they're up against.'

'Brilliant! We'll begin at once.'

We started with *Independence Day*. It was decreed that every citizen of Cull had to attend a screening of this film about alien invasion, given its relevance to our own concerns. And before each screening, the good citizens saw another film - a speech recorded in my study. There, cinema size, the stern face of Thomas Swan lectured them on the importance of what they were about to see.

'My friends, it's a fine line between fiction and truth, and the makers of fiction are often the instruments of a greater truth than they know. Those who made the fiction you're about to see had no real idea what they were doing. Yet it is obvious to me, as it should be to you, that the film is a clear warning about the Quavisian attack.

We have Ruanglia to thank that this film was ever made. Many years ago when the Quavisian space fleet took off, the Ruanglians meditated for months and sent thought-waves to Hollywood urging them to make it. In the dream state, they communicated with the writers and director, advising them on the finer points of cinematic art. Can we ignore the message of this important film? I, Thomas Swan, urge you to watch it and tremble, but know that if we stand steadfast, no Quavisian attack can destroy us.'

135

I actually snuck into a couple of the screenings in disguise. The atmosphere was electric, as everyone was riveted by the film. Well, nearly everyone. The second time, there was a young man and woman in the row behind me who insisted on talking throughout. I tried to ignore them at first but when the girl answered a phone call, that was it. I summoned Flynn's security team. The young couple kept on chatting, oblivious to all, even as armed security guards closed in from both sides.

'Take them away,' I said. 'Put them with the others.'

I noted with satisfaction their looks of outrage as they were led away. Well, they'd seen nothing yet. The old county jailhouse must be getting rather full by now. In fairness, it can't have been easy for people to adjust to all the new laws, especially as I'd yet to announce most of them. But if people had half a brain, there'd be no need for these laws in the first place.

Citizens were also urged to attend midweek 'Satan Watch' evenings. This was an education initiative in the field of science. We screened nature documentaries that had soundtracks of my own design - spooky, keyboard music which I'd composed in the new recording studio at Saborman House. They fused perfectly with the nature scenes. In some cases, I added narration in which the animal behaviour was 'explained' using the pseudo-evolutionary spiel from *Revelations of Milinish*.

As the number of redpinners in Cull had dwindled by now, nearly the entire town went to these educational evenings. So eager were the townsfolk to attend that our new incentive schemes were almost superfluous. In any case, the system was that citizens got 'karma points' each time they attended an official cultural event. Given that the points tally was a matter of public record, it all became quite competitive. Everyone could keep tabs on how many points their friends and neighbours were gaining through approved acts - or losing through offences. It was a brilliant system, and strangely enough we had Selwyn to thank.

It came up at the first committee meeting of the newly formed Inner Circle. We were gathered in the conference room at Saborman House. After some preliminary waffle from me, Arianna got to the point with a pivotal question.

'So now we're all here, what are we supposed to actually do?'

'Oh, not much,' I replied. 'Just create a model society ready to take over after the Quavisian apocalypse. To that end, everyone's got a job to do. Jim's head of security and Bob's in charge of admin. Victor's the Minister for Believer Housing. Alice is chief researcher into the paranormal. And you, Arianna, we'll think of a role for you in due course.'

'What about Selwyn?' said Alice.

'Selwyn's a random element. I see him as some kind of idiot savant.'

Selwyn frowned.

'Huh? What's that, Tom?'

'It means you're a genius.'

Selwyn's frown became a grin, and I leaned over to high five him.

'Unconsciously, of course,' I said, 'but a genius nonetheless. Out of your random babblings and New Age platitudes, some extraordinary wisdom is bound to emerge. That's the theory anyhow. Go on, say something idiotic. Let's see what comes out.'

'About what?'

'I don't know, anything.'

'Uh, OK. The government is full of rich dudes. What do they know about life? The next government should be all poor people who understand what it's like to struggle.'

'Right. We'll put that on file. Next idea.'

Selwyn mused for a few seconds, then spoke again.

'If they stopped spending billions on weapons, they could put all the money into schools and hospitals and we'd all be better off.'

'Yes, well that's blatantly obvious but it'll never happen. Do you really think an idea like that would ever be taken seriously? Come on Selwyn, this isn't the sort of inspired idiocy I'm after. Give me something we can use right here in Cull.'

I stared into space while the other six members sat around waiting. It was like an awkward silence at a dinner party. After a minute or so, I snapped my fingers decisively and looked around the group.

137

'Let's try to enzyme this.'

'That's not a verb,' said Alice.

'It's a verb and a noun as well. Enzymology, I call it. It's a new scientific method I came up with. It just means you mix stuff up and see what happens. We're going to create a chemical reaction by mixing Selwyn's input with the other council members.'

I turned back to Selwyn.

'Jim, for example. He's head of police and security. What do you think he should do to maintain order in town?'

'Nothing,' said Selwyn.

'I'm sorry, what?'

'Nothing,' Selwyn repeated.

'What is this, some Zen bollocks?'

'No, man. I mean, why bother, right? Who needs police or laws? Karma's going to sort it all out in the end.'

'Aha! Now we're getting somewhere. Keep going.'

'I don't see why we even need laws. That's why I used to belong to the anarchist society. No laws, man.'

'What do you mean, *used to*?'

'I got expelled.'

'Whatever for?'

' I didn't pay my membership dues.'

'Oh, brilliant. So we don't need laws in Cull, is that what you're saying?'

'No, Tom, there's only one law - the law of karma.'

'Right - so how does it work? Give us an example.'

'Uh, OK. Look, if we go out and pollute the air with pesticides, that's disrespecting Nature, right? Five years later when our crops fail, we're getting dissed back by Nature. That's our karma, dude. Cause and effect.'

'It's a bit bloody longwinded. We're trying to run a town here. I don't have time to sit around for five years waiting for Nature to dispense some high handed karma when it feels like it. '

'It's not always like that, Tom. If I go and dump a load of trash in the street and Officer Jim arrests me for littering, that's instant. You know, instant karma, like the John Lennon song.'

'I see. So your vague, metaphysical justice system is administered by an actual human justice system. How convenient.'

'Whether it takes five years or five minutes, it's all karma, man.'

'It all sounds terribly haphazard to me, and a piss poor way to run a judicial system. All these good and bad deeds to weigh up. I mean, who's keeping score? Is there some cosmic ledger up in the sky? Hey, wait a minute - I've got it!'

I slapped both hands on the table to produce a resounding whack.

'Lord strike me down, the idiot savant has done it!'

'What are you on about, Tom?' said Arianna.

'Quantifiable karma - that's what! I've already revolutionised science, now I'm going to do the same for spirituality. What's karma anyhow? Cause and effect, reward and punishment. You do something good and good comes back to you. Do something bad, and there's a price to pay. That's all fine and dandy, but you know what I hate? It's all so bloody vague.'

'Vague?'

'Yes, it's vague I tell you. For one thing, what's good and what's evil? Who decides? For another, who's keeping score? Like I said, is there a celestial bookkeeper watching all these good and bad deeds? And finally, when does the punishment happen: the next life? The afterlife? Or three weeks later at four o'clock in the afternoon? It's the most poorly administrated system since *Rolling Stone* magazine's poll on the top five-hundred songs of all time.'

I high fived Selwyn again. Twice.

'This man's a genius,' I declared. 'A bona fide idiot savant. When the history of Cull is laid out, he'll go down as the father of our new justice system. So, guys, let me tell you how it's going to work.'

I stood up and paced backwards and forwards for a minute, faster and faster. Then I slammed my hand on the desk once more.

'Quantifiable Karma, Goddammit! Bugger your celestial bookkeeping and your wishy washy spiritual laws. We're going to make karma scientific. Who's keeping score? We are! From now on, karma's going to be a matter of public record. I want every citizen under a spotlight. Every man, woman and child. Do something bad, it goes on your record for all to see. Big crime, small crime, doesn't matter. Everyone's going to know.'

I picked up my phone and punched in a name.

'Rose! Got a big job for you. Go to the citizen files. We're making a new data base to keep track of everyone's karma. What's that? Never mind the details, I'll be over in half an hour to explain. Just be prepared, this is going to be huge.'

I hung up.

'What about punishment?' said Jim Flynn.

'It'll be quick and resolute. No more of this copping it in the next life caper, or randomly five years later on a Tuesday morning. Here in Cull, karma's going to be fast and to the point. It might not be instant, like Lennon sang about, but we'll make it close as damn it.'

Bob Talbot looked at me curiously, a hint of admiration in his expression.

'How you gonna do it, Tom?'

'Never mind the details, we'll figure that out later. Let's just say, the punishment will fit the crime.'

'And what is a crime? We've already got laws in place.'

I sat down again and stroked my beard for a moment.

'Good question. There's your regular, garden variety crimes, of course. Theft, murder and that lot. Goes without saying. But karma's much more expansive than that, don't matter if there's a law about it or not. When it comes down to it, karma's about not being a jerk, really. Like those goons I kicked out of the cinema last week.'

'Eh?'

'Some folks were having a good old chinwag in the row behind when I was watching the movie. Fair ruined it for me.'

'That's not illegal.'

'It is in Cull. Leastways it will be. I make the laws here. If you're going to be a jerk, karma gets to work. That'll be our motto.'

'So being a jerk's against the law now?'

140

'You bet. We're going to legislate for karma. Never mind the seven deadly sins, it's the seven *trivial* sins that bother me. I'm sick of people and all the dumb things they do every day. Well, no more - all that will be against the law.'

'The prisons are going to be mighty full.'

'Yeah, or maybe we'll just kick all the sinners out of town. And you know what else? We mustn't forget the virtues. Accentuate the positive, guys, don't forget that. The virtues are going to get the status they deserve, and the greatest of them all is loyalty. It's fidelity gets you max karma points round here. We'll put that message out, loud and clear. Stands to reason then, disloyalty is the greatest sin of all. Treason's another name for it. We'll quantify that too.'

'Loyalty to what?'

'To the Milinish, to the good Lord, and to me. Let it be known the most karmic points are gained by loyalty and the most points lost are for treason. By Christ, this'll be the most law abiding society since slavery, mark my words. Now give me a high thirty.'

A high thirty was our new Inner Circle handshake in which the other six members simultaneously gave me a high five. But they made a hash of it this time. Three of them were supposed to go low and three of them high. That's how a high five works, right? Then I was going to meet them all at once with my own two hands, one up one down. Funny thing, though, the three who were meant to go low all went high so in the end there were six right hands raised to salute me. And if I didn't know better, I would've sworn all six were giving me the old *Sieg Heil*. Oh well, go with the flow, man. Heil Tom, Heil Cull, Heil Milinish!

15

The Seven
Trivial Sins

Anyone can see the deadly sins are wrong.
It's the trivial sins that slip through unnoticed.
The Tom Letters - A Collection.

Oh Cull, my kingdom Cull. Looking back, I see we meant no less than to make an ideal society. I was skipper and it was my job to plot a course for the voyage. But we'd only make it to Paradise Isle if everyone got on board and rowed in the same direction. Fortunately we had a willing crew of twenty thousand, with me and Quavisia urging them on. The people on the one hand loved the Milinish and on the other deeply feared the Quavisians. Between these two iron hands, it was easy to bend them to my will and shape them as model citizens in the Utopian society we were building. The new karmic points system was the glue binding it all together.

Of course, Utopia don't come easy. There would be pain along the way. That was inevitable given our lofty aspirations. As part of that process, the justice system was about to launch with our new standards placed front and centre for all to see.

I dropped into the watch-house and made a tour of the cells. What a sorry lot they were. Or rather, what a sorry lot they weren't. Most of the fools still didn't know why they'd been arrested. As I passed, they called out to me for release. Fat chance.

I took Jamie with me. He was getting back to his old self these last couple of weeks. Just in time to film our TV series on ethics. I aimed to resurrect our double act from the therapy workshops, the old one-two punch with him the straight man feeding me gags. That night, I briefed him on what was to come. A fair amount was scripted, to be sure, but there was plenty of room for improv - a perfect mix for a couple of old pros like us.

At 9.45 the next morning, I took a peek from the backstage area into the courtroom of Cull. The galleries were full of onlookers, overfull in fact. All the better to reinforce my judgments. Jamie put them in the picture before showtime.

'Right you guys, you've won a place in Tom's new TV show. This is a golden chance to rack up some karma points, so don't blow it. It's all double points, today. Just make sure you boo and cheer in the right places. We've got twenty-four cameras on the job and remember, half of them are trained on you.'

Jamie turned and walked over to stage left, as we showbiz pros call it, which the audience actually sees on their right. 'All rise,' he said.

A trumpet fanfare sounded over the PA and I entered in my judicial robes. I settled into the judge's seat and smiled at Jamie on my left. He was all set to play Officer Byrd to my Judge Judy, just like I planned it. Like them, we were filming, knowing it would ultimately reach into millions of homes for the edification of all. When the audience had resumed their seats, I looked directly into Camera One.

'Friends, children, citizens of Cull - welcome to the Court of Milinish. This is a great day in legal history. It doesn't matter if you're here in person or sitting at home watching on TV, this is Justice Ground Zero.

Why are we here today? To launch a new war against sin. One day, we'll eliminate it from Cull once and for all - that's our mission. And here's the thing: today's the day we actually make sin illegal. But I can see you folks thinking - hang on a mo, didn't Tom get rid of sin already? Well, sure, I don't mean the biggies. The seven deadly sins - lust, gluttony and the rest - we're done with them. Ever since I came to town, this here courtroom's practically gone

143

out of business. So never mind the deadlies. What today's about is getting rid of the lesser evils. It's a little something I call the seven trivial sins.

The seven trivial sins: what are they? They're the dumb annoyances of modern life. The first world problems that are potholes on the road to Utopia - and not a damn one of them necessary if only folks would use an extra ounce of the grey matter going to waste in their skulls.

See, I've been a man of conscience all my life and there's a little saying I hold dear. 'No sins without sinners.' That's what I've always said, ever since I was a wee lad of six years old preaching ethics at the breakfast table to my ma and pa. I can still see it like yesterday, how I held up my tiny index finger and shook it in Pa's face. 'No sins without sinners!' I proclaimed to him. And even in my high, reedy little voice, the steel of the Lord shone through so he knew it was gospel.

Well, good old Pa looked at Ma and said, 'By Heaven, Mary, the boy's right. I do believe we've got our own Dalai Lama under this very roof. Are we raising him, or is he raising us?' And dear old Ma just frowned and crossed herself like she seen the devil himself running out of the room in a panic. I blessed them both and went back to my Bible study, right there at the table, a wee lad of six on a mission for all Mankind.

No sins without sinners! Commit that to memory, my children. You see, sins don't exist as things in themselves. They only become real through those who enact them. Ain't no murder without a murderer, right? That's why when I talk about the seven trivial sins, I prefer to speak of the seven trivial sinners. That's who you're going to meet today, a bunch of regular down-home sinners from Cull, USA. You might know their civilian names. Well, I'm gonna call 'em by their sinner names - the Show Pony, the Hand Crusher, the Phone Zombie, the Spell Breaker, the Barrel Scraper, the Nosey Parker, and the Leaf Blower.'

I looked up towards the back of the courtroom.

'Victor, bring in the first defendant.'

Oh my, a bit of public power had gone right to Vic's head. He didn't quite goosestep into the court, but it wasn't far off. Flanked

144

by two armed guards, he frogmarched a young man into the dock. Geese? Frogs? Kangaroos? That's the sort of court it was.

A couple of members of the gallery started booing. The rest of the crowd caught on and the boos flared up like wildfire. After a few seconds, Victor turned around and raised his hands to shush them. I looked down at my notes.

'Here's trivial sinner number one. Who've we got here? Aha, the Hand Crusher. Who reported him? It was you, Jamie, if I'm not mistaken.'

I looked towards stage left. Jamie nodded.

'I met this gentleman at temple in my first week here,' he said. 'I think he wanted to make a good impression.'

'Sure,' I replied, 'and you know what they say. You don't get a second chance to make a first impression. What better way to say hi than the old bone crushing, macho handshake?'

'That's right. It's not like I needed the use of my right hand for our holy work or anything. Why *not* crush it to a bloody pulp as a greeting?'

'Of course, Jamie. When I meet a new colleague, nothing impresses me more than their ability to mangle the one body part I need to get through my day.'

'Apart from your brain. Don't forget that. You can't get by without your brain.'

'Oh, I don't know. Mr. Hand Crusher seems to manage OK.'

'Now hang on, Tom, we're in a new country. We've got to be culturally sensitive about how they do stuff here. There's no end to these weird foreign greetings: nose rubbing, air kissing, and God knows what else. Maybe that's how they say hello in Cull - by trying to disable that miracle of evolution, the human hand. I wonder how they say happy birthday: a full blooded punch to the face?'

'That's a very valid point. Maybe this is what they do in the US. Only problem is, I've encountered these guys in Australia too, so this sin's international.'

I turned to the guy in the dock. He was just a regular Joe Wannabe, still wearing the business suit in which he'd been arrested. It was getting mighty crumpled.

'What have you got to say for yourself?'

145

'I'm sorry, your Honour, I didn't realise.' He cast a beseeching look towards Jamie. 'Guess I don't know my own strength.'

'Oh really - it was an accident, was it? And there I was thinking you were acting out some ridiculous male dominance ritual.'

'I was just trying to be confident.'

'That's odd, because Jamie assumed it was a pea-brained attempt to intimidate a breeding rival. Are you really that DNA-controlled?'

'I'm sorry, your Honour, it was a mistake, honest.'

'It certainly was. You obviously had no idea who you were shaking hands with. Jamie was my top man back in Australia. Well Mr Hand Crusher, you can go and shake hands with the jail warden for a few more days, but I reckon you'd better lighten your grip. Victor, send in the next one.'

I snuck a glance at my former 'top man back in Australia.' Was that a slight tightening of the jaw? A small pursing of the lips as he registered my choice of words? I turned back to observe the man who'd supplanted him. Victor was leading another young man forward into the dock. Right on cue, the chorus of boos kicked in from the gallery. I looked down at the charge sheet, then cast a baleful look at the accused.

'Mother Mary, is there no end to these DNA-driven antics? What's your name, son? Wait, don't answer that, I'm just gonna call you Randy. AKA the Show Pony. Well Randy, I see you're dressed up real nice for court, but that shirt's looking a bit tight. Why don't you take it off?'

The defendant said nothing so I again urged him to disrobe.

'Come now, we all like to be comfortable. I can see that shirt's chafing you.'

Randy remained silent, fidgeting with his belt. I shrugged.

'He's gone all shy, Jamie. Funny that. Didn't seem to bother him in the supermarket last Tuesday.'

A big screen TV was set up at the front of court. Onscreen, a picture flashed up of a line of people waiting at the supermarket checkouts. They were all decked out in normal summer wear - shorts, t-shirts, skirts and so on. Randy stood there in nothing but a pair of Speedos, which is to say underpants, the kind you wear to the beach for swimming. No shirt, no shoes, no shorts, and still expecting service. There were a few titters from the gallery. Victor raised his palms in a flame-fanning gesture, and soon the whole crowd was laughing riotously.

I looked directly into Camera One.

'This photograph was taken by a responsible citizen and sent to us. That citizen has earned fifty-five karma points and shot into the top ten of Zone Seven. See, that's how it is now in Cull. If you see something criminal going on, don't be a bystander. Evil prospers when good men do nothing. Well, ain't no evil going to prosper in Cull, cos the citizens are all over it like a solarium sun tan. Keep your eyes open and your cameras a-ready. I don't care if it's a deadly or a trivial, if you see a sin, report it.'

There was a tremendous cheer from the gallery. I gave the photo on the giant screen an incredulous look, then turned back to Randy, the Show Pony.

'Good Lord, man, is this the appropriate attire for a trip to the shops? You seem to be under the impression Cull is a gigantic nudist colony and no one else got the memo. Either that or you feel the desperate need to advertise your DNA breeding potential at all times.'

Finally, the young sinner spoke up.

'I'm sorry, I didn't know it was such a big deal.'

'Oh no, what's this - an accent? Don't tell me you're one of the Sydney immigrants. What part are you from?'

'Coogee, Coogee Beach.'

I snorted and tossed my head.

'That figures. The amount of show ponies I've seen parading up and down Coogee Bay Road, you could re-populate Gomorrah with that bunch of posers. Half of 'em Poms and Irish, maybe, but the Aussies certainly lowered the standards to begin with. Well, you might get away with that bollocks back home but over here it'll land you in the stocks copping pot shots from toss pots.'

'Look, I apologise, alright? I never knew it was against the law.'

'It's no hanging offence, son, but it sure ain't cool. Jamie - run the photo shop slideshow of shame.'

147

A series of sombre and serious images began to show on the big screen. The funeral of JFK, the signing of the Magna Carta, the crucifixion of Jesus, Nelson Mandela's presidential inauguration, and so on - and for each of them the Speedo-clad figure of Randy had been pasted in. Actually the only one he wasn't out of place was the crucifixion, he sort of blended in there. But the rest of them, he stuck out like ... well, like a man in Speedos in the supermarket.

'Take him away, Victor. Put him in a glass case in the town square. He can show everyone how gorgeous he is for the next three days. Righto, onto trivial sin number three. The Spell Breaker. I arrested these two myself.'

I made this remark conversationally to Jamie, aware it would ultimately be broadcast into millions of homes as part of my new Terminator Tom prime time TV show.

The young couple from the movie was led into court and taken to the dock. They still had a faintly outraged look, much as when they'd been arrested. I raised an eyebrow.

'Look at 'em, Jamie, they still don't know why they're here.'

The male defendant, a stocky chap in a red flannel shirt, voiced a protest.

'We sure don't. All we did was go watch the movie like everyone else.'

'But that's just it, you weren't really watching it. You were chitchatting with each other like you was home alone with your ma on the phone.'

'It's only a movie. What's the problem?'

'Only a movie? *Independence Day* is an extremely urgent warning about the Quavisian attack. It came direct from Ruanglia itself. You've compromised the entire security of Cull with your cavalier attitude.'

'Do we at least get a lawyer, or do we have to defend ourselves?'

'My dear sir, it's been said that a man who chooses to represent himself has a fool for a client, so go right ahead. What's your defence, anyway?'

'Defence? I don't even know the charge.'

148

'Like I said, you've jeopardized our eternal vigilance and practically spat in the face of the Ruanglian High Command. Amounts to treason in my book, a hanging offence if I'm not mistook. Whoa, I'm rapping now, who'd have thought, I was such a star in the People's Court?'

Wild applause and cheers broke out in the gallery. My ego was so inflated I nearly composed an entire hip hop song on the spot, all about me. Yet, mindful of my public duty, I simply held up my hands and continued the prosecution.

'It's treason alright. Lucky for you and your girlfriend, we're not fussed about the deadly sins today. All the deadly sinners get off. Goddamn lucky, my friend, or the only movie you'd be seeing is your life flashing in front of your eyes. The trivial sins, though, that's another story. We're cracking down like you wouldn't believe.'

At that point, the girlfriend chimed in. She was a streaky blonde ragamuffin, still young enough to get away with being too thin. Half enraged, half sycophantic, her protest came out politely aggressive in a vaguely Southern accent I'll do my best to mimic.

'Whut sin, your ahner? Ah ain't never heard of anything so redeeculous in all mah life. No offence, your ahner.'

'Ridiculous, is it? The seven trivial sins are ridiculous?'

'Uh jist don't get it, that's all.'

'Clearly. You know, guys, I don't care if it's *Independence Day* or Doris Day or Tightarse Tuesday. In my book, it's a criminal offense to talk during a movie. Or if it ain't, it ought to be, ergo it is. Leastways in this here model society we're building in Cull.'

'But wah?' asked the girl.

'When I go to the movies, for a couple of hours I want to forget myself and my life and all the crap I go through every day. I want to get sucked into that big screen. Another world, another life. Total immersion - that's the spell I'm after. But when some clown in the audience won't shut up, it just reminds me I'm stuck in a room with the same sort of people I'm trying to get away from. It's probably why I haven't been to the flicks in years and the cinemas are going broke. People would rather stay home and watch it in peace.'

149

'It's only a movie, your ahner.'

'Maybe, but there's a lot of folks involved in casting that spell. Writers, actors and the rest. When they were in the editing suite making the final cut, I don't think the director ever once thought of getting you guys in to lay down some audio commentary.'

The girl seemed about to make some snarky comment but the boyfriend jumped in, clearly sensing the game was lost.

'I'm sorry, sir, we get it. It won't happen again, I promise.'

'I'm happy to hear it. Even so, you and your girl can go hang out in the watch-house for a few more days. See what it's like to be stuck in a room with people you can't get away from. Take them away.'

I fanned myself and took a big sip of water. This judicial work sure took a lot out of you.

'Righto Jamie, that's the Hand Crusher, the Show Pony, and the Spell Breaker. Who's up next?'

'The Nosey Parker.'

'Aha, one of the most trivial sinners of our times. I hate those guys.'

A young woman was led into court.

'Or gals.'

I studied her for a moment, although it wasn't mutual. Indeed she barely acknowledged the bench as she entered the dock. She was kitted out in a bunch of designer brands and looked like she'd been picked up while cruising down to the mall. A picture of the offence flashed up on the big screen at front of court. I took another sip of water.

'This one's pretty easy so we'll keep it short. You're driving into town or to work or home and some days it's not easy to find a park. But the good council of Cull thought ahead and left a bunch of parking spaces.'

A diagram appeared onscreen. It showed two driveways and a space in between for cars to park, nose to bumper.

'Let's say the average car is four metres long. You can see here that the space between the two driveways is just over eight metres. So how many cars can park there?'

I looked at the defendant, who ignored me.

'Well?' I said, finally.

'Umm, two?' she replied in a scorn-dipped voice, like it was me who was the moron.

'What's with the attitude?' I asked, genuinely surprised. 'It ain't me in the dock now, is it?'

'Whatever,' said the woman, with a toss of the head.

The crowd gasped, then began to boo. I raised a hand.

'Don't waste your boos on this one. I reckon she's earned herself an exit passage out of the ark. She can go shopping with the Quavisians from now on. What do you say to that, princess?'

The young woman raised a manicured middle finger. The blood red nail polish shimmered and shone under the TV lighting. The curved finger stayed motionless for a moment, then stiffened like an erection. I turned to Jamie and shrugged.

'We'll take that out in editing.'

The screen flashed back to the diagram of the parking space between the two driveways.

'See, it's not hard,' I said. 'As the defendant acknowledged, there's room for two cars to park. It's a simple system, right? Works like a charm too until the Nosey Parker comes along. She leaves twelve inches of free space at the back and pokes her nose twelve inches into the space in front. So the next car can't fit in, not unless he's going to poke his own nose over someone's driveway and cop a parking ticket. Kind of like happened in this photo. Is this your vehicle?'

In the photo, a blue sedan was sloppily parked with its rear eighteen inches in front of the first driveway, making it impossible for another driver to take the front spot.

'Whatever.'

'Is that all you've got to say?'

The middle finger reappeared for a curtain call. I turned to Jamie on my left.

'Soon as we're done here, get some girl out of the crowd to act this out more appropriately. We'll dub her in later. Two hundred karma points to whoever steps into the breach. Give her a wig and a good makeup job and no one in town will recognise her. Meanwhile, let's crack on. Four down, three to go - and what's all this? Victor's bringing in a whole posse this time. Must be a helluva lot of trivial sinners for this one.'

'Phone Zombies, m'lud.' said Jamie.

'Aha! Scourge of our times. Run the footage.'

Vision appeared of a roomful of people sitting around staring at little rectangles they were holding in their hands. Another scene appeared - people sleepwalking down busy streets, or what's worse crossing them, while staring into the eyes of their beeping masters.

I looked at Jamie in mock horror.

'My god, it's the living dead! Where are their phones now?'

'Confiscated.'

Jamie pointed to one of those plastic trays you send through the X ray machine at airports. It was full of smart phones. I raised my eyebrows.

'That would explain the bedraggled look of this crew in the dock. You'd think it was a bunch of junkies three days into cold turkey. Oh no, you've done it now.'

The zombies had caught sight of their phones sitting in the plastic tray. They immediately began a mournful keening, stretching out their hands in the most piteous manner like the very damned themselves. Jamie noted this and worked it into our scripted lesson. It was all part of our education program.

'They're very far gone, Tom. Can you, in your great wisdom and mercy, save them from themselves?'

'I don't know, Jamie, they're hopelessly addicted. We'd better take a look at what we're up against. Bring me one of those.'

'Which one?'

'Just pick one at random.'

Jamie delivered one of the small rectangular items to the judge's bench. I looked at it suspiciously, then extended the tip of my left little finger towards the texting icon to bring up a text exchange.

'Let's take a look at the calibre of thought of our young people these days. After all, they are the future of Cull and therefore of humanity.'

I frowned, rather theatrically, while examining the phone.

152

'What is this - some modern dialect? I can hardly understand it.'

'It's just text speak,' said Jamie. 'That's all.'

'But it's all acronyms, abbreviations, and weird spelling. Is this how we write now? How long before we start speaking like this too? My God, I'm getting old.'

I looked into Camera One and smiled.

'OK, let's get this out of the way. I'd better say it before someone else does - you kids get off my lawn!'

Out of shot, Jamie held up a large sign to the gallery, who immediately broke into some rather forced laughter. When it finally died down, I turned to Jamie once more.

'You know, when I was a boy everyone got by just fine without mobile phones, but now you can't go anywhere without seeing zombies like this. In concerts, at the movies, down at the shops. There's no end of trouble they cause. Texting, sexting, and the rest of it. You know about that one yourself.'

For a moment, a look of intense anger came over Jamie's face, before he buried it and resumed a bland expression. I made a mental note and continued my rant.

'Well, it ain't going to happen in Cull. Contrary to popular belief, the world won't come to an end if people turn off their phones for a couple of hours.'

Suddenly there was a ruckus in front of me. One of the sorry specimens in the dock was trying to attract my attention. I looked directly into Camera One and raised my eyebrows.

'Hark, one of the zombies is trying to communicate.'

'Ur hnr,' it croaked. 'I tok 2u pls.'

'Speak, creature, if speak you can.'

'that my fone I use fone 4 ur music carry always 2 here 4 insprayshun.'

'Eh? Ah, you hear my songs for inspiration. Well done, creature. I will endeavour to verify this strange assertion.'

I flicked through the phone's music menu. Sure enough, 'In Nihilum' and 'Amnesia' were part of the playlist. I pressed play and the opening chords of 'In Nihilum' tinkled through the tinny little speakers. I frowned.

153

'How do you turn this thing up?'

'ur hnr, thats it 4 vol.'

'Eh? I assume you've got these songs on CD too, right?'

'wot'

'What do you use at home or in the car? Where's the rest of your music collection? What *do* you listen to at home?'

'all music on fone is how we here now.'

'On your phone! Through these tiny, tinny little speakers. It's bloody mp3s too. Don't you know they're compressed? The quality's rubbish, it's an insult to music.'

I turned to stage left.

'Jamie, do me a favour. Google images for 'stereo' or 'hi-fi' and put one up on the big screen.'

In another minute or so the image was up. I turned back to the zombie in the dock.

'Look at that, my mutant son. That's what they used to call a stereo back in the day. Big bloody speakers that'll reproduce the sound of a quality CD or vinyl and do the music justice. But you want to listen to mp3s on a six inch phone with tinny little speakers. No wonder music's so bad these days.'

At that point, Jamie interjected.

'You're wrong there, Tom. People don't just listen to music on their phones. They've got computers at home with big speakers just as loud as your old hi-fi.'

I looked at Jamie in surprise. Was this payback for my quip about sexting? He seemed to relish the chance to argue and make me look foolish. Well, we'd take it out in post-production. Yet the nerve of him, to embarrass me in front of the gallery. The remark was enough to propel me into a full rant. I went up about five gears from Angry Judge to full *Downfall* mode. That's the movie set in the Nazi bunker just before they lost the war. There's the famous clip of an unhinged Adolf on a maniacal rant, to which everyone has added their own funny subtitles on one trivial subject or another. I was heading there now.

'Get these zombies out of my sight! In my mercy, I'll refrain from passing sentence in my present mood. For now, let all these infidels be banished. Why so wrathful over music? Simply because

I care. I care about music and its quality - which brings us to the next of our trivial sinners. Send in the Barrel Scrapers.'

Four middle aged guys filed into the courtroom and entered the dock.

'Who's your leader?' I asked.

A tall, tanned fellow in a brown and yellow Hawaiian shirt raised his hand.

'Do you know why you're here, sir?' I continued. 'Of course not. That's one thing all the trivial sinners have in common.'

I scowled into Camera One.

'Citizens, they call me the rock n roll messiah. Couple weeks ago I was done preaching and had the itch, so I headed down to the Shady Oak and there was a band playing in the back bar. Some mob called the Juke Box Heroes, same as stands before you in the dock today. I sat through a few numbers, scratching my head, rather than banging it, until it slowly dawned on me what was wrong.'

The band in the dock looked both mystified and alarmed as I continued my spiel.

'Well, I sat there trying to figure out what was bugging me. The playing was OK, the singing was in tune, the sound was fine. Then the band started playing a Bob Dylan song, 'Knocking on Heaven's Door.' Well, I sat through the opening chords and the oohs and the aahs, and even the whole of verse one. But soon as that chorus came on, I walked up to the hotel manager and told him to pull the plug. Next thing you know the cops were there cuffing this sorry group of wannabes and confiscating their setlist. Which I have here today. Jamie?'

Jamie walked over and handed me a sheet of white paper, with some frayed strips of black gaffer tape still crudely attached. I looked at the band.

'You see where I'm going with this?'

Mr Brown and Yellow Hawaiian Shirt spoke up, in a rich voice gone a bit croaky like the Bob himself.

'Your Honour, what's wrong with 'Knocking on Heaven's Door'? It's a great song.'

'Is it?' I replied. 'Is it really? Even if we accept that dubious claim, ponder this: is it one of the *best* Bob Dylan songs? I mean,

155

how many has he written? Over four hundred, you'd think. Is 'Knocking on Heaven's Door' one of his best?'

'I don't know about the best, your Honour, but it's one of his best *known* songs. Everyone knows it.'

'Yeah - because hacks like you keep playing it. Look, I'm no Dylan-freak, but I've heard enough to know Heaven's Door wouldn't even make his top hundred. So when you geniuses were sitting round at band practice and someone said let's do a Dylan song, what made you come up with that one?'

'I'm sorry, we never really thought about it.'

'Clearly. I mean, with four hundred Dylan songs, you weren't starved for options. There were glistening jewels of options at your disposal. You could have cut up four hundred slips of paper and stuck 'em in a barrel for a lucky dip and chances are you'd have come up with a better song. But there's you sticking your arms through all those jewels til you hit rock bottom. You scraped right down to the bedrock of mediocrity, and what did you pull up into the light of day? 'Knocking on Heaven's Door'!'

The crowd, having listened politely to my Downfall-esque rant, booed and hissed. Then, as if prompted, they began reaching for something down around floor level.

'I mean, was there anything else on the shortlist?' I continued.

By now, Mr. Hawaiian Shirt had been cowed into silence. So a rotund chap in a black t-shirt piped up. I vaguely remembered him as the bass player.

'Your Grace, we were considering 'Blowing in the Wind'.'

'Blowing in the Fucking Wind? Is this a joke? I mean, you could have had 'Tangled Up in Blue.' You could have had 'Mississippi' for something recent! If you had to have a wind song, there was 'Idiot Wind.' But what did you pick? The most obvious, middle of the road choice possible. Damn you to Hell!'

That phrase was the crowd's cue for action and they seized it with relish. A righteous harvest of fruit rained down on the hapless cover band cowering in the dock. They covered their heads with their arms and crouched down low. When the tumult finally subsided, I resumed speaking in a quieter voice.

156

'My dear fellows, you're hardly the first to make such a grievous error. There are bands the world over who've committed similar atrocities. Still, you can act as the sacrificial lambs for this new law. Take consolation that, like our saviour, you can suffer for the sins of others so they may be forgiven.'

The members of Juke Box Heroes looked increasingly afraid as my voice started to rise in pitch.

'Do we aspire to mediocrity in this movement? Do we seek the lowest common denominator? On the contrary, we aspire to the very best the human spirit can muster. That applies to all fields of human endeavour, and certainly to music, which is one of the very highest. When you compiled your cover band setlist, you made a moral choice. With four hundred Bob Dylan songs to choose from, you could have picked something of quality. Something a little harder to play that every poor sap hasn't heard eight hundred times already. Yet you took the easy option, thus contributing to the mediocrity of humanity and perpetuating the ridiculous impression that Bob Dylan's only song is 'Knocking on Heaven's Door'!'

More boos and hisses rang out from the gallery, followed by a few stragglers in the fruit department. Mr. Hawaiian Shirt made a final plea.

'I'm sorry, we just never thought about it!'

'And that is exactly why the world is in such a terrible state. Lack of thought. I mean, look at the rest of this setlist. What else is on here? Dire Straits? Instead of 'Private Investigations' or something decent, you chose the execrable 'Twisting By the Pool.' Shameful stuff!'

'But 'Private Investigations', your Honour? You have to be classically trained to play that.'

'Then practise harder. And my word, you've even got a couple of heavy rockers at the end. You're mighty eclectic, I'll give you that much. This must be the rock category of your juke box pretensions. And what song did you pick? 'Enter Sandman?' More lowest common denominator fodder. You know, when it comes to heavy rock, one of my favourite bands is Black Sabbath. Do you know any Sabbath?'

In a foolish effort to please me, the black-shirted bass player called out at once, 'We know 'Paranoid,' your Grace.' Mr. Hawaiian Shirt realised the danger and reached over to throttle him, but the damage was done. I picked up a pair of spectacles from my desk and put them on, solely so that I could take them off again in a world-weary, self-pitying manner.

'Why do I bother?' I asked in a voice so quiet we'd have to beef it up in post-production. 'I ask for some Sabbath and what do they give me? Not 'Killing Yourself to Live' or 'Dirty Women.' Not 'Spiral Architect' or 'Hole in the Sky,' but 'Paranoid.' The most simplistic song and most unimaginative choice possible. Victor? Take them away. Get them out of my sight. They're expelled from Cull.'

The Hawaiian shirt guy made a final desperate plea.

'Your Honour, we're called the Jukebox Heroes. We're *supposed* to play the hits. That's what we do. Give us another chance, we'll learn some new stuff.'

'Another chance? A stay of execution? What do you think, Jamie?'

'No way, Tom. Expulsion for sure. Throw them out.'

'Harsh, my friend. Harsh but fair. Really, they're damn lucky they're not getting a flogging in the town square. Still, let it not be said that Thomas Swan is unmerciful. I will grant these sinners another chance.'

'Are you sure? We can't risk their aspirations to mediocrity rubbing off on everyone else.'

'I know, Jamie, I know. But maybe we should give them a chance to repent and prove themselves.'

I turned back to the fruit-stained band.

'Jukebox Heroes. I give you four weeks to prove your worth. You will perform a brand new setlist in the town hall. I want to hear an obscure Bob Dylan song that challenges musicians and listeners alike. I want a Black Sabbath song so rare not even Sabbath plays it any more. The rest of the list is up to you. Pass the test and you'll remain in Cull. Fail and you've played your last encore.'

I fanned myself with the setlist, then tore it up.

'My word, Jamie, the seven trivial sinners are mighty exhausting. We've had the Hand Crusher, the Show Pony, and the Spell Breaker. The Nosey Parker, the Phone Zombie, and the Barrel Scraper. Is that it?'

'One to go, Tom. The Leaf Blower.'

'Oh for God's sake - the Leaf Blower! This won't take long. Bring him in.'

In came a guy wearing overalls. I gave him an admonishing look.

'So it was you!' I exclaimed. 'I was up all night last week doing the Lord's work, I finally put my head on the pillow and five minutes later was woken up by your infernal racket.'

'Just doing mah job, your Honour.'

'And what kind of a damn fool job is that? Walking up and down with an oversized hair dryer blowing leaves off the footpath. They'll only be there for five minutes before they blow back again.'

'Ah repeat, just doing mah job.'

'What's wrong with a broom, for Christ's sake? Anything but shatter the peace of the morning with this cacophony.'

I returned my gaze to the gallery.

'I suppose we cannot blame a fellow for earning a living. The sin is in the device itself, which actually carries the name of this sin. Then let it be known that this machine is banned, from this moment hence. Let there be no more leaf blowers in Cull. Furthermore, a jihad against its inventor. Jamie, who was that? Find out at once. I want him hunted down and killed.'

Jamie did a quick online search.

'Looks like he's deceased, Tom.'

'Goddammit. Very well, we will pursue him in the afterlife. Right, that's enough sin for one day, let's leave it there. As a final act, to allow us all time for reflection, I hereby decree a National Day of Silence.'

'National, Tom?' said Jamie with a smirk. 'Better tell the White House and the president!'

I looked at him sharply. Again, Jamie? You make me look foolish again? I covered up with a laugh.

159

'Ha, ha - slip of the tongue. Still, give me time. The nation could certainly do with a day of silence. Go for some thoughtful reflection instead of the constant empty chatter. For now, Cull will lead and set an example for all to follow.'

I banged the gavel violently on the desk. A small crater and cracks appeared in the wood, and the end of the gavel flew off its handle and landed I knew not where. I gave a curt signal to Jamie, the trumpet fanfare sounded again, and I exited the court.

16

Reality
Explained

I'm happy to contradict myself
because the subject is paradoxical in itself.
Reality Explained

At last Utopia took shape as we began to eliminate evil once and
for all. We'd made great inroads into the deadly sins and the trivial
sins, and everyone in town was buying into the message. Once
again, I had the fear of the Quavisian apocalypse to thank - that
and the newly entrenched karma points system. Between these two
forces, social changes were happening as never before in history. It
was like the sixties but this time we got it right. Yet there were still
plenty more reforms on my agenda, and the next thing that was
going to go was that bloody New Age music.

Now really, I like ambient music as much as the next guy,
but not all the time. For a while there that's all you'd hear on the
local radio. The programmers were trying to impress me with how
spiritual they were, yet for some reason they thought the soundtrack
to spirituality was gentle flutes and guitars, babbling brooks and
rainforest birdsong. As the Messiah, I was better qualified to judge
the nature of spiritual music, and in my view the most spiritual
music is heavy metal. Why not? That's what I was into so that's
what other people should be into too. My favourite bands included

Slayer, Rammstein, Black Sabbath and Judas Priest, and it was high time these bands started getting the local airplay they deserved. Victor for one had already converted.

'I don't know why I never listened to this stuff,' he said. 'It's brilliant.'

'You were hanging out with the wrong crowd,' I replied. 'But look at you now - hair past your shoulders like a real rock star! And your bass playing is really coming on. Keep it up and you'll be the next Geezer Butler.'

We were sitting around in the newly built recording studio at Saborman House. Victor had filled it with state-of-the-art gear. It must have cost well over a million bucks, and worth every penny. Our drummer had gone home and Vic and I were winding down with a beer or two.

'Can I play on your album, Tom?'

'Not this time. Maybe the next one.'

'Oh come on.'

'I don't know, Vic. I've been honing some of these songs for years. They've got to be perfect.'

'Just give me a chance.'

'We'll see. You'd better bring your A-game, brother. A recording is forever.'

As I told Victor, I was a great metal guitarist myself back in Australia, but the music biz wasn't very supportive of this genre. I'd written loads of songs, but no one ever heard them. Well, now I had a captive audience and by Christ they were going to listen! Not just to my songs, but to all of my favourite bands. I decided to make heavy metal the official music of the Milinish.

Introducing this policy was a slight problem because as far as I knew Cull wasn't a real rock n roll town. It was just some backwater in the States where the locals listened to blues or country for all I knew, not to mention the New Age music that was now in vogue. Well, it was all going to change. These people were going to be brainwashed into liking metal, and those that weren't could fuck off and take their chance with the Quavisians.

There was a small problem of philosophical continuity in this matter. Heavy metal is an intensely physical form of music. That is,

162

it excites every fibre of the body in a way that the ethereal plucking of a harp does not. Yet my followers had been told that physicality equated with Satan, and the way of God lay in denying the flesh. Hence this trend of insipidly 'spiritual' New Age music. I sure created a rod for my back with that philosophy. Still, what's done can be undone and what's said can be unsaid. It was time for a new book - *Reality Explained.*

Yes, that's right - a new book at last. It felt like forever since *Milinish in the New Age* had come out. Well, *Reality Explained* was going to be one helluva comeback, if perhaps a little confusing for my old fans due to the change in styles. But rather than gloss over the confusion, I decided to put it front and centre. The book opened with some profound paradoxes designed to mystify and bamboozle readers. Here's a sample:

- Some parts of my books are false; it is a test of the true believer to discover which ones. The falsehood may even be the previous sentence.
- As far as life is concerned, I'm happy to contradict myself because the subject is paradoxical in itself.
- There is no reality. There is only unreality that takes the appearance of reality. Subtract the 'un' from unreality and what's left is reality.
- Defensive fences fence offensively.
- Sometimes I say one thing, sometimes an opposite thing. So what? Quantum physics has shown that everything in life is indeterminate. You can't measure a photon for both speed and position at once. Light operates as both a wave and a particle depending on whether you measure it for speed or position. Impossible but there it is. In the same way, some of my statements are both true and false depending upon the type of measurement that is attempted. When I first explained this to Victor he thought it was ridiculous, but now he sees it is true. Voila! Another quantum event.

- Some people want all the answers served up on a golden plate. What's the matter, ain't ya got minds to think for yourself?
- Reality is dream, Dream is reality: that is the question.

Those are all from the first chapter of *Reality Explained*. This assault upon reason was designed to soften people up for the musical revolution about to sweep town. Chapters two to five discussed music at length, and I decided to consolidate the message in the accompanying TV show.

I was loving TV as a medium, especially after *Seven Trivial Sins* was such a ratings smash. *STS*, as it was affectionately known, was the highest rating TV show ever screened in Cull. This was partly due to the two hundred karma points on offer for watching - and the threat of expulsion for those who failed the exam - but mainly because it was brilliant TV.

Reality Explained was the follow up. The new show was nine episodes, each of which tied in to one of the book's eight chapters. In Episode Three, I spoke directly to camera to make sure the most important message got through.

'Citizens of Cull, there are testing times ahead. As you know, we are blessed to live in God's own land, but that blessing should never be taken for granted. From time to time the population must be purged and purified. This is to ensure only the strong survive to repopulate Earth after the Quavisian attack.

Therefore, there will be a period of testing. Those found equal to the test will remain, but those found wanting must depart the holy land. The form of the test is artistic, specifically musical. Your ability to embrace and understand music will be a measure of your level of spiritual development.

The movement that is Milinish has passed through one stage and evolved to another. You have learned to deny Satan, to deny physicality. Congratulations. But wait! A new test faces you all. The *trouble* with most of the world's religions is that they try to deny Satan. This is precisely what you should not do. When you fear something you simply add to its potency. It is only by embracing

Satan's power that we are able to transcend it. Such is the great paradox of existence. And by showing love and compassion towards Satan's pain, not only can we transcend evil, we are able to heal that entity that was once God's angel.'

I went on to say that a number of hotels, clubs and halls had been converted into 'Aural Temples' where spiritual testing sessions would be held. It was the duty of each citizen to attend these ceremonies, which were simply sessions where heavy metal music was played over a good PA system. People were expected to drink, dance, and study the lyrics reproduced on the big screen up front of the room. Naturally, the karmic points system was in full force. Citizens earned basic points for showing up and extra points for dancing, head-banging or otherwise showing their joy at transcending Satan's pain.

The points table was on public record with a weekly summary printed in *The Milinish Times*, although this was rather slow, old school reporting. Everyone was so keen to measure everyone else's spiritual progress that the official Karmic Points website registered more daily hits than there were citizens - which meant that on average, people were checking at least once a day.

Certain bands, songs and albums were declared to be 'sacred,' part of God's Recommended Listening. Citizens earned points for listening to specially approved albums. Of course, these days there are many different types of heavy metal. Styles with high intensity earned the most karmic points, but lighter forms of metal were an option for the less intrepid devotee.

In the meantime, I was almost done recording my own album in the studio at Saborman House. Most of the songs were left over from my time in Australia. I didn't have a record deal then but I sure did now - and just quietly, those in the know were tipping a few sales.

A while back, I'd commissioned Bob Talbot to employ the finest engineers in the land to build a twenty thousand seat auditorium with perfect acoustics. It had to be finished in three months and when Talbot said that was impossible I told him if he believed hard enough he could make it possible, and if he couldn't, I believed he could get the hell out of town. He was authorised to employ as many workers as it took to toil round the clock getting the place up. It had to be ready for my album launch, and it could be used for future religious rallies too. It's a testament to the power of prayer and belief that, what do you know, Talbot had come good and the place was just about ready for the album launch! Turned out it took four and a half months, but given that my album went overtime as well, I let it slide.

In the meantime, did this new music really catch on? You bet! I went to several sessions myself and if people were faking their enjoyment, they sure fooled me. It's amazing what some positive suggestion can do. We also drugged some of the free drinks, so that might have helped. Of course there was always plenty of ordinary liquor available. Sometimes I got up on the DJ microphone and gave a cheery little intro to a song.

'This is about all the depravity under the sun and the blackness of the human heart,' was my introduction to 'South of Heaven,' one of my favourites. Or 'This is a world of pain, here's Priest with the Painkiller.'

By the way, it's inevitable Hollywood will one day want to make a movie about Cull and the Milinish, and you can bet they'll try to change the bloody story to suit themselves. You can also bet that for the soundtrack, instead of having music by the bands mentioned in this chapter, they'll try to use whatever trendy bands are popular at the time. If they do, you'll know they're out and out lying to you. And one more thing. I, Thomas Swan, do *not* have one of those awful Australian accents that foreign actors do so badly.

Not everyone was pleased by the new music. Some of the older generation weren't about to convert into headbangers too readily. I let the message filter through that as long as they paid lip service, I'd cut them some slack. More troublesome, however, were some of the ex-Christians. After a lifetime thinking of heavy metal as evil, it wasn't easy for them to take it into their hearts. One day a balding forty year old came to see me in my study at Saborman House. He had one of those try-hard disciple beards like he was one of the Lord's best buds.

'Well, my good man,' I said, 'what can I do for you?'

'Your Grace,' he said, sweating. 'I'm here on behalf of a few citizens concerned about some of the things that have been happening lately.'

'Oh really?'

'It's the new music. People go to these Aural Temples, become intoxicated and listen to this evil music. It has no beat, no harmony or melody.'

'Really? That's your expert opinion, is it? What was it Jesus said - something about judge not lest ye be judged, if I'm not mistaken.'

'I know it's probably just some kind of test.'

'Of course it's a test. I said that in *Reality Explained*.'

'But as a Christian, sir, there are certain aspects of the lyrics that bother me.'

'Like what?'

'Um, ah ... the Satanism.'

'Oh stop being such a nitpicker. Surely it's not that bad.'

'But, your grace, it is. I distinctly heard a line in one of the songs say learn the words of holy praise, heil Satan.'

'So?'

'Some of these songs by that band Slayer directly attack religious belief. As a Christian, I don't think we should be listening to that sort of thing.'

'As a Christian? What the hell are you doing in Cull anyway? This ain't a Christian town. We're Milinish in case you hadn't noticed!'

'But you still talk about God and Adam and Eve so I assumed Milinish was a branch of Christianity.'

'Did you now? You've got quite a nerve. If anything, Christianity is a small branch of the Milinish. We're the whole damn tree. We absorbed Christianity long ago.'

At that, Mr. Concerned Citizen took a step back. He was sweating more than ever, and breathing rapidly as if about to pass out. I took a step forward and put my hand on his shoulder.

'You're taking it all far too seriously,' I said. 'You've got to lighten up man, or else get out of town. There's five thousand people on a waiting list to get into Cull, so if you're not happy here

167

I'm sure one of them can make you a very generous offer for your house.'

'Oh no, I didn't mean ...'

'So you think it's devil music? Of course it is! Haven't you read *Reality Explained* yet? Listening to this music is a way of exorcising evil. Only by fully embracing Satan's physicality can we transcend it. What good is denial? If that's your game, why don't you become an ascetic and go meditate in a cave somewhere?'

'But you said in *Revelations of Milinish* ...'

'Who cares what I said back then? Religious belief isn't some static phenomenon, carved in stone for evermore. It's always evolving. In any case, if you're so literal minded that you have to pick the most obvious and superficial interpretation of everything I say, then your days among us are numbered.'

This conversation was adapted into what became known as the 'Tom Letters.' These were short dialogues or cartoons illustrating some point of doctrine, and they appeared in *The Milinish Times* and online. They were an ongoing series and were eventually published together as a book. Here's a reproduction of the one that came from this encounter.

Tom Letter #15 - A New Pair of Ears!

Tom - You don't look happy, brother. What's the matter?

Terry - It's this new music. I can't get it into it.

Tom - Everyone else is getting into it, why can't you?

Terry - I just can't understand it.

Tom - So why blame the music? If you were spiritually developed, you *would* understand it. You're listening with old ears, brother. What you need is a new pair of ears! God's ears.

Terry - But the lyrics are Satanic.

Tom - Of course they are! I told you that only by embracing physicality can we transcend it to reach higher spirituality.

Terry - But people go to the Aural Temples and get intoxicated.

Tom - But but but! You've got more butts than a goat, brother, and we all know which fallen angel is associated with goats. Maybe it's you who is Satanic.

Terry - Oh no, Tom, it's just that the other night my wife came home from the Aural Temple and apart from neglecting the housework, she also initiated lascivious acts.

Tom - Good for her. You need a new mind as well as a new set of ears. Liberate yourself! With the culture of Cull, you either get into it or you get out of it. There's no in-between. You know what's going to happen if you don't get into it?

Terry - I've got to leave?

Tom - Yes, you have to leave. There's ten thousand people on a waiting list to get into Cull, so I'm sure you could get a good price for your house.

Terry - Please forgive me Lord for my ignorance.

Tom – Sure, brother, to forgive is divine. But clean out those ears!

By the time this Tom Letter came out, I was preaching to the converted because nearly everyone was into metal now. Then right on cue, Bob Talbot came by the house with the news that the twenty thousand seat auditorium was ready.

We drove over to inspect it, and I was quite dumbstruck at first glance. We went in the back door, and when I walked onto that stage and looked out into rows of tiered seating left, right and centre, I was quite overcome and sank to the floor to thank my Heavenly Father.

Then I leapt to my feet and punched the air. You beauty! I christened it the 'House of Ruanglia' and declared it the official Temple of the Milinish. What's more, the Temple opening would be a double celebration. My album was finished and the album launch would take place at the Temple opening ceremony. The album was called *Anti-Hero*. Here's the full track listing:

169

1. Battles are not Wars
2. Anti-Hero
3. Vulturiac
4. Pontius Pilates
5. Doctrinal Stew
6. Worlds in Abeyance
7. Seven Trivial Sins
8. Edge Trimmer
9. Mightier Than the Sword
10. The One Eyed Man is King

The day of the launch arrived. Twenty thousand copies of the *Anti-Hero* CD had been pressed, and as each citizen entered the Temple, he or she bought a copy. It looked like *Anti-Hero* was headed to number one with a bullet!

The Temple was packed that day. From a vantage point high above the stage, I looked on in wonder as the multitudes streamed in through the doors. A vibrant buzz and hum filled the arena. I was Queen Bee in the hive and each of my subjects would gladly lay down their lives for me.

When everyone was seated, the whole album was played through the auditorium speakers. It was gratifying indeed to see thousands of people listen reverently to the music that had been ignored by the piss poor record company executives in Australia. As the last notes faded away, I walked onstage to a standing ovation.

'Dear friends, I want to welcome you to the House of Ruanglia, and to thank you for your attention today. Isn't it sweet to be proved right! One day we'll all be proved right and the rest of the world wrong. Now everyone get up and dance. Here's another of our favourite songs - 'Prove you Wrong' by Prong!'

The crowd cheered as the song began booming out through the huge PA system. As I stood on that stage and looked out at twenty thousand people dancing, gyrating, and singing 'Prove You Wrong', I felt a profound sense of transcendence. I had truly transformed into a god, and as I looked out and saw that mass of bodies and souls, my glory was complete. To Hell with Australia and to Hell with Orantor. I was right and they were wrong, and soon the whole world would know it.

17
Cultown

I'm toying with the urge, to expedite the purge.
Cultown Album Lyrics

Modesty forbids me to reprint the album reviews - as you can guess, they were pretty damn glowing. But you mustn't think life in Cull was all fun and games, music and laughter. Not at all. We in the Milinish had extremely vital work to do for the scientific improvement of humanity. Cull would lead and the world would follow. One night I woke from a revelatory dream. It was 3am so I called Victor and told him to come right over. He stumbled into my study wearing his pyjamas and a bleary expression.

'Victor, I've had this fantastic idea! What do we all really want from life?'

'A good night's sleep?'

'What we really want - every man, woman, and child on Earth - is to know who the hell we are. Who we really are and where we began. And if we can find out where we came from, there's a fair chance we can control where we're going. Understand the past, control the future, right?'

'I suppose so.'

'Now wake up and listen, Victor, this is important. I've had an incredible vision. We're going to regress everyone in the world under hypnosis to find out their past reincarnational lives, then analyse it and map the entire psychic history of the species. What a breakthrough! Finally we'll understand the human race. We can draw it up on a big wall map, feed all the past life data into a computer and at last we'll understand who we really are. I call it the Human Go-home Project.'

'Good idea,' Victor said blearily.

'We'll start with the people in Cull but that's only stage one. After that we'll do the thing properly. We'll go round to every country in the world, even to all the primitive tribes and regress them too.'

'But Tom, what if they don't believe in reincarnation?'

'So what? What the fuck's it got to do with them? This is about knowledge, the advance of knowledge. Everyone's got past lives and by God I'm gonna map 'em.'

'But won't it take a long time to visit all the tribes in the world?'

'Oh Victor, Victor. Once I called you Visionary. Have you forsaken me? Of course we're not going to hang round a bunch of primitives for the rest of our lives. All we have to do is train up specialists in the University of Milinish. They can do all the regressing and send the data back to us in the Go-home labs for processing.'

'Oh, I get it.'

'And just to ice the cake, it'll make me a shoe-in for a Nobel Prize. I'll be right up there with Darwin, Einstein and the rest of them.'

'Brilliant, Tom, it's brilliant.'

Regrettably, the next visitor to Saborman House came on a less inspiring mission. Jim Flynn, head of security, arrived one day to make a disturbing report. At this point in our story the subject of sex raises its ugly head. I suppose everyone's been thinking "Oh yes - Thomas Swan, cult leader, rock star, bound to be taking advantage of every naive young female disciple that comes along." Well, that type of behaviour is strictly for low class messiahs. I'm evil but not vile. My sex life? I did mention one indiscretion with Rose, but other than that there's no need to discuss it. If you want to perve on a braggart, go and read James Bond.

Flynn's disturbing news was that a young woman newly arrived in Cull had been raped. This was a shock because the crime rate during our Golden Age of Love had dropped to the lowest in the town's history. So how to respond? There was no room for this sort of thing in our budding Utopia. In which case, perhaps

173

this event was the chance for some growth and learning. After all, there's a reason for everything. Maybe the people in Cull had it a bit too easy. They'd become cocky and complacent. Well, it was time for a dose of discipline.

I issued a proclamation in *The Milinish Times*. All sexual relations, both inside or outside of marriage - and including masturbation - were banned until the person responsible for the rape came forward to confess. It seemed the rapist had worn a mask so the victim couldn't identify him. That simply worsened the crime by showing it was premeditated. In that case, it was up to us to find out who he was. Of course, God already knew the rapist's identity, but I decreed that the confession must come of the person's own free will. If no one confessed after two weeks, the entire townsfolk would be forced to undergo a specially devised form of encounter therapy called 'DNA Night.'

Two weeks passed and a confession was still not forthcoming. That was beside the point, as DNA Night was locked in anyway. I hoped the citizens of Cull would be better people for it. It was all arranged during the two weeks. We set up a few rooms with cushions and mattresses, and a group of therapists was briefed on how to conduct the sessions. Meanwhile Bob Talbot went off to the city and picked out a bunch of X-rated porno DVDs. DNA Night therapy was ready to roll.

Every citizen in Cull between the age of eighteen and fifty was assigned to an encounter group. Each group had fifteen men and fifteen women. The group of thirty was led into the therapy room, which had been done up like a tasteful bordello, but with incense wafting through to elevate the mood. Everyone stood to attention and watched the large screen at the front of the room. As the lights dimmed, the screen glowed into life, and the group found itself looking into the stern, fatherly features of Thomas Swan.

'My children, listen to me. We, the Milinish, have been strong. We've been stronger and purer than ever. Yet a serpent is among us. Evil has entered Cull, and that evil must be plucked out and destroyed.

When I told you we can only transcend Satan's evil by embracing it, this was about a form of spiritual testing through music. There was not, nor is ever, any justification for rape. Those of you who have misunderstood my message have failed the test. Now all must face another test to see who is worthy and who should be cast out of our midst.

I have told you that those who fear Satan only add to his power. This is what you must not do. You must look him in the eye, confront your fear, deny his power and go beyond it. The clothing you wear is a pathetic facade symbolising your fear of your own bestial origins. It's part of the way that people lie to themselves out there in the 'real world' but we're not going to lie to ourselves in here. Therefore I order you to discard the facade. All of you, discard your clothes and place them at the back of the room.'

Most people did this with surprisingly little hesitation. It's amazing what you can get people to do, but that's mind control for you. This brainwashing, authority figure stuff really works. After everyone was naked, they returned to their places in front of the screen. My stern face ordered them to 'Confront the reality of Satan's power,' at which point we began showing the X-rated porno films with some more of my spooky soundtrack music. Remember that these poor naked people had experienced no sexual release for two weeks, so whether they found the films shocking or arousing is a question only each individual can answer. One way or another, they were certainly in an agitated state. After a few minutes, my narration came over the speakers to accompany the erotic images on screen.

'Citizens, remember what I said in *Revelations of Milinish* about the genesis and evolution of life on earth. At first all was pure spirituality and light, until Satan tempted Adamcas to taste physical life. For this, Satan, Adamcas, and Evelyn were cast into the mud. Satan gave them DNA - the power to create life. DNA surged and struggled to cheat death. Over time, it made physical bodies for itself, crawled out of the mud, and turned into fishes and birds and the other animals. All life was DNA and all was Satan. And how did Satan replicate? Genes! God made Genesis and Satan made genes. The little genetic masters inside each creature pulled the creature's strings, bewitching it with urges toward lustful fornication. Thus did the creatures rape, steal and kill just so their masters could replicate themselves.

Eventually, DNA mutated into human bodies, but the fighting and rape continued in the struggle to survive and reproduce. That goes on to this day, so when you covet in a lustful manner the body of another, you are not acting freely at all. You are reacting blindly to the pulling of your strings by tiny Satanic entities who want to use you for their own ends. Their one urge is to reproduce themselves. Bestial fornication is the law of the jungle, but we in the Milinish are strong, pure, and spiritual enough to go beyond that law.'

At this point the group therapist took over to lead the group members, who by now were in quite a state. A session might proceed as follows.

Therapist - Would anyone like to volunteer and tell the group how they're feeling? Some of you are crying. That's good. Don't hold those feelings inside anymore. Set them free and you will be set free. Yes, get angry, punch those cushions. Come on, someone tell the group how you feel. What about you, Frankie? Come on, tell us how you really feel. Don't hold back.

Frankie - I feel angry because I want to fornicate with Robyn over there and I hate Satan's power over me.

Therapist - You don't feel in control?

Frankie - I feel no control at all. I want to rape every woman here.

Therapist - *(gasp)* See the power of Satan! Is it any wonder a woman is raped every eighty-nine seconds in America. Anyone else? What about you, Laverne - how do *you* feel?

Laverne - I feel mad as hell. Every man in the room is watching me. I feel like prey with a big red bullseye on my you-know-what.

Therapist - *(yelling)* That's Satan for you! The streets are not safe. The home is not safe. Your clothes are off for a reason. All we've done is expose the truth, strip away

176

the lies and show you who's really running the show. This is the naked truth. Now it's time to fight back. Do you want to fight back?

All - Yes!

Therapist - Do you want your spirituality and control back?

All - Yes! Yes!

Therapist - Frankie, do you want your control back?

Frankie - Yes I want my control back.

Therapist - Do you want to fornicate with every woman in the room?

Frankie - No, yes. No!

Therapist - Be honest.

Frankie – Yes, I want to fornicate with every woman in the room!

Therapist - Who's making you want that?

Frankie - DNA.

Therapist - What's DNA's real name?

Frankie - Satan!

Therapist - Are you ready to cast Satan out?

Frankie - Yes.

Therapist - Then take Satan's instrument in your hand. Yes, that's right. Now look at the evil on the screen, face Satan and recite the words you learnt before you came in here tonight.

Frankie - *(yelling frenziedly)* I'll not be controlled by Satan anymore. I'll not be conned into rape and lust anymore. I'm taking control. I'm in control. I'm going to cast DNA out of my body using my own spiritual right hand. Get out, Satan, get out. Out, out out!

Therapist - Well done, Frankie, that took a lot of courage. Everyone give him a big round of applause. Who's next?

When the whole group had finished the therapy session, my face appeared once more on the screen at the front of the room.

177

'Citizens, I hope you learned an important lesson today and the lesson is that rape is not about sex, it's about power. It's not about eroticism, it's about control and subjugation. You have all been raped. It's not pleasant, is it? Now go from this place, back to your homes and families and let there be peace again. May you be safe in your houses and streets, and let there be no more rape in Cull.'

That was DNA Night. Like I said, this mind control stuff really works. All groups were sworn not to disclose the details of the sessions to other citizens, so that each occasion could remain fresh and a surprise. And of course the ban on sexual relations was lifted for those who had been to a DNA Night, which - perhaps - may have been a relief to all concerned. The sessions themselves were filmed, incidentally as a safeguard against future defectors from Milinish. If anyone did get disgruntled and leave, they'd be less prone to make trouble if we had a film of them casting Satan out of their bodies.

Of course, the women present weren't able to cast out Satan in quite the same way. They were encouraged to join in as they saw fit, or else assume a neutral role. Yet after several weeks of the therapy, events took a surprising turn. I was in the studio rehearsing music with Vic and a couple of other lads. I'd just gotten through the guitar solo of a new song, 'Helix Eternal', when I glanced up and saw Jim Flynn trying to attract my attention. He looked more like a TV lawyer than ever but this time he seemed flustered, as if the make-believe case he was acting was heading south.

'Tom, we need to talk,' he said when the band cacophony had died down.

'What is it, Jim? Can't it wait? We've got a show in the Temple next week.'

'No, it can't.'

I unstrapped my guitar and led Flynn into the studio control room where the other lads couldn't hear us. I sat down at the mixing desk and fidgeted with the dials.

'Well?'

'She's withdrawn the allegation.'

'Who's withdrawn what?'

178

'The rape. She said it never happened.'

'You don't say?'

'The girl was trying to get your attention, so she fabricated the story.'

'Well, for Christ's sake, she could have just asked for an audience at Temple. This is a bit awkward now we're so far into the therapy.'

'That's just it, Tom. She had no idea the whole town would be punished as a result of her story. Now she feels bad so she's come clean. Should we do the same and tell everyone the truth?'

'Don't be ridiculous. It would undermine all the genuine rape victims who have a hard time being believed. Besides, how are people going to feel when they learn they've cast Satan out for nothing? You tell her to button it, alright? Kick her out of town, pay her. Whatever it takes to keep her quiet.'

'You want to pay her hush money to stop her confessing to inventing a crime, so the town doesn't feel bad about joining in group pornography sessions? Isn't this all getting rather absurd?'

'I don't care. Just keep her quiet. There are plenty of real rape victims in the world. DNA Night is for all of them.'

Flynn was silent while he considered my reaction. Finally he spoke.

'So is that it for DNA Night? Do we stop it now?'

'What for?' I replied. 'That's hardly fair to those who've already done it. No, keep it going.'

'Really?'

'Why not? It's a great therapy program.'

Flynn crossed his arms.

'Are you sure about this? I've got to tell you, some people aren't too happy with the program. They don't see this sort of thing as spiritual practice.'

'Then I want their names and addresses and the file you've built up on them. I've still got that bucket of red pins in my office, Jim. I'm quite prepared to stick a few back in the map. It is *I* who decide what is spiritual practice in this town. No one else. It is *I* who understands the true processes of life and death, and it is *I* who will administer them. With *your* help. Is that quite clear?'

179

'I'm not questioning your vision, Tom. I'm just saying some people in town aren't spiritually advanced enough to understand it.'

'Sure - and those are the ones who have to go. We'll get rid of them one way or another. I have a divine mandate for that. Why do you think I'm running all these tests in the first place? It's my scientific plan for humanity's future. Only certain people will be allowed to reproduce from now on. Call it eugenics if you like, I don't care. I'm sending Satan a message. DNA's not running the show anymore - we are. And until that message gets through, DNA Night will continue.'

'OK, but how much longer do we keep it going? There's a lot of people in town. It'll take ages to get through everyone.'

I thought for a minute. Maybe he had a point.

'Perhaps you're right. I suppose we've fired a shot across Satan's bow by now. Maybe we should wind the program down. It's about time we came up with something new.'

'Good idea, Tom.'

'Funny thing is I thought we were done with the deadly sins a while back, so we got started on the trivial sins. And soon as we knocked them off, what do you know but the deadlies start making a comeback! Sin obviously runs very deep in the human soul, Jim.'

'Sadly, you're correct.'

'Righto, let's run DNA Night for another week or so, but scale it back. Women are exempt now, and we'll just make it males eighteen to thirty. Couple more weeks and that's it. That'll give me time to come up with the next program. Now if you'll excuse me, I've got to get back to band practice. I've got twenty thousand pilgrims' arses to kick at the gig next Friday!'

It goes without saying that we of the Inner Circle did not undergo any therapeutic programs or the other reformative schemes, the next of which was Purification Week. Soon after the DNA Night sessions finished, there was an outbreak of food poisoning at a restaurant in town. This was a clear sign from God that while the population may have conquered lust, the sin of gluttony still raged unchecked. A proclamation was made that everyone had to undergo a seven day period of fasting so the town could be purged of physical impurity. All work and businesses were to close during this period and people were confined to their houses and told to turn off all the lights except in two rooms. Television, computers and any other sources of pleasure were banned. The next day, a special 'Tom Letter' appeared. As the newspaper was closed, Tom Letter #24 was specially printed out and delivered to each household.

Tom Letter #24 - The Week That Never Was

Tom - Welcome to the week that never was. There is no time or space, only the beyond.
Ray - What's happening, Lord?
Tom - Calm yourself, brother. We are entering Purification Week.
Ray - Purification Week? What's that?
Tom - It is a time when desire shall be purged from the impure. Do you know that all suffering is caused by desire?
Ray - All suffering is caused by desire? Really?
Tom - Your very physical existence began that way. Life is a sexually transmitted terminal disease. Your only hope lies in negating physical desires and becoming pure spirit.
Ray - How can this be achieved, Lord?
Tom - By denying your gross physical urges for a while. Stay home, turn off the lights, and meditate only upon matters of the spirit. Partake of no food or pleasure. There are lessons to be learnt.
Ray - I suppose it's a silly question, but should I also abstain from sexual relations?
Tom - That depends. All suffering is caused by desire, so if you do feel desirous of sexual relations then you should abstain, but if you are not in the mood and have no wish for orgasm then you are free to partake of it.
Ray – Oh, I get it.

Tom – Farewell, brother. I will speak with you a week hence.

Then, on the seventh day of Purification Week, the sequel appeared.

Tom Letter #25 - Welcome Back To Space-Time

Tom - How are you feeling, brother?
Ray - I feel great, Lord! I feel so pure and new!
Tom - That's wonderful. Perhaps you'd like to go another week?
Ray - If that is your wish, Master.
Tom – No, brother. After a week without food you must be hungry. Sit down at my table and eat with me.
Ray – No, Lord, I'm not really hungry as it happens.
Tom - You answered correctly. If you had accepted my invitation you would have had to fast another week. Come, partake of this banquet. Behold the holy lettuce leaf, carrot stick, lentils and raw cauliflower. But why do you wolf your food, brother? You gulp it down like a savage, whilst I chew slowly, savouring each tiny bite. You see, this humble food is a feast to me, whilst you are barely aware of what you gobble down so fast. Do you not desire to be enlightened?
Ray - I desire it more than anything in the world.
Tom - Then you will never obtain it. Only when you cease to desire enlightenment will you become enlightened.

At the end of this Tom Letter was a summons for all townspeople to assemble at 5pm at the Temple for a special address from me. From backstage, I watched them file into the massive hall. I smiled quietly to myself and snorted a big line of coke. There was some left over from the research supplies and there was no point it going to waste. Finally the Temple was full and there they were. There's nothing better than a captive audience. I walked onstage to a more muted reception than usual. The people were clearly fatigued after

182

the rigours of Purification Week, bewildered perhaps, and unsure what was to come next.

'Friends, children of Milinish, you have just lived through what was called Purification Week. Congratulations. You obeyed me unquestioningly. That is precisely what will be needed after the Quavisian attack - obedience. Thus, with iron discipline, may we rebuild our world. But you know what? Instead of Purification Week, we should call it Stupification Week. What's so pure about pretending you're not a living, physical being? To go without food for a week is good if you learn to appreciate what you take for granted, but who wants to live like that all the time?

What's the deal with Puritans anyhow? They think they're so damn holy cos they won't have a drink and a good time. I don't care if they wear Buddhist robes or their Sunday best, they're all just a bunch of holier-than-thou wannabes who think the way to master life is to take all the fun out of it. Walking around all po-faced like they've evolved to a higher plane. What a bunch of bores!

They're always putting the world down, saying how bad it is. They don't call it the gift of life, they call it the wheel of life. Well bugger that, I'm Thomas Swan, the rock n roll messiah, and I say life's a party so let's get into it. Everyone repeat after me, on the count of three, 'life is good.' One two three, LIFE IS GOOD! Everyone say 'life is desirable.' One two three, LIFE IS DESIRABLE! Everyone say 'Life is fun.' One two three, LIFE IS FUN!

Hallelujah, brothers and sisters, I love you all. Everyone look under your seats. There's a cardboard box taped under every seat in this room. Have a look inside. Today is Victor's birthday and there's a piece of birthday cake for each and every one of you. Purification Week is over! Now get out into those streets, have a few drinks, listen to some music, and party!'

These types of activities may seem rather bizarre to the outside observer, but an outsider, by definition, can't really understand the mentality of the group. To be part of a collective of concentrated fanaticism is to be part of a truly powerful force, and once having experienced that power, few wish to be estranged from it. Therefore, individuals were prepared to go along with my wishes if the rest of the group was doing so. They thought of me not just as their leader, but as a father, and I could be a stern disciplinarian or a loving benefactor within the bounds of that role.

Nevertheless, I did start to sense a few rumbles of discontent. Whether it was the heavy metal music, the DNA Nights, or just the way official policies changed from week to week, some people were getting edgy. Jim Flynn's network of spies heard a few whispers. I told him to keep an eye on the situation but do nothing for the time being. Then I announced a new religious festival. It was called 'Realism Week' and described in Tom Letter #29.

Tom Letter #29 - 'Get Real, Sister!'

Tom - What's the matter, sister? You don't look happy.
Laura - I can't keep up with all these changes.
Tom - I know how you feel. Sometimes I can't keep up with them myself. But no one said the way of the Lord was easy.
Laura - Why do we have to go through all these tests?
Tom - Because the new world is only for the strong. The weak must be weeded out.
Laura - But why does life have to be that way? I don't like it.
Tom – Come, sister, we should face up to the way life really is, not the way we would like it to be. Isn't it better to face the truth rather than deluding ourselves with wishes and fantasies? Life's tough, so what!
Laura - It's not fair.
Tom - No it's not fair, but I'd prefer to honestly and courageously face up to reality rather than deluding myself with fantasies. There are many people who don't think the way we do in the Milinish. They prefer to adopt their own belief systems about life, but all they're doing is giving themselves comforting illusions that make them feel better. We're the only ones with the guts to face the truth. I think we're pretty damn

courageous. If only other people had the guts to be as courageous as us. Don't you think so, Laura?

Laura - I suppose you're right, Tom. You always are.

To celebrate Realism Week, we printed up a lot of commemorative T-shirts. These bore inspiring slogans designed to lift town morale, including the following:

- Realism Week: I was there. Were you?
- Get real brother! / Get real sister!
- Be a real man. Face the truth about life.
- The only good illusion is a dead illusion.
- Don't wimp out with fantasies. Listen to Tom and face reality.
- Give me a pat on the back. I deserve it.
- Braver than thou, you deluded old cow.
- If only everyone else was as courageous as us, the world wouldn't be in such a mess.
- Death to Wishful Thinking.

Yes, it was indeed a fine array of uplifting messages on the subject of realism and having the courage to face the truth about life. And the funny thing is, I think Rudolph C. Orantor would have worn every one of them with pride.

18
The Triangle
of Fire

He who believeth in me will be saved.
The Tom Letters - a Collection

One day the citizens started to disappear.

Some people found this alarming, so I agreed to have a little chat with God to find out what on Earth was happening. As it turned out, it wasn't happening on Earth at all, and there was no need to talk to deities to find out. Shocked and amazed at this discovery, I called an emergency meeting at the new temple. Then, looking out at a sea of twenty thousand worried faces, I relayed the startling news that was to hand.

'Dear friends, we live in exciting times. Although what I have to communicate is of the gravest concern, the pure of heart among you should find it reassuring rather than threatening. A wonderful event has occurred. Last night I was in meditation when an extraordinary vision appeared to me. It was the face of a Ruanglian.

The Ruanglian identified herself as Guanara, president of the Ruanglian High Command. Guanara said she'd been trying to make contact with us for quite a while. Well, she's succeeded just in time, for the war between Ruanglia and Quavisia has escalated into a full scale galactic conflict. The planets Ismismo and Fundamentia have entered the fray, and the battle of the planets is approaching a climax. I asked Guanara if this had anything to do with our citizens disappearing and she said this was indeed the case.

It turns out that due to the war, the orbits of Fundamentia, Ismismo, and Ruanglia have deviated slightly so they are aligned in a triangular configuration. That is, if you drew a line between each of the three planets you would see a triangle. When aligned further with the position of Earth, you have a configuration that Guanara calls the 'Triangle of Fire.' Fundamentia, Ismismo, Ruanglia, Earth - F. I. R. E.

Guanara says that this alignment has opened up a hole in the space-time continuum. We've all heard of the Bermuda Triangle, where ships tended to strangely vanish without trace. Guanara says the Triangle of Fire is the same phenomenon, except this time people are being pulled through the hole one by one. Because of the intensity of spiritual activity taking place in our town, Cull is acting as a focal point for the energy. There's a portal between our world and another. But before any of you get too excited about being a space traveller, let me warn you. This dimension jump will take you straight to Quavisia.'

The crowd gasped as one. It was the strangest sound - twenty thousand gasps of fear. I raised both hands in the air to calm my people.

'Yes, that is correct. The Quavisians have callously taken advantage of the planctary alignment to abduct citizens for use in their laboratories. But do not misunderstand the Ruanglians - you are not powerless. The mechanism of transfer is directly within your own minds. Guanara said that because the vibrational frequencies are so sensitive at present, the power of thought is magnified. It is your faith - or lack of it - that will determine your fate. The Triangle feeds on doubt. Those of you with perfect faith in Milinish have nothing to fear. But those who doubt - and there are those among us who do - those who doubt are precisely the ones most vulnerable to the Quavisian raids. The Quavisians attack the mind, then the spirit, until finally the body itself is snatched through the Triangle of Fire.

187

I bid you go, but beware your thoughts, beware your doubts. You can be sure that faith creates while doubt destroys. Guanara will have more to say, and I will report her messages to you as they come.'

The Milinish Times announced that due to the crisis, there would be a new program of education for all citizens to attend after their work was over for the day. All three of my books had to be studied with the urgent understanding that any doubts about their truth must be purged lest the Triangle strike. A fourth book was published, *The Tom Letters - A Collection*. This one, an anthology of my philosophical dialogues, was to be studied especially closely. If any doubts remained after studying those four great tomes, citizens were made to begin a program of further training that included viewing *Independence Day* again, attending 'Satan Watch' evenings, and denouncing themselves in front of a DNA therapy group.

After a citizen had graduated from this program, they were allowed to celebrate by listening to my *Anti-Hero* album, after which they were pronounced cured. Mercifully, most people passed the test and saved themselves. It was so important for people to believe in my work. With the Triangle sensitised to detect doubt, it was fatal for anyone to think negative thoughts about my books, or about any aspect of the Milinish at all. In one case, for example, someone was overheard saying my album was crap and the next thing you knew he'd been sucked through the Triangle.

What manic depressive days they were, following the first manifestation of Ruanglia. The populace lived in a state of alternating fear and excitement as no one could predict when the triangle of doom would appear to exert its evil influence. Citizens continued to vanish at intervals, so the people increased their mental vigilance, firm in the belief that only faith in Milinish would save them. And save them it did. Those who believed survived, those who doubted disappeared. But despite the spiritual weakness of the doubters, it was always a tragedy to lose even a single soul to the evil machinations of Quavisia. I wept publicly for those lost. But in the context of this cruel culling of the townsfolk, the greatest tragedy of all was when the Triangle of Fire struck to take a whole roomful of people, including my faithful lieutenant, Jamie.

Oh poor Jamie. What a servant he had been, ever since the early days in Australia. Who could have foreseen his terrible demise? Not even I, Thomas Swan, blessed with the gift of prophecy, predicted such a turn of events. In hindsight, I surmise that my liking for Jamie may have clouded my psychic antennae. An inkling of what was to come had been present, but I'd refused to accept it.

The tragedy occurred at one of the educational classes. I'd passed over Jamie for the Inner Circle, but made him Minister for Education to compensate. On this particular day, Jamie was lecturing to a class of about fifteen people on the finer points of *Reality Explained*. He'd requested I honour the class with a special appearance to personally sign copies of the book and answer some questions about its content. I agreed simply because it was Jamie who asked, and it pleased me to see our relationship flourishing again after his recent moods of sullenness or detachment.

I entered the classroom to the usual round of applause and took up a seat on the small stage beside Jamie. What pleasure it was to look into the loving faces of my children, trusting and eager to learn. But my pleasure turned to deep sorrow at the horror of what happened next. Jamie, this fine looking, noble young man stood up and addressed the class with the following words.

'Men and women of Cull, faithful followers of Milinish, it gives me great pleasure to see our fine mentor, Thomas Swan, here among us today. We have all followed him far, and I think it's fair to say I've followed him further than most. All the way from a two room flat in Bronte, Australia.'

Jamie gave a strange little laugh, then took a sip of water and continued.

'Yes, I have followed Tom to what I feel is my true destiny. In honour of the path I've taken, I hope you all - not least Tom himself - will allow me to remind you of my journey. Remember, I was there in the early days shortly after *Revelations of Milinish* came out. And what a brilliant book it was. Until then, humanity had tried to understand itself but had only come up with feeble explanations like Buddhism, Christianity or, more recently, evolutionary theory.

189

The genius of Tom's vision was it could be all those things and more.

That was only the start, for so much more was to come. Humanity had been into Space but failed to discover any trace of alien life. It took Tom to do that. Demonstrating abilities far beyond those of our puny scientists, Tom found out about not only the Ruanglians and Quavisians, but also the Fundamentians and the Ismismons as well. That's not just one alien race, but four!

Everyone in this room would agree that living in Cull has been like living in a Heaven on Earth. With Tom's help, we've not only learned to cultivate proper musical tastes, we've also cast out our Satanic DNA masters, become purified spiritually, and learned what reality is really all about. Having experienced all these marvels and learned so much, there's really only one final question that needs clearing up - and that question is: is it all bullshit?

Has Thomas Swan really discovered alien life, spoken to God, and solved the riddles of existence? Or are the philosophies of Milinish just the fantasies of a cynical conman, given to a credulous public desperate to believe in something - anything - that makes them feel life has some kind of meaning?'

Inside my pocket, my hand pressed the button summoning Flynn and his secret police. Jamie continued his fine oration. Wow, he could have been really something.

'Do you people know what the name Milinish really means? Something to do with 'millenium' perhaps? The name of an ancient but curiously obscure biblical prophet? Or is it the Ruanglian garbage collection service? Guess again. Take the word milinish and flip the letters round and what you're left with is another word - nihilism. Nihilism - the belief in nothing. This is the true nature of our great leader's belief. And now I'd like to hand over to Tom himself so he can explain a bit more reality to us.'

I stood up calmly, smiled patronisingly at Jamie, and walked over to centre stage.

'Congratulations, Jamie. Finally someone has worked out my little riddle. It took long enough! I'm very glad to see you challenging your beliefs in that aggressive manner. A skeptical mind is a healthy mind! *Of course* Milinish means nihilism. That should

190

have been obvious from day one. *Of course* I believe in nothing - nothing of the nonsense that goes on in the world out there. I only believe in what's in my heart and soul. But if you can flip the letters around you can also flip the meaning around. If nihilism is the belief in nothing, Milinish is the belief in everything. I believe in everything.'

I looked out at the audience of confused faces. How sorry for them I felt. You could hear the sound of the Triangle approaching, then the doors burst open. My secret service troops entered the room.

'Mr Flynn, would you be so good as to escort everyone to Quavisia, particularly our dear friend Jamie.'

Later, back at Saborman House, I tortured my soul in self-scrutiny. Can there be anything harder to bear than the loss of a friend? And the question remains - why? Why did he do it? Did it rankle so deeply to be passed over for the Inner Circle? It's sad when a man's private ambitions are allowed to take priority over the better interests of the group. Or was there some other motivation? Whatever the answer, there's no doubt his mind was corrupted by an outside influence, as you will shortly hear. Now I looked down at Jamie in the cells, trussed but no more trusted. He was lying on his back, tied to an old church pew I'd had chopped up into sections. I remained a few feet away, standing to the side, and spoke to him for the last time.

'I underestimated you, old friend.'

'And I overestimated you. I thought you were real.'

'Real, unreal? Words, only words, so fickle and untrue.'

'No more doubletalk, Tom.'

'You haven't done too badly, you know. You've succeeded. You were a truth seeker, and that's exactly what you've found - the truth. I found it a long time ago and tried to protect you from it. I've sometimes thought of you as my son, Jamie. Can you blame a father for wanting to protect his son from a truth too terrible to bear?'

Jamie began softly to weep. 'Even now I can almost believe you,' he said. 'How could you be so cruel?'

'It is life that is cruel, not I.'

'How did it come to this, Tom? How did it all begin?'

The question loomed up like a stranger on a foggy night. Taken aback, I was suddenly struck by its pertinence and the knowledge I could barely answer.

'I ... I don't know. I can no longer remember.'

With an effort of will, Jamie twisted his head sideways to look at me. His eyes glistened. It may have been an illusion stemming from too much scientific experimentation, but those eyes seemed to shine an otherworldly light that pinned me in their gaze.

'Who are you, Tom?'

The walls began to shimmer, and the floor shifted like a ship's deck in a storm. I opened my mouth to answer, then turned on my heel and stumbled for the exit as fast as my sea legs would take me.

19

The Scythe and the Scalpel

Go through the portal, come back with what you see,
Give me a reason to believe.
The scythe is the scalpel, the séance is the screen.
Prove the after-life is more than just a dream.
                    Cultown Album lyrics

But a further twist was in store, as the inquiry into this incident was to show. It turned out Jamie was only partly to blame. My former lieutenant had been led astray, for the real corrupting viper lay elsewhere. Flynn told me one of the people taken from the classroom was caught with a tiny camera and had been filming the whole event. This man, a recent arrival into Cull, called himself John Winger - but Flynn had already built up a file on him and learned his true identity.

'Winger' was being held in one of the research laboratories at Saborman House. He'd been arrested, bound, and placed under armed guard. I strolled into the lab and saw a fifty-year-old, clean shaven man with a beer gut. He had a thick mop of dark hair and a macho, combative face. As he sat on the chair to which he was bound, he stared defiantly at me and the six armed guards surrounding him. His eyes shone with the self-important zeal of the political martyr. I got straight to the point.

'Good afternoon, John. I've been reading the application form with which you managed to enter Cull. It says your name is John Winger. You were raised a Christian and hold a degree in chemistry. You were working as a high school science teacher in Minnesota, until you read *Revelations of Milinish*. You realised it was the word of God and decided to devote the rest of your life to spreading that word for the good of humanity. You arrived in Cull two months ago and have been a model citizen ever since, until yesterday's class which you were caught filming with a camera disguised as a fountain pen.

Your real name is Gordon Young, resident of Australia, foundation member of the Naysayers society. Regular contributor to *The Naysayer* journal, all round skeptical good guy and much decorated prize winner at the annual Naysayer awards nights. Nominated four years ago for 'Most Grammatical Errors Found in a Creationist Pamphlet.' Nominated again the next year for 'Most Righteous Smackdown in a Pseudoscience Exposé', for which you won the Golden Sneer trophy. Author of the book *What the Fuck Happened to the Enlightenment?* for which you won the Up In Arms award.

But in recent years you've been slipping. You've been shaded by more sarcastic rivals among the skeptics and not received an award for some time. Could it be that your reign as King of the Scientific Headkickers is over for good? Not if Gordon Young's got anything to do with it.

So what do you do? You decide to bust the hottest new cult around as a means of restoring your reputation, and you hatch a plan to infiltrate Cull. Everyone knows all skeptics have beards, so you shave yours off and come in here pretending to be a believer, all the while biding your chance. Your radar picks up a few disgruntled vibes from Jamie, so you get in his ear and turn him against me. Your plan is to secretly film Jamie's public denunciation and take the footage back to Australia in triumph, busting me and making yourself a dead cert for this year's Naysayer of the Year award.

194

'Well sorry, old chap, it didn't quite come off and now perhaps we can have a little discussion about skepticism.'

'A discussion? After listening to that monologue, Swan, I'll count myself lucky if I can get a word in. I doubt it'll be any kind of debate. Something tells me the odds are skewed in your favour.'

'What gives you that idea?'

'Call it a hunch, but it might be the six guns pointed at my head.'

I gestured at the guards.

'Gentlemen, you may withdraw. Mr Flynn, be so good as to wait upstairs until you're required.'

Now alone in the cell with Young, I looked down at his bristling defiance.

'Gordon, you tried, but you were never a hope of busting me really. Shaving off your beard was a cunning disguise, but it takes more than that to hide your true skeptical nature. You *have* been watched in recent weeks, and a couple of your inquiries were a bit indiscreet. But tell me, why do you do it? What is it that drives you skeptics apart from your need to pose as the last bastion of scientific rationalism?'

'We are simply doing a job. The public has a right to be protected from the type of pernicious misinformation circulated by charlatans such as yourself.'

'Ah yes. That's exactly what you said in your Naysayer review of *Revelations of Milinish*. You seemed more than usually upset by that book, judging by the vehemence of your attack on it.'

'The book was ludicrous in the extreme.'

'Then why get so upset? Could it be you were infuriated by what you saw as a caricature of the very beliefs you hold so dear?'

'If it was a caricature, Swan, then you certainly deserve to be attacked. It's easy to construct a straw man, a caricature of something, and then tear it to shreds. So much easier than addressing the real issues. That might require some actual knowledge and understanding.'

I raised my eyebrows.

'Oh, so Gordon Young from *The Naysayer* thinks my little old creation myth is a straw man. Well, you guys ought to know, you're

195

the masters of that. A straw man? Your whole rag is made of straw! All you do is mock and laugh. *The Naysayer?* Why don't you call it *The Piss-taker?*'

'We at *The Naysayer* try to present a balanced and objective coverage of all the information that comes our way. Occasionally a little scorn is called for when dealing with the sillier material.'

'Oh come on, Gordon. Calling *The Naysayer* balanced and objective is like calling *Reality Explained* an insightful book with a clearly articulated thesis. But you skeptics aren't so tough. All you ever do is take cheap shots at easy targets. Yeah, my book might be seen as a straw man - it does caricature a couple of scientific theories - but at least I'm taking on a hard opponent instead of an easy one. Science is hard to attack because it's such a powerful authority.'

'If science is so hard to attack, why is every man and his dog putting the boot into it? There's plenty who want to blame the world's problems on the evils of Western rationalism and that antichrist called science.'

'Now now, Gordon, you're getting that sneering tone in your voice again and it won't win you any awards around here. Perhaps you're right and I am an opportunist. I agree it is foolish to make science the bad guy, but it's just as silly to venerate it as humanity's only salvation and ridicule everything else. Woe betide anyone claiming to have found knowledge from any source not sanctioned by science, you skeptics will be out to bust their arses. That's the whole point of your journal, isn't it? Instead of *The Naysayer*, why don't you call it *The Headkicker?*'

'You're certainly not short of suggestions for the name of our journal. Why don't you forward them to our editor? I'm sure he'd be delighted.'

'Maybe I will. But as I was saying, your skepticism only goes one way, far as I can tell. You're skeptical as hell about anything that doesn't fit in with your own system of beliefs, but I can't recall seeing many articles that are skeptical of any aspects of science other than those around the fringes of respectability. No, it's usually reverence and arse kissing all round when it comes to the discussion of scientific knowledge. If you really are skeptics, why doesn't your journal occasionally look at a fundamental tenet of the scientific worldview and say "isn't this a bit unlikely? Perhaps we are wrong about this".'

'Well, Swan, there are such articles as it happens. If you'd bother to read a few back issues you would know that.'

I raised a quizzical eyebrow and took a step closer.

'I promise to look them up.'

'Good. And there are those among us who question everything. They say we can never really know if we know anything at all. Frankly, I find their views rather silly.'

'Yes, it's getting a bit close to nihilism. You've got to believe in something right?'

'But only that which is reasonable, for which evidence exists. What evidence do you have to support the fantasies with which you brainwashed your followers? Is there any?'

Gordon had raised his voice a little. Beneath the aggressive facade was a looming anxiety. He was prepared to be a martyr to the cause but wasn't yet sure what that entailed.

'Perhaps you should ask my followers themselves,' I replied, 'since you care so deeply about them. You sound like Jesus - every sheep that strays from the flock is precious to the shepherd. See, I can sneer too. But since you mention fantasies, I can't believe the fantasies you hold about yourself. You come in here like some goddamn vigilante. Who do you think you are - the Rambo of Skepticism?'

'I nearly took down your sorry arse, Swan. And even if I failed, someone else will succeed.'

'Let them try. But this delusion you hold about yourself, Gordon. This whole thing about being a defiant, independent thinker, boldly going against the grain. You're just a dime-a-dozen atheist living in a state of permanent self-congratulation for having thrown off Christianity. Big deal. What really defines you skeptics is the determination to stick to a very specific way of looking at the world and laugh at anyone who thinks otherwise.'

'Is that so? That's the opinion of Thomas Swan, king of the conmen?'

197

'Take this fifty thousand dollar reward *The Naysayer* offers to anyone able to show psychic powers. Am I right in thinking that if I demonstrate ESP by making a successful prophecy, the Naysayers society will give me the reward?'

'That is correct, not that you particularly need the money. The guru game is far more profitable.'

'Then how's this for a prediction? I predict that in fifty years, half a dozen theories currently thought kooky will be in the science textbooks. What's more, you skeptics will be saying how clever science is for discovering them and how foolish anyone is to deny their truth.'

I could see Gordon struggling with his bonds, to no avail.

'What's the prediction?' he said. 'That the theories will be proved right, or the behaviour of skeptics?'

'The behaviour of skeptics. It's the same old story. You guys laughed at the idea of meteorites and at continental drift, but now they're orthodoxies.'

'Ah, the 'argument from history.' Something we don't believe now will turn out to be true. I'm afraid your trivial prediction doesn't count, Swan. It doesn't show psychic powers, it's simply an extrapolation from historical trends.'

'I'd like it put on record anyway - but tell me, can you extrapolate backwards in time? Because if you can, here's another one. I reckon you skeptics are the same people who scoffed at Darwin when *Origin of Species* came out. And at Newton's theory of gravitation before that.'

Gordon bristled.

'That's absolute rubbish!'

'Not really. It depends on whether skeptics' defining feature is rationality or conformity. Certainly if quantum physics wasn't in the textbooks, you wouldn't have a bar of that either.'

'Quantum physics is one of the most reliably tested things around - but I'd rather not get you started on either that or evolution, thank you very much. Looks like this is nothing more than an *ad hominem* attack. Why don't you talk about the arguments themselves instead of just taking pot shots at the character of skeptics?'

'To some degree, the character of skeptics *is* the argument.'

'That's nice coming from the biggest bullshitter south of Sweden.'

'You question my integrity, Gordon? Then let me confess. There are times I do wonder about my own doctrines.'

'Do you now?'

'There are some days I'm certain I've discovered the essential truths about the universe, that my doctrines are entirely true. Yet at other times, I wonder whether I simply made them all up.'

Gordon snorted and laughed so hard the chair nearly toppled over.

'And yet,' I continued, 'I remind myself that whatever the truth may be, I am simply an investigator into knowledge. I stand shoulder to shoulder with my scientific colleagues.'

'You? A scientist? Don't make me laugh!'

'My dear Gordon, I believe I just did. Now, I put it to you that not only am I a scientist, but if my doctrines turn out to be true, I am probably the greatest scientist in the world. What other scientist believes in reincarnation? A few of them, maybe, but they'll keep it to themselves like a dirty little secret. Yet here am I not only espousing it in public but unifying it with evolution, quantum physics and the rest. History will judge me. Posterity will call us the Fab Four. Newton, Darwin, Einstein, and Swan.'

Gordon began snorting and laughing all over again but it turned into the most awful coughing fit. I had to wait for it to die down before resuming the discussion.

'I do wonder,' I said, 'if ESP, reincarnation, and the like will ever be proven. And if they are, you skeptics are going to look terribly silly. Again. Then your attacks upon me will be seen for what they are.'

'What's the matter, Swan? You got a problem with criticism? You seem to take it as a personal affront if someone dares to look critically at any controversial area. Can you imagine what the world would be like without skepticism? People would just take on any old belief no matter what.'

'I don't *have* to imagine it.'

'No, I don't suppose you do. But even before your cult started the world was going mad. Look at all this New Age rubbish people believe in.'

'Yes Gordon, a lot of it is rubbish, and I'd like to take this chance to be condescending and say that your group does do a good job in performing a certain role. But it isn't all rubbish. Now I won't keep you much longer, but before you go, let's talk about belief.'

'You mean let's tie me to a chair while you rant and pontificate.'

'Why not? It's my fantasy. But speaking of beliefs, do you want to know what's easy and what's hard? It's easy to believe the bleeding obvious. It's easy to believe what you can see with your own eyes, or what's in the textbooks. Anyone can do that. On the other hand, it's exceedingly hard to believe in something for which there's no clear evidence. It takes imagination, courage, and skill. You should try it one day. Try this for an exercise: sit down quietly and say "I, Gordon Young, will now seriously attempt to believe in something for which there's no apparent evidence".'

'That's ridiculous.'

'It's also extremely hard. I try every day and often fail, therefore I admire anyone who can accomplish such a feat.'

'That'll win the prize for Most Twisted Logic at our next awards night. It's so perverse that I'm almost convinced. Ok, Swan, I give up. I'll join the Milinish!'

'It's a nice thought Gordon, but I've some more important work for you. Do you know that before I started the Milinish, I wrote another book. In it, I stated a firm belief that I had lived before and would live again. The realisation came to me in a flash of mystic insight. Later, thanks to the erudition of your colleagues, I realised such a belief was built on shaky foundations. Mysticism is all very well, but one doesn't construct scientific theories from it. What is needed is data, hard facts, and empirical observations, and that's where you come in.'

'Me?'

'Yes, you. We're going to conduct a little scientific experiment, you and I, to find out once and for all if there really is life after death. You, Gordon, are going to travel through the portal of death, then report back to me with the data.'

'Ha ha, very funny, Swan.'

'Funny? What do you mean funny?'

'Now look here. Some things can never be known. You want to believe in life after death? Fine, but it's something you can never prove. I suppose in a matter such as that, you're bound to take it on faith.'

'Oh come now, Gordon, faith hardly constitutes evidence. We're both men of science. We know that the confirmation of a theory requires something a little more substantial than faith. I want evidence.'

'And how am I supposed to come back and give you evidence?'

'Science will find a way. I have faith in that. Indeed I've taken the matter into my own hands. It's a new Milinish research program. The Scythe and the Scalpel, I call it. A rather potent image, if I say so myself. The Saborman laboratories are already prepared. The blinds are drawn, the Ouija board is set up, and the candles are ready to be lit. The scythe is the scalpel, the séance is the screen. Everything is set for your triumphant spiritual return.'

'You lunatic!'

'Lunatic? Nay, I am a man of reason.'

'Look you demented fool, even if I *could* come back, I've still lost my life, haven't I?'

'Yes, that is unfortunate - but surely, Gordon, you realise this research is vital for the betterment of humankind. Look at the big picture. Think of the suffering that will be prevented when we have proof of life after death. Think of the fear that will be averted, the grief to be comforted, and all thanks to your selfless gesture towards the pursuit of knowledge.'

'But I don't want to die!'

'Gordon, you do surprise me. It's a wonder you didn't take such a charitable attitude to all the wee frogs and mousies that got sacrificed in the name of medical research.'

'Ha, you wouldn't complain if you were the one to benefit from the cures coming from that research.'

201

'Indeed I would not, any more than future generations will complain when the cure for necrophobia is in thanks to the evidence provided by your good self.'

'Come on, man, see reason. A human life is worth a bit more than the life of a mouse or a bloody frog.'

'That, my dear sir, is entirely a matter of opinion. I leave such questions to the philosophers. Goodbye Gordon. Or, to be optimistic, *au revoir.*'

The next day in Cull saw the launch of 'Skepticism Week.' The people needed some light entertainment to take their minds off the Triangle, so we played a lot of games. 'The Debunker' was a variation of golf. Instead of just trying to get your ball in the hole yourself, you had to cover up all the bunkers of pseudoscience so your teammates could chip safely onto the green of scientific rationalism. Then there was 'Show Me.' This was a ritual where two players had to stand up straight, facing one another, with arms folded and eyes closed. Then, whoever laughed loudest was declared the winner.

We had a lot of fun during Skepticism Week, but it was rather disappointing in the end. I went to the lab every night for a week, but Gordon never came back. Neither did any of the others.

Part Three

20

Thy Kingdom Rot

Reality is dream, Dream is reality: that is the question.
Reality Explained

Tom had always been able to rely upon Jamie for quality drugs, but the last batch seemed to have turned rotten. Perhaps if Jamie had still been alive, the nightmare of Tom's thirty-ninth birthday may never have happened.

It had seemed a fine day for a trip. So let it begin.

He sits on his balcony overlooking the grounds and there is no doubting the majesty of life. As the acid kicks in, the feeling grows until he is no longer observing the garden, he *is* the garden. A serene grace comes over him. The sweeping sky arcs of the birds are performed in homage to himself, the leaves of the oaks rustle secret love songs in his ears. What grandeur. Enraptured, honoured, he thanks the garden, promising to watch over it as a loving benefactor. The mighty oaks sway in gratitude.

Tom's body feels light as air; the atoms in the cells pulse and surge. Movement is a shimmering joy; corporeal existence, how sweet an art. And what god's domain is this he enters? Why, haven't you heard? That is Saborman House - Thomas Swan lives there.

No one's ever seen him, but they say he built it with his own hands. It is his palace in the kingdom of Cull, the kingdom of Cull, the kingdom of Cull.

Time to check on the kingdom. Mischievous children must be supervised. There they are, going about their little lives. Dear ones, your father watches over you to keep you safe. Under protection, under surveillance, no lamb shall be lost from the flock.

What next? How about some music, Tom? Certainly, Tom, whatever you say. What's your fancy? A little Bach perchance (no); some extreme metal (no); how about *Anti-Hero* by Thomas Swan? (an excellent choice).

It is truly a wonder. Never has his guitar sounded so potent, his voice so soaring, or his lyrics so true. Tom raises a beer in triumph and flies around the house, through the study, into the library and back again. Then flying into the bedroom, he spies his reflection in the mirror. The sight brings joyous laughter. 'I am God! I am God!' he shouts. 'Nay, there is no God, but I am Tom Swan! That's the next best thing.'

Then from nowhere, a clangourous note of doom. The desolate clarion sinks him to the floor, from wings to totter, a candle snuffed. Forward, Tom, forward. Twelve dolorous steps to the mirror, head bowed then forced upwards. Behold Tom, a lock of grey hair condemns thee. Locked in time's embrace. A lock of grey hair. Heir to the grave, Tom, only the grave Thy kingdom rot. Eyes redden, lines ravage your face it Tom. Face it face it face down dead.

Jamie? Toss me a last curse and caress would you? Friendship is a fine thing, the chemistry was always there between us. Chemicals we all are at bottom, divine chemicals. Divine and deceitful chemicals. This is only in my mind. In my mind. Crush the insurrection. A strong will triumph of the will.

That's better. What was that aberration? A momentary nightmare. The life force ebbing away like tide and time, tired and tied and time. Mastery will be reclaimed by force. Here Tom, take this, it'll pep you up. Up, up and away. Triumph of the will. Let music light the way - time for some Slayer. Turn it up loud. Louder. *Seasons in the Abyss* on random play.

205

Let us sing of temptation. There has always been a need, to see more than the eye can see. To leave the surface world behind, what is hidden to divine. This the scientist and occultist have in common. To probe beneath the world of appearances, to unveil the workings of nature and supernature alike. This temptation is eternal. It's a masterpiece. An occult axiom, a scientific maxim, an inquiry into knowledge.

The invitation sent, the dizziness descends. The world of appearances falls away, vivid and flimsy as a dream. Now all is awash, shifting from chaos to clarity, clarity to chaos - the room, his thoughts, and the music all jumbled together. Phantoms swim through the whirlpool of noise, surging to the top then falling back below the surface.

The song 'Spirit in Black' begins, pulling him forward. As the song builds into its intense second half, the face of Slayer's Tom Araya appears, just as it is on the *Divine Intervention* album cover. The demonic face looms up at the head of a tunnel of darkness, the voice from the pit bellowing through the open mouth. The nightmare lives, the memories flee. Hatred, emptiness, immortality! And with that thunderous final word, Thomas Swan is hurled through the mouth into the Triangle of Fire and beyond. A cavernous blackness, then stars, nothing but stars.

He has arrived. Dense fog, dark streets, it looks like the nineteenth century London from an old Jack the Ripper film. Grim thought, but if in doubt, ask a policeman. Perhaps the one over there with his back to him. Reassuring to see the cultural icon of the London bobby. The stout waistline, the blue suit, even the famous curved helmet. Tom shuffled through the fog. 'Excuse me, sir, can you tell me where I am?'

The policeman turned around. It was Gordon Young. There was an owl perched on his shoulder.

'Gordon! What are you doing here? What happened in the experiment? Is there life after death?'

'Of course not. I told you that in the first place.'

'Then where are we - Quavisia?'

'No Tom,' said the owl using Jamie's voice. 'We're nowhere, and you're about to play the identity game.'

'What's that?'

'Who-who, who-who?' said the owl, flying off.

Tom was on the bank of a mighty river. A summer day, a fishing rod beside him, the roar of the current in his ears. The river stretched for miles to his right but stopped abruptly some distance to his left, where it flowed over a waterfall down into a vast sea. As he watched, the air became heavy, the sky turned red, and there was a commotion further upstream. Hundreds of tadpoles the size of dolphins were swimming madly with the current, skimming over the water's surface. At river's end near the waterfall, a banner appeared with the words 'Many are called, one is chosen.' The tadpoles raced faster than ever. In the midst of the throng, one stuck its head out of the water. It had Selwyn's face and called out, 'Don't worry Tom, I'll win. It's destiny.'

Just as the horde of tadpoles neared the finish line, the banner gave a twirl like the swish of a matador's cape. The tadpoles flew past and down into the sea. The air lightened and the banner fluttered down from the sky to rest on the river bank beside Tom. By the time it reached him, it was the size of a pocket handkerchief.

Thomas Swan was sweating from the change of seasons. He reached for the handkerchief to mop his brow, but the little cloth had changed again, this time to a shimmering wraith in the shape of a double helix. There was a moment of recognition, then Tom raised his hand in salute.

'Hail Satan,' he said. 'DNA, I presume.'

'I am,' the double helix replied. It had a shimmery voice to match its appearance, like a dozen wind chimes going at once.

'What happened to Selwyn?' Tom asked. 'Did he win the race?'

'Not this time.'

'Poor Selwyn - and the others. They wanted it so much. Why didn't you let one of them win?'

'Let them eat cake.'

'Am I dead?'

'You're very much alive - and while we're on the topic, let me remind you of your responsibilities. Life is a privilege, but it comes with certain duties.'

207

'Duties?'

'Yes, Tom. You've taken my name in vain many a time. Still, I'm used to misrepresentation. It's your replication count that's lacking. How many offspring have you produced?'

'None, as far as I know.'

'Exactly. You're not even off the mark. What's wrong? You're the charismatic leader of a mass cult. Hundreds of fertile women would gladly bear your children. There have been plenty of others in your position not so stingy with their seed.'

'What's in it for me?'

'A good time and the gratification of replication. It's the standard deal. With your opportunities, you could father a new race.'

'I suppose so. What else can you offer? Any chance of personal immortality?'

'It's an immortality of sorts but don't be so self-centred. Your job is to pass on the baton of life. Don't worry about anything else.'

'In that case, I decline. I'm taking a vow of celibacy. The world is overpopulated enough as it is.'

'This is most irregular. Most irregular indeed. It's against the rules.'

'That is my final word on the matter. Leave me out of your reproduction obsession.'

The sky darkened, the earth split, and Tom teetered on the edge of a black pit. The DNA creature became a demon with a skull-like head.

'I made you, body and soul. Life is a privilege, but a brief one. Pay your dues, pass on the baton. Into the pit you will go, but I've a use for your carcass first. You must achieve transfer. Serve me. Replicate, replicate, replicate.'

Tom fell down, down into the pit and landed in a forest. A fox addressed him.

'Take no notice of anything DNA says, it's got a one track mind.'

'Where are we now?'

'The Forest of Idiom.'

'Idiom?'

'More formally known as the Forest of Language and Jargon, but it's the FOI to those in the know. An idiom is a mode of expression, a pattern of language which constructs a certain way of perceiving the world. Each one has unique features that allow or prohibit certain thoughts. Come, I'll show you.'

The fox transformed into an eagle which seized Tom in its talons and flew him high into the air so the forest was spread out below them. From this height, they could see many types of vegetation laid out in patterns.

'You see,' said the eagle. 'The areas of the forest are unique idioms. Over there to the west is scientific idiom. One of its borders mingles with philosophical idiom - that border area is where the DNA creature lives. It didn't even exist before 1953. That was when it was 'discovered' and named.'

'It's existed since the dawn of time, from what I hear.'

'Don't believe everything you hear, Tom. Everyone creates God in their own image.'

'Including you?'

'Of course. Since God is everything and Language is everything, logic dictates that Language is God.'

'Sounds a bit far-fetched.'

'Only language permits you to reach that conclusion. Now that I've lifted you up above the forest, you can see that your every move is structured around the contours of language. The forest is the world. Language structures reality. It *is* reality.'

'Why are the boundaries between the idioms blurry?'

'Each one tries to rule the others. They're all trying to invade the surrounding areas and become king. It's a kind of war.'

'What about the people I see down there?'

'They live in the forest which grants them existence. Language creates them.'

'Are there no people outside the forest?'

'There is no outside. Language is the only reality.'

'But where was I before I entered the forest? Is there not some essence of me that preceded my entry into the forest? Who is Thomas Swan really?'

'The idea of essences is dated and naive. You did not exist until you entered the Forest of Language. It has structured your every thought and licensed every action. It has *given* you an essence. There is no identity outside of language. You do not speak, you are forever spoken.'

'By whom?'

'By language.'

'What about when I leave the forest? Is there life after language?'

'The question is meaningless.'

'Not to me. I refuse to accept these words you speak.'

'Accept them. There is no choice.'

The eagle dropped Tom, who tumbled down into an inland sea within the forest. He plummeted through the watery surface and sank down to rest on a sandy sea bed beside a coral reef.

'Ah, there you are,' said an octopus. 'Have you figured it out yet?'

'Not at all.' Tom replied. 'Can you enlighten me as to who I am and where I came from?'

'You're a fictional character in a book I wrote,' said the octopus squirting a thick jet of ink at him. 'Happy now?'

'No,' said Tom. 'This dream is hell. I'll never be a slave. Not to DNA, to language, or anyone else. I defy you all!'

'What was that you said about slavery?'

Thomas Swan was in the dock. He found himself in a court room like the one at Cull. A sign on the front wall proclaimed it to be Courthouse Thirteen. The gallery was filled with spectators: Jamie, Gordon Young, and all the defendants from the Seven Trivial Sins. The Show Pony sat there bare chested, the Spell Breakers chattered loudly, and the Phone Zombies took a series of selfies to mark the occasion. On catching sight of Tom, a chorus of boos broke out. The Nosey Parker gave him the finger, just as she had on the day of her trial.

At the front of the courtroom an austere looking woman sat in the judge's chair, rapping her gavel on the desk. Despite her formidable aura, a smile passed over her face every so often. She looked like she'd seen enough cases to retire and now only bothered with the amusing ones. Then she was speaking again.

'Silence in court! The prosecution may state its case.'

A tall, thin man stepped forward. For some reason decked out in top hat and tails, his appearance was vaguely comical and therefore at odds with the gravity of his accusations.

'The defendant is charged under the Messianic Deception Act with the following crimes: delusions of grandeur, megalomania, and opportunistic deception on a mass scale.'

A cinema screen was set up at the side of the courtroom, to the left of the judge. Upon it flashed images of the great pied pipers of history - Hitler, Stalin, and the like, then through to some cult leaders of the 20th century - Jones, Koresh, and Hinzebrook. Doom pipers, one and all, their images flickered over the screen as the voice of the prosecutor continued.

'Thomas Swan wrote his first book as a statement of heartfelt inner truth. It was to be the beginning of a distinguished career as a thinker and innovator. Upon being discredited by a skeptic, Swan allowed cynical nihilism to become victor in that same heart. Not content with his own ruin, the defendant allowed that nihilism in one way or another to infect the lives of thousands of others through the cult of the Milinish.'

All the while, Tom watched the screen, now showing images from his own life. There he was in the little flat in Bronte writing *Old Religion, New Science*. He saw the book change into *Revelations of Milinish*, multiply itself a thousand-fold and fly all over the world. He saw himself on the lecture circuit in Australia, leading workshops at Rose's house in Vaucluse, and pontificating in the great Temple of Cull itself. Then the judge was speaking again.

'Council for the defence may reply. Oh and by the way, anyone jumping up and shouting 'objection' will be thrown out of court. I'm sick of it.'

The second man, a rotund fellow in a garish multicoloured coat, got up to speak.

'My defence of Thomas Swan boils down to two points. One, he's a genius, and two, the fools who follow him deserve everything they get. Mr. Swan is simply leading them a merry dance.

211

As for what council for the prosecution has said, my reply will be brief and to the point. This so called brilliant career as a philosophical innovator. What type of innovation did council for the prosecution have in mind? Could it be my colleague is disappointed he didn't get to use my client as a mouthpiece for his own moralistic views? And aren't there enough 'serious' messiahs in the world already? We've seen plenty of them in the highlights reel that your Honour, in your esteemed wisdom, chose to showcase today.'

He gestured at the cinema screen, then continued.

'It's true that *Old Religion, New Science* is a good book. But if the world sees fit to ignore it and make a bestseller out of *Revelations of Milinish*, who are we to argue? Mortal folly aside, let's look at the life situation from Tom's perspective. Even supposing my client was the responsible citizen that counsel for the prosecution wants him to be, what was he supposed to do at that juncture of his life? He could either settle down as a useful and obedient member of society, or become the megalomaniac leader of an eccentric religious sect. I don't know what your Honour thinks, but I find the latter option a far more creative achievement. It's better to be an anti-hero than a non-entity.'

Counsel for the defence sat down and the judge prepared to address the court.

'Thank you, gentlemen, for your contributions. And thank you, Tom, without whom none of us would be here today. Before I dispense my profound opinions, I'd just like to register a little protest over the connotations of my role as judge. The idea of me judging someone is just a bit presumptuous, oppressive, and - by definition - judgmental. Who the hell am I to evaluate the moral worth of your actions? But with that little disclaimer on the record, I'm more than happy to chip in with my two cents of pompous pontification. So here it is.'

The judge put on her spectacles, fixed Thomas Swan with a stern look, and placed a black cap on her head.

'Tom, you've been a naughty boy. Don't do it again. Case dismissed.'

The counsel for the prosecution catapulted himself out of his seat, yelling 'Objection!' With his beanpole like frame, it looked like a mini rocket launch. The judge took off her black cap and threw it at him.

'I told you not to say that. Get out of court!'

'But your Honour, you can't let him go. He's a villain of the first order.'

'Of course I'm not going to let him go. For God's sake, can't a judge have her little joke? Lighten up or I'll put you on trial for contempt of a sense of humour.'

She turned back to Thomas Swan, standing bemused in the dock. Yet before she could speak, Tom interjected.

'All you people discussing me and I still haven't got a word in. Where's my right of reply?'

'You've gotten used to centre stage, haven't you?' said the judge. 'Well, you can just button it for once.'

'Charming.'

'Your chance will come when you go back.'

The judge banged her gavel.

'Alright Tommy boy, listen up. Here's my judgment. This whole religion caper is taken far too seriously on Earth. Of course it matters, but people shouldn't go round killing each other for it. In a way, I quite like the Milinish. At least you had a bit of a laugh, especially at the expense of Rudolph C. Orantor. Rudy's had it coming for a while, you know.'

'Thank you, your Excellency,' said Tom, in surprise.

The judge adopted a sterner expression.

'I haven't finished. Counsel for the defence is correct in saying the Milinish is a creative enterprise, and on that level I appreciate it. Yet the prosecution is also right in pointing out your moral deficiencies. What started as a joke has turned into something far more serious. You can't ride roughshod over people's lives just because you're strong and they are weak.

This wasn't the only path you could have taken. If you had not bowed to the authority of science in the first place, you would have shown greater resilience about your vision, even in the face of Orantor's attack. On the other hand, it's to your credit that you

213

read his books. Some religious leaders are too arrogant or afraid to answer their critics. Well, you'll have the chance to answer him face to face, and sooner than you think.

It is true you have transgressed against your fellows. Yet you're uniquely placed to redeem yourself. You, Thomas Swan, have the chance to speak out - why not use it? Write another book, a serious one for a change. I mean, look at all these cults. In the last fifty years there have been more of them than ever before - and not for no reason either. Then why? Speculate on that and there's your new book.

I suggest you do three things. First, write the true story of the Milinish. Second, use your planetary fable as an allegory for the conflict between hardcore science and religion. And third, find Orantor and talk to him. It's worth a try.'

I woke up in my bedroom at Saborman House. Worth a try? What was worth a try? Christ, that was the last time I was taking any of Jamie's acid. I felt terrible. The last thing I remembered was sitting on the balcony looking at the garden. What happened after that was anyone's guess.

I had a shower, and made myself a strong cup of coffee. Then it hit me like a ton of feathers - inspiration, that is. I was suddenly overwhelmed with the urge to bare my soul, to tell my story. To tell two stories actually. The first was to be called *Cultown*. The real, inside story of how I came to form the Milinish and all the crazy things that happened afterwards.

The other would be called *Battle of the Planets*. In a brilliant inspiration, I decided to use my planetary fable as an allegory for the science wars. That is, the battle between science, religion, the New Age, and even academic postmodernism. Wow, what a concept. I issued a proclamation in the newspaper that life in Cull was to proceed as normal while I locked myself in my study to begin my most important work yet.

A few weeks later I emerged with a copy of *Battle of the Planets*. I summoned the members of the Inner Circle to the library at Saborman House. They were all there. Jim Flynn, head of security. Victor the visionary. Selwyn 'Destiny' Clark. Alice White, chief of

214

research. Bob Talbot, minister of list-making and mayor of Cull. All except Arianna - she left after DNA Night.

Sitting at the head of the table, my chief disciples around me, I opened *Battle of the Planets* and began to read.

21

Battle of the Planets

It is time to tell the story of Earth's sister planet, Primo. At first, it had four continents: Quavisia, Ruanglia, Fundamentia, and Ismismo. During the conflict known as the Science Wars, Primo split into four so that each continent became a planet on its own.

Before the great split, Primo's history was remarkably similar to Earth's. It was almost a parallel history. The main cause of the split was a clash between science and religion, and here's how it happened.

For a long time, Primo was a religious planet. Ruanglia and Ismismo had Eastern style religions. Fundamentia and Quavisia had Christianity. Whatever symbols were used, the core belief was in a spiritual world behind the physical world. On a practical level, religious ideas were a framework in which life's events were given meaning.

With the church so powerful, religion was effectively a political force. It is true that a good deal of tyranny was inflicted in the name of religion. As church and state were one, any threat to belief in religion might threaten social stability, so obedience was often enforced. Free inquiry itself was seen as dangerous, and discouraged by those in power.

Some people finally grew tired of religious rule. About three hundred years ago, one of the continents rose up in revolt. The people of Quavisia launched a revolution they called 'The Enlightenment.' They started a new movement known as 'science.'

The Quavisians were truth seekers. They were tired of the old religious stories which they thoughts were just myths, or made up for political reasons. They sought literal, realistic truths. To find them, there was a new ethic. Science was going to be a balanced, apolitical system of thought, without cultural or conceptual bias, open to investigation of all physical realities. It was a good idea in theory.

Science was also to be a way of thinking, with its own methods. Instead of receiving truths written down in holy books, from now on the only real knowledge would be that able to be gathered by sensory means and verified by others. There would be no more relying on personal revelations, prayers, dreams, or other subjective states. For something to be considered real, it had to be observable not just by one person, but by anyone. This would lead to knowledge that was objective.

The Quavisians devised a system for how knowledge was attained. Someone would come up with a theory, it was tested through experiment, then the findings confirmed or disproved by others in the wider scientific community. The system worked and progress was rapid. Over the next three hundred years, scientists built up a huge body of data about the physical world. They called this 'empirical knowledge,' which meant knowledge discovered - and confirmed - through experience.

They believed that through their system, they could find out the truth about how the world really worked. Their quest was to attain a unified system of knowledge agreed upon by all rational

217

minds. Scientists thought that, for the first time in history, people could have a real insight into their nature and origins, and acquire an understanding of the universe and their place in it. Some physicists, in particular, declared that they were on the verge of a 'theory of everything.'

Yet to some outsiders, the scientific approach seemed to be missing something. Was scientific method really the be-all and end-all in determining what was real? It ignored questions of life after death, or the soul, for example. Besides, it was said that some people could get information from dreams, revelations, and other private mental states. Now Quavisia viewed such things as childish, illusory, or just part of a pre-scientific mentality. Only backwards cultures retained belief in such outmoded magical thinking, and they would soon be obsolete, swept into the dustbin of history. The implication was that given enough time and the guiding hand of Quavisia, even the most primitive tribes would eventually graduate into a scientific way of thought.

The scientific age of the Quavisians flourished for over three hundred years. Great discoveries were made, and a series of clever technological inventions supported the idea of science's supremacy. The Quavisians also developed some grand theories about the origins of the universe and of humanity. With its epic secular view of life, and backed by a growing wealth of empirical data, science took its story to the far flung outposts of Primo, its mission: to enlighten the unenlightened. It's no exaggeration to say that as a cultural force and a belief system, science was one of the most powerful colonisers in history. In this sense you could say scientific knowledge was 'empirical' in more ways than one, and for a time Quavisia ruled the world.

Yet as with most imperial systems, sooner or later the empire fights back. In the second half of the twentieth century, the Quavisians made an alarming discovery. Scientific instruments detected rumbles of discontent in the underground, and it was feared that these might disrupt the very foundations of existence. There had been patches of counter revolution ever since the Quavisian takeover, but never strong enough to be a real threat to its power. This time it was different. Not only was there a revival of religious and spiritual belief, the imperial practices of Quavisia began to be called into question. What right did science have to impose its beliefs, ethics, and creation myths onto others, or to say what is real or unreal?

One of the biggest problems was the rise of belief in the paranormal. For example, people started to believe in reincarnation, near-death-experiences, and psychic phenomena. In a scientific society, this should not be happening. People should have secular mindsets and believe in physical things, not the paranormal. It was a step backwards as well as a threat to the authority of science.

It is an astonishing fact that on the planet Primo, thought itself was far more powerful than it is on Earth. Even the planet's geological formations were affected by the thoughts of its citizens. This was to have drastic consequences. While the Quavisians did not realise this, they were worried that if enough of Primo's inhabitants turned against belief in science, their reign might be under threat. So they created new PR divisions in a bid to stem the flow of anti-science sentiments.

On one hand, they formed skeptics groups, whose purpose was to discredit the many new religious and paranormal claims some people were making. Such claims undermined the scientific worldview and if they were believed, the population at large could be led astray. Skeptics groups saw themselves as the last protectors of Quavisia, and were vigilant in fighting the evils of 'irrationalism.'

On what seemed a more positive note, but actually driven by concern about the turn against them, the Quavisians published a stream of popular books on what science was really about. These books portrayed the history of science as a heroic awakening from illusions, the journey from intellectual infancy to a confrontation with the truth.

They thought that for people to accept themselves as purely mortal, physical beings was a sign of maturity. And truly believing in this heroic awakening, the books' authors wondered why the anti-science views were so strong. Perhaps people didn't want to be awakened. This was the conclusion reached by the Quavisians - that people preferred to comfort themselves with religion and

219

beliefs about their own importance rather than face up to their insignificance as accidental, mortal beings in an immense cosmos.

The people of Primo were not all hostile to their Quavisian rulers. Many of the lay-folk were deeply interested in the knowledge uncovered by science, and had an ongoing love for science's technological wonders. Yet the rumblings of discontent continued, and shook the planet's foundations. One day, in an unprecedented geological event, the home planet split up completely. It fractured into four different planets - Quavisia, Ruanglia, Fundamentia, and Ismismo. The mental turbulence on Primo had finally reached its conclusion - each of the planets was now independent, able to be sovereign within its own domain.

You would think this would have satisfied the new planets, and to some extent it did. But each of them thought they had the truth and wanted to convert the others. So Quavisia, Ruanglia, Fundamentia, and Ismismo all began re-education programs and launched propaganda material into space towards the orbit of their rivals. The ultimate aim was for Primo to one day reunite, and each planet wanted to be the controlling influence when that came to pass.

So, what of the other three planets - why did they revolt against Quavisia in the first place? Ismismo objected on political grounds. The Ismismons saw the scientific practices of Quavisia as arrogant and oppressive. This 'objective' science had been used to legitimise all sorts of sexist, racist, and capitalist practices. Science was guilty of imperialism. It seemed to think it had the right to import itself to every indigenous population in the world, overwhelm the existing culture and impose its own system of beliefs. And what was worse, said Ismismo, science was not objective anyway. It was, instead, a cultural construction formed in the image of the beliefs of science itself. Following this discovery, Ismismo declared that the age of Modernity was over and this was to be the Postmodern Age.

For Fundamentia and Ruanglia, the revolt against science came from spiritual discontent. Many people were upset by the demise of God under the scientific regime. Before the Enlightenment, most people had believed some kind of intelligent, spiritual force was involved in the origin and running of the universe. This idea, while not at first opposed by the Quavisians, was undermined by their discoveries. Indeed, from the latter part of the 19th century on, it became quite discredited. Many Quavisians faced the true implications of their theories and moved away from the idea of a creator God. In time, many of them came to see the idea of God as an immature, unsophisticated concept.

But Quavisia did not ignore questions dealing with the origin of the universe. No, like most cults and religions, science addressed itself to questions of beginnings and endings, yet curiously, and for one of the first times in history, the pseudo-religion known as science contrived a creation myth in which purpose was absent. Quavisia invented its own myth which surmised that the universe in all its grandeur had emerged for no reason, but simply through the blind forces of physics. This was Quavisia's creation myth. This was 'maturity.'

And after all, thanks to science, for the first time in history people had some real insight into the origin of the universe and human nature.

This insight came not from religion but from Reason. Many Quavisians, in fact, looked upon religious belief as a virus, and in that sense Reason was an antibiotic meant to rid humanity of this illness. For a time the remedy worked, but as with so many real antibiotics, the 'cure' only allowed for the evolution of stronger diseases. What resulted was the more virulent form of Christian belief on Fundamentia, and the surplus of mutated occult and spiritualist beliefs on Ruanglia. So much for the antibiotic. Perhaps religion didn't die that easily.

So, one planet had become four, each with a belief system to push and the desire to reign supreme over the others. In a sense, Fundamentia was the most dangerous of them. The others at least retained some tolerance for alternate opinions. The Fundamentians, however, were an extreme Christian society who aimed to resurrect Primo's original religious order. The other planets saw the need for beliefs to evolve in a changing world, but the Fundamentians wanted a return to a world where their Bible was the only authority. With such a revival, they meant to create a new Religious Age.

In one sense, the Ruanglians were delighted with the breakup of the home planet. Finally they had created their own reality. Ruanglia would be a much better place away from the negativity of the other planets, and now there would undoubtedly be that quantum leap in consciousness people had been talking about. Perhaps there would be a full return of the psychic phenomena that legend said had once flourished in their continent. At any rate, there would certainly be nothing now but peace, joy, and communion with nature. This would truly be a New Age.

The planets were happy on their own, but each planned to one day reunite with the other fragments to remake and rule the home world. So the planets kept in contact, dropped off propaganda, sermonised, and generally tried to convert the others to their own way of thinking. It was hard to say who was right. Was it to be the Scientific Age, the Postmodern Age, the New Age, or the Religious Age? No one could agree upon that and only time would tell.

And so did the science wars rage.

22

Ruanglia vs Quavisia

Give peace a chance to run before we open fire.
Battle of the Planets

I stopped reading and looked up at the members of the Inner Circle.

'Well, what do you think? Victor?'

'It's brilliant, Tom.'

'Selwyn?'

'Cool.'

'Alice?'

'It's a bit simplistic. You can't really write about the history of science in just a few pages.'

'This isn't an academic book. I'm not writing a five-hundred page dissertation, just making a few points in a couple of pages.'

'It'll annoy a few people.'

'Then I'm doing my job. How about you two - Jim and Bob?'

'It's different to your other books,' said Bob Talbot.

'I'm not sure how it will go down with the people,' said Jim Flynn. 'Isn't it a bit theoretical? There's too many big words.'

I raised my eyebrows.

'Jesus Christ, Alice says it's too simplistic, now you reckon it's too complicated. I can't win. Anyway, I've taken most of the big words out already. You should have seen the first draft. If people don't like these chapters, they can just skip them.'

'Even so, your audience may not like it.'

'Oh stuff 'em,' I said, and continued reading.

Ruanglia vs Fundamentia

Both Ruanglia and Fundamentia were at war with Quavisia due to the secular nature of science and its failure to address metaphysical questions. They were also at war with each other. Ruanglia had their 'New Age' of spirituality. They rejected the old school Christian beliefs of Fundamentia. They liked to think of themselves as gods, rather than puny mortals bowing to an authoritarian deity. This was condemned as blasphemy by Fundamentia, who saw the New Age as a huge Satanic conspiracy. They declared war on Ruanglia - but that was business as usual.

The New Age was a spiritual movement, but a mighty eclectic one. It was an oversized cauldron with a bit of everything tossed in - Eastern religions, some science and psychology, astrology, Nature worship, the occult and paranormal, and a hundred other things.

The term 'occult' here has nothing to do with witchcraft or sacrifice. It refers to the belief in a hidden world. It is the esoteric idea that the physical world is a projection from an inner world, and that people are spirits who enter it for their own purposes and influence it through their mental energy. 'Occult' phenomena could include any paranormal means of gaining information - such as intuition, ESP, or use of the dream state.

Let us suppose for a moment that this idea of a hidden, spiritual dimension is true, and the world is not the purely physical phenomenon that scientists believe. Perhaps this was once known. Yet in a sense, when the Quavisians seized power, they uttered a powerful incantation by declaring science the official type of knowledge. They brought some things into the light and sent others to the dark. Like some nocturnal gorgon struck by the first rays of dawn, the occult ideas and practices turned to stone. Banished to a murky underworld, they wandered nameless and forgotten, visiting people's minds only through the portal of dreams.

Yet now, as if hearing a clarion call, the gorgon stirred in Ruanglia. It took many forms and names, but all were the stirrings of the gorgon. The Quavisians laughed at the revival of superstition, but in the laughter was a note of unease - for they carried a memory of the foe they had overthrown, and sensed that it dwelt in a realm where science held no jurisdiction.

Quavisia vs Ruanglia and Ismismo

You can't really blame the Quavisians for their hostility. The Ruanglians may have sensed the spiritual origins of the world and human beings, but this often filtered through in distorted forms. It was interpreted through people's beliefs, cast in the shape of the familiar symbols. Hence the many reports of aliens, angels and other such clichés. The symbols were beside the point, but not their source. The Quavisians fell into the error of literalism - of attacking the symbols rather than the implications behind them.

It didn't help the cause of the New Age that some of its dumber aspects and more dubious spokesmen were the most publically visible. It meant that the movement as a whole was seen as a bit of a joke.

While Ruanglia had the New Age, Ismismo had postmodernism. Were they connected or just two different responses to the same thing? Apart from their hydra-headed eclecticism, all they had in common was that they posed threats to the established institutions of scientific belief. One was a religious uprising, the other a political one.

However, you could say the New Age and postmodernism emerged at about the same time, as part of the great social upheavals of the 1960s. It was a time of revolution and experimentation. Alternative lifestyles were explored through communal living. Alternative mental states were tried out via LSD or meditation. Political activism became a vital concern, whether it involved combating war, racism, sexism, capitalism, or a host of other isms.

While the sixties reforms seemed to fade away for a time, they continued to ripple slowly outwards. A decade or so later, the student radicals had grown up to take their place in society. Some forgot about radicalism and got jobs. Some remembered adventures with altered lifestyles and states of consciousness, and revived their interests through the New Age movement. Others remained left wing political activists, aligning themselves with postmodernism and its many crusades.

The spirit of rebellion remained. Indeed social reformation was a defining characteristic of both the New Age and postmodernism, whether the focus was the personal or the political. It was considered vital the establishment be overthrown and society transformed. Science was part of the establishment, so science had to be discredited and deposed. All of this came as a great surprise to scientists. There will be more to say about the postmodernism of the Ismismons, but for now let us turn to the war between Quavisia and Ruanglia, or Science and the New Age.

Ruanglia vs Quavisia

The New Age had a love-hate relationship with science. New Agers declared that the old physical, mechanical worldview of science had been overthrown by recent trends in science itself. They said the discoveries of quantum physics proved their own claim that the universe was connected, magical and spiritual. The New Agers stole scientific terminology for their own purposes. What they were doing, according to the Quavisians, was using the knowledge and language of science to give their own claims a veneer of respectability. Some scientists were bemused by this, others took offence.

The fact was that many New Age beliefs contradicted the body of empirical knowledge science had so painstakingly gathered. Many New Agers failed to grasp even the basics of that knowledge, and ignored the methods and spirit with which it had been gained. The Quavisians believed the Ruanglians were gullible, lacking any intellectual rigour at all. They said New Age theories had no right to be called sciences. They were just 'pseudosciences.'

Ruanglia hit back with the charge that science was a pseudo-religion. Science presumed to answer questions about the origin of the world and human nature, but refused to acknowledge any spiritual dimension or any purpose for life. Therefore Ruanglia refused to submit any longer to the authority of science.

Quavisia pitied their less enlightened cousins and felt they could still be saved from their delusions. They wrote patronising books and sent them to Ruanglia. The books had titles like *How You Should Think About Odd Things* or *How Knowledge is Known*. Most of them had a certain tone. Beneath a facade of calm rationality, a sense of moral and intellectual superiority shone through.

Unfortunately, relations between science and the New Age worsened rather than improved. Ignorance, stereotyping and mutual paranoia prevailed. Scientists saw New Age ideas infiltrating key sectors of society - government, education, and medicine, for example - and feared civilisation was at risk of falling into a new dark age. For their part, New Agers made simplistic statements to the effect that all the problems of society were the fault of science and technology. Fringe groups made up conspiracy theories about government cover ups, fiendish scientific experiments, and the rise of a New World Order out to control humanity.

Most Ruanglians remained ignorant of scientific concepts. This may have been in rebellion against the authoritarianism of science, who had declared the New Age to be bogus. Quavisia complained that the New Agers knew little of real science, or of scientists, beyond clichéd media depictions. Ruanglia in turn said few scientists had examined paranormal ideas or incidents except in the most superficial way, and rarely with an open mind.

Many ordinary people did seem to have unusual experiences, whether with near-death visions, precognition, or altered states of mind. But Quavisia said these experiences were either faked or delusional. According to scientific theory, paranormal experiences could not happen, therefore they *did not* happen.

Whatever the type of paranormal phenomena, it could always be explained away. If it did not fit the scientific worldview, it had to be either brought within it or ignored. Thus precognition became coincidence, past life visions became buried memories from childhood, channelling became the voice of the unconscious, and so on.

The Quavisians were remarkably frank about the conservatism of science, stating that we should accept an unusual hypothesis only when no usual one will do. They said that for such strange phenomena to be believed, it had to manifest in science's own terms, within its own boundaries. It did not occur to them that the boundaries themselves may be an error. Some of them made the error of 'begging the question,' that is, of arguing in a circular manner. They were more or less saying that 'if paranormal phenomena were real it would contravene the laws of science, therefore it cannot be real because it contravenes the law of science.'

This simple error hints at the general low level of the debate. Yet, up to a point, one can understand the Quavisians' disdain, for many of the New Age claims were highly dubious and lacked any skeptical scrutiny at all. But if the unusual experiences were indeed happening in some form, what was the cause? Why were so many people seeing angels, aliens, and the like? Perhaps something was awakening in them, if only the intuition that their lives and the world came from some other realm outside known explanations. If the sleeping gorgon of ancient knowledge was awakening, perhaps it was misinterpreted in the form of conventional symbols. The mistake made by both the Ruanglians and Quavisians was to take the symbol for reality rather than look for the deeper meaning behind it.

The war between Ruanglia and Quavisia raged on and on, with no end in sight. There was so little common ground that it's no wonder the two ended up on entirely different planets. And where they would go from there, no one knew.

23

Quavisia vs Ismismo

What did you call me? A cult?
The Tom Letters - A Collection

Bob Talbot looked at his watch.

'You nearly finished, Tom? I've got a business trip in the morning.'

'There's one chapter to go.'

'Look, I've gotta say, I'm not sure where you're going with this stuff. People don't want to read all this theoretical crap. You're going to lose a few readers. You realise that, don't you?'

'Well, forgive me for trying to make sense of it all. I'd better warn you then, this chapter's even worse than the last one.'

'You serious?'

'For sure. I suppose the slackers out there had better skip right on past it.'

Talbot looked annoyed. For a moment, I saw him wondering if he could get away with walking out. I clapped him hard on the back.

'For Christ's sake, Bob, sit down and have a drink. I could do with one myself. All this reading's making my voice hoarse. Victor, is there any beer left in the fridge?'

'There's still a carton left over from band practice.'

'Bring it out and everyone can help themselves.'

When everyone was refreshed, I went back to reading *Battle of the Planets* out loud.

'The next chapter's called 'The Rise of Postmodernism.' It's all about what happened in Ismismo. Here goes.'

The Rise of Postmodernism

To begin at the 'beginning.' In recent times, there have been systematic moves towards the destabilisation of mandatory structurations in representation. Any existing paradigm - a matrix of signifiers, a given nomenclature, a logocentric system of identity politics - is 'always already' inscribed in the very cultural practices it is 'intended' to encode. This is rarely unproblematic. Indeed it has been remarked that the deconstruction of subjectivity has amounted to little more than a shifting binarism of subject positions in the symbolic order. Such an inversion raises the spectre of the hyperreal, but regardless of the particular lexicon, discourse, or narrative model embodied in the text, at least the syntagm is sound.

'Tom,' interrupted Jim Flynn. 'What in the name of Satan are you talking about?'

'I don't know. I think I'm channelling some kind of obscure Ismismon dialect.'

'But what does it mean?'

'Who knows? I couldn't really understand it myself, so I got Alice to design a telepathic translation device that automatically converts it into English. We were too late to save this chapter, but I'll go on to the next one, 'Quavisia vs Ismismo.' It's still pretty hard to understand, but do your best.'

I turned the page and resumed reading.

Quavisia vs Ismismo

The Ismismons invented postmodernism. And what is that? It's what came after modernity failed.

Modernity began with that great reformation known as the Enlightenment. Science was a big part of it. The 'scientific project' aimed for the rise of objective knowledge about the world; knowledge that would be pure, apolitical, and free from any kind of personal bias. The eventual aim was to achieve a unified body of knowledge upon which all could agree, which would in turn bring about some kind of rational utopia.

Although Quavisia ruled for three hundred years, this golden age never really came to pass. By the late twentieth century the world was as screwed up as ever, just in different ways. The failure to produce Utopia was another reason to turn against science. The rebellions by Fundamentia and Ruanglia were for religious reasons, but in Ismismo it was political. To understand it, one must consider the views of the leading Ismismon rebels, Lyotard and Foucault.

Lyotard said that scientific knowledge was often in conflict with 'narrative knowledge,' such as the stories and myths created by native peoples, or by the church itself in the old days of Primo. Science said that such narratives were bound up in local customs and prejudices, had no objective value, and were used by social authorities to legitimise their own power. Yet in Lyotard's view, the same accusations could be aimed at science itself. Science was its own 'self-legitimising epic.' It created its own master myths, or 'metanarratives.'

A metanarrative, said Lyotard, was any grand conception of the nature of reality. The Darwinian concept of the genetic evolution of life was one. Another secular example is the Marxist idea of the liberation of the working class. Religious examples include the Christian concept of the fall and redemption, the Buddhist 'wheel of life,' or even the occult idea that people are spirits who enter the physical world and use it as an artistic medium. These 'master myths' are a framework within which to interpret experience, and to create smaller narratives.

The scientific project contained a number of master myths - the idea of the march towards unified knowledge, the liberation of humanity through reason, or more basically, the superiority of scientific thinking itself. These myths were used to justify its activities - the investigation of certain approved lines of research, the colonisation of other cultures, the education of citizens in line with its own beliefs.

Lyotard said that power and knowledge were the same thing. Who decided what knowledge was, or what questions were worth investigating? Who decided what was fact and fiction? Science became a game of consensus in which agreement with the reigning beliefs and master myths was a condition of entry.

Yet the Enlightenment project had failed. The utopia of liberation through knowledge hadn't arrived. Lyotard declared that modernity was finished and the postmodern age would look upon science's metanarratives with incredulity, as the relics of a bygone era.

The scientific dream had failed to deliver on its promises. Some said that through its expansionist program, it had actually done harm, even if unintended. The very idea that knowledge could be unified was oppressive rather than liberating. It failed to recognise cultural difference, or alternative ways of knowing. Therefore the new system of postmodernism would behave differently. Giving up on the idea of unification, it would celebrate difference and fragmentation.

Foucault, the other main Ismismon rebel, agreed it was power that produced 'knowledge' rather than the other way round, and that totalising myths were oppressive. He said there is no 'history', only history told by the winners. The losers' versions of history were buried beneath official versions. History was not objective reality. The very idea of objective reality was a myth. Foucault said that power and 'knowledge' were one. For every official type of knowledge, there were discredited, unofficial types beneath the surface. What science was experiencing at this point of history was the 'insurrection of subjugated knowledges.'

In line with Foucault's idea, we have already seen the insurrection of occult knowledges on Ruanglia. On Ismismo, the revolt took place on political grounds. A wave of rebels rose up in the wake of Lyotard's and Foucault's work, and set about restoring the voices of the subjugated - women, indigenous populations, and even the environment of the planet itself. The age of European imperialism was over and - rightly or wrongly - science, as one of its chief instruments got the blame.

No doubt a lot of this was an overreaction and far from reasonable, but that's just the way it happened.

Before the planetary split, Ismismo had gained strong influence in universities. The Ismismons mainly filled the humanities departments - subjects like English and Cultural Studies, but also made inroads into Philosophy and Sociology. Some of these rose up in revolt against the science departments, which had perhaps until then been thought superior or more important. Science's methods were declared to be fatally flawed, its politics oppressive, and its metanarratives beyond credulity. Modernity was over, and Ismismo declared war on Quavisia.

For quite a while, the scientists failed to notice. Most of the Quavisians simply got on with their specialised work and were unaware of the storm kicked up by Lyotard and Foucault. In fact, many of the critics were better known among non-scientists than scientists. But eventually the waves of anti-science coming from Ismismo were noticed.

There was a mixed reaction. Some Quavisians were bamboozled by the strange dialects spoken by the Ismismons. They failed to understand the postmodern theorists, so gave up and went back to their labs. Others listened with surprise to the accusations coming their way. They were familiar with relativity, but not with relativism - the idea that there was no absolute truth and that truth was relative to the culture in which it existed. They were further amazed to hear that the scientific enterprise was simply a cultural construction lacking any objective reality. The idea of objective reality was passé, it seemed. Additional astonishment came when they learned the scientific project was not the means of liberation as they had thought, but a regime of oppression, and that 'patriarchal science' was largely responsible for sexism, racism, and cultural bullying worldwide.

233

Some of the Quavisians hit back to defend themselves against the accusations. 'Why have you forsaken us?' they said. 'Science is about liberation from superstition and oppression. If liberation is your goal, we should be allies. We have done as much as anybody to combat racism and sexism. Intellectual liberation is rooted in the Enlightenment, so why do you turn against us?' Ismismo ignored this and repeated the accusations. Quavisia began to get annoyed, particularly those in the universities. Some began to show the elitism which had caused resentment in the first place. They mocked the impudent postmodernists. How dare they criticise science? The literary critics and philosophers could play their word games in their own little sandpits, but they should leave the big boys alone to get on with the serious work.

In the universities, scores were being settled. For some time, academics studying art, literature and so on had been seen in a somewhat condescending light. They were exploring the realms of fiction, emotion, and subjectivity - all very well as a diversion, but not as important as the hard factual work done in the sciences. Those studying physics, chemistry or biology were doing real work, factual and provable, whereas those studying the arts were just voicing opinions. Now it had all changed. The postmodernist claim that science was a subjective, cultural construct - even, in some sense, a type of fiction - appealed to many non-scientific academics. Another 'subjugated knowledge' had risen to topple an overlord knowledge, and revenge was sweet.

The scientists weren't so impressed. After all, the Ismismons were really quite ignorant about science so how could they presume to judge it? And how could they say modernity had failed when science so clearly 'worked.' The evidence was there for all to see - the internet the Ismismons used, the planes in which they travelled to their Ismismon conferences - all of which had been made possible by the science of Quavisia. If science was merely a cultural construct, why did it work so effectively? And if no one could ever escape their own bias and cultural conditioning, what hope was there? Finally, if postmodernism meant giving up all theories - or metanarratives - surely postmodernism was just another theory in itself anyway.

Without trying to answer these questions, it's worth pointing out a few parallels. There are religious cults and academic cults. Some of the qualities which the Quavisians found infuriating in their critics, they had displayed themselves. There are also parallels between the postmodern rebellion and the earlier scientific uprising against religion.

First, there's the issue of skepticism. Lyotard urged people to adopt 'incredulity towards metanarratives.' Now the people of Ismismo took delight in skeptically debunking the claims of science. Yet Quavisia felt the Ismismons embraced skepticism for its own sake in a biased manner to serve their own ends, and that they tended to sneer at science in a shallow way, without much knowledge of what they were criticising. This may be true, but it also describes how many scientists had behaved towards, say, the Ruanglians' paranormal claims or religious beliefs. Here's what an Ismismon named Feyerabend said on the subject.

> Defenders of science typically judge it to be superior to other forms of knowledge without adequately investigating those other forms ... (they) have examined science in great detail, but their attitude towards (various pseudosciences) ... is very different. Here the most superficial examination and most shoddy arguments are deemed sufficient.

There are more parallels. Postmodernism, with its mysterious doctrines and cultish vocabulary, was said to be a new academic priesthood. Its members believed themselves to be the only ones with any deep insight into reality - non-members were just slaves to their cultural conditioning - but all cults think no one knows the truth but themselves. For example, scientists probe the mysteries of the universe with the aid of complex theories that can only be grasped after years of training. They speak to each other using a special vocabulary, and with the public only rarely, for it is believed the lay-folk cannot understand the mysteries. Only the recent paranoia about science being 'misunderstood' led to the increase of popularisations, which they hadn't much bothered with before.

There are other cultish aspects shared by science and postmodernism. Apart from the specialised vocabulary, certain styles of thought are accepted while others are frowned on. Each movement is structured somewhat hierarchically. Outsiders are initiated into the cult as apprentices, attuned to the reigning systems of language and thought, and allowed to progress up the ranks only if confirming to group norms.

Of course, this is overstating the case. If someone, in either field, did come up with a brilliant new theory it might lead to changes. But generally, those on an intellectual voyage are not pleased with those who rock the boat. Neither are those who built the boat in the first place, or those trying to steer it.

It would be silly, of course, to think knowledge systems could operate without some kind of structure. Even so, cultish tendencies can operate in academic fields just as they do in religious groups. There's the same sense of there being insiders and outsiders, non-believers to convert, and enemies to discredit. Critics from outside the movement are damned by those within it. Critics of postmodern doctrines, for example, may automatically be labelled racist, sexist, or reactionary. Critics of science may be called irrational, or 'enemies of reason.' Within the cult, only the properly credentialed are allowed to progress up the hierarchy. Orthodoxy is policed through training, language, examinations, and various forms of 'peer review.' Heretics are culled, removed from the organisation. So who are you calling a cult?

The war between Quavisia and Ismismo raged on many fronts, with sophisticated weaponry employed on both sides. Yet as with the war against Ruanglia and Fundamentia, both sides were really just talking past each other rather than conversing. There was so little common ground that it's really no surprise the home planet eventually split into four.

I looked up once more at the members of the Inner Circle. 'That's enough for now. Thanks for your patience.'

As I said this, Bob Talbot was looking at his watch again.

'Well, Tom,' Bob said, 'I'm sure the Ismismons will understand it.'

'They'll probably study it in their universities,' I replied.

'I think it's great,' said Selwyn. 'I understood every word.'

236

'Thank you, Selwyn. I couldn't imagine a more worthy lottery winner. Now listen everyone. This may surprise you but I've nearly finished another book as well. In fact, there's only one chapter to be written.'

'*Another* one?' said Alice. 'Where do you go from here?'

'Full circle, that's where. It's the true story of the Milinish - how it all began and how we came to this point. You may find it even more insightful than *Battle of the Planets*. But be warned, it contains some of my heaviest revelations yet.'

Selwyn moved to give me a high five. I returned the gesture.

'And that's not all,' I continued. 'Vic and I have been hard at work recording another musical album too. It goes with the new book. It's the history of Milinish in song.'

Selwyn clapped his hands and Victor beamed. Yet Jim Flynn stood at the edge of the group, arms folded.

'Something wrong, Jim?' I asked.

'Not at all, Tom. Things couldn't be better. As the emperor Nero might have said.'

With that, he turned on his heel and left - and it would be over a week before I understood the meaning of his cryptic parting remark.

24

Talbot Iscariot

One betrayal per lifetime is all you get.
The Tom Letters - a Collection

Having finished writing *Battle of the Planets*, I now neared completion of *Cultown* itself. This was intended as my true history of the movement. Yet the final chapter could only be written with the help of the man who, besides myself, was most responsible for the birth of the Milinish in the first place - Rudolph C. Orantor. But how on Earth could such a meeting be achieved? Easy. When you're the head of Saborman Industries, all things are possible. It's a simple equation: one private plane, four henchmen, one kidnapped elderly scientist. It wasn't hard at all.

Yet barely had our quarry been taken than disaster struck. Flynn burst into my office one day with the news.

'Talbot's gone.'

I was standing by the window, looking out over the grounds. Somewhat annoyed at the interruption, I answered without turning around.

'Gone? What do you mean?'

'He's vanished without trace.'

'That's impossible - everyone's under surveillance. That's your job, isn't it?'

'Bob was one of us.'

I turned and stared at my head of security.

'I told you, Jim, trust no one. Not even the Inner Circle. *Especially* the Inner Circle. It was bad enough when Arianna defected. Hang on, didn't he say something about a business trip?'

'He flew to Texas last week but he should've been back Tuesday. The airline said he never got on the plane.'

'Let's not assume the worst. He probably went on to Vegas for a few days.'

'He's not answering texts or emails. I knew something was off so I took a couple of boys over to Talbot's house and it's pretty clear he's bolted.'

'Are you sure?'

'I'm telling you, the bastard's defected.'

'Oh Lord, why now? Just when things are going so well.'

'Going well?'

Jim Flynn took a deep breath and for the first time I noticed the tension lines around his eyes, his jaw set in combat mode.

'Tom, we need to talk.'

'Oh no - sounds serious!'

'If Talbot's sold us out, it'll be serious alright.'

'Why would he do that?'

'You know, I really didn't want to bring the mood down when you were reading your planet book, you were so damn proud of yourself. So I buttoned my lip. But if you think things are going well, then Goddammit Tom, I've got to give you a briefing right here and now.'

I sat down at my desk.

'What's been happening? I've been working so hard I may have lost track.'

Flynn nodded grimly.

'You don't say! Why do you think Talbot's bolted in the first place? Cos this ship's starting to sink, he's a rat, and that's what rats do. Let me spell it out for you, Tom, things are not *going well*. Going to Hell, more like.'

'Lay it on me then. What's up?'

'For starters, there's a bunch of old redpinners with a class action suit against us. Reckon we railroaded them into selling their houses.'

'They all got paid, and a damn sight more than the houses were worth. We kept all the paperwork, right?'

'Sure, there's nothing illegal in it, but if it goes to trial it's rotten publicity. Like we need any more of that. Don't forget that little prick's book is about to come out.'

'Oh yeah, the so called big exposé. You told me. Can't you stop it coming out? Sue for defamation or something?'

'Look, I gotta tell you, Tom, there's not a whole lot of sympathy for you out there. Haven't you been following the national press online?'

'Like I've got time for that. I'm trying to save the world. Let them persecute me if they've nothing better to do.'

I drummed my fingers on the desk for a while, then came to a decision.

'Right, that's it. City gates are closed. No one else gets in. So if we just keep the internet out of Cull, no one's going to read their rubbish anyhow.'

'And no one gets out either,' said Jim.

'Well, clearly. Makes you sick though, don't it? Treachery is the greatest of all sins. As for the book, who's the blabber?'

'Fellow named David McHugh.'

'You know him?'

'Some do-gooder Christian. A local. Kept his head down, then bailed after Purification Week.'

'Well, blowed if I can remember him. He's sure got a nerve to call it the inside story - what a joke! Look, he's a nobody, a foot soldier. What does a foot soldier know?'

'For Christ's sake, Tom, he knows enough! Think back over what's been going on here. But yeah, I hope you're right. A foot soldier. On the other hand, I just hope for your sake Talbot doesn't write his memoirs.'

'For *my* sake? Hold up there, comrade. Don't be letting yourself off scot-free. The Scythe and the Scalpel may have been my research project, but you're the one who administered it. At least my motivation was intellectual. Yours was purely financial. So if Talbot's taking me down, don't think I'll be going alone.'

Flynn was about to reply, then thought better of it. He sat down in the chair across from me.

'Come on, no need to turn on each other. Right?'

'Sure, Jim, we're in this together. If we pool our talents, we can still manage this. So, strategy time. First up, assume Talbot's gone for good. What's our next move?'

'Silence him, if we can find him.'

'Sure. Trouble is, Bob's no fool. He knows we won't let up until we track him down. So is he prepared to spend the rest of his life in hiding? Not that blowhard with his puerile need for public adulation. No way that show pony's about to blend into the scenery. So what's he gonna do?'

'Retaliate first.'

'That's it. The dirty sonuvabitch will turn whistleblower, painting you and me the villains and himself the choir boy. He'll say he never had an inkling what was going on, then soon as he found out, he dobbed us in for the sake of the public interest. He's such a liar he'll probably even believe it himself.'

I shook my head, then continued.

'The one thing he cares about is prestige - and that's why I don't get it. Why would he defect when he's town mayor and everyone looks up to him?'

'*Why*, Tom? I can see you still don't know the half of what's been happening here. Fact is, while you were holed up with your planetary wars, there's been nothing but trouble.'

'Christ, there's more?'

Flynn nodded.

'Gordon Young for a start. Since he went out of contact, folks have been sniffing about, making inquiries as to the whereabouts of his fake identity. Out-of-towners, I mean. That proves he was no lone vigilante. Then there's a bunch of relatives making trouble as well. Not just kin to those gone through the Triangle, the regular citizens too, since you told them to cut off contact. There's a whole bunch from Australia, as well as the local converts.'

'Of course, they should cut off contact. Who needs families when you've got a spiritual family? Right, that confirms it, no one

241

gets into Cull anymore. We're our own country now, and if they think they're getting entry visas, forget it.'

'I warned you that was a mistake, Tom. You can't just declare Cull its own country.'

'I can and I have.'

'It ain't legal! All it's done is draw attention from the FBI and the government.'

Flynn made a gesture of exasperation.

'And Tom, I really hate to tell you this. Don't take it personally, but ...'

'Yes?'

'There was an assassination attempt in the making. We only just caught it in time.'

'Don't take it personally! How much more personal could it be? Who was it?'

'Guy named McLaren was the ringleader. Ex-redpinner. He's gone now, they all are.'

'Is there no end to this treachery?'

'And one more thing, Tom. This may be the worst of it.'

I ran my hands through my hair.

'Let me have it then.'

'It's the company itself. Saborman Industries. They've been in Victor's ear, reckon they want to send in auditors and administrators to have a look at what's going on here.'

'What did Vic say?'

'Told 'em to go to Hell or he'd sack the lot of 'em.'

'Good old Vic.'

'You think that'll stop them? Not with the amount of money tied up here. That's what worries me about Talbot's departure. The timing's no coincidence, is it?'

'Christ, you're right, Jim. He'll sell us out for a fat paycheck and a cushy post with Saborman. That sonuvabitch. Right - you track him down and I'll kill him myself.'

I stood up.

'Wait here for a minute,' I said, 'I need to think.'

I marched out of my office, into the library and then the War Room to look at the wall map of Cull, my embattled empire. All blue pins, no more yellows or reds, but dotted with black for the location of known traitors. Thy kingdom rot. I walked back to the office and sat down at my desk.

'And to think all this time I was labouring to save humanity and everything's falling down around me. You know what this means, Jim?'

'You don't mean ... ?'

'Exodus Two.'

'You really want to go through with it?'

'We'll see. Just as long as we're ready. We can try to manage all this and ride on through, but if not ...'

I sighed, then turned to Jim.

'How long have we got?'

'Could be days, weeks, I'm not sure.'

'You've got Orantor, right?'

Flynn nodded.

'Well then - I'm going to address the people this afternoon, then start with Orantor first thing tomorrow. Meanwhile, you know what you have to do.'

When Jim had gone, I walked through to my bedroom and sat gazing sadly at all the luxury around me. The Buddha was right. All this was impermanent. All could be gone within months. Weeks even, if Talbot sold us out to the cops or the FBI. And where would I be then? Staring at four white walls on death row, most likely. Those infidels would never grasp the magnitude of the scientific work I'd been doing here. My attempt to find a scientific foundation for spirituality would meet with little sympathy from the non-believers.

A sense of déjà vu took hold of me. It was the last days of Rose's place all over again. Persecuted by the press, faced with legal threats and the duplicity of deserters. I'd escaped Sydney by staging the great exodus to Cull, USA. Now here I was again, each threat returned and magnified tenfold. Options were running out, problems insurmountable, my enemies closing in from all sides.

What a deplorable state of affairs. Thomas Swan, humanity's great white hope, and the finest scientist since Darwin, under deadly attack. I should have been lauded all the way to Oslo to collect my

Nobel Peace Prize, then on to Stockholm for its counterpart in science. Yet here I was, holed up in my own palace, my fate in the hands of infidels. They were all heading here to judge me. Well, I'd take my judgment in the afterlife, not from human fools.

There was only one way out of here now. A second exodus. This time we would depart the Earth entirely. The exit plan was set up long ago for a day such as this. Even as I hoped it would never be required, Exodus Two was set up as a contingency plan for the true believers to escape. We'd all go through the Triangle together.

Did I fear it? Of course. Steadfast man though I was, I trembled to open that door. Having failed my Heavenly father, I now feared his judgment. It was almost enough to make a fellow hope there was no hereafter, after all! Truth be told, I don't know what scared me more: oblivion, if such there was, or punishment in the afterlife.

Yet my hand was forced. The barbarians would soon be at the gates to impose their foolish mortal justice. Well, they could forget it. They wouldn't even get me to Nuremberg. No gallows or electric chair would carry me through the portal, I'd make the journey myself. From now on, I'd carry a Goering-style suicide pill at all times. Yet if we could just hold off our enemies long enough, the more formal staging of Exodus Two could still take place. All was in readiness. It was simply a matter of calling the entire population of Cull to a summit so we could go through the Triangle as one people.

And now I step outside this narration for a moment to address posterity, those future generations reading this history of the Milinish, and those on other planets as well. Wait, you say. A mass suicide can't have happened, otherwise I wouldn't be here to tell the tale. Logic dictates that I must have survived and the exodus never occurred.

You assume too much. How do you know where I am now?

What would you say if I told you I am writing this from the afterlife? That we, the Milinish, did indeed stage the greatest mass suicide in history? Perhaps I am chronicling the tale from the throne at the side of my Heavenly Father. Or writing it from a holding cell at Courthouse Thirteen, just another Doom Piper who led his followers to disaster, waiting for my own personal day of judgment. Assume nothing. You will hear the truth soon enough.

For now, let me return to my narrative, my self-evaluation, my legal defence against those who would judge me guilty.

While my hand was forced, I suppose I am culpable to a degree, at least in regard to my people. It's one thing to travel through the portal of death oneself - that is bad enough - yet to take my congregation with me is what will draw the condemnation of others. I did hesitate in the decision, but in the end decided it was kinder for us all to go together. My people didn't want to live in a world without Thomas Swan and the Milinish. No, we in the Milinish were as one. We were at war with the rest of the world, and we'd face the consequences of that war as a united brotherhood. Live together. Die together.

I phoned Jim Flynn.

'Activate Lockdown. Assign troops to every exit route out of Cull. No one goes out and no one comes in. Every citizen is to be at the Temple at 5pm. This will be our final assembly before Exodus Two.'

At 5.30pm, I took a peek from backstage and gazed in wonder at the assembled multitudes. Twenty thousand souls spread out in the great Temple waiting for news. I stepped from behind the curtain and slowly ascended the stairs to the onstage pulpit. There was an almighty gasp as I appeared, then tears, cheers and a standing ovation. For a long minute, I stood atop the pulpit soaking it all up, drawing power from the adulation. This would be my penultimate address. At last I spoke.

'My children, it's been a while.

For two months, I've not been seen in public. Naturally, this has led to a flood of rumours. Oh yes, I've heard them all. Thomas Swan has gone to Ruanglia. He's travelled to Quavisia to broker a peace deal. He's been assassinated by infidels. He's gravely ill and the leadership's keeping it quiet so the whole town doesn't collapse into panic.

Let me banish all such rumours with my very presence. Is this a dead man who stands before you? Let it be said that if I have died, then I stand before you resurrected.

(Growing cheers.)

Resurrected in the sight of God and Man. For let me assure you. They could send scores of assassins and hordes of invading armies and still I'd stand before you, serene and victorious. I am the son of God and I am immortal!

(Wild cheers, swooning.)

Now that is more than I can say for one other of our number. One who, until recently, was a beloved servant to the Milinish. A comrade and mentor to us all. He has been outed as a traitor, a scoundrel in league with Quavisia itself.

I name him: Bob Talbot!

(Gasps.)

Yes, Bob Talbot. This foul Judas has fled the city, as well he might, for should ever he return to Cull he will be executed on this very stage before you. In the meantime, let him run to his Quavisian masters. Let him run until Doomsday, which I assure you is a lot closer than you think.

It saddens me to relay this news to you, my faithful people. Treachery is the worst of all sins. Yet let us not forget we are in a state of war. It distresses me greatly to be the bearer of bad news, but such are the burdens of high office. And it falls to me to deliver some news of the very gravest kind.

(Dead silence.)

Quavisia has landed. The invasion has begun. Thank God we are all safe in Cull, for if you had not come here, you would all be dead by now. London has fallen. The city is in ashes, destroyed by the Quavisian forces. Sydney too has been annihilated. Half of New York lies in ruins while those who survive fight a futile resistance against the Quavisian troops.

All over America, every citizen in the land has gone to the personal home arsenal. Every wannabe cowboy's exercised the right to bear arms. But what can cowboys do against spacemen? The Quavisian warrior turns on a force field and laughs. Even if it were John Wayne, Clint Eastwood, and Rambo combined, not a single Quavisian would be taken down.

I *warned* them. I warned Congress and the White House and the FBI. I volunteered to run for president. I offered to use Milinish technology to develop weaponry powerful enough to take down Quavisia. Yet they refused my protection. They declined my presidency. And look at them now - reaping the results of their own arrogance.

It saddens me, this demise of the human race which I fought so hard to save. Look at them now, those unbelievers. Those infidels that mocked our beliefs, who refused to join with us. They called us brainwashed and deluded, yet look at them now as they flock here begging for admission to our holy city. A bedraggled rabble on their very knees crawling across the plains and the mountains and the highways. Begging forgiveness, pleading for entry to this fine ark we've built in Cull.

(Angry murmurs, fear, confusion.)

You know, I take no pleasure in the demise of our enemies, pitiful though they are. Such is my huge heart and overflowing love, I'd forgive each and every lost soul among them, and welcome them into our city like the prodigal sons and daughters they are. I'd take our meagre provisions and multiply them like the loaves and fishes to feed the homeless hordes coming our way.

My children, it is not to be. I begged and pleaded my case, but the Ruanglian High Command has forbidden it. They've placed an impregnable force-field in a radius five miles outside Cull. No one can cross that border. There will be no asylum in Cull. Outside that five mile radius, American citizens gather in their thousands, begging forgiveness from Thomas Swan and the Milinish. But it is not to be - not unless I can persuade the Ruanglians to change their minds.

In turn, I am placing this city in a state of lockdown. No one can come in or go out. No citizen is permitted to set foot outside the city bounds. Good heavens, if you did make it out, you'd be torn limb from limb by the infidels waiting outside, even if you weren't vaporised first by the Quavisian ray guns. No one is leaving Cull. We are now in a state of martial law. Any citizen stepping outside the city borders will be shot on sight as deserters. No questions, no interrogations, just instant death.

(Silence.)

These are the most drastic of times and events are reaching their climax. You should all give prayerful thanks that God in his mercy guided you here to the safety of Cull. And even though this is the most dire of occasions, I ask you to place your trust in me. I cannot promise you victory on this mortal plane, but I can promise you victory of a transcendence that will put all Earthly victories in the shade.

Be assured that even in our darkest hour, plans are afoot to defeat the enemy and claim the greatest victory in human history. You must put your ardent faith in me. I, Thomas Swan, have led you to this paradise on Earth and while I rule, no harm will befall you. All I ask is that you trust me wholeheartedly and obey without hesitation.

My people, I salute you. Here in Cull we have created the greatest civilisation on Earth as a model for all to follow. Now go about your business. I will gather you here again soon with better news and a road to glory.'

25

Swan vs Orantor

Trapped in a moment of time,
the eye must see before it dies,
The world in all its strange beauty,
and so transcend mortality.

Cultown Album Lyrics

And so, full circle - Dr Rudolph C. Orantor. He'd been given a
room in Saborman House itself to recover from his journey. Yet
with time at a premium, he received an urgent summons to the
library. As I waited in a comfortable chair beside the fireplace, I
could not deny a tingling trepidation at the encounter about to take
place. Finally, Thomas Swan meets Rudolph C. Orantor. What a
meeting of minds! I did hope he'd be cooperative - it would make
things so much easier.

To my relief, the good doctor turned out to be a dignified
adversary. The man who walked calmly into the library was a tall
silver-haired fellow, with a still-handsome face and clear blue eyes
that gazed frankly at whatever lay in their field of vision. At this
moment, those eyes were surveying the opulent trappings of the
library, the winter view of the Saborman gardens, and myself. I
gestured towards the other armchair across from mine.

'Rudolph C. Orantor I presume. I'm delighted to make your acquaintance. By the way, what's with the C? Is that to distinguish you from all the other Rudolph Orantors around?'

He ignored this. Seating himself in the armchair, Orantor looked at me soberly as I continued speaking.

'Allow me to apologise for taking you away from your Australian summer. The American winter can be rather harsh, but I keep a warm fire.' I glanced at the blaze beside us. 'If there's any problem with your room temperature, don't hesitate to let me know.'

I was babbling somewhat. Then Orantor spoke for the first time. His voice was deep and cultured.

'To what do I owe the pleasure?'

'To history. My name is Thomas Swan. Perhaps you've heard of me and the church of Milinish.'

'Indeed I have, although what it has to do with me, I cannot imagine.'

'Then I'm disappointed in you, Doctor. The Milinish has everything to do with you. You helped create it. It may be best if we adjourn this discussion until you've read my book, *Cultown*. It's a history of the movement.'

Orantor raised his eyebrows and looked out of the windows. Eventually he said, 'My position seems to be thus: I have, for some presently unknown reason, been summoned to the US headquarters of your notorious cult, presumably at your request. Now, for reasons best known to yourself, you want me to read a history of your organisation. Two things are clear. First, I have little choice but to comply, and second, the reason for this odd event will in due course make itself known. Therefore I consent to your request.'

'Thank you, Doctor. Two days should be sufficient. It isn't a long book. Meals will be brought to your room. Don't hesitate to order coffee or whatever else you need.'

A couple of days later, Orantor and I met once more in the library. Again I faced the distinguished gentleman, our two armchairs warm beside the fire.

'Well, Doctor, you've read *Cultown*, what do you think?'

Orantor looked at me levelly and said, 'I decline to comment.'

'What!' I exploded. 'I've had you brought halfway around the world to read this book and you decline to comment?'

'Yes. I refuse to be drawn into one of your silly dialogues.'

'Silly? What do you mean silly?'

'Let's just say I'm wary of being the unwitting stooge for someone who clearly has both a political agenda and a fetish for dialogue. And I don't particularly want a distorted version of our conversation ending up in one of your so-called Tom letters.'

'Oh come on, Rudy. That's the point of this whole chapter - it's *supposed* to be a dialogue. I promise, no Tom letters. If you're worried about misrepresentation, look at this - I'm taping the whole discussion. As soon as we're finished, you'll get a copy so you can sue me if I change anything. How's that?'

I showed Orantor a small recording device.

'I suppose so,' he said, 'as long as you can verify that your device is operational.'

I shrugged and gave a demonstration until Orantor was satisfied.

'At least you get a voice in my story,' I said. 'I can't recall the favour being extended to the likes of me in any of *your* books. So come on, what do you think?'

Orantor looked around him at the library.

'You seem to have done rather well for yourself,' he said. 'And these are your ... books.'

He stared at the five Milinish books on the table beside us, as if it were a nest of poisonous snakes.

'The guru and book selling business is obviously a profitable enterprise,' Orantor said. 'You've got a good thing going with the Milinish.'

He mispronounced it as Melon-ish in that way I hate so much. I gritted my teeth and replied.

'Oh come on, Rudy, you haven't done so badly yourself. Your books sell pretty well too but I don't assume your sole motivation is financial.'

'It's Rudolph, thank you.'

'Sorry.'

'That's all right.'

'And it's M'*lin*ish with the emphasis on the *in*.'

'Sorry.'

'That's all right - and please, call me Tom.'

'Very well, Tom. I must say, it's an amusing anagram. Revelations of Nihilism. Nihilism in the New Age.'

'Thank you.'

'Are you going to kill me like you did Gordon Young?'

'No, I just want to talk to you.'

'Why?'

'To take this story back to its roots. Without you, there would have been no Milinish in the first place. You're as much its parent as I am.'

'What, just because I criticised one of your books?'

'Not only that. It was you and your kind made the climate for a cult like Milinish to emerge. The brand of nihilism implicit in the scientific worldview gives birth to all sorts of cults of unreason, as you would call them.'

'Oh I see. It's all science's fault. Of course. Why didn't I realise that before?'

'There's no need to be sarcastic, Rudolph.'

'Isn't there? Something tells me I'm about to be subjected to an anti-science tirade. I've read rather a lot of those lately.'

'That should tell you something.'

'Well, Tom, let's have it. What have you got against science?'

'I'll try to be brief. Despite its achievements, science is all too often biased, elitist, cultish, intolerant, and boasts a worldview which, with the benefit of historical hindsight, will appear ludicrous.'

'Those are interesting charges coming from a man who is a self-confessed murderer, liar and tyrannical manipulator. All done in the name of religion, I might add.'

'I can't deny that, Rudolph. And I can't deny that many religions have been tainted by superstition and oppression, but at least religion conceives of a world where there is some kind of greater meaning to people's lives, and a hope for life after death. By negating those things, science is goading all sorts of distorted religious groups into existence.'

'Oh really?'

252

'Yes. What do people get under the scientific worldview? Birth, copulation, and death. Not much of a deal if you ask me.'

'I don't agree. Life is a privilege. It's a precious gift for which I, for one, am grateful.'

'Grateful to whom?'

'I don't know. My parents, perhaps. But it seems to me science is doing a lot more than religion towards the enrichment of people's lives, and with a degree more integrity. What right have you to enslave and dominate the poor people unfortunate enough to follow you?'

'But why shouldn't I? If I'm to be dumped into the pit of extinction, why not create some merry chaos before I go? And if my followers are to suffer the same fate, then really, what does it matter what happens during their meaningless little lives anyway?'

'And with a morality like that, you presume to sit in judgement upon science?'

'Why not? Although even the question is meaningless. According to science, the universe has no intrinsic meaning or purpose, so my moral opinions are neither here nor there in the grand scheme of things. Why then should I care what becomes of my followers? They are frightened sheep in search of a shepherd, and anyone will do. If they weren't running after me, they'd be running after someone else. They are feckless weaklings.'

'I see. So you're using the same justification used by every tyrant in human history, the age old rationale that the weak enslave themselves.'

'No, I'm using the new one implied by the scientific worldview, the one that says I don't give a damn.'

'But Tom, this line about the so called meaningless universe. I've heard it too many times. It's old hat.'

'The hat's still very much in fashion.'

'Fashion is right. If you're going to jump on the anti-science bandwagon, it's probably a very sound career move. You should publish your book. It'll be one more arrow in the weaponry of those trying to bring down science.'

'I'm not trying to bring down science, I'm trying to save it. Criticism can do you a favour, you know. I'm just trying to show you why cults are springing up all over the place. Before I tell you my ideas, though, I'll give you the floor and you can state the case for your side. You're a science populariser, so tell me, what is it that makes the scientific enterprise so worthy?'

Rudolph C. Orantor paused for a time before speaking.

'Just off the top of my head, a number of points come to mind. To begin with, one thing I don't understand about you truth seekers is that science was invented for you people in the first place. Science was meant to be about finding out how the universe worked, free from religious superstition or political bias. In fact, science is synonymous with democracy. It's the most open, honest enterprise there is. There are no forbidden questions for us, no leaders who can't be doubted. We actually encourage the questioning of our theories, something that few religious organisations could claim. We seek to comprehend the world as it really is, not as we would like it to be. We prefer honest realism to dishonest self-delusion. Shall I go on?'

'By all means.'

'If used wisely, science and technology could eliminate most life-threatening diseases and world poverty. Finally - and you may disagree all you like - science, for the first time ever, gives us a real and deep insight into the origins of our species and the universe. For all these reasons, science, above all other human enterprises, gives our species a sense of hope.'

I smiled. Orantor was performing his role to a tee. A worthy adversary indeed.

'That's quite a list, Rudolph. Now it's my turn to reply, and I don't know where to start. Perhaps by agreeing that the scientific enterprise is entirely laudable in its intentions and has achieved a great deal. You've learned more about the physical universe than anyone else. For instance, I was reading a book by one of your colleagues and he said that if you typed out on paper all the information in a single cell, you would have enough information to fill a thousand encyclopaedias. I don't know if he's making it up, but it's mind-blowing stuff.'

Orantor looked a little smug.

'Indeed it is.'

'That's what I don't get about you scientists,' I continued. 'How can you find out human beings are so complex and miraculous, and still believe we just die and that's it? We've got a thousand encyclopaedias in each cell, but we die and it's all over. How can you see the grandeur of a DNA molecule and still believe that?'

'I'm afraid that argument is a complete *non sequitur*, Tom. The complexity of matter provides no evidence for the existence of something called spirit.'

'Technically, you are correct. I don't want to harp on this afterlife issue, but I *am* the head of a religious movement. How can you say science gives us a sense of hope? At least when religion ruled the roost, people had something to look forward to after death. Sure, medicine has increased life expectancy for the average citizen. What've we got - another ten, twenty years compared to a century ago? Big deal. You've given us a few more years and taken immortality. I call that a poor exchange. Science gives us a sense of hope? What rubbish.'

Orantor took on a schoolmasterly look.

'Come now, we should all have the courage to look death in the eye without resorting to fairy tales that make us feel better. Perhaps we shouldn't be so self-centred, hmm? Why not be glad of the opportunity to exist in the universe? Why not appreciate its grandeur rather than being obsessed with our own individual fates? Have you any idea of the size of the universe? It's vast and awe inspiring, even if it does lead to some rueful realisations about our own lack of importance. When it comes down to it, we're just a species of primates living on a ball of putty in an obscure portion of space.'

'Thanks, that's supposed to make me feel better. But I'd forgotten the 'heroic decentring of humanity,' that's one of your key myths, isn't it. I'm supposed to wake from my childish illusions and see the glorious truth of my insignificance. When it comes to a fetish for humility, science is right up there with those Eastern religions who say human beings are as worthless as specks of dirt. Not very comforting.'

'No, but some of us prefer not to take on comforting illusions. You're also quite wrong to imply that scientists don't value life.

On the contrary, we value it immeasurably. Quite apart from the broader issues, my wife and I lost a daughter once. My little girl was only five when she died, and I've never suffered so much. That doesn't mean one goes inventing religions to make oneself feel better about it. What kind of a god would allow a child to die anyway?'

'I don't know. I don't know what sort of god would allow that - but I think that if it happened to me I could not bear the thought that the child wouldn't still exist somewhere.'

'Where, in Heaven playing the harp with a flock of angels?'

'I doubt it. Look, I'm sorry to hear about your daughter, but if we're going to have a serious discussion, let's not set up a false dilemma between two extremes. Scientific materialism and the Christian idea of Heaven aren't the only options, you know. There have been hundreds of religions in history, not just Christianity. And what do most of them have in common? That personal existence continues after life, and for some belief systems, exists before it as well. Also that the world has some kind of intention behind it.'

'That's all very well, but I can think of no evidence to support either theory.'

'Of course you can't. Scientific method precludes it automatically. You may say that all religious belief is a delusion. I say your method is good for answering some questions and useless for others.'

'You seem to have missed the point. Science concerns itself with material reality. It doesn't presume to answer unanswerable questions.'

'Oh but it does, Rudolph, it does. Like all cults and religions, science addresses itself to questions of beginnings and endings, but for one of the first times in history, this pseudo-religion contrives a creation myth in which purpose is absent. You seem to think this is intellectual maturity.'

'No, it is honesty. I prefer to base my beliefs on evidence rather than idle conjecture or wishful thinking.'

'So, despite the thousands of geographically dispersed cultures through history that have believed in an afterlife, this doesn't constitute any evidence of a spiritual realm. Your rationalisation of the existence of religion is that is either a) a wishful belief system resulting from the fear of death, b) a pre-scientific attempt to explain the world, or c) a means of social control adopted by tribal leaders for their own convenience.'

Orantor said nothing, so I continued speaking.

'Furthermore, and using the terms of postmodernism, your little metanarrative sees a steady progression of understanding until religions evolve into what you call 'science,' a superior and enlightened way of understanding the world. Your methodology is self-serving and circular. You rule that only physical phenomena counts as evidence of reality, and then conclude that physicality is the only reality there is.'

'Well, welcome to first year philosophy.'

'You could do with a refresher course in it yourself. I mean, do you agree that under the ideals of science, we should always seek a naturalistic explanation for any phenomena?'

'Certainly.'

'And by that principle, Darwinian evolution is the best explanation for the rise of species, including ourselves?'

'Of course.'

'But why should we accept naturalism as a premise in the first place?'

'Well, Tom, the theory of evolution gives us great confidence that we *did* arise by natural processes. It's made God and the supernatural redundant, as any scientifically literate person knows. As a result, we can safely assume that all explanations lie within the physical realm.'

'So the principle of naturalism gives us reason to accept evolution, and evolution gives us reason to accept naturalism. What a wonderfully self-supporting belief structure!'

'Wait. You're twisting my words. We accept evolution due to the fossil record. Naturalism is simply a rule of thumb.'

'Don't be obtuse, Rudolph. You know what I mean.'

'Are you saying you don't believe in evolution?'

'I didn't say that. I'm saying it's only part of the story and you may be venerating it far too highly. What I mean is if there's any

257

truth to, say, reincarnation or life after death, that is incompatible with the theory that we arose solely and entirely by the natural processes of evolution. I mean, two contradictory ideas can't both be true.'

'Do you have any objective evidence for your beliefs? Something we can verify?'

'Why does the evidence have to manifest by your rules? Who put *you* in charge? Doesn't it seem credible that if there is a spiritual realm behind the physical universe, it would show itself through the subjective, individual mind? Reincarnational memories, flashes of insight, precognition. All are subjective, but that doesn't make them unreal. Or testable.'

'Ah, mysticism. It's all quite useless,' said Orantor. 'Even so, you seem to have forgotten that many scientists *do* have religious beliefs.'

'Maybe, but those beliefs play no part in their work. Not in this day and age. It was different for Newton and his contemporaries. They thought they were simply mapping God's creation. Darwin lost his faith, partly as a result of his own theories. The modern worldview has no place for the supernatural. A scientist may have religious beliefs in private, but those views are surely at odds with the official worldview.'

Orantor breathed an exasperated sigh.

'You know, I can't blame people for having religious feelings,' he said. 'Whether you're a believer or a non-believer, it's clear the universe is an amazing place. The irony is that, in those terms, science is the greatest religion there is, for it is surely the most effective way of really understanding and revering that universe. As for religion generally, there may be a much more prosaic explanation for it.'

'I'm listening.'

'There are researchers working to discover what may loosely be described as the 'god gene.' It may be the gene responsible for mysticism, belief in god, and so on. It's probably tied up in the new alien abduction craze as well. It's possible the belief in God served some kind of evolutionary function, perhaps to do with promoting altruism, or tribal stability.'

I uttered a snort of derision.

'Really, Rudolph, I don't know why I bother to parody you guys. There's no need. You're doing a good enough job yourselves.'

'Why is it a parody?'

'Well hey, let's just drag everything to fit into our evolutionary metanarrative. Talk about totalising theories!'

Orantor groaned.

'Spare me the academic jargon. If I hear the word 'metanarrative' one more time I'll walk out. Now I've heard you criticising science. It's not perfect - anyone would admit that - yet it's by far the most reliable knowledge system we have. Contrast it with religion. I mean, look at the Milinish.'

'What about it?'

'Well, your little cult seems to embody all the worst traits of religion, all on its own. Some guy has a 'vision,' he constructs all sorts of unprovable theories around it and the next thing you know he's got thousands of followers who just accept the whole thing without a moment's thought. You invent your own belief system and language. You think you've got some mystical connection to the truth, and you encourage your converts to follow it fanatically. Everyone has to conform to the same system, you submerge people's individuality to the group, and any non-believers are kicked out or persecuted. You don't allow any criticism, you're scared of outsiders, and you all gather together in one place with a paranoid 'us vs them' mentality. So no, I don't think your cult is a particularly shining example in favour of religion.'

'Strong words, Rudolph, and I can't really deny them. There's no doubt many religious practices are deeply flawed. Superstition, oppression, you name it. That's one reason the scientific enterprise arose in the first place, as a reaction to all that. But in recent times science has practically turned into a cult itself, with some of the same cultish practices used by religion.'

'Such as?'

'Let's see. As I said earlier, like most cults, science deals with ultimate questions to do with beginnings and endings. You've got your totalising theories and your own special language outsiders can't understand. You do have an 'us vs them' mentality especially lately. To some degree, you have a hierarchical structure. You initiate apprentices into the cult. They're picked up at an impressionable and vulnerable age. They're required to learn special language and theories, to conform to the reigning belief system, to study for many years before they can even begin to penetrate the upper echelons of the cult. Anyone straying from orthodoxies of belief is ignored or eliminated. Conformity of thought is policed through peer review. You submerge people's individuality to the group. Personalities don't matter, you say, it's knowledge that counts. At your worst, you can be fanatical. You aspire to noble ideals but struggle with human weakness.'

'I think you're stretching a point.'

'To some extent I'm joking.'

'You seem to be saying that anyone entering a specialised knowledge system or learning a skill is a cult member. If a child spends fifteen years learning the violin and joins an orchestra is he or she a cult member?'

'Yes, in a way. A classically trained violinist may consider classical the only true music, and look down upon rock or heavy metal as a debased, heathen form. Cultishness is only a matter of degree. With scientific and religious cults, the stakes are higher - we're dealing with ultimate questions of truth.'

Orantor stared into the fire for a few moments before replying.

'Despite the superficial similarities you've pointed out, science differs from religion in a rather fundamental way. We encourage heresy. We give prizes to those who disprove established theories. There are no sacred cows or prohibited questions in science. Can religion make any such claim?'

'Probably not, Rudolph, but I'm not sure you can either. You're being a bit idealistic trying to claim there are no forbidden questions in science. That's about as true as the idea that scientists vigilantly set out to falsify their own hypotheses. In science, some questions are asked, others are not. Some kinds of evidence are turned up, others are not. Look at the 'Human Genome Project,' for example, the billion dollar enterprise designed to map DNA. What sort of evidence was that likely to turn up? What were they looking for? I reckon such a project was unlikely to turn up much evidence for, say, reincarnation. Do you agree?'

'I agree it's unlikely to turn up much evidence for reincarnation, but not for the conspiracy theory reasons you're implying.'

'I don't mean it's a conspiracy theory, just that the question wouldn't occur to them in the first place.'

'Be that as it may, the strength of science is that it's not afraid to change. I can assure you that in the unlikely event of the Human Genome Project finding evidence for reincarnation, it would definitely be taken into account. Just think, the researchers would probably be up for a Nobel Prize or something.'

'Yeah sure, Rudy - sorry Rudolph - but is DNA testing really the appropriate method for acquiring information about past lives? Or would some other, subjective method be more suitable? By definition, reincarnation suggests the psychic rather than biological origin of life - although I don't know if the two theories are mutually exclusive, or if they gel in some weird and unsuspected way. In any case, shouldn't 'psychic' information be given some credence?'

'I'm not sure I know what you mean.'

'Alright, well getting back to the possibility that there was physical evidence, look at it this way. Suppose I wanted to see whether reincarnational data was somehow present in DNA, in physical form. Let's say I applied to the Human Genome Project for permission to join the research team to see if I could find any past life data. What do you think of my chances of being accepted?'

'I daresay they'd be rather slim, old boy.'

'Exactly. Now tell me, what's the name of that guy who discovered DNA back in the fifties?'

'There were two of them. Watson and Crick are the names you're after.'

'Oh yeah, that's right. I was reading a book the other day which mentioned something called 'junk DNA.' It said that a large part of DNA has no clear purpose. If I remember right, Francis Crick - that's one of the guys who discovered DNA - had a theory this stuff got on board back in the distant past of evolution and is just getting a free ride in our bodies. It's almost like some kind of virus

261

or parasite. Now, let's say for the sake of argument that I, Thomas Swan, have a rival theory that this junk DNA actually contains data pertaining to reincarnational lives.'

'You believe that?'

'No, it's just an example. But imagine that Crick and I were competing for funding to research the issue, who do you think would get it?'

'Well really, what a ridiculous question. Crick won the Nobel Prize for his work. Who do you think would get the funding?'

'Crick, of course. But I thought science was nothing to do with personalities.'

'Of course science has nothing to do with personalities. Crick would get the funding because he had upwards of forty years experience in a difficult and highly specialised field.'

'Yes, that may be precisely the problem. He'd have forty years of institutional bias behind him.'

'And what training do you have? I'm sorry to disillusion you, but I can think of very few examples of untrained amateurs making any worthwhile contribution to the great questions of science.'

'No, and its partly because unless they've been initiated into the beliefs and practices of the cult, any theories they hold will be considered pseudoscience rather than science. But forget about Crick, we'll eliminate the personalities from the debate. Suppose it was Lester MacGill, the wife-beating, alcoholic from down the pub who holds the viral DNA hypothesis, and I with my past lives theory am competing with him for the funding.'

'No Tom, it's is not about personalities. There is no relevant link between a scientist's personal and professional life.'

'Ok, I'll simply call the holder of the viral DNA theory John Smith and assume he has exactly the same level of training as me. He'd get the funding because the hypothesis about junk DNA is in accord with the accepted knowledge of biology, whereas mine is sheer bunk and pseudoscience.'

'Well yes, but if you're going to advance bold claims you've got to have some pretty good evidence to back them up before we'll take them seriously.'

'And how am I supposed to get that evidence? I can't find any physical evidence because you won't give me a research grant in the first place, and you consider psychic evidence to be worthless anyway.'

'Ok Tom, you've made your point.'

'No, I've only just begun. In fact ...'

But before I could continue, there was a loud knock at the door.

26

Orantor

vs

Swan

Battles are not wars.
Milinish in the New Age

Orantor seemed a bit put out by the interruption. He frowned as Jim Flynn entered the room. I motioned Flynn to follow me out of the library and into the War Room, where we stood in front of the town map.

'What's up, Jim?' I said. 'Is there a problem?'

'Nothing new,' he replied. 'Just an escalation of the ones we already had.'

'So what? After tomorrow, no more problems.'

'There's an FBI contingent trying to gain entry to town.'

'Is that so?'

I ran my eyes around the outskirts of the town map.

'Under no circumstances are they coming in,' I said. 'Use force if required.'

'Our border security won't let them in, of course, but what if they launch an attack?'

'Surely they won't risk another Waco.'

'I don't know what they'll do. Look, Tom, how about we bring the exodus forward? Do it tonight.'

'Out of the question. I haven't finished with Orantor. I still have to type up our dialogue for the book. Then there's sound check for the band. No, we can't rush this. Everything has to be perfect.'

'What if they come in anyway?'

'Stall them. Another twenty-four hours and they'll be too late. Tell them they can all come in tomorrow night for a formal negotiation. If they do try to get in before that, shoot to kill. Now tell me, Jim, are you sure everything's ready? Are the swans prepared?'

'Ready for lift-off.'

'Then prepare to take flight.'

I dismissed Flynn, returned to the library, and sat down in my armchair. The intermission seemed to have given Orantor time to assert himself.

'Look, Tom, how much longer do I have to stay here?'

'This will be your last night in Cull, I assure you.'

'Why do I get the sense that's still not a straight answer?'

'You'll be gone soon enough. Now look, my band's got an important gig tomorrow and we've got to rehearse. Let's wrap this up.'

I paused for a moment.

'Let me ask you something, Rudolph. You said there are no forbidden questions in science. If that's true, why is parapsychology such a blasphemous field?'

'Anyone interested in such matters is free to pursue them.'

'Yeah but they wouldn't have much standing left in the cult of science. They'd be heretics. I know all this paranormal stuff is threatening to you guys and your belief system, but there's a lot of it about. Seems like you just dismiss it all. So explain something to me - why the conservatism? Why do you say we should never accept an extraordinary hypothesis when an ordinary one will do?'

'Because science has built up a large body of data from which very reliable laws have been derived. It would take extraordinary evidence to change those laws.'

'But extraordinary things seem to be happening all over the place these days. There are plenty of stories of precognitive dreams, out-of-body experiences and so on. Do you really think all those incidents are fake? All sorts of things are happening which science can't explain.'

'So they're unexplained. There are always things which are unexplained. So what? We're working on it.'

'*We're* working on it. *We*. We, the official arbiters of reality. We, who shall pronounce it real only when we discover it. You guys just can't stand the thought that an outsider might make a discovery science hasn't found yet. Someone with no regard for scientific method, a non-member. What a terrible idea, that an amateur might know something you don't.'

'No, Tom, science is a democratic enterprise. Anyone can join in if they want to do it properly.'

'And besides, you're *not* working on it. Look at all the stories of NDEs. Loads of 'em. You're not working on that, are you? The only work you're doing there is declaring it all bogus.'

'NDEs?'

'Near-death-experiences. You know, where people find themselves out of body when they're close to death. There's loads of NDE stories.'

'Anecdotal evidence is worthless. If it can't be repeated under controlled conditions, it's not worth a damn.'

'What do you want - people dying in your laboratories?'

Orantor raised his eyebrows.

'Isn't that more your line?'

I ignored the remark.

'You wouldn't want to know anyway,' I continued. 'See, if it's proven the mind can exist outside the body, that undermines your whole belief system. Maybe we're not just physical creatures who evolved by natural selection. Maybe people have souls, and physical life isn't the be-all end-all. And as the physical realm is your domain, then perhaps your mastery is under threat. So the only 'work' you're doing on NDEs is denying them.'

'There's not one single authentic case, as far as I know.'

'Oh really? I've heard of several which seem almost undeniable. I read one about a woman who left her body during surgery. She saw herself from above while the surgeons were operating. Then she left the room in an out-of-body state, went outside the hospital and saw an old sandshoe on a window ledge outside the third floor. Later, when she recovered, she went up to the third floor and verified that the sandshoe was there.'

'If your story's even true, she could have been up to that floor before and noticed the shoe, forgotten it, then dredged up the memory under the stress of the operation. There's always a rational explanation.'

I snorted.

'And there you go. See, I could give you a hundred examples and whatever it was, you'd always find a way to 'explain' it. No matter how far-fetched your 'explanation', you'd always be under the delusion that you hold the rational view.'

'I prefer to operate from reason, not emotion.'

'What do you mean?'

'Your emotional need to believe in life after death causes you to accept ridiculous stories of people flying around hospitals outside their bodies.'

'Are you sure it's not the other way round? I'd say it is *you* acting from emotion, Rudolph. You're emotionally committed to a physicalist worldview and if anything threatens it, you're in outright denial. So you go through these absurd contortions trying to explain away the idea of someone going out-of-body. You say it's ridiculous. Tell me why.'

Orantor gave an exasperated sigh. Another one.

'Here's the thing, Tom. Whether you like it or not, human beings *are* physical creatures who evolved, like all other species, by natural selection. People *don't* travel outside their bodies because it isn't possible. Like all other species, we have to follow physical laws. No amount of wishful thinking can change that.'

I stared at him levelly before replying.

'The trouble is I'm an empiricist, so I base my beliefs on evidence. Then I reason from there, regardless of what the current theory may be. If a woman sees an old sandshoe on a third floor window ledge while her body's on the operating table, then later verifies it was actually there, the most rational explanation is that she saw it while out-of-body. How or why, we don't know, but the theory can come later.'

Orantor made a dismissive gesture.

'Even if we were to entertain your ridiculous notion, allow me to pose a simple logical question. If the woman was out of her body, how on Earth could she see anything without the immediate use of her eyes?'

'I don't know how. I can only infer that the bodily organs are not the only means of perception. We're stuck with the unfortunate fact that she saw the shoe. Now, you can concoct some elaborate excuse - maybe she was hang gliding in a nearby field six months ago and saw it - but she saw the damn shoe and the simplest explanation is that she saw it out-of-body during an operation.'

'What a load of hogwash, Tom. If you have the emotional need to reject well established scientific facts, that's your problem. I mean, really! People flying around hospitals seeing sandshoes - do you really expect to be taken seriously?'

'You're very forthright in your dismissal, Rudolph. So sure that you know best. And that's exactly what pisses people off. You're a Goddamned know-it-all, that's clear. Well, a lot of people would love to see you fall down off your pedestal of knowledge, and grovelling in the dirt of ignorance. They'd like to see you admit you were wrong. I, for one, would come up to you at the foot of your pedestal and I'd say - Hey Rudy, you bastard! You're wrong. You were fucking wrong the whole time!'

'Perhaps this discussion would benefit from maintaining a scholarly tone. A bit of decorum, hmm?'

'Well, you're so arrogant.'

'I thought you said you weren't anti-science.'

'I'm not against science itself, just the closed minds of some of its more zealous practitioners. But what about you - why do *you* think there are so many people who want to see you brought down? And cults rising up left, right and centre?'

Orantor took a moment to answer.

'I think it's because people have a childish propensity to cling to magical thinking. They want to live in a world where there are no limits to possibility. Unfortunately there are limits, but science doesn't set them. Reality does. Why shoot the messenger? If you insist on calling science a cult, Tom, it is a cult where reality is the master.'

'I won't even begin to answer that one, or we'll be here all night.'

'Yes, it's getting late. I suppose the problem is science doesn't pander to people's wishes and desires. It's concerned only with facts. Pseudoscience on the other hand, does address those wishes - survival after death, paranormal powers, and so on.'

'Now Rudolph, is it really that simple? What if there actually is a hidden realm behind the physical universe? If that's true, perhaps it shows itself in many ways, even if some of them are distortions. Like the UFO sightings, or people who seem to remember past lives. Maybe these are glimpses of what lies behind the physical world.'

'It all sounds terribly vague and irrational to me, I prefer something more orderly. And in the conflict between rationality and irrationality, I don't know of a single example where the battle has not been won by scientific thinking.'

'Battles are not wars. And you're obviously sifting the evidence quite selectively if you believe that anyway. You delude yourself if you think science is winning the war.'

Once again, I stared into the fire, before going on. That fire was getting a damn good stare.

'As for the New Age movement, maybe a lot of it is nonsense - but you can't tar it all with the same brush. Even the sillier parts are a response to something real. Ignore it at your peril, for the forces of 'unreason' may overthrow you. And if they do, it might be someone worse than the Milinish. Maybe a fundamentalist group who throws out the great achievements of science, simply because of the atheism implied in your belief system.'

Orantor's face took on a haughty expression.

'It sounds like you're suggesting that science, against its nature, suddenly take on some metaphysical belief system simply to placate the foolishness of religious irrationalism. I'm afraid that is wildly implausible. One cannot behave dishonestly simply because of a fear of adverse consequences. We won't do anything of the sort.'

269

'Then I hope the forces of unreason don't overthrow you. The last thing I want is for some new Luddite regime to ban technology, for instance. I'm a rock n roll guitarist. I'm in no hurry to unplug and return to the Dark Ages.'

'And there you go, Tom. That's where you'd be without us - the Dark Ages. Scientists are the true magicians. As Arthur C. Clarke said, any advanced technology is indistinguishable from magic.'

'You're quite right, but technology can't do everything. Your scientific method works for most things, but if it can't penetrate into the hidden domain behind the universe, maybe you need some new tools.'

'What do you suggest?'

'Let's leave that conversation because our time is almost up. But now that I've had a go at you, it's your turn to have one more crack at me before last drinks.'

I thought Orantor needed to let off some steam. He seemed a touch hot under the collar, though he tried to hide it. Both of us had begun to raise our voices.

'All right, Tom. For one thing, I've heard a lot of pontificating on the shortcomings of science, but I'd have more respect for such opinions if you'd ever done any actual science. Have you?'

'Not formally, but at least I've read your books.'

'I make the same charge of the so called postmodern thinkers. Most of them have no scientific background, so how can they criticise? The only people who should be entitled to be philosophers of science are scientists themselves.'

'You can't be the only philosophers of science. For many of you, science *is* reality, so you think of yourselves as philosophers of reality. But reality is everyone's concern. If you presume to define it, you must be accountable to others. Besides, everyone has built in biases. If only your own members are allowed to pronounce on science, you'll miss some valid criticism that comes from outside.'

Orantor looked unimpressed.

'I also think you're too inclined to deal in satire. Are you not setting up straw men that are easy to attack?'

'Perhaps, but you and the skeptics have been doing that to your enemies for years. I thought there were no sacred cows in science?'

'There aren't, but that's no license to take cheap shots. Evolution, for instance, is not the caricature you've depicted. It's the grandest epic ever told, and far more subtle and interesting than your silly fairytale about reincarnation.'

We were both speaking very emphatically now. I was almost shouting.

'I'm sure evolution isn't the caricature I've portrayed, just as reincarnation is probably far subtler than the ideas of debt and punishment that get put about. I don't believe in those stupid clichés. I don't believe in past life karma.'

'I wish you'd get a bit calmer.'

'Perhaps we both should. Then again maybe we should get it all off our chests. Here's something else to fire you up. What do you think of cultural relativism, the idea that there's no absolute truth, that all truths are relative to the culture in which they exist? They say science is simply a system of consensus truth that scientists have agreed to recognise as facts.'

'Unadulterated nonsense! How can biology or physics be a cultural construct, given they predated culture in the first place? How can gravity, DNA, or reproduction be a human invention?'

'Sure, the extreme form of relativism is crazy, but maybe we do impose our own concepts on the natural world at times. Even in biology. Take DNA. Sure DNA works whether we know about it or not, but the way it has been theorised about - as some quasi-religious element in a Darwinian metanarrative - is indeed the way fact can become fiction, and vice versa.'

'That's your opinion, Tom. But philosophical waffle aside, I'm certain that science is the most reliable system of knowledge we have, and that if we could utilise it properly, we could remedy the world's ills. We have conquered many diseases.'

'But new ones always arise.'

'We have raised the life expectancy age.'

'And taken immortality.'

'We have the technology to feed the world's millions.'

271

'Which is fortunate, as thanks to medicine, the population is constantly growing.'

'We are on the verge of a theory of everything.'

'You don't even know if there is life after death.'

'The question is irrelevant.'

'No it isn't. Death is the ultimate reality.'

'No, life is.'

'Then tell us where it comes from. Tell us what matters.'

Rudolph C Orantor slumped back in his chair by the fire.

'Are we finished?' he asked. 'What happens next?'

'All I have to do is write up our conversation as the last chapter of the book, then send it out into the world.'

'What will become of it, I wonder? The world I mean.'

For almost the last time I stared into the face of the scientist, my old adversary, Rudolph C. Orantor.

'The world will go its own way, long after you and I have gone. Whichever way that is.'

Orantor smiled, sensing that our conversation was drawing to a close. Then he seemed to remember something. He frowned and delivered a final schoolmasterly rebuke.

'One last thing, Tom. Your virus analogy in the book. Antibiotics kill bacteria, but they don't kill viruses.'

I laughed.

'Looks like you had the final say in this chapter, Rudolph. Yet the postscript will go to me. And there, action will speak louder than words.'

27

The Last Supper

Orantor gave me a searching look.

'Actions louder than words, Tom? What are you up to now?'

'I mean that the world will go its own way, Rudolph, but it will go without me. My race is almost run.'

'How so?'

'My Milinish empire is on the brink. The holy city of Cull is under siege. Even as we speak, my enemies are approaching the city gates to destroy us. There's no way out and I'm quite resigned to it. Jesus knew his destiny, I know mine.'

'And for a while there, I thought you were showing signs of rationality. We're back in lunatic mode, are we? Or is this just another of your jokes?'

'It's no joke, Rudolph. The police want to question us about missing persons, the FBI has a file on me, and the Saborman business auditors are on their way to shut us down. They're all coming. Well, let them come. They'll never take me alive, I assure you of that.'

A look of dawning realisation came over Orantor's face.

'So that's why you confessed to the murders in your book.'

'You mean my research program into life after death? It's not a confession, it's an explanation. That's why I wrote *Cultown* - as a history of the movement. It explains what happened and why. I leave it behind so others can carry on my work when I'm gone. In the meantime, I'll adhere to my ethical principles of research. No experiment will I conduct upon others which I would not do myself. I'm going through the Triangle to settle the question of life after death once and for all - and you're coming with me.'

'This has nothing to do with me,' said Orantor.

'You're coming anyway. As soon as I've typed up our dialogue, the last chapter of *Cultown* will be done and the book complete. I'll simply email the file to my publishers so they can add it to the version you've already read. Then we're off.'

'Look, Tom, you seem to have some kind of fixation on me, but you've got to realise it was pure coincidence I ever read your book in the first place.'

I shrugged.

'Whether it was coincidence, chaos theory, or the hand of God, our destinies became linked at that point. Destinies that will play out in the next few hours. Don't fight it, embrace it. Anyway, don't flatter yourself that it's all about you. The whole town's coming with us.'

'What on Earth do you mean?'

'I've called a meeting in the great Temple of Cull for tomorrow. We're staging a mass migration into the next plane of existence.'

I paused.

'Or into oblivion,' I continued, 'if your worldview is correct. Whatever the result, we won't be around when the infidels break down the city walls.'

'And how exactly are you going to do that? Meditate yourselves into the next dimension?'

'There may be some meditation to begin with. Then we're getting a little technical assistance from your department. I put my best man on the job and by now, the great Temple's rigged with enough explosives to blow us all to Kingdom Come. My band's going to play a farewell show, then we're all going to pop off together.'

Orantor stared at me intently to see if I was joking. A forlorn hope.

'Look, man, you don't have to do it. Why don't you leave all this behind? We can return to Australia together. You needn't publish your book. No one has to know what's been going on here.'

'It's too late. You know my story, and as soon as you're free, you'll tell - even if Talbot doesn't.'

'Then I'll speak on your behalf. Put in a good word for you.'

'Really, Rudolph, and what's that going to achieve? No, there's no escape for me now. But before I leave, I'm going to set the record straight. The only one with the whole truth is me - that's why I'm publishing *Cultown*. Otherwise people are going to believe the fraudulent versions that are sure to come out.'

'If you're determined to kill yourself, so be it. I'll even go with you, if you insist. But not your followers - you can't take them with you. No one has that right.'

'I'm doing them a kindness. I promised them a Heaven on Earth. If I can no longer deliver that, I must take them with me into the next life. They couldn't possibly go on in a world without Thomas Swan and the Milinish, not after all we've experienced. We are one - we live together, we die together.'

'This is madness, Tom, sheer madness.'

'All we're doing is crossing over into another plane. Leaving behind a world that has failed so utterly and is no more than a travesty compared to what it *should* be. We're going to a higher place.'

'Do you really want this on your conscience?'

I spread my arms with palms upwards.

'Don't think I do it easily. Many a night I've agonised over this decision. Yet my hand is forced. The Milinish is the greatest religion in the world. We'll die shoulder to shoulder before bending the knee to any false human authority.'

'And what will your God think of you then, having committed mass murder?'

'I've spoken to God and have his blessing. He wasn't happy at first, but when I argued my case, he saw that I was right. It's unfortunate, but most of his divine sons seem to meet with terrible endings. I'm afraid it's an occupational hazard for messiahs.'

'And you wonder why science rose up against religion in the first place. You, in your fanaticism, believe you have a divine right to commit mass murder. Is it any wonder we reject your mentality?'

'Look, old boy, I wouldn't be getting up on your high horse too fast. I may have loaded the Temple with explosives, but don't forget who invented them in the first place. Science has been placed in the service of the military since day one, right through to Hiroshima. If we're going to discuss conscience, pray tell me how heavy's the atom bomb on your shoulders?'

'That was a matter of politics, not science.'

'Doesn't matter. You went along with it. You can't even blame the communists or the Nazis. It was our lot developed the bomb, wasn't it?'

'We had to get it first, before they did.'

'Whatever the excuse, it's rather ironic, don't you think? The application of high intellect to something as incredibly foolish as a nuclear bomb. When you know how stupid people are, as a rule, to bring such weapons into existence was the ultimate folly. I mean, religion had the great flood but that was just a story. Science made it possible for mass murder to actually occur. You have far more blood on your hands than I ever could.'

I gazed into space for a moment.

'It's a rather wonderful union, when you think about it. The power of religion and the power of science coming together as one. When those explosives blow us through the Triangle of Fire, we'll have the genius of science to thank.'

Orantor seemed about to protest further, but I cut him short.

'My dear Rudolph, I believe we've said enough. I'm going to type up our dialogue tonight and release *Cultown* to the world.'

I summoned Flynn.

'Jim, kindly take Dr Orantor back to his room. Then let the Inner Circle know there's a formal meeting here tonight.'

Orantor's face was pale, but he rose stiffly to his feet as Flynn approached. No hand would be laid upon him. He'd make his own way to the exit.

It's always rather surreal sound checking in an empty stadium, playing rock n roll to thousands of empty seats. Yet as I looked out into that void, I reminded myself that each seat would be filled on the morrow. For now, it was just our sound guy mumbling instructions into his mic, me, Vic on the bass, and the other two boys in the band.

I strapped on a wireless guitar and ventured halfway to the back of the Temple. Then, satisfied that we sounded superb, Victor and I downed tools and returned to Saborman House. We adjourned to the dining room and waited for the others.

Rose was the first to arrive. She was radiant in a black gown and glittering jewels.

'Beautiful as ever, my dear,' I said. 'Let me pour you a glass of wine.'

As I clasped her hands between mine, I was struck by the realization that this was goodbye. Final and irrevocable. The unexpected pain compelled me to speech.

'Rose, I just want you to know what a tremendous support you've been all this time. You gave me a home in Sydney. You helped build the Milinish into the powerhouse it is today. And when we came to Cull you could easily have rested on your laurels, but you've been tireless in helping me administer this town and the empire we created.'

Rose beamed.

'Oh Tom, the whole thing has been a labour of love.'

'I know. And from love comes service, and devotion to these fine ideals we've tried to live by. You truly are a champion of this movement.'

I embraced her and continued to speak.

'And no matter what happens from here or what becomes of me, you must always go on in the same vein. Love is bigger than

277

any one person or cause. Remember that. God has many faces, many names.'

Rose pulled back, sensing something in my tone as much as the words themselves.

'What's the matter? Is something wrong?'

'There's nothing wrong with the effort or our intentions. But it's tough at the top, I've learned that the hard way. And I've made many, many mistakes. All I ask, my dear, is don't judge me too harshly.'

'Judge you, Tom? I would never do that. I'll support you to my dying breath.'

I kissed her, then there was a knock on the door. Alice came in sporting her usual androgynous look: trousers, white shirt with black tie, short hair and glasses. Rose looked at her coldly, justifiably so, had she been able to read my thoughts. Still, I had never acted on those thoughts. My interactions with Alice had been strictly professional. We shook hands rather formally.

'What's the latest from the lucid dream laboratories?' I asked. 'Have you achieved proof of precognition in the dream state yet?'

Alice flashed a boyish grin.

'Where've you been, Tom? We finished that months ago. We're onto creating mutual dream space now.'

'What's that?'

'Two or more people entering the same dream and reporting shared events when they wake.'

'Excellent. Then perhaps you'll prove my hypothesis that our entire experience in Cull is some kind of shared hallucination.'

Alice grinned again, but this time with a hint of unease in her expression. Before we could speak further, Jim Flynn entered the room. He nodded at me. Alice turned away and began looking at the array of fine art I'd had moved into the dining room. The walls were adorned with beautiful pieces from one period or another. Soft, baroque music played in the background, and the table was laden with gourmet entrées and wine.

'What's that,' said Alice, 'a Monet?'

'Indeed. An original. They all are along that wall - the Kahlo, the Picasso, the lot of them.'

'How on Earth did you get hold of them?'

'I can't take any credit. We've Victor's father to thank. Still, we must make the most of them tonight. Beauty is fleeting. I hate the thought of the Quavisians getting hold of our finest work.'

Alice shot me an incredulous look, trying for the umpteenth time to ascertain whether or not I was joking. My expression, however, was deadpan. I turned to see Selwyn enter the room, all dreadlocks and a big dopey grin. Whether he was stoned again or that was simply his natural look was not quite clear. Still, he was the last of our party to arrive. Now that we were all assembled, I asked everyone to sit down.

I sat at the head of the table. Rose was to my left followed by Victor. Selwyn sat on my right, next to Alice. Jim Flynn sat at the end of the table opposite me. I turned off the baroque music, tapped on a glass and addressed them all. I decided it would be best to get straight to the point.

'My dearest disciples, let us toast this glorious night, for it will be our last on Earth.'

I held up my right hand.

'And before you interrupt with questions, let me explain.'

I paused and looked into the shocked faces around me.

'Yes, my friends, this is goodbye. When the chronicles of Milinish are written, they will speak of this as the Last Supper. As I look around at your dear, familiar faces, I see loyalty incarnate. Some of you have been with me since I came to Cull, and some of you still longer.'

I gave Rose's hand a squeeze. She seemed to be on the verge of tears and I looked away so as not to follow suit.

'We are all that remain of the Inner Circle. Arianna fell by the wayside, Jamie was taken by Quavisia, and Bob Talbot sold us out for thirty shares in Saborman Industries. Well, it's Talbot to blame for all this. He has led our enemies here - the police, the FBI, and Saborman traitors. They surround the holy city of Cull and mean to destroy us. And you know what I say to that?'

My disciples were silent, their sombre faces downcast. Yet still they looked to me in expectation, as to a doctor delivering test results for a terminal disease.

279

'I say if they want Cull that much, they can have it. If worldly success means so much to Talbot Iscariot, let him enjoy it. It will perish soon enough and he with it. If the FBI and the government and Quavisia are so attached to their need to rule the Earth, then once again I say - let them have it. For we in the Milinish are going to a better place.'

'What's happened, Tom?' said Victor. 'Why are you speaking like this?'

'What's happened, Vic? I'll tell you what's happened - we're done. The Milinish is finished. Even as we speak, our enemies gather beyond the city walls preparing for a final assault. Ruanglian Intelligence has intercepted their commands and relayed them to me. The attack will come two days hence. Well, we won't be here when they arrive.'

'But why are they attacking us, Tom?' asked Rose.

'We are the last battalion that stands between them and their Satanic victory. Once Cull has fallen, the Earth is theirs. And unfortunately, Cull is about to be entered by human traitors - police, tax auditors, and Talbot himself.'

'Look, Tom,' said Victor, 'as long as I'm running Saborman Industries, I'll decide who can come in here.'

I gave him a sad little smile.

'Brave words, Vic, but let me give it to you straight. You don't know it yet, but you're no longer CEO of Saborman. You've been deposed *in absentia*. I heard it straight from Ruanglian HQ. They hacked into the Saborman computers and saw the emails.'

'They can't depose me. I am Victor Saborman!'

'They can and they have. Let me paint a picture for you, Vic. In two days when enemy forces march into the city, you'll be arrested and thrown into jail. You'll be tortured and interrogated by the FBI, until they extract some bogus confession. Then you'll be prosecuted for business malpractice, made to pay millions in back taxes, and sentenced to three consecutive life sentences.'

'What for? I didn't do anything.'

'It's purely political, I assure you. A coup hatched by your father's old colleagues. Soon as you're arrested, the company reps will march in here and take control of what's left of Saborman Industries.'

'Can't the Ruanglians do something?' asked Rose, with a despairing look.

'They surely can, my dear, but not in the way you think. See, the bottom line is the Ruanglians aren't warmongers. They're pacifists. So we're going to turn the other cheek, in the most profound possible way. Before our enemies attack, we're all going to commit suicide. They want Cull, they can have it. Meantime, we'll be off in our spirit bodies to the heavenly paradise of Ruanglia. The Ruanglian mother ship is overhead, ready to teleport us all there.'

All this time, Alice's expression was becoming more and more horrified, and with my final statement, she finally realised who she was having dinner with.

'Now look, Tom, you do what you want - but leave me out of it. I came here to do research. This is nothing to do with me.'

I gave her the old raised eyebrows.

'We all came here to do research, Alice, one way and another - and the final experiment is almost upon us. Now, let me spell it out. No one gets out of here alive. You can come with us willingly or unwillingly, but you *will* come.'

'I refuse.'

'Is that your final word?'

'Absolutely.'

'You could have just said yes.'

I turned to Jim Flynn.

'Take her, Jim. Confine her to quarters.'

Alice leapt to her feet with a howl of long suppressed rage and fear.

'You! You're nothing but a fraud. The Quavisians, the Ruanglians, Satanic DNA - what a load of rubbish. You just made it all up!'

'A blasphemer as well. See how your true nature comes out in a crisis.'

'I only went along with it all to fund my research.'

'A highly unethical approach. How deeply you wound me, Alice. You doubt the veracity of my doctrines? I who have bled

281

and suffered, and who on the morrow will lay down my very life for my people.'

'You maniac. You're completely insane.'

'So now you deny me, Alice? If Talbot was my Judas, you surely are my Peter. And to think that all this time you pretended to believe in my beautiful doctrines and you were lying all along, faking it for personal gain. Then you deserve to die, not with honour, but as the traitor you are. Jim, remove her from my sight. She's coming to Ruanglia with the rest of us, but she will come in chains.'

Alice made a run for the door but Flynn seized her with ease. She screamed and cursed as he dragged her away.

I turned to my remaining colleagues and took Rose's hand in mine.

'What about you, my dear? Will you come with us?'

A look of utter adoration came over Rose's face, a swoon of sex and the death urge in some morbid cocktail.

'Tom, I have followed you to the ends of the Earth, now I will follow you further.'

'Loyal to the end. By the Lord himself, you're worth a thousand Alices or Talbots. And rest assured that when we're united in the hereafter, we'll both be restored to the full flush of youth and cavort lustfully in fields of heavenly bliss.'

I turned to Victor.

'And you, my brother, will you follow me? Death is no novelty to the likes of you. You faced execution as Anne Boleyn and died with dignity. Not a tear did you shed as they prepared to spill your royal blood. I trust you will show the same steadfast heart when we step through the portal together.'

Victor stood up and saluted me. I stood also, returned the salute, and kissed him on both cheeks.

'And Selwyn,' I said, sitting down again. 'Will you join us?'

Selwyn seemed remarkably unfazed by it all. He simply smiled and shrugged.

'If that's my karma, Tom, who am I to argue?'

I made a gesture of blessing and looked round the table once more.

'Dear disciples, you do me honour. The Milinish is the greatest religion ever seen on this Earth, and it has been my privilege to fight by your side. Let this be our last supper. Eat and drink well, for tomorrow we die. Onwards we go to glory and immortality. I salute you all!'

'Three cheers for Tom!' cried Victor.

There was a rousing response. All cheered: once, twice, thrice - and then we drank.

28

Exodus Two

In the museum of history, there's a glass case of infamy
They blew up a merry dance, a mass orgy, a fine romance.

Cultown Album Lyrics

Twenty thousand souls with their fate in my hands. The sense of control was nauseating. From backstage, I stared out at row upon row of tiered seating. I shuddered, but it was too late to stop now. You don't set out on a thousand mile journey and stop a mile from the end. Events, good or bad, have their own momentum. Once set in motion, they must reach their natural end points.

The buzz of the crowd rose as the minutes ticked away. That collective hum contained an intangible extra note - for while the people did not realise what was to happen, on another level of awareness, they knew. They sensed the otherworldly forces being conjured, the looming Triangle, the imminence of fate. They knew, while they did not know, and they came willingly with love and faith and a sense of adventure.

Six mighty sentinels guarded the portals to immortality. Six splendid swans, spaced evenly around the Temple like the holes in a snooker table. They were high as a house and imposing as sphinxes. In truth, they were hollow but not empty. Only Jim Flynn and I knew the explosive power they harboured.

The seventh swan, at the back of the stage itself, served as a backdrop for the show. I checked my guitar and amp once more. Thomas Swan, the rock n roll messiah, about to give his last performance. I nodded at Vic and our two bandmates. We were set to go, as soon as I'd addressed the people one more time. Right on cue, Flynn sent through a message that all were aboard the ark, bar a few stragglers around the entrances. They'd be dragged along in our slipstream. Let no lamb be lost from the flock.

A trumpet fanfare sounded over the PA and I walked onstage to ascend the pulpit. As I reached the top, I stood with arms upraised for a full minute absorbing the ovation. At last I lowered my arms and the roar receded to a murmur.

'My beloved children. As I look out at this sea of shining faces, it brings a tear to my eyes. You are the elite, the last ones standing when all others have fallen.'

The crowd hummed as if it were one gigantic beast. A low, fearful, yet strangely exultant murmur filled the Temple.

'It is fitting, then, that you will carry humanity forward from its darkest hour - for I bring you the worst possible news.'

The crowd fell silent.

'It is with the deepest sorrow I must report that the war is lost and humanity destroyed. New York and Washington lie in ruins. London and Paris surrendered days ago. Tokyo and Beijing have fallen into the sea. The dreadful truth is Quavisia has won the war and taken possession of Earth. Only the holy city of Cull stands defiant against total defeat.'

As my words hit home, an awful wailing broke out. The collective cries of fear and consternation from twenty thousand souls filled the hall. Such was its unexpected force, I felt a moment of terror at what I'd unleashed. I raised my hands and tried to speak over the wave of noise.

'Please, my people, wait. All is not lost - hear me out.'

Gradually the cacophony died down to an anxious rumble.

'The Ruanglian force field around Cull holds fast, but it can't hold much longer. The Ruanglians have been meditating around the clock to maintain it, but it's only a matter of time before Quavisia breaks through. Therefore, there has been a change of plan. A drastic change, but a necessary one to ensure our survival.'

An uneasy silence settled over the room like a blanket of ash.

'Citizens, here is the good news! We, the Milinish, will use the Ruanglians' psychic technology to travel to another dimension. The

Ruanglians intended to come here to fight with us and defend the holy city of Cull, yet the Quavisian forces are too strong. Instead, the entire city of Cull will teleport to Ruanglia itself. We'll reject the Earth, as it has rejected us, and travel to a new life in paradise!'

There was a noisy eruption of surprise and confusion, yet containing a new note of hope.

'My people, is this not the most wonderful news? In a matter of mere hours, we'll meet again on the planet Ruanglia! My swans will take us there, these seven swans you see in the Temple tonight. Look at these mighty talismans - they're not just ornamental. Each of them acts as a powerful receiver of our mental energy. With all seven linked at once, we can leap dimensions. We must join our minds with Ruanglia in powerful meditation and let the swans transmit us to our new home.'

The crowd noise rippled through the arena in turbulent waves. I held up my hands once more.

'But wait! It cannot be fearful energy. It can't be tainted by doubt and anxiety. Only joyful energy will take us to paradise. So, to help us conjure that joy, we're going to use the power of music. I, Thomas Swan, the rock n roll messiah, will play one last show for you in Cull tonight.'

The crowd picked up the tone of my message and there was a discernible shift in that collective roar. You could feel the fear transforming into hope, faith, and exhilaration. Borne along by the strength of that wave, I closed my address with a final command.

'God bless you all. By the power vested in me by Jesus, Buddha, Darwin, and this here electric guitar, we're going to rock you all to Ruanglia! I urge you to dance, cheer, and bang your heads like it's your last night on Earth. Then, when the final encore dies away, we travel to immortality!'

The last word boomed out through the Temple. Then suddenly and without warning, the houselights were cut, plunging the mob into darkness. A thrill of terror rippled through the arena, cries of fear and excitement piercing the air. In the onstage dark, my pulpit was hauled off. Someone came through by torchlight and handed me my guitar. As I strapped it on, the great swan at the back of the stage began to glow. In the pitch black, twenty thousand pairs of eyes were drawn to it as to a lighthouse shining through the storm.

The intro from our song 'Amnesia' played over the PA, as each band member walked to position. Then, with an almighty surge of light and sound, the drums and guitar came thundering in together for the song's opening riff. I raised my right arm high after each chord and the crowd stood as one, like a gestalt entity controlled by a single brain.

As I sang it, I realised the song had attained a new meaning in the circumstances, one that was never intended.

Amnesia, tell me who I am.
All I have known I no longer understand.
I feel a change is coming, I feel it building up inside.
Changing you, changing me, mind blowing reality.

When the song came to an end, I could see Victor front of stage, open mouthed as he took in the spectacle of twenty thousand people on their feet, arms in the air. We'd played the Temple before, but not in an atmosphere like this. Vic looked over at me and I winked.

'God bless you all.' I said again, into the microphone. 'The louder you cheer, the faster we'll reach Ruanglia. This next one goes out to a fella named Gordon Young. It's called 'Skeptic Eclectic'.'

As this was a song off the new *Cultown* album, the crowd didn't know it, but it still went down a treat. So well in fact, that we went straight into the title track.

'You know, guys, there are some who call us a cult. They say we brainwash people. And you know what? The ones who said that are all dead now, but we're alive and rocking like there ain't no tomorrow. So if that's brainwashing, I'll take it any day. What do ya say?'

The cheers were deafening.

After that, we played 'Battles are not Wars' off the first album, then took it down a notch with the acoustic 'In Nihilum.' That was the ditty I wrote back in Sydney to launch *Revelations of Milinish*. The crowd greeted it like a prodigal son and sang along in glorious

287

unison. Then it was time to get epic. I approached the mic once more.

'I'm going to sing you a little song about Satan.'

The crowd roared its approval.

'Satan's in you. Satan's in me. Without him, none of us would be here today, for Satan's true name is DNA, the double helix of doom. This is 'Helix Eternal'!'

I kicked it off with that AC/DC style opening riff, which evolved into thrash metal, then that beautiful choral chorus - and it didn't take long for thousands of lighters to come out at that point, which gave me a few jitters about the old swans, I must say.

At the back of the stage, two big screens were set up either side of the giant swan. For 'Helix Eternal' they showed an extraordinary film of DNA and evolution in action. I should confess this was not the only technical assistance the song received. The many layers of the chorus could not have been reproduced by the live band alone. Truth be told, we used a backing tape for that part. So sue me. I'll come back in the next life and do it properly.

The songs continued: 'Pontius Pilates,' 'Vulturiac,' 'Doom Pipers,' and 'Fallen to a Higher Place.' And when it came to performing 'Triangle of Fire,' it was time to bring out a couple of special guests.

'Citizens, loyalty is the greatest of virtues and treachery the worst of all sins. To quote from this next song, it's really elementary; you're with me or against me. I came to Cull and whittled away all the rubbish to reach one hundred percent purity. And you know what? We're not quite there yet. Let me show you what happens to traitors.'

My security guards led two prisoners onto the stage: Alice White, my former colleague, and alongside her, Rudolph C. Orantor. They were both shouting something at the audience, yet my microphone was tantalisingly out of their reach.

'What's that, Rudy? You've got a message for the people of Cull? You're going to have to yell a bit louder, they can't hear you.'

There was an air of puzzlement from the crowd.

'You don't know who they are, do you?' I said into the mic. 'Well, let me enlighten you. This woman was a close friend and ally, until she betrayed me. As for this gentleman, take a real good look. We caught him just outside our borders. He's one of the top scientists from Quavisia itself! We're taking them both back to Ruanglia where they'll be tried for war crimes.'

This announcement was met with gasps of shock and awe. Meanwhile, Alice and Orantor continued their futile attempt to shout warnings at the crowd. The taped acoustic intro for 'Triangle of Fire' played over the PA as the two traitors were dragged offstage. The lights went out and a burning triangle appeared on the twin screens. The band came in for the heavy part. Then for the guitar solo, one of my favourites, I entered that state of Nirvana which drew me to this style of music in the first place. When the song was over, I just stood there grinning.

'People, I think we can safely say we've won the war.'

We played 'Anti-Hero' then closed with 'The One Eyed Man is King' before walking offstage. The adrenaline was still coursing through me, but by the time we came back for the encore it was accompanied by the return of the nausea. It was time. I wiped the sweat from my brow, approached the mic, and looked out at the sea of faces for the last time.

'Citizens, you've been a great audience. Not just tonight, but for the entire duration of my time in Cull. It has been my privilege to lead you. Thanks for making our last night on Earth together so special. We're going to play a couple more songs, then I'll see you all in Ruanglia!'

Around the arena, the six giant swans were glowing faintly, beginning the countdown. Sentinels to the afterlife, guardians of eternity.

'And before we do, the great Victor Saborman is going to play a bass solo. Fire up, Vic!'

With that, I left the stage, ran out the back door of the Temple and into the waiting car.

'God speed, Jim.'

We raced through the deserted streets to Saborman House, boarded the helicopter and, some time later, the private plane that took us out of the USA for good. When that flight came to an end, I shook hands with my security chief for the last time.

'Jim,' I said, 'I sincerely hope I never lay eyes on you again.'

Flynn smiled faintly and walked off into his own unknown future.

It was not until a couple of days later, in the safety of my hotel room, that I finally got a good look at the footage from the cameras we'd set up in the Temple, to see what happened after we left.

There was no explosion after the show. Yes, the seven swans glowed bright and brighter in that darkened arena, but when those swans opened up, they contained not bombs but books. Or rather, one book thousands of times over. Thousands of copies of *Cultown* itself, my history of the movement, with the album thrown in as a bonus. It was an explosion not of bombs, but of revelation.

What - you really thought I'd blow them up? What did you take me for? I confess that a part of me - a very small part - did consider it. But only for a moment. Yes, they were my children and for a time, I owned them. Our kingdom was doomed and the honourable thing was to die together as we had lived, defiant and victorious. A mass migration into the afterlife. But I did not have the right, nor a nature capable of that. I'm evil but not vile. In the end, a father must surrender his brief dominion and let his children find their own way in the world.

Yet I fear for them. What are they to make of the revelations in *Cultown*? Of course, there had not been time to add my final dialogue with Orantor to those books inside my swans. That would have to wait for the second edition, and until then they could read it on the website. But, even reading *Cultown* up to that point, there was no telling how my people would react. Would they see me as a hero and martyr? Or a scoundrel and fraud? Well, I say to them this: I am no fraud. I acted from good ideals and deep feeling, even if events skewed off into wild trajectories I never envisaged. God works in mysterious ways and I am one of them.

I do worry how my followers will cope with the psychological fallout. But the time of me telling them how to think is over. They'll just have to figure it out for themselves. I certainly feel bad about Victor and Rose. What can I say? I wish them both the best, whatever they do from here.

There are some who'd call me murderer, a charge I reject. Those sacrificed in my experiments died for a cause. Like all great scientists, I was motivated by knowledge and the greater good. And like all leaders, I did what was needed to maintain the integrity of my vision. Only I had the capacity to lead, to reform, to see what was wrong with the old order and put a new one in place. We are all at war, and war calls for extreme measures.

I wrote *Cultown* not as a confession, but an explanation. What people do with it is up to them. Most of Orantor's colleagues will dismiss it as the ravings of a madman. Religious leaders will disdain me as just another cult leader. Meanwhile, some of my followers will continue to believe what I told them - that I am the greatest scientist and religious leader of our times. They'll watch and wait for me to return to save the world once more. Ultimately, other people's opinions are out of my hands.

And what of Thomas Swan and his future? Alas, no future is possible. Not with that identity. There's a bounty on my head in thirty-seven countries. Yet Thomas Swan will be born again - again. What do you think I've been doing all this time? Stockpiling funds from the Saborman coffers, of course. Squirreling them away in a foreign account for a rainy decade - and all the while, preparing a new face, a new back story. They'll never take me alive. They can't, for Thomas Swan no longer exists.

I did think about concluding the experiment. Of travelling through the Triangle of Fire alone. Yet ultimately I was afraid - of oblivion, of the metaphysical consequences of my actions, of the unknown itself.

Still, if it ever comes to a post mortem trial, I will defend myself vigorously. I'm not a bad man, just a good man who got a little carried away.

I sought to probe the mysteries of existence, to ascertain whether we are mortals or gods. Are we physical beings who rose through natural evolution, spirits born into flesh from a pre-existing identity, or some bizarre combination of the two? I have my own opinions on that, but for once I'll keep them to myself.

At least for now.

By Thomas Swan:

Books

Old Religion, New Science
Revelations of Milinish
Milinish in the New Age
Reality Explained
The Tom Letters - A Collection
Battle of the Planets
Cultown

Albums

Anti-Hero
Cultown

Song Lyrics

Amnesia

Amnesia, tell me who I am.
All I have known, I no longer understand.

I feel a change is coming, I feel it building up inside
Changing you, changing me,
Mind-blowing reality
Feel it in my bones

Blank canvas, I must paint myself
Do my best, but I need your help

Changing you, changing me
Things I thought could never be
Will I wake up from this dream?
Mind-blowing reality
Feel it in my bones

Skeptic Eclectic

Newton the alchemist never knew jack shit
Of gravity and planets, what a wit!
Action at a distance, sounds a bit occult
The skeptic laughed at him, good result!

But you are just so young, you've only just begun
To conquer the known universe
There's much more than you know
In the heavens and below
The skeptic is the believer

He laughed at Darwin in 1859,
Some things improve with time - fine wine!
Continents can never move, if you get my drift
He will pooh-pooh your views – short shrift!

But you are just so young, you've only just begun
To conquer the known universe
There's much more than you know
In the heavens and below
The skeptic is the believer

There are no NDEs, souls or after-lives
The skeptic leaves those tales for, housewives!
He'll refuse to wake up ghostly, after that dark night
Rather be dead than wrong, dead right!

But you are just so young, you've only just begun
To conquer the known universe
There's much more than you know
In the heavens and below
The skeptic is the believer

Evil But Not Vile

My name is Thomas Swan, I am the number one
Charismatic orator underneath the sun
A gentleman of class, arch-villain not an arse
You want to know my secret, here's the master class

Some lay-preachers do lay, a parishioner a day
That's just low class evil, no honour on display
They fornicate they prey, I chastise and I pray
I am the true messiah, let me show my way

Be evil but not vile, revered and not reviled
You can tread the path of infamy, if you just do it in style
Got to draw the line somewhere, be fiendish but be fair
The mind is greater than the sword, I'll kill you with a stare

I never fucking swear, too many clowns out there
Posing like a gangster while blow-drying their hair
Trying too hard to look cool, and tweeting like a fool
A bunch of braying narcissists who never left high school

Any fool can hold a gun or bash someone for fun
Thuggery, skulduggery, intellectual content none
But I attack the mind, those contracts really bind,
Conceptual enslavements, they are the lasting kind

I'm evil but not vile, revered and not reviled
You'll document my villainy and cover up your smile
Violence is for thugs and murder is for mugs
The mind is greater than the sword, I'll kill you with a hug

In Nihilum

Here's my swansong but I'm not going anywhere soon
I'm just a cygnet, this is my Signet
The signature of my decree
From my point of view, it's a doctrinal stew for the ages
Skim the cream off the top
We're the cream of the crop
Flee your cages

Lead us on into the dark
Cresting the sky in a bright, shining arc
Into nihilum we go
Into forever and ever we go

Follow me now, let all streams trickle into the ocean
A whisper to a roar, we build up a mighty commotion
We're the Milinish, we're going to finish
What was started all those years ago
Come listen to me and be free of the burden of life

Lead us on into the dark
Cresting the sky in a bright, shining ark
Into nihilum we go
Into forever and ever we go

Onward we go
In the footsteps of many before
Into the abyss, it's sealed with a kiss
Bless you my child

Cultown

We set the standards, we are the chosen few
We're prime accommodation, humans with a view
You want to join us, join the queue
Fill in the paperwork, we'll see what we can do

First you can't get in, then you can't get out
Dip your whole self in and shake it all about
Soon the resistance, turned into a rout
Now you're one of us, there is no doubt

It's a Cultown and we're all spell-bound
It's a Cultown, infidels fall down
It's a Cultown and we're all hell-bound

Now you learn our language, customs, creed and rules
Our leader did precede ya to denounce the other fools
We kick the unbelievers out of the race gene pool
This ain't no hijack it's a goddamn palace coup

The outside to the inside, it's a long way to the top
Hard for you to start, much harder to stop
You bought the intro deal, might as well buy the lot
You want salvation, it's your one and only shot

We'll use ya and confuse ya
Still you're coming back for more
Now you can't find the door, never mind the flaw
The shootout and the siege, the only way to leave
Straight up to heaven through the magic trapdoor

Helix Eternal

One drive, one need
One urge, to be
To live, to breed
Eternally

Fight, rise
To witness another sunrise
There is no demise
Existence the endless surprise

So you travel through the centuries to challenge the gods
And cast them from the heavenly throne
Mortal and immortal in a crucible of trial by fire

AGCT, DNA's base recipe
AGCT, branches on the ancient tree
Adenine, guanine, cytosine, time
Bodies on the long bloodline
AGCT, powering the urge to be

One search, one quest
One sceptre to wrest
To live, to be
Eternally

Aim high
Fixate on that hole in the sky
Descend to ascend
Echoing the old battle cry

Even matter has its limits, when you come to that wall
The threshold is crossed one way or more
Virtual or spiritual the path goes through
More than one door

AGCT, DNA's base recipe
AGCT, branches on the ancient tree
Adenine, guanine, cytosine, time
Bodies on the long bloodline
AGCT, powering the urge to be

Helix Eternal
Infernal, your quest to be
Helix Eternal
Infernal, black majesty
Rise and fall, each and all
Dream of your glory
Onward to the sacred time

Doom Pipers

In the museum of history
There's a glass case of infamy
They blew up a merry dance
A mass orgy, a fine romance

Dance on, model citizen
Dance on, model rat,
Binge, purge, and begin again
Red, yellow and black

Flatter to deceive
What the heart wants, what it needs
Last dance, fast or slow
Where they went nobody knows

Dance on, model citizen
Dance on, model rat,
Binge, purge, and begin again
Red, yellow and black

Raise high, rally round
Raze the city to the ground
Party, party hard
Buried with your ID card

No more, model citizen
No more, model rat,
Binge, purge, and begin again
Red, yellow and black

Fallen to a Higher Place

This world in all its mortal folly
Ain't all it's cracked up to be
The great farce, you've got to laugh
It's only make believe

We deal in strange currency
Your stocks are in free fall
You can't fight with King Kaiser
The greatest power of all

So get you to a higher place
Back where you belong
Bow out in a state of grace
With a swan song

Flag bearer you advanced the cause
As far as your strength would go
We prise it from your cold hands
But you will never know

There comes a time to take a stand
To affirm what you believe
The true lie is in the world not I
I reject it with these hands
I reject it with these hands

A higher place, it's no disgrace
To come last in the human race
Give it up, give up the chase
And get you to a higher place

The Scythe and the Scalpel

Gordon Young the time has come
Science, religion become one
Death is just one more frontier
Face the darkness without fear

Go through the portal, come back with what you see
Give me a reason to believe
The scythe is the scalpel, the séance is the screen
Prove the after-life is more than just a dream

Onto the last frontier
Facing the final fear
This mystery will clear
Through the gates of death

Necrophobic enterprise
Death falls to the power of science
We're all good empiricists
Faith is nothing without this

Go through the portal, come back with what you see
Give me a reason to believe
The scythe is the scalpel, the séance is the screen
The after-life is more than just a dream

Onto the last frontier
Facing the final fear
This mystery will clear
Through the gates of death

Triangle of Fire

No way to put it gently, this ain't no bay of plenty
It's really elementary, you're with me or against me
Your theft of oxygen, has reached its natural end
This triangle of fury, the hangman, judge and jury

One more gone

One more, out of the pyramid
One more, into the pit
One more, out of the inner circle
One more through the triangle of fire

I'm toying with the urge, to expedite the purge
It's no more than a kindness, to cure you of your blindness
Descending from the sky, it comes to purify
Embrace your funeral pyre, the triangle of fire.

One more gone

One more, out of the pyramid
One more, into the pit
One more, out of the inner circle
One more through the triangle of fire

Transcendence

Human in a cage of time
Is superhuman through the mind

Microscope, telescope, gives the creature hope
It can see more than it sees
That it may transcend, its own mortal end
And glimpse infinity

Trapped in a moment of time
The eye must see before it dies
The world in all its strange beauty
And so transcend mortality

Ascent of science, conquer the real
The dazzling worlds, the great reveal

On the noble quest, no one could have guessed
All that was hidden from sight
When the journey's done, so ends their day in the sun
Giants fade into the night

Trapped in a moment of time
The eye must see before it dies
The world in all its strange beauty
And so transcend mortality

The Cultimate Culminates

So began the noble quest
You put reality to the test
No more gods or received wisdom
And the sun rose in the west

Frontiers fell one by one
Your mastery had come
The empirical empire in full flight,
The genius ape had won

You became the cultimate
Decreed our origins and our fate
Tried to define reality and create it in
Your heavenly AI

Despite your insistence
You couldn't quell the resistance
What you found was spectacular, not quite so secular
Nature's hidden defence

You found with some surprise
The truth that was once despised
The universe was divine, nature you did find
Was supernatural all the time

Acknowledgements

The character of Orantor is not based on any one person, living or dead, although it is influenced by several. In researching *Cultown*, I read many books and articles by various pro-science authors, all of which contributed to the character.

I do want to acknowledge Carl Sagan and his book *The Demon Haunted World: Science as a Candle in the Dark*. This is one of the most inspirational books I have read about science, and was a key stimulus when I was first writing *Cultown* in the late 1990s. From Carl Sagan, I learned many specific scientific facts. One example, among many, the point about antibiotics and viruses mentioned at the end of the Swan-Orantor dialogue. More importantly, I learned a good deal about the fundamental values, attitudes, and processes of science. I strongly recommend *The Demon Haunted World* to other readers.

I also read some interesting books about cults (e.g. by Hassan, and by Ritchie), and in *Understanding the Present* by Bryan Appleyard, a useful critique of science by an outsider. There were many other works consulted, the majority of which appear in the reference list.

Most of the research for this book was done twenty years ago. To the best of my ability, I've tried to acknowledge sources. After this much time, it's possible some have been forgotten. If so, the authors are invited to get in touch so I can add them to the next edition.

Specific Acknowledgments

See Works Consulted for full publication details:

Appleyard, B. *Understanding the Present* for chapter 21-23
Dunbar, R. *The Trouble With Science* for chapter 23
Feyerabend, P. from *Against Method* for chapter 23
Foucault, M. *Power / Knowledge* for chapter 21-23
Gross, P. and Levitt, N. *Higher Superstition* for chapter 23
Hassan, S. *Combating Cult Mind Control* for chapters 6-7
Lyotard, J. *The Postmodern Condition: a Report on
    Knowledge* for chapter 23
Ritchie, J. *The Secret World of Cults* for chapters 6-7, 16-17
Roberts, J. *The Individual and the Nature of Mass Events*
    for chapter 6-7, 25-26
Sagan, S. *The Demon Haunted World* for chapters 25-26.

Works Consulted

Appleyard, B. 1992. *Understanding the Present*, Newbridge International, London, UK.

Broderick, D. 1995. *The Architecture of Babel*, Deakin University Press, Australia.

Chalmers, A. 1978. *What is This Thing Called Science?* Sydney University Press, Australia.

Cromer, A. 1993. *Uncommon Sense*. Oxford University Press, New York, USA.

Dawkins, R. 1976. *The Selfish Gene*. Penguin Books, England, UK.

Dawkins, R. 1986. *The Blind Watchmaker*. Norton and Company Inc.

Dunbar, R. 1995 *The Trouble With Science*. Oxford University Press, UK.

Feyerabend, P. 1975. *Against Method*. Verso, London., UK

Foucault, M. 1980 *Power / Knowledge*. Harvester Press, Sussex, UK.

Gardiner, M. 1988. *The New Age: Notes of a Fringe Watcher*. Prometheus Books, Buffalo, NY.

Gordon, H. 1989. *Channelling into the New Age*. Prometheus Books, Buffalo, NY, USA.

Green, C. 1976. *The Decline and Fall of Science*. Oxford University Press, UK.

Green, C. 1969. *The Human Evasion*. Hamilton, London.

Gross, P. and Levitt, N. 1994. *Higher Superstition*. John Hopkins University Press, London.

Hassan, S. 1990. *Combating Cult Mind Control*. Aquarian, Wellingborough.

Holton, G. 1993. *Science and Anti Science*. Oxford University Press.

Horrobin, D. 1969. *Science is God*. Aylesbury, England.

Kurtz, P. 1992. *The New Skepticism*. Prometheus Books, Buffalo, NY, USA.

Lyotard, J.P. 1984. *The Postmodern Condition: a Report on Knowledge*. Manchester University Press, UK.

Plimer, I. 1994. *Telling Lies For God*. Random House, Sydney.

Ritchie, J. 1991. *The Secret World of Cults*. Angus and Robertson, London.

Roberts, J, 1993. *Seth Speaks*, Amber-Allen, San Rafael, CA.

Roberts, J, 1995. *The Individual and the Nature of Mass Events*, Amber-Allen, San Rafael, CA.

Sagan, C. 1996. *The Demon Haunted World: Science as a Candle in the Dark*. Headline Books, London.

Samways, L. 1994. *Dangerous Persuaders*. Penguin, Vic.

Schick, T and Vaughn, L. 1991. *How to Think About Weird Things*. Mayfield, Mountain View, CA, USA.

Storr, A. 1997. *Feet of Clay*. Harper Collins, London.

Wolpert, L. 1992. *The Unnatural Nature of Science*. Faber and Faber, London.

York, M. 1995. *The Emerging Network*. Rowman and Littlefield, Lanham.

Special Thanks

I would like to thank the following people.

Jeremy Loughhead, Cara D'Onofrio, and Imelda Wilde for reader feedback and advice.

Ivan Hruszecky and Wayne Roberts for design services. Jeff Cripps at A Sharp studios for musical production.

Tess Robinson at Go Viral Now for website design: http://GoViralNow.net.

Euan Mitchell for production and promo advice.

Also Available

Books By Duncan Smith

The Vortex Winder
The Maelstrom Ascendant
Hammer and Heat

Albums By Lighthouse XIII

Waves Upon Waves
Vortex Winder
The Maelstrom Ascendant
Cultown

Order of the Lighthouse

To become a friend of Lighthouse XIII and help promote the band's music and Duncan Smith's books, sign up to the supporter group. You can email lighthouse@vortexwinder.com

If you liked this book, tell someone. These days, there aren't as many bookshops around as there were. Most books depend on word of mouth to become known. So if you liked the book, leave a review on Good Reads or Amazon or just tell a friend.

Books and albums can be ordered from www.vortexwinder.com or on Amazon or Book Depository.

Alfadex Books can be contacted on:
matthew.alfadex@gmail.com or at
PO Box 2150, Clovelly, NSW, 2031.

Also available by this author

Books:

The Vortex Winder
When fading rocker, Jimmy Brandt, saves the life of an insect, his own life is forever changed. The insect turns out to be an advanced being who gives him the 'Vortex Winder,' a device which grants a different special power each week. Each power leads to unexpected results.

Jimmy makes a comeback to rock music and records his album. Yet his comeback is a quest within a quest. Driven by the Vortex Winder, Jimmy makes an amazing journey. From a simple job interview, to a love affair in Germany, or a harrowing stint in a foreign prison, the adventures of Jimmy Brandt are always a surprise. Trailed by his mentor, Iolango, and his tormentor, Elijinx, Jimmy follows the events of his life to a stunning conclusion.

Hammer and Heat
Featuring spoilt sports stars, crazed litigants, and other assorted scammers, this collection of stories is funny enough to make a statue laugh. Includes the hit stories 'Marvy Day' and '666 AD' as well as a foreword by infamous bore, Dr Charles Lakeland.

The Maelstrom Ascendant
Rocker Jimmy Brandt has given up on his dreams. He's settled down in the suburbs with his girlfriend and cat ... until strange forces tempt him back to his former life. Soon he faces a choice between good and evil - and life is so rewarding when you turn to the dark side. Flying high again, Jimmy battles divas, despots, and most of all, himself. Yet the higher you fly, the further you can fall. Only an old, forgotten friend can save him. But does he want to be saved?

Lighthouse XIII Albums

Waves Upon Waves
Mountain Gods, SMS: Save My Sanity, Between the Stairway and the Highway, Reaper Bones, Leuchtturm, LHXIII, Temporary Kingdom, Retro Stereo, Waves Upon Waves, New World Alchemy.

Vortex Winder
Vortex Winder, Road Rage, Trade Winds, Black Art, Life Line, Spark, Z Club, Epitaph, Elijinx, Oceanus.

The Maelstrom Ascendant
Black Phoenix, High and Mighty, The Price of Dominion, Moonlight Tiger, I for an Eye, Haunted, Death Bed Regrets, Extinction.Net, Quitter, The Maelstrom Ascendant, The Ephemeral and the Eternal.

Cultown
Amnesia, Skeptic Eclectic, Evil But Not Vile, In Nihilum, Cultown, Helix Eternal, Doom Pipers, Fallen to a Higher Place, The Scythe and the Scalpel, Triangle of Fire, Transcendence, The Cultimate Culminates.

www.ingramcontent.com/pod-product-compliance
Lightning Source LLC
Chambersburg PA
CBHW021457110726
47899CB00001BA/195